RedScottBlue RedScottBlue RedScottBlue RedScottBlue

Red Scott Blue

...a disorienting work of experimental literature.

unfortunately written by

Ty Jordan

Table of Contents

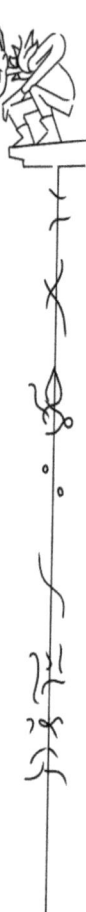

The last Epilouge, we promise.

Acknowledgement

A **H U G E** thanks to Tahara Saron. Without her, this story may never have been told, especially not the way it is now. With her help and encouragement, this book grew to a much larger scale than I ever imagined. Thank you for giving me a chance.

We support Saint Tahara in this house.

Also, shout out to Unique Williams, the first person I talked to at BlackGold Publishing. She thought my idea was special and sent it up the chain, so in a sense, this is her fault too.

I, also, acknowledge that I'm addicted, to using commas,,,,,,,, I definitely ate too much pizza and Chinese takeout within the three years I was writing this book.

Anyone involved in the editing process is the real MVP.

Dedication

To the wonderful who supported me throughout these past few years, both those that are still here and those that have since passed away. I will take the time to thank as many of them personally as I can.

For my cousin Angelo, a skilled poet that was even more excited than I was when I told him I was going to be a published author.

To you dear reader, make time for your loved ones. Check in with your friends and family. Go forth and enjoy life!

CHAPTER I

Wind would wind in an empty home just to push over a young freeloading junkie named Scott Blue. He sat on the edge of a countertop, counting stacks of caps. How many bottles has he had in the last ten minutes, and how could he drink so fast? "Scott Blue is my name or at least I proclaim" he shouted at a squirrel in a soda can. The squirrel turned his back and umped- sorry-I mean jumped three times. "Roswell The Squirrel. RAAAAAAAAWZWEEEEEEELL" the little squirrel replied. "Roswell, good friend how does thyeth fare on such a day, in a place....... such as this?" "No, no, my name is Roswell, *The Squirrel*. Don't refer to me as just Roswell" the little squirrel replied angrily. Scott was now very confused. "My friend, I didn't call you Just Roswell, I called you Roswell. No need to be upset my friend."

The squirrel put his face in his palm and sighed. "Call me by my full name, Roswell The Squirrel, got that?"

Ah, so the little squirrel wanted to be called Roswell, The squirrel. Tedious, sure, but otherwise Roswell seems like a reasonable pers- I mean squirrel. To keep the peace, Scott decided to call the little squirrel Roswell, The Squirrel.

"Roswell, The Squirrel, where are we exactly. I don't remember anything before counting bottle caps and I know I haven't been here all of my life. And I certainly know there was no time when I sought friendship from a squirrel. "Roswell, The Squirrel, stared at Scott and he stared right back for what seemed like hours, or a few minutes, or a lot of seconds; I'm honestly not sure at the moment. Then the squirrel finally broke the silence. "You dropped from the floor and fell on the countertop. When you woke up you were drinking bottled sodas for two hours, counting the caps after each one you drank. All the while I've been in my house, but you imposed conversation on me, and I'm not sure how to feel about this." This was an odd squirrel indeed. In fact, this is an odd world. Where is Scott right now? I'm trying to figure this out as well, but I'm not having much luck. Your guess is as good as mine folks.

Scott got up from the- no that's not right. Scott got off the counter and began to explore the house. He was surprised to find that there was no furniture in any room. There were no appliances, no pictures, not even any dust. As he walked, he couldn't hear his footsteps, until the lack of sound was replaced with shattering glass.

He took two more steps to see if he was really the one making those horrible sounds. Two loud crashes followed each step, so he stopped immediately. There was a door and a window in front of him, so he could see if the world outside was as strange as it was in the house if he could get out. While he could walk to either, the sound of shattering glass would be unbearable even if it was just for a little bit. He had to find a way out of the house; hopefully the little squirrel would be nice enough to help him.

"Roswell, The Squirrel," Scott said angrily "would you mind helping me find a way out of here without taking another step? I can't bare that sound anymore." The squirrel stared again and without a hint of emotion he replied "Yes I would mind, thanks for asking" then casually strolled up to the window and flew out of it.

Scott was overwhelmed by the amount of luck he was having. He had a severe headache, glass shattered every time he walked, the room was catching on fire, he had no idea

3

where he was or how he got here. "Wait, the room is on fire? When did this happen?" No, no, the room isn't on fire, it's in the *process of burning*. It is currently *catching on fire* meaning that you have nothing to fear! "I gotta get out of here, man!" Ignoring what I said along with the sounds of shattering glass, Scott charged at the front door with the hopes of barging through it. Unfortunately for Scott the door was not real and he ran right into a brick wall.

The wall was extremely upset that someone would hit it, so it grew arms and legs to fight back. Scott wasn't sure how to react to this, or anything else for that matter. Scott already found this world off-putting and he hasn't even left the house. Speaking of, he had to get out of the house alive if wanted to see the rest of this horrible world, or at least get back to his. The wall was reaching for him and the fire was getting closer so he took a dive out the window without a second thought.

At first the ground looked closely but it started to get further and further away until that grassy, green lawn disappeared completely. He was falling slower and slower but time never seemed to actually stop. Scott felt like he was spinning rapidly but there was nothing but darkness all around him. He was panicking like he never had before and panicking is absolutely one of his most notable traits. "How did I get into this mess?" he spoke without a hint of hope in his voice. Perhaps the most terrifying thing about the situation was his inability to remember how he got there.

During his fall, a soda can, a carton of cigarettes, a bottle of Sazerac, red wine in a box, a flask, and a box of knock off Frosted Flakes surrounded him. The fall got even slower until he seemed to come to a complete stop. He carefully examined each item starting with the soda can, and he made his way to each taking note of anything unusual about them. "This can look just like the one Roswell was in. It's just a different color, I think." He looked at the rest and found nothing out of the ordinary except for words written on the Sazerac label. "Take a dive in the water and you'll still come out on fire. Come on down and have a drink, it's on me. By the way, I'm glad you can read." He assumed that nothing would happen unless he used one of the items and he wasn't sure how to feel about smoking again. Besides the Sazerac had a note on it and it was the only thing he's never heard of.

Why not try it?

He popped off the cap and drank like he hadn't done so in days. Perhaps he was much thirstier than he or anyone else could've guessed! As he drank, he heard water shooting down from as though it was coming from a faucet. He took a breath and wiped his mouth after chugging a quarter of the bottle. When he opened his eyes, he saw water slowly rising at his feet and panicked. This panic however, was different from any other that he has ever experienced. The intensity of the situation and the lack of another place to go left him with no choice but to stay where he was. It was at this moment that he decided another round of Sazerac wouldn't hurt.

While downing more of the bottle he heard the water shooting out much faster than before. "A beautiful time I'm having in this wonderfully strange place. Surely this is a punishment for my consistent inconsistency. I swore by my life that I would stop drinking, but yet I find myself relinquishing my relinquishment of alcohol without hesitation. I suppose I should feel ashamed of myself, but this isn't even close to how I feel. Maybe I deserve this death; to have my lungs refurbished by the cleansing water. A long and painful death for a disappointing man such as myself is fitting. But who am I to wallow in self-pity? This stuff is too good!" He drank more the very moment he finished his words. "Although I really wish that this water would rise faster. It sounds like the water is falling much faster than it's rising which... actually kind of makes sense, but just not for what's happening here."

There was definitely something to what Scott was thinking. The sounded like it was coming down significantly faster than the rate at which the room was flooding. This world is presenting itself in a way that makes its whimsical nature clear as day. Scott continued to drink and continued to be melodramatic until his wallowing was interrupted by six growing whirlwinds of fire appeared around him. They grew until they were of an unimaginable and astonishing scale. The clouds of black and gray were being wrestled by fires of orange, red, blue, and white. They moved at such rapid speeds that the struggle appeared to be more of a passionate dance. They hovered closer to Scott until they passed over him. He caught a glance at the inside of one of the pillars of fire and was stunned by the glaring white light he saw.

There was no way for him to understand what was happening around him, but he felt it was beautiful regardless. Soon the water started rising above his ankles and before he knew it water was all the way up to his chin. He knew in his heart that it must've been time for him to die, so he closed his eyes for the last time. Or at least what he was sure would be the last time.

II

T HE SOUTH AND THE FIREMAN

CHAPTER II
THE SOUTH AND THE FIREMAN

Scott awoke on a pile of dead leaves, but he wouldn't even dare to think about how he got there. He had already woken up in a strange land before, but this seemed normal enough, so maybe he was back in the real world. For his sake, he'd better be in the real world. It is at this time that we are in the present and because I'm not omniscient I have no as to what happens next. From here forward your guesses are as good as mine. "What the fuck? *What the fuck*? What the fuck?! What the fuck?! I never asked for this! I never asked to be whirled away to God knows where! I'm not sure why me of all people was put in this...this...it's stupid! But maybe it isn't as bad as it looks? Really, it doesn't seem bad at all...kinda. Nothing too strange happened yet-well-but I'm still not sure how to feel about this. Why the fuck was I talking like that, all weird and stuff? Everything is still really fucking weird and I should be freaking out and I don't know why I'm not."

Scott is obviously confused by his strange predicament. "Who said that? Who's there?" Scott heard a voice somewhere around him and is now looking anxiously at the woods nearby with terror and anticipation. "Who are you and why the heck are you announcing everything I do?" Oh ok, so you just decided you can hear me now? That's great. That's just *soooo* amazing. Absolutely wonderful. "I'm gonna ask you one more time; who the hell are you?" Ooo we've got a badass over here folks; I'm shaking in my boots. Well Mr. Sassypants, if it's really that big of a deal to you I'll tell you what I know. I'm the narrator of this story, and this story is *supposed* to be a children's book. I handle fairytales with morals, but for some reason I was assigned to you. If you're upset with me, and I'm sensing that you are, there's not much you can do about it. In fact, the only thing that you can do about it is reach the end of the story and learn whatever lesson the author has for you.

I am not physically there and I never will be. As for why you're in this world...I have not a single clue. "So, let me get this straight..." Scott said folding his hands and putting them to his nose. "Hey cut that out, will ya?" Hey man, I'm just doing my job; disregard that and please continue. "So right now, I'm in a children's book?" Well, now it's a book that children *can* read; yes. "Okay, so I'm in a children's book and I can't get out until I learn a lesson of some kind?" That is correct Mr. Blue. "Can't you just teleport me out of here or something? If you do, I promise I won't tell anyone about this." Look pal, I don't like you any more than you like me, but you have to reach the end of the story to get out. Trust me, I really want you out of my life because you're already getting on my nerves and you've hardly had any lines yet. I'll help you as much as I can because I honestly don't see the point of you being here. Do your job, I'll do mine, and you'll be out in no time; this I can assure you.

"Fine by me; the sooner I leave the better." Agreed. Now I've noticed that you're in a wooded area with some swampy waters to complement it. Paired with the lights and that white mansion not too far from you, my guess is that you're somewhere in Louisiana. Now I know that any old state can have these things, but something about the vibe of this place is shouting Louisiana. Don't ask me why I think it's the Big Easy; just trust me on that one, Scott. Feel free to explore the land, but I suggest you get to a more *established* area first. Now I can't give you much more than that, but keep in mind that this is a fantasy story. Anything can happen since you're operating in a world without rules.

"Alright I'll keep that in mind." Hey Scott, one more thing before you go. "Shoot." You have to do your best to ignore me when I'm narrating. I'm not exactly sure how you can suddenly hear me, but since you can, you have to act like I'm not here. If I stop doing my job you won't be able to get any further than where you are. The story will fall apart if I stop, understand? "Completely; I'll do my best to tune you out." That's the ticket. Well, I'll leave you to it.

He looked down at his left hand to find that the Sazerac was gone, but he knew better than to question that. He could ask as many questions as he wanted, but they would only push him deeper into confusion. Right now, he just wanted to relax for the first time in a while. He wanted to rest his weary brain and try to live in the moment. He's here in this world and he's not sure why, but there is at least some beauty in it. This Louisiana being more fantastical than the real one would make for a truly unbelievable and unforgettable time. This is plausible, being that he is in a fantasy world.

He took a deep breath of the fresh air and slowly rolled out of the pile of leaves. He warmed up to how the ground felt on his skin once he stopped worrying about how he would get back home. Maybe home isn't the best place for him to be right now. And I can tell from the grimace on his face that he hates every second of my narration. After ignoring my presence again, Scott rolled on his back and sprawled out on the dingy green grass. He gazed at the stars sparkling in the night sky and they seemed to be doing a dance of some kind. He knows he must be high on something to be like this. Maybe it's acid; on account of how long it took for him to lighten up. If he was drunk, he was positive he'd know by now, noting the seemingly infinite amount of times he's been drunk. "Yeah, this isn't what happens when I drink."

Suddenly he heard the powerful burst of a wailing trumpet and the shock from the velocity hammered his ears. He felt an immense pain in his head but he soldiered through it to go see where it was coming from. Running was obviously much faster, but he only moved a few steps until he felt to weak and lost momentum. He continued to walk on hopes of getting to the source of the sound without putting too much stress on his body. In a combination of laziness and determination, Scott trudged down a short hill and found that a ferry was the source of the music. The large white boat was a beacon of light in an otherwise dark river and it led a charge against the mundane with vibrant, wild jazz.

Scott assumed that the ferry would stop since he appears to be the main character of this tale. He stood and waited by the side of the river with pride and confidence. When the ferry was moving towards him he stepped forward but he started to get worried when it passed by. "Maybe it'll stop a little bit ahead of me." Unfortunately for Scott, the ferry kept going as it had before. He began walking after it expecting it to at least slow down, but it continued down the river. He quickly picked up the pace until he was sprinting after it. The ferry was definitely moving faster the closer he got to it. He jumped on the back of it, but his footing was almost completely off. He was barely able to hold on to the rails.

He didn't bother pulling himself up to the main deck because he wasn't supposed to be there. Under the current circumstances, he figured that it would be best to lay low for a while. The last thing he would want is to be in the spotlight of a play he didn't know the lines to. You know I'm not completely sure about that one but I'll roll with it. "You're doing great. Just try not to veer too far off whatever the script says, okay? I don't want this to drag on." Right, sorry about that one.

Not long after clinging to the railing, Scott couldn't help but look at what was going on. The people he saw were dressed in fancy clothes of many colors, wining and dining on what was no doubt expensive food and liquor. The tables were small, square, and covered with white cloths. The chairs were large rolling chairs that oddly had an appearance of regality. The band itself was unusual being that it had two violinists, a pianist, four trumpeters, two trombonists, a drummer, an electric bassist, a kazooist(?), and a 'percussionist' (he only plays the triangle). Another odd thing is that they weren't dressed like they were supposed to be playing at the same time, especially not at this venue. The bassist was wearing a blue Christmas sweater, the pianist wore a red suit jacket with sweatpants and loafers, and the most bizarre of all was the percussionist who was dressed in a onesie, a green hoodie, track shoes, and a scarf. This reassured Scott that this world wasn't normal at all.

They still played jazz, but it quickly turned into something much different from what he heard earlier. Scott was so captivated by the unusual spectacle that he hadn't realized someone noticed him. BANG! BANG! Two bullets fired off, missing him by a hair. "Get off this boat you filthy heathen!" A man decked out in a vanilla white tuxedo yelled at Scott. This man was horribly tall, towering over the average joe at seven feet tall. He had slicked back dark grey hair, a handlebar/ goatee combo of the same color, blue tinted monocles, and red beady eyes. He held a golden flintlock in his left hand a twenty-gauge sawed off in a holster. His first thought was to jump into the river, but he scrapped the idea when he caught wind of an alligator's back rise from the waters.

He moved to the other side of the ferry as fast as he could, but the man shot at the rails so much that they became too weak to hold Scott. The railing broke, but he gripped the edge of the floor to keep him from falling. The goliath in white was still in the same spot as before and he had a clear shot at Scott, but he didn't take it. "Pardon my inhospitality; I'm really starting to become a rather rude host. I tend to freak out when I see an unfamiliar patron aboard *The Lady Well*. I take it you haven't paid for your evening ride on this fine vessel, but I'm willing to let that one slide if you would accept my invitation to my formal Junta Jubilee tonight. It would be nice for a young man such as yourself to have some powerful friends and become acquainted with some of the finest gals of Louisiana. What do ya say partner?"

"Would you shoot me if I said no?" Scott asked jokingly, but he took on a nervous laugh when the man responded "*Most certainly*. What's your name partner?"

"Scott Blue; I'm nineteen years old. I'm not from ar…"

"Well I didn't ask you all of that. I just wanted to know your name; mostly so I could introduce myself. I'm Atticus Bellamy, head of the Junta State of Louisiana. You'll be staying at my mansion down in New Orleans for at least a day, but you're welcome to stay as long as you like. My posse and I will accompany you while you're getting the proper attire for the celebration because you certainly can't go in that… less than elegant attire."

"What's wrong with what I'm wearing? Chinos and a leather jacket don't do it for ya?" Scott put on a smug smile and voice. "They are black, yes, but I would like this to be a more elegant affair. That jacket doesn't fit the dress code." Atticus had a stern, crusty, gruff, demanding voice, topped off with a deep southern accent, which commonly made his audience feel something between fear and compliance. Scott is no exception.

Atticus motioned Scott to follow him to the front of the ferry, which Scott did hesitantly. A moment ago, Atticus was trying to kill him, and now he's an esteemed guest. He had every right to be skeptical, but protest was out of the question if he wanted to live. "Ladies and gentlemen of The Great Coterie, I would like to introduce you to a special guest. This young man is the first to cross me and live! Let's get a standing ovation for this brave young man!" He laughed heartily but he wasn't joking at all. Everyone got up and clapped and cheered for Scott immediately. This was unsettling, but somewhat gratifying.

"Thanks. Thanks a million guys." Scot spoke nervously while he looked closely at the cheering crowd. Was Atticus really so terrifying that people felt compelled to do what he wanted? It didn't seem like it at surface level, but there was something eerily intimidating about this man even when he wasn't holding a gun. After all, Scott hadn't gone against even one of the man's requests so far.

He carefully examined the crowd until he noticed a young woman he found very attractive (to put in the simplest terms). Her skin was dark with some lighter patches along the side of her neck, and the side of her forehead not covered by her hair. She had a mild undercut with long wiry, kinky hair. It was mostly in the area of onyx, but there was one white streak near her left eye. Said eye is dark brown while the other is fairly pale; all graced with the beauty mark on the left side of her nose, but that's all he could see of her because of the crowd. Okay, that may have sounded just a little weird. Like, seriously, how good is his vision?

Scott smiled and waved and she winked at him then disappeared into the crowd. He felt in his gut that he had to talk to her, so when Atticus told everyone to "resume the festivities" Scott went around as quickly and casually as he could to find her.

As he passed by some of the guests patted him on the back, which made him feel completely and utterly uncomfortable, but he ignored it the best he could.

He was sure she was somewhere deep in the crowd, but he was contemplating whether or not it was even worth pushing through all those horribly pretentious human beings. What if she was one of those pretentious human beings? Scott decided it was worth the risk since he literally had nothing better to do. He awkwardly maneuvered around the patrons until he got out of that crowd then he let out a huge sigh of relief. It seems that Scott isn't the most sociable person you'd ever meet. "For God's sake, SHUT UP! I'm working on it, geez." Scott was so busy flipping a lid that he didn't notice that the woman he was looking for was actually pretty close.

"Who are you talking to?" she asked playfully with just a hint of concern. Scott was flipping out on the inside, but that was mostly due to his fear of making a bad first impression. However, he was able to give the impression that he was keeping his composure. "I was… thinking out loud. I do that sometimes but I'm trying to cut back. Sorry if I freaked you out or anything like that." Scott was displaying so much confidence that he almost believed what he said.

"We all have our quirks. Believe it or not, that's not even one of the really weird ones." Her voice could be described as smooth, but...nah I'll just go with smooth. Scott nodded then just stood there and looked at her for a few seconds until she broke the silence. "So, what's your name? Where are you from? You don't have to start with those if you don't want to." "No, you're fine, it's just that I can be a little awkward sometimes. I'm Scott, by the way. I'm not from here, but I do think Louisiana is pretty cool. I just didn't expect Louisiana to be so terrifying on my first visit." "The brochures are hardly ever right. My name's Faaghira, but you're free to call me Fae. So, how'd you end up on this ferry anyway? I've never seen you around and from what I know you have to have some kind of connections to even sneak on board." "Well, the thing is, I'm not from around here."

"It's been a long time since I've heard anyone say *that one*." Fae jokingly crossed her arms. "I mean I'm not from a place where Louisiana has some militant aristocracy with a gun toting maniac." "You're telling me there's another one? Are you sure you're not crazy? Last time I checked, this is the only Louisiana, and *it is currently run by a gun toting maniac*." Fae pursed her lips and gave Scott a severely stern look. Also, she said that last part so loud that there's no way Atticus wouldn't have heard her.

Scott leaned close to her and whispered in her ear. "I would love to explain everything, but something tells me that this isn't the best place for stories." She nodded then reached out her hand.

"Dance with me." He was totally confused but he placed his palm in hers, and their fingers were soon intertwined. "Trust me on this one." She had a tight-lipped smile but a vulnerable look in her eyes. She let go of his hand and put both her arms over his shoulders. "Usually anybody around this area that Atticus doesn't recognize is declared a terrorist and they disappear in an hour or less. But for some reason you're different. That doesn't mean that you should get too comfortable though. I thought I saw some contractors somewhere in the crowd, so you're still in danger." Scott was even more confused than before. Why would someone has it in for him if he just showed up? How was that even possible? It had to be some mistake that he was dropped into this confusing and horribly paced chain of events. "How can you tell who the contractors are? I don't see anybody that's even remotely close to standing out."

"That's the point. You have to look at gestures rather than aesthetic when you're looking for someone. Their job is to look like they fit in, but they never act like they do. I can't explain much more than I have already, well not right now. Not sure I'll tell you later though." "Why not? Is it part of a top-secret conspiracy or something?" "Wanna try something?" Fae had a playful smirk, but there was also fear and anxiety in her eyes. She kissed him on the neck then slow worked up to his cheek.

"See if you can one-up me."

"With pleasure" Scott grinned." Without getting into extrancous details, they kissed passionately and seemed to really enjoyed it. This whole scene seems pretty pointless to me, so I'm not sure why it even happened. I suppose that's why I don't write the stories. "What prompted the spontaneous makeout? I'm not complaining; I'm just curious."

Fae's face seemed to hold conflicting emotions but it unlike the other times, it was easy to see. "I don't know, maybe I felt like being spontaneous. It was the right moment for it, I guess. Is that good enough for you?" "For now; until you let your guard down that'll be good enough." "Good luck trying to catch me doing that. And just to make things tougher…feelings can be weird just like people, and while we're on the topic of weird people, who's the weirdest person you've ever met?" For once she got really close to bearing a genuine smile but her expression was still riddled with deceit. "It's between you and this one guy named Zach Hurst." Scott smirked but Fae was clearly unamused so he continued with his story. "When I was in Middle School, he went around telling people that he was too fast for the track team. It didn't matter whether he knew them or not, he just talked and talked like everyone's lives depended on it. He had this whole geeky, awkward demeanor, his voice cracked all the time, all his pants were highwaters, he was a mouth breather, and not a day went by where he didn't walk at an uncomfortably close distance behind complete strangers."

"Sounds hot if you ask me. Wearing highwaters *and* breathing out of your mouth are signs of a bona fide lady killer! He was probably sleeping with all the girls, but he didn't tell the other guys so they wouldn't feel bad. Also, and this *might* not be right, but I wouldn't be surprised if he picked out his highwaters to show off those kankles. Though in all seriousness, he's probably grown a lot since then. Nobody stays the same for that long."

"He hasn't changed a bit since I last saw him. That's pretty big because the last time I saw him was yesterday. It was like, a party or something." She simpered, resulting in conflicting desires to laugh and remain mysterious. "Okay then, so nobody stays the same for that long except for him." Scott hadn't known her for more than a few minutes but it made him feel good whenever she almost genuinely smiled. "One thing I will give the guy is that he was more confident than anyone I've ever seen. I'm not sure if he wasn't aware of society or if he just didn't care, but if I had even half the confidence of that guy, I'd be able to retire next year. A Lack of confidence can make the world a pretty scary place to be. And while we're on the topic of scary things, what's your biggest fear?" Any trace of a smile immediately withdrew from her face. She was completely and utterly mortified. "Hmm, touché; there's one thing…" She took a moment to flip the script. "The ferry will be stopping pretty soon, so we can go somewhere and talk in private. Did Atticus say that you were staying at the estate?"

"Yeah, I don't trust the guy one bit but I don't have anywhere else to stay." "Now you do; I'm telling Atticus that you're staying with me, come on." She held out her hand and he took hold of her wrist. Fae led him through the crowd and they went straight to the cockpit were Atticus was keeping a close watch on his guests.

"Scott, I see you've met Fae, my inauspicious niece. I sincerely apologize for any trouble she may have caused you. She can be quite the brash one." Fae scowled at Atticus and mouthed something at him that we can assume was the vilest thing she could think of. "Scott is staying with me. I'm not asking you; I'm telling you. You know good and well that that ringleader crap you like to pull doesn't work on me, so cool it with that shit, alright? He's staying at my place and that's that." Atticus put his right hand on his holster while Fae stood unflinching, loosening her grip on Scott's hand.

Atticus and Fae continued to give each other Stern looks until Atticus put on a glaringly fake smile. "Did you even ask the man what he wanted to do? I didn't hear a word out of his mouth that went along any of the nonsense you're spouting out." "Did you ask him? Did you ask him or did you tell him what would happen, Atticus? I already know

19

which one it is, but I'm here to prove a point." Atticus was processing the normally impossible circumstance that he was in. He couldn't resort to fear to gain the upper hand this time. He couldn't use the one thing he functioned on, and one of the only people he couldn't kill was his niece.

"I suppose it wouldn't do any harm if *you* accommodated Scott while during his stay. However, I do expect him to be at the Jubilee. Though you are my kin by technicality, I wouldn't mind if *you* didn't show up at the party. After all, it is supposed to celebrate successes, not mistakes and disappointments." The tall man smiled in an irritatingly smug way but it didn't have the effect that he'd hoped for. All Fae did was roll her eyes before she led Scott back outside the cockpit. As the ferry got closer to the docks it was met by strands upon strands of fairy lights that lined the tree trunks and branches. The luminescent reds, blues, yellows, greens, and whites were a perfect complement to the white lines of light that adorned the ferry. Most of the crowd was captivated by the beautiful sight, but there are always those folks who couldn't care less.

Fae glanced at Scott and noticed how amazed he was by the light. However, she was very careful not to be noticed looking at him. She's had conflicting feelings the whole time; from a playful vamp to a starry eyed hopeless romantic. She didn't seem to be sure how she felt about him. Heck, at this point she hadn't known him for more than an hour. "Leaving the ferry is always my favorite part of riding down the river. Something about seeing the all these beautiful lights welcome you to the docks is just so magical! It's still one of the most captivating experiences for me even though I've seen it dozens of times."

"It must be amazing to see this every night, or every other night, or however often you're on the ferry. The only thing I've experienced regularly was one of my cousin's horrible pickup lines. He would stroll up to some girl and he'd use the deepest voice he could make. He'd slick his hair back and say 'Girl, if I could rearrange the alphabet, I'd put you and me together.'" Fae giggled then quickly cover put her hand over her mouth and pretended to look around.

"It's okay to smile and it's even better to laugh; especially when you laugh like a drunk hyena." She smiled and playfully pushed his shoulder.

"You're such a duface. Anyway, we're about to dock soon so let's get to the bottom deck before everyone else does. If we wait too long, we'll be stuck on this boat forever. She led him through the crowd and back down the stairs. They ran to the railing at the bow and rushed off the ferry as soon as it reached the ramp. They walked and talked for a while, still holding hands and Scott still wasn't sure why. Not that he minded, of course. She checked her phone here and there but for the most part they talked without any distractions. "Man, I lost track of time; the limo's been here for a few minutes already! Come on Scott, I don't want to keep my driver waiting any longer!" Scott was trying his hardest to keep up with what was happening. He started off in a battered house doing odd things like talking differently than he normally does and trying to hold a full-on conversation with a squirrel. Next, he drowned; then somehow, he ended up in Louisiana. He was almost shot to death by a freakishly tall, trigger happy man. Afterwards, he met a mysterious and charming young lady who is the niece of said maniac. Now they're about to go somewhere in her limousine; something about this seems too good to be true for Scott. I really can't blame him, though. She pulled him along to the limo and the car moved as soon as Scott closed the door. "Sorry I'm so late X, I met a new friend tonight. So, Scott do you play any instruments?" Her driver (their name is actually X) checked his rear mirror to see Scott but was silent otherwise.

"I'm a pretty sick triangle player and I can play the mess out of a kazoo. Why asking?" She got excited and reached behind her seat to get a colorful pineapple shaped ukulele that she started to idly strum. "I'll play us a number or two on the ride to my place. It's not a mansion but it's more than enough for me; I digress again. The reason I asked is because I have tons of instruments at my place. Saxophones, trumpets, violins, basses, drums, xylophones, cellos, lutes, guitars, violas, harmonicas, banjos, a grand piano, a sitar, a veena, a kora, a seperewa, a gravikord, and of course a bunch of ukes! I really hope you like it!"

It's crazy seeing so many different sides of one person in one night. One minute she's mysterious and alluring, the next she's so gentle and vulnerable. Scott was still unsure how to feel because something about her was so magnificent to him, but he couldn't put her on a pedestal because he saw how normal she was. She had quirks and flaws just like everyone else and she wasn't trying to hide it. Anyone can see that he's got some kind of feelings towards her, but it's a bit too early to tell if it's love, lust, or infatuation. I'm sure he wouldn't deny that she was beautiful if you asked, but right now there's no telling what he'd be willing to admit.

Fae closed her eyes and gave the ukulele one hard strum before she burst into song.

"The tide has come and parted with me
She was the beauty of the moon
To be so far and leave so soon
I knew that she'd get too close
Gravity would bring the crashing of the sea
The love was there but hope was gone
Or was it absent all along?
The balance that could never be…"

She abruptly stopped playing but it didn't bother Scott at first. He was sure that she just forgot the rest of the words. Her eyes were still closed but they were watering up a bit. "Sorry… I guess I forgot a word or two. I get really upset when I forget lyrics. I'm *sooooooooo* dramatic for no reason." She wiped her eyes with the back of her hand and smiled. She's a tough one alright. She knows that isn't the truth, and she probably doesn't expect Scott to believe her at all; it appears that her game isn't about fooling people.

"We all forget things sometimes; that's just part of being human." Scott responds in a modest way, mostly as a hint that he knew exactly what she did.

"Don't worry; I'm not always such a mess. Life's just been a piece of work these days. Oh, my stop is coming up. It's that complex on the far right." She pointed briefly to a set of extravagant buildings that towered over the streets. And when he saw the high rises deeper in the city, they paled in comparison. It's hard to believe that this is Louisiana; even if it is in an alternate reality, it's not at what I'd imagine it would ever look like. And to believe Scott's luck; not even a day in and he's around luxury. It all seems a bit *too* good. "I know it can seem overwhelming at first, but this is kind of like a small town once you've been around for a while. I would ask if you want to see some of the city, but I'm sure you're exhausted. Today was pretty wild for a lot of us." When the limo pulled up to front of the tall condo Scott was almost too overwhelmed to open the door.

The building was way bigger than he thought it would be; it looked more like some gargantuan hotel rather than a condominium. Of course, he knew this kind of stuff existed in the real world, but he never thought he would see it in person. Being an average nineteen-year-old guy, he hadn't had many run-ins with luxury (being black and not rich hadn't helped either). At the most it's been a decent hotel here and there. Such a drastic change in luck can give anyone a good reason to be skeptical. Even though I'm not omniscient, I know for sure that Scott could pass for the definition of skeptical right now. Things are changing so much for him here that there's no way to get a legitimate read on anyone or anything. He stood staring up at the complex for a few moments until Fae wrapped her arm around his. "What's wrong?" She gave him a focused but gentle look, showing him that she wouldn't let up until he answered. "It's just hard to believe that you come home every night to this. Now I'm here at a place like this and it's just so surreal."

"You're lying, but it's a good lie. Though, you should know that I have all night, so you should probably tell me what's wrong and just get it over with." She smiled in a way that would've been obnoxious if anyone else did it. Scott nodded, wanting to make a smart remark instead, but he couldn't think of anything on the spot. They walked inside the lobby arm in arm and by Fae's suggestion they took the stairs rather than the elevator. "I feel lazy whenever I use the elevator. It's always really confined and awkward, and everyone does that weird thing where they walk in and turn around. I don't think technology should barge itself into

24

something as simple as getting from one floor to another. Besides, I've never heard of anyone getting stuck on the stairs."

"Alright, no argument there. What about escalators? You do know those are stairs too." A frown plagued her efforts to hold a smile. "Only by a technicality. They don't actually count from my point of view. I know that what I think isn't the be all-end all of anything, but it makes sense when you think about it. You can move at any speed you want on stationary stairs. Meanwhile, escalators have a predetermined speed which can be much slower than you would normally use on stairs. And which are we on right now again? Oh, that's right, the stairs." Her tone hadn't changed one bit while they talked which partially annoyed Scott. Maybe it's because she was always quicker to the punch. She was sassy but it never showed in her tone. "We're only on the third floor and my place is the eighth. Still beats an escalator though."

"Don't you mean it's on the eighth?"

"No. It *is* the eighth floor. So, since it'll be a couple minutes and you're not too good with small talk I'll give you a choice of two stories: I can tell you about the only thing I'm afraid of or how Louisiana ended up like this. Remember, it's your choice and that you'll get to hear the other story later."

"Sure, that'll work. As much as I want to know what you're afraid of since you dodged it earlier, I'm more curious about what's going on. I'm completely lost on how this could ever be Louisiana." "Alright dude, brace yourself for some really weird and seriously messed up happenings. A little over twenty-five years ago a para military group showed up after

25

terrorists bombed the French Quarter. The group was welcomed with open arms at first, but after they made quick work of the so-called terrorists, they stayed. If you could see the reports of what happened, you'd know that everything was too perfect for it to not be an inside job. There were already some corrupt officials and law enforcement around, but from what I hear the whole justice system was flipped on its head after the attack. There were these lists of suspected terrorists a day or two after the bombing; not even the F.B.I was that fast! My take is that the group, The Junta was planning a coupe de etat for a long time and they guaranteed a win by playing both sides. This is the twenty-fifth anniversary of it and today was the end of the national election; he won, like always."

"So, from what I'm gathering here, the government found a legal way to completely take over a state. Am I right?" Fae put her palm over her mouth and shook her head in disagreement. "Not exactly. I'm not so sure that the Junta was involved with the government before taking over the state. Again, maybe I'm wrong. One thing I do know for sure is that there was a huge reduction in state social spending, along with lower incomes across the board; except for the Junta and its supporters, of course. It took out the upper middle class and left three tax brackets. These days you're either below the poverty line, above the poverty line, or the bourgeoisie. If you haven't guessed already, I'm in the last one." "People in the lower classes must not like you too much." She stopped at one of the steps for a second then she kept walking. "Funny story about that one. There's been a resistance group ever since The Junta got in a seat of power. I've been helping them on and off for the better part of five years, but I've recently cut ties with them. The people that know I helped certainly don't hate me, but I'm still rich while they're…not. Everyone else straight up hates my guts, but I'm tolerated when I go to the inner city. Mostly because Atticus is the leader of The Junta and I openly hate him."

"So, what you're saying is your uncle is the reason for all of this?" Fae sighed and rolled her eyes. "Ugh! Don't remind me I'm technically related to that halfwit. Okay, fifth floor! That's basically the past twenty-five years in a nutshell. Any questions?" She was trying to keep the conversation going but Scott wasn't giving her the easiest time. He's not the greatest with words, as I've mentioned before. In fact, the only reason I'm bringing that up again is because it got on Scott's nerves the last time. The best part is that he can't say anything about it because only he can hear me. He doesn't want to seem strange around Fae and telling her that they're in a story and there's a narrator only he can hear. Maybe she wouldn't think much of it, but maybe she'd ditch him as soon as she could. Scott didn't want to risk finding out what would really happen so he tucked that thought away.

"Why did you end up leaving the resistance? People usually don't get up and leave a rebellion behind. What made you quit?" She kept walking up the stairs but she didn't say a word until they got to the seventh floor.

"Conflicting interests; I still believed in the cause, but one of the cats in charge and I butted heads on a lot of things. She told me to leave the resistance, but I still helped out from time to time without her knowing. When she did find out, she went off on me like I've never seen her do with anyone. I still don't see why she was so mad; we were still on the same team, but she kicked me to the curb. Now I couldn't care less what happens to them. I don't hate them, but I don't support them anymore. I thought they were about equality and a fair society, but apparently, I had them all wrong. I like a fair economy as much as the next guy, I really do, but I couldn't care less about her… and the rest of them now. I'm sure some of them are still good people, but I'm just not down with the group anymore. With that being said, I do think they would be a better alternative to the greedy idiots running the place right now."

"I was hoping for more details, but I will say that you dance around topics quite nicely." She seemed to completely ignore his comment. "Oh look! We're at the eighth floor! I told you the stairs would be better. We had a nice chat and got from the first floor to here in the blink of eight hundred cat eyes." She opened the exit door for the eighth floor (cool rhyme, right?) and promptly welcomed Scott to her home. "So, which one is it? There's a bunch of rooms up here." "Pick a unit, dude. I own the entire building and I specifically kept the eighth floor off limits so that I wouldn't have any neighbors. I don't have any instruments in any of the rooms up here; they're all cooped up in the den. I'll show you that room later. There's stuff in some of these, but I'm a minimalist for the most part. Compared to everyone else here I don't live a very lavish lifestyle."

"So, are we just gonna pretend this isn't excessive at all?"

Fae rolled her eyes then went back to her playful smirk. "It's only too much by a *very* small margin. Now I want to show you my least favorite room first: unit number four!"

"Don't you show off the best room first?"

"Nope. Why would you say I'd do that? You don't know me." "Whatever." She took him by the hand and they went into the fourth unit. It was mostly an open area but it had two rooms… or three. The room was dimly lit by lights on the ground and the ceiling which provided a chill atmosphere.

The kitchen was in a corner near the door and was modest compared to the lavish interior he expected. The appliances were your run of the mill modern stainless steel. There was no way to see what colors most of the things in the room were without turning on the main lights, but that would've totally ruined the mood. The glow from the busy city shone through the large window that overlooked the skyline.

Fae motioned for him to sit on the couch facing towards the glass. "At nights, whether I'm at home or at least somewhere with a window, I like to sit back and take in the sights. A lot of bad happened there, but a lot of good happens there every day. Most of that is ignored for the sake of news headlines and tabloids. At night it's clear to see that we're all regular people and the constructs that divide us are our own faults. Sometimes I wish the next day would never come so that we wouldn't have to keep putting on this charade."

"The charade never goes away. All of that is wishful thinking, Fae. It's admirable, but everything is still the same when the lights go out. In fact, it may be just a little worse because it's easier to hide when you're in the dark. Life is just one big charade. It might even be worse because there's no light to shine on any shady deals. I wish it wasn't so bad. I wish that wasn't the reality, but those things we make stick with us at any part of the day. Life never really stops sucking, it just sucks less sometimes."

Fae pursed her lips as if she were contemplating something, but she nodded in agreement instead. "Wow. That's pretty deep dude. Are you secretly a philosopher or something? If you are, feel free to shoot down a couple more of my hopes." She crossed her legs, folded her arms and grinned slightly.

"That would make my whole world. Okay, so slight

digression here; what's that thing you're afraid of?" The color slowly started to fade from her face. "Hmmm… I had a feeling this one would come back to bite me at some point. I knew I shouldn't have mentioned that; I actually don't know why I even told you." She uncrossed her legs, put her hands on her knees and sighed with disgust. "Okay, here it goes. There's this legend that's been going around for a long time about this 'thing' that lives in a mansion in the Old Quarter. It's a twenty-minute walk from here."

"Twenty-minute walk? You allergic to driving there or something?" Scott interrupted her, assuming that now was the greatest time to joke around. From what we've seen, Fae loves to be silly and give people a hard time, but this was different. She was almost scared stiff every time she even started talking about whatever this thing is. She gave him this steely look but she kept talking after a moment or two. "Cars don't come back from there. A good number of cars are sitting near the grounds. They're not damaged, they're not out of gas, but nobody drives out of there. Walking is the only way off the estate, so anybody that goes their walks. It's a real creep show, but it's a local hotspot for some reason." "What's the thing you're afraid of?"

"Geez, give me a second; I'm getting to that part soon. So, there's this thing there that isn't a monster per se, but it isn't a person. It's apparently a fire demon, but nobody's ever gotten a good look at it. The Fireman is what it's called by most of the folks who know about him. Every once in a while, you'll see someone post a blurry picture somewhere of it, but there's not much out there aside from those. I was obviously too little to remember anything that happened that day, but I've been having nightmares about this monster ever since I was a kid. I'm pretty sure that day had something to do with it but I've been too scared to go back there."

"I'll go with you if that'll make you feel any better. If anything is there I'll rough 'em up a bit and teach him not to mess with you. It might actually turn out to be nothing at all." "You being there would actually make it scarier. You're alright, but you can't do anything. This…it's more than just a legend; it needs to be more than just a legend; all those nightmares had to come from somewhere! I can't be crazy! It has to be real!" Fae was leaning over staring at the floor, resting her forehead in her palms. She was so different when she talked about her fear. It's like seeing a whole new person; as if her tough shell cracked and she was left terrified. "Look Fae, I know I haven't known you for even like, two hours, but this doesn't seem like you at all. I also know that you aren't too keen on me going with you to that mansion. Since you're a complete mess when you talk about this, you need to face your fear. Tonight, we're going to that mansion and you'll see that there's nothing to be afraid of. After all, you weren't even old enough to remember what really happened." Scott was sure that whatever she was afraid of couldn't be real. He's experienced at least two unexplainable events in the past few hours, but somehow, he doesn't believe her. I didn't have a reason to think he was a hypocrite before, but he sure showed me!

"Tonight, wouldn't be a good night. My uncle invited you to that party and he'd be pissed if you didn't show up. I'm not a fan of the guy myself, but he's one of the last people that you'd wanna be around when he's lost it; I really do appreciate the offer though. Come on we should get to that party. We can talk about this sometime later." Fae got up from the couch and rushed out the door. Scott wasn't in such a hurry to leave but he didn't see a reason to. Atticus was a strange and vicious man, but Scott's sure he's not nearly as bad as Faaghira says he is. Scott already showed that he's

31

not a very good judge of anything.

"Hurry up you tart! We've got somewhere to be!" Fae yelled at him from outside the door. "Yes master." Scott yelled back and smiled slyly. The smile didn't really have much of a point because she couldn't see it, but he found his comment funny enough. However, he rushed to the door after he shared his remark because Fae didn't seem like the kind of dame that would put up with anyone's crap. She was waiting at the elevator when he opened the door which genuinely surprised him. I'm sure he would've made some idiotic comment but the look on Faaghira's face told him that she had absolutely no time for that. They went in the elevator as soon as it opened because she being on time to this party is a big deal to her. There was one other person on the elevator who tried to spark some conversations with small talk, but he shut up after nobody said a word about any of his random topics. When the elevator opened Fae and Scott got out as fast as they could. The pulled him through the lobby and out the main doors, where a burgundy muscle car was parked. "It starts sometime after twelve but we'll get there before then. I'm letting you know ahead of time that I'm ignoring the speed limit for somewhere around five minutes. If you're a backseat driver shut your eyes and cover your ears. I'm not much of a talker when I drive, but feel free to run your mouth on anything."

"Sweet wheels! What year is this one?" Fae popped the doors open then started the car. "Don't know, don't care. It's not even mine to be honest." Scott left that alone without another thought. He started to go into the backseat but she told him to get in the passenger's seat and he went without protest. The engine let out a loud, raspy howl while she waited for Scott to close his door. Right after he did, the car growled and sped off with sheer force. She sped out of the parking lot at a solid fifty. Scott didn't know how to react to feel about her driving so fast. Her stern face told him to leave it alone before he asked her why. After a few minutes of silence, he asked her whose car it was. "Someone who probably wouldn't lose sleep over it. Is your golden heart hurting because of my *blatant sinning*?" She was playful as she normally was, but she didn't do as much as crack a smile.

"Not one bit. I've never been able to consider myself a saint. It's just that stealing an entire car is a bit much." He expected at least a trace of a smile but her face still didn't move a muscle. "I hope you catch on to the whole class disparity thing we've got going on here down in New Orleans. The poor are really poor, the rich have more money than they know what to do with, and the middle class can't move up without getting into rackets. I'm not downplaying anything when I say that they probably won't miss the car. You're gonna need to chill out if we keep hanging out. When you're with me you always live the high life; take a load off and live a little!" The contrast between her voice and her expression was confusing. She sounded so excited but was still stone faced. Scott was a little creeped out by the lack of matching emotions.

"Shut up!" He whispered angrily at me. Faaghira was too focused on driving to comment on anything that wasn't clearly directed towards her.

I hoped that she would catch him talking to me so that she would see how weird that guy is. Fae drove to Atticus' house in a terrifyingly fast period of time. Poor Scott only got to see the city as a blur of colors. Despite the fact that she was a speed demon on her way there, she didn't hit a thing. Her driving was flawless but utterly terrifying. This obviously wasn't her first time driving that far at such high speeds. The thing that really worried Scott was if she always drove like that. She drove so smoothly that it was almost like a roller coaster. The potentially scary part was if she made even one turn a bit too early, they would crash and probably die.

Scott was panicking at the thought of dying so young. He was getting heavier anxiety the more he thought about it. "The heck are you so sweaty?" Fae took a rag from the glove compartment and wiped beads of sweat from Scott's face. "I told you the speed limit didn't matter. Don't tell me that you're not the thrill-seeking guy I thought you were."

"You were going *eighty* freaking miles per hour. Let that sink I for a second. *Eighty*! We could've died if you made one bad turn!" Faaghira shook her head at Scott with an arrogant smile.

"*But I didn't,* so you're alive to complain about something that didn't even happen. Perhaps I drove a little *too* well this time." "Faaghira, I don't get how you could be so nonchalant about this. You could've hurt so many people and crashed into so many things, but here you are, brushing it off like it's nothing. I'd like to put emphasis on the fact that *you could've* gotten us killed! I could've been so freaking dead right now." "So, is there like a strict no cursing rule or something wherever you're from? Did your mum tell you not to curse because you'd have to stand against the wall and think about how much of a bad boy you are?"

"My 'mum' has been dead for years! What would you think if I told you that I'm trying to quit cursing because it's what she would've wanted?" For the first time Fae showed concern. "I'm so sorry! I didn't mean for it to come off that way; it was just a joke." Scott's cold expression was replaced by a smile and a good laugh.

34

"Nah I'm just pulling your teeth. Both my folks are still alive. I haven't talk to them in a little over a year though. Now since we're here we better stop wasting time. We'd better go find your uncle before he finds us." Fae was still stunned from the fact that she actually believed Scott. I'm sure she would admit that he got her pretty good if she weren't the prideful type.

"You're a class A asshole, you know that? Or, or, even better... a classhole!" Scott shook his head in disapproval.

"Nah I don't like that one." "Yeah, me either. I'll keep trying; but seriously, you're a dick." "You do that." From there they set out to Atticus' excessively large house. The posh building is adorned with large white columns as well as a seemingly infinite amount of stairs and windows. It can easily pass for a slightly smaller courthouse. There were fireworks of all kinds going off behind the mansion. At first, they were just red, white, and blue, which led Scott to believe that it was a patriotic event. Hey, there's nothing wrong with a little patriotism here and there. However, he was confused by the numerous other colors that burst into the sky. The different shades of greens, yellows, oranges, and purples made him unsure of what the event was celebrating. So basically, if you're Scott Blue, the only fireworks that are acceptable are red, white, and blue ones. Anything else is *obviously* a sign of a freedom hater.

She took his hand and walked him up the steps to the front doors. She sat down at the top step as if she was waiting for something. "So, are we *not* going inside now?" This was Scott's way of asking if something was wrong. He didn't want to lose the whole witty thing he's been holding up this whole time. Faaghira is that kind of person that'll bust your chops at any given time. It can be hard to tell when someone like that is having a legitimate problem. There's not always a clear difference between when it's time to be serious and when it isn't. "Can we sit and talk for a minute? We're already early." Fae didn't seem worried or concerned with anything. She was actually very casual for once.

"Umm…sure. Okay. What's up?" He was careful when he sat down and wiped his pants to get rid of any dust that might have got on them. "Why are you… never mind. I feel weird because I haven't really asked you anything. Nothing important to be exact. I've told you more about me than I normally do and the only thing I know about you is your name. You don't even know what's going on and here I am pushing some more issues on you. I haven't really thought about you as a person until now. You have your own life, your own problems, and your own dreams. None of that occurred to me until just now."

"What did you look at me as before?"

She smirked again. "Someone that would be a little bit of fun. A guy that I could string along for a week or two. Mostly as another guy that would catch feelings who I could lead on till I got bored of him. Maybe a benefits situation; you're one of my types. I actually didn't have any interest in you as a person and I didn't want to."

"Why? Were you afraid that you'd like me?"

"No, that's not it. I was sure you'd turn out to be a douche. There aren't a whole lot of people I get along with so I didn't expect you to be any different." "Oh, okay. That's not what I was expecting to hear at all. So, what did you want to know?" He shot Fae an awkward smirk as if someone put a

36

gun up to his head and told him to smile. She chuckled either because she thought his awkwardness was cute, or she was trying to make the situation less awkward. He noticed how perfectly white her teeth are. He noticed the black scarf that was draped around her neck. In fact, he noticed a lot of important things that he should've noticed before. She had the same dark red blazer and dark grey high waisted skinny jeans the whole night. She had this formally casual aesthetic all this time and he hardly noticed it. It's not that he didn't see her clothes. Wait… that sounds a little off now that I think about it. I'll just skip over that one too. From her hair down to her boots, there's not a bright color to be seen, save for an off-white blouse. That's not really bright though. "Asking where you're from is too cliché. Hmm…let's see. What about your day before you came here?" "What about it?" "What were you doing before you ended up here? You had to have been doing something."

Any trace of a smile jumped off his face, much akin to Fae's reaction to The Fireman. "Running away from my problems. Not physically though. I was still in the same old town I've always been in. I was having a couple of drinks with some people I met senior year. I won't go calling them my friends because they aren't. I down a bottle or four and next thing I know I'm in a pile of leaves by a river. I saw the ferry and you pretty much know the rest of the story from there." As you might've noticed, Scott left out some details. This doesn't come from a lack of trust. There are certain people that can't handle the whole truth, especially when the truth is essentially wild fiction. At this time, he's not sure if she can and this may not be a good time to find out.

"What were you running from?" Fae voice had a sincerity that showed she was genuinely concerned. Scott was still trying to figure out why she even cares about him as much as she does. Why was he such a big deal?

"The future. My parents want me to go to college and get a degree in something that's supposed to pay well. I'm pretty sure it's just for bragging rights. At a family function or at work either one of them want to say 'My child is a insert high paying job here! They make a six-figure salary and have an ultimate superior doctorate degree from the one of the most pretentious schools in the country!" Fae laughed so hard at his impersonation of his parents that snot ran out of her nose. She promptly pulled out a napkin from the inside of her blazer, wiped her nose, and let it drop on the steps.

"Do all the rich people here leave their trash for other people to pick up? And do you guys always dress up so much? Makes me feel like I should've at least worn a suit or something."

"Nope, I just *really* hate Atticus. I leave all sorts of stuff lying around whenever I'm here. This is an outfit I just threw together; just some of the cheap stuff I have laying around in some of my closets. Now back to you and that future you're running away from. Something's telling me that there's a bit more to it than your folks pushing for you to get a degree." Fae has eerily good senses. "I wouldn't mind so much if I could afford it, and I wouldn't have to worry about affording it if they'd help me with it. Both in and out of school everybody was shoving college down my throat. I'm surprised I didn't suffocate from all the pressure."

"Looks like somebody's gotten over that gag reflex." She winked at him after inserting a strong double entendre into the conversation. He briefly nodded his head to show that he acknowledged but didn't care for her joke.

"Everybody wants me to go, but nobody wants to help me pay for it. I know scholarships are a thing, but most of them don't help enough. It's not fair that colleges are becoming the center of a lot of people's lives. If one of the requirements for the highest paying scholarships were to make a make an eighty-minute twerking video, at least twenty thousand would be up in the next hour. College is becoming mandatory for a lot more jobs but the prices are shooting up. It's the biggest racket of all if you ask me. I'm lucky to have help dealing with that part, but that's between us." Fae was laughing hysterically when he made that comment on scholarship requirements. "You're killing me, dude! Twerking videos? I'm *beyond* tired of you!" She couldn't stop laughing while she talked. Scott was contemplating whether or not he should tell her the last thing he felt was weighing on him. She was laughing and he didn't want to ruin that with some depressing issue. But she was able to tell when he was holding back the first part of the story. Chances are she'd to do it again without hesitation.

"Fae, how's your relationship with your parents?"

"Umm I'm not really sure. I like them a lot better than Atticus. I don't see them very often but aside from a couple of times we've always been on good terms. Is yours not too hot?" "How much time do you think passed while we were out here? I see some cars pulling up." Scott made a mission out of avoiding his problems. His diversions aren't exactly smooth, but they get the job done.

"Oh man, you're right! We should head inside now before the crowd gets in." Faaghira caught wind of what he was doing, but she decided it was best to drop their conversation now and pick it back up later. She rolled over to push herself off the ground then she pulled Scott up. They never let go of each other's hands when they walked through the front doors. They were greeted in the main hall by two smiling men in crisp white suits. They were armed to the teeth with pistols on their hips and rifles on their backs. Despite the excessive number of arms, they were very nice. They both shook hands with Scott and one of them tipped their hat at Faaghira. The four engaged in some friendly but mundane small talk for a minute or so until they dismissed themselves and returned to their posts.

The main hall is a gigantic white room with classy gold lines that adorn parts of the staircase and the floor. The room is made almost completely of highly polished marble. The ceiling is covered by a renaissance style painting of Atticus accompanied by farmers, businessmen, women, and children, decimating some grotesque looking people. A heap of fire and smoke sits in the corner the people portrayed as monsters are retreating to. It's a brutally violent mural that sticks out in an otherwise elegant room.

The low hanging chandeliers near the staircase bring some attention away from the gruesome centerpiece. They have a beautiful shine that comes from the crystals reflecting the various lights around them. Some of the light they reflect land on the tall golden candelabras on both sides of the staircase. The extravagant fashion of the room is carried on by the sculpted scene the candelabras have at their bases. The whole theme of violence is subtly spread across the hall throughout paintings, vases, and tables that hug the walls of the room. It's not necessarily a room like regular people would call it, but I'm not really sure what else to call it. Using hall over and over again is a bit too repetitive and using 'room' makes it seem smaller than it actually is.

The gold isn't the cheap looking kind that most people see

in a run of the mill interior store; it's sharper and more refined. Of course, not all gilded things are what they appear to be. This beautiful place is owned by a foul man and was built on the backs of the lower classes in a period of serious economic disparity. Those nice men are part of the reason that Louisiana is like this now. The horrors they brought to this state were rewarded with a cozy lifestyle. Was it right to take part in any of this when you knew what was really going on? These are the kind of things that have Scott wondering if Faaghira is good at all.

"This place sure changed a lot in a matter of months. Last time I was here the ceiling was solid white. Somewhere along the way he must've gotten someone to paint that all that creepy junk up there. And speaking of creepy junk, Atticus is right over there by the staircase. Let's go say hi before he can. Whoever starts the talk gets to leave first and I'm pretty sure you'd rather shove a cactus in your eye than wait for him to finish yapping." This time Scott led Fae to the place they were going to. Atticus was sitting on a golden throne with velvet cushions at a table with white legs and a golden top. Across from him was a dark-skinned black man with a low fade hair dressed in a blue pinstripe suit. His scruffy beard, sunglasses, and unsmiling face are a direct contrast to the men in the white suits.

"Scott's here just like you wanted. Can you please leave us alone while we're here? The guy needs a break."

Atticus didn't fully turn around because he recognized Faaghira's voice. "I appreciate that very much niece, but I don't recall asking for you too." They stared each other down for a second before sending each other blatantly fake smiles. The animosity between them is exponential but it can seem insignificant to the untrained eye.

"Is the music room still here or did you scrap it during the renovation?" Atticus smoked a cigar he pulled from the inside of his jacket and puffed a ring of smoke at Fae. She squinted but otherwise stood unfazed.

"Of course, darling. I know it's your favorite room so I'd never ever get rid of it. Not like you wouldn't put all that stuff back if I took it out. Left wing, second floor; same place as always. What brings up the question?" "I'm going to show Scott the music room here. I didn't get to show him at my place because you wanted him to be at your stupid party. He's here and now he's going to see the music room." Atticus put on a fake smile that may have passed for a genuine under bad lighting.

"Does that poor man ever get a say with you? Excuse my manners. Please disregard that question, niece. It makes it sound like I actually care. Enjoy the party you two." The man in the blue suit threw up a peace sign as Fae and Scott began to walk to the left wing. His expression never changed, which made Scott a little uneasy. The man and Atticus instantly started speaking in hushed voices when Scott and Fae walked further from the table.

When Scott slowed down to eavesdrop Fae tugged on his arm and whispered in his ear. "Let's go slowpoke. If anybody here finds out you heard something you shouldn't have, you'll be gone without a trace by tomorrow morning. Now look at me like someone just wrecked your car. I'll explain what I can in the music room." Scott gave her a stunned look with eyes as wide as he could make them. He didn't put any thought into the reason behind it because...trust. He hasn't met anyone else here that he would even consider putting the tiniest bit of faith in.

42

Besides, the gesture seemed harmless enough.

The hallway to the left wing appears to be even more extravagant than the main hall. Busts and paintings of Atticus and others are scattered throughout the long marble path. The walls are bare compared to the main wall because of the smaller dose of Atticus. Not to downplay the amount of Atticus centered artwork; it's still excessive and very creepy. Complex designs take place of a mural on the ceiling. It adds to the regal feel that makes the area feel more welcoming. Faaghira paced through the hallway to get to the music room faster. The elegant decor was nothing new to her. Scott wanted to take in the sights but he didn't want to say that to her. She's clearly not in the state of mind to slow down to see things she's seen dozens of times before. If she didn't stop to show it then it really can't be much of a big deal. "We have to come back through here anyway. I promise we'll go sightseeing when we're done in the music room. It's just that nobody else knows about this room and I want it to stay that way. Some people always find a way to ruin something good. We won't have too much time in there though. Even though I don't like the term, I am technically social royalty. I have to keep up appearances so nobody invades my private life. With my luck Atticus will tell all the guests that I'm already here, and there's no doubt they'll come looking for me. Sorry if I'm coming off a little bitchy about it." Scott assured her that it wasn't a problem then he went walked the rest of the way at the same pace as her.

The larger room that houses it is very reminiscent of a museum. There are life-sized sculptures of scenes from myths of all types placed around the room. They ranged from a wizard and curious cat all the way to drunken men with eighty-seven bottles on the ground and twelve left on the wall. They can come off as a little silly because they were all crafted in the ever-dramatic baroque fashion. There are a few other displays of paintings of documents, but Fae told him not to pay too much attention to them. "The real treasure is over here. It's a secret room-get this-in a secret room. It can be a pain in the ass to find sometimes but that helps spice things up a little. It's not always in the same place and there's a whole system behind it. I know the ins and outs of how it works but I don't think I could simplify it for you."

"Womansplainer." Scott joked and grinned at Fae but the gestures weren't reciprocated. She wasn't mad or upset, but her folded arms and her face clearly read 'over it'.

She walked over to the wall across from them and ran her fingers across it until she suddenly came to a stop. The wall doesn't appear to be any different from the others, but I suppose that was done on purpose. She knocked on the wall three times then moved to another part of the wall. She made the motion to knock but her hand went right through it. "Hurry! Get over here, Scott!" She motioned for him to follow quickly, but this time he hesitated to move. If he continued in the same pattern, he's been going in then he would've gone immediately. However, more than half of her body had disappeared behind the wall. This reminded him that he wasn't his regular world. He wasn't sure why he was seeing that; he hadn't had even a sip of juice since he was in that abandoned house.

After seeing the 'unimpressed' look on her face, he followed her as he normally would. When she disappeared completely behind the wall he tried to put his hand in the wall to see if it was solid. His hand fell right through which shocked him to say the least. After finding that it wasn't real he went through the wall like it was an open door. There was a slight chill when he passed through but other than that it had no effect. "Was that a hologram?" "Cool, isn't it? I made it myself. Most of the kinks have been worked out but it still gets faulty every other blue moon. I built it to hide this closet that the music room is in. I purposely left out the idea of a plain old lock and key because locks can be picked. Nobody looks for an entrance they don't know is there. Anyway, the music room is downstairs; I'm really excited to show you all the rad stuff in there." She passed through another wall, but Scott didn't follow. He took a moment to look around the closet even though there isn't much in it. It's small and but it's not so small to where it's cramped.

The closet is dark, but patches of light from the music room creep in. All the walls have some light on them except for the holographic ones which were almost pitch black. "Must be one of those kinks she was talking about. "He made an utterly pointless observation to, at least I assume, postpone going to the music room. And why wouldn't he be so keen on going? Perhaps the situations he's found himself in have been far too strange. Trying to disregard these things or play them down can't work forever. Sooner or later he would have to come to terms with the fact that he's been nothing above a push over for most of the time. Yes, Faaghira is cool but she tends to impose her best interests on him whether he wants it or not. He as a person has not been given much consideration by a single soul this whole time. Had he met someone in his reality that was more or less the same as he is now, they would be ridiculed at the very least. However, I will commend him for showing the dominance of a poorly educated sheep.

"Will you shut up already? Being here is like being bilingual in a foreign country where they don't speak either language. I don't know what's going on, and when somebody offers to help me out I'll take it. I don't really know who's good and who's bad; I just want to get back home so I'm playing the game until I can bow out. You really think I care about all this other shit?" Okay, I didn't see that one coming. Around people you're a doormat, then you're a complete wad to me. I love it! Why aren't you like this with everyone else?

"Look, I don't want to talk about this here okay?"

"Okay, we can talk about it in the music room." Scott heard Fae's voice from behind the wall and rushed through it to see what she was doing. "Oh, hey Fae. I didn't see you there. I thought you already went downstairs." Scott was legitimately scared by her sudden appearance. Mostly because he was afraid, she would think he's a nut job. That thought may actually be right though. Hey, I hardly know the guy myself.

"I did, but while I was opening the door, I heard you talking. I brushed it off at first, but then you started getting riled up I had to come and see who you were getting so mad at. I don't see anybody else here but that didn't sound like the kind of talk someone would have alone. Who were you talking to?" She didn't sound sarcastic or weirded out when she spoke; an odd reaction to an even stranger predicament. And Scott wasn't sure how to answer without sounding crazy. The truth is that he was talking to me, the narrator of a story he's stuck in. But of course, that would mean that she is a character in said story. A good lie could be any of the following:

1. I'm crazy
2. I have a split personality
3. I talk to my dead uncle when I get upset. He's still annoying even in the afterlife
4. Sometimes I talk at myself when I'm stressed
   And don't even get me started on the number of bad lies:

46

1. Someone found the secret closet and I was trying to stop them from finding the music room.
2. You're hearing things; I never said a word.
3. The wall was talking to me. I think your holograms really do have some kinks that need to be worked out.
4. I was singing my favorite song and there's this weird talking part in it. I love the song so much that I even say that part too.
5. My girlfriend contacted me telepathically because she had a feeling I was cheating on her. I guess she's kind of right.
6. I found a bug the F.B.I put in here. I had to let them know I was on to them.
7. I was defending your honor in some way, shape, or form.

Then there's my favorite defense; it's not a lie, but it's beautiful regardless:

➢ What are you talking about?

The list could literally go on forever. Let's see which one he'll go with.

"It's a long story; I don't know if we have time for it. Maybe we should move on to something like music. Music is awesome; let's go do that right now."

But this time Fae wasn't letting him off the hook so easily. "Oh don't worry, we have *lots* of time between now and when I have to leave, *and I happen to love long stories*. I was planning to tell a few myself but those can wait. Since you're trying to push it to the side it must be a good one." She put on the arrogant smirk once again then went back downstairs. I have a feeling he would've shot me a middle finger at the very least, but I'm not physically there so the most he could do is shake his head. He finally went downstairs before Fae would have a reason to check on him again.

The steps were carpeted and the walls were a faux stained

brown flamed maple. It has a very seventies vibe going on with it that's interrupted by a very futuristic looking door at the base of the stairs. The door is open but there's a glowing vertical keypad next to it indicating that it isn't your run of the mill door. I know it may seem like one of the more pointless observations I've made, but I do have to paint a mental picture. Faaghira was already picking out an instrument when he came in. The wall of instruments was the first part of the room to catch Scott's eye. The wall is covered by black foam and rectangular steel panels with a faux wood finish. Different instruments of all kinds were either hung on the wall or near it. Violins, guitars, basses, and a drum set, but mostly ukuleles. The room isn't as grand as Faaghira described hers as.

She was sitting on a stool near the drum set, idly plucking at an electric bass. It was plugged in to a large Marshall stack but it wasn't powered on. The bass is a violin type that has a severely worn golden finish on the top and a faded cherry color on the back.

"You can't go, don't leave me
  Not 'cause I'm desperate, but because you're easy
  I can't talk to my friends again; they'll read me for filth
  Not that they would make me feel any guilt"

  She sang in a smooth voice which is very close to her speaking voice but with a light accent that is reminiscent of something, but I'm not really sure. I tend to stick with smooth when describing her voice because using words like 'velvety' or 'buttery' would sound creepy to me. For future reference: I'm not one of those narrators that describes everything in painstaking detail. I'm also guilty of excessively using commas, but it just so happens that I need them most of the time. "Damn it! I keep getting this wrong.

You can't go, don't leave me
Not 'cause I'm desperate but becasue-

Damn it! I messed up again. One more time from the top."
She started over without a hint of the anger she had just a
moment ago. Scott was fascinated by how fast she ran
through emotions.

"You're a pretty good bassist. You're also a crazy serious
perfectionist. Are you sure you want me to be here?"

"Don't worry; I'm not always a perfectionist when it comes
to most music, just the stuff I write. Actually, you should
throw out what I just said. I'm *always* a perfectionist when
it comes to any type of music. If you see me look disgusted
or if I tell you to start over, please ignore me; we're here to
have fun. Go ahead and pick one of the guitars up there."
Scott didn't move a muscle because he was trying to take in
his surroundings. He must not have been in a nice studio
before. "All these guitars… it's crazy. *Is this a fifty-nine Les
Paul*? I've been gassing for one of these ever since I first
heard the sound that comes out of these tone monsters."

"You've been *what*?" Fae stopped playing her bass to squint
at him in confusion. You know GAS: Gear Acquisition
Syndrome. It's when you feel you need a certain amplifier
or guitar." She was no less confused after his… stellar
explanation. "And *tone monster*? I wish you could
objectively hear what you're saying right now. It's just a pile
of wood, metal, and plastic mashed together. Doesn't sound
like much of a monster to me." She smiled because she was
very confident that he would go on a tangent because of what
she said. "Mashed together? *Excuse me*? A fifty-nine burst

49

is not simply wood, metal, and plastic haphazardly mashed together. It's a fine piece of unique and elite craftsmanship. The fifty-nine burst is the holy grail of electric guitars!" Fae rolled her eyes halfway through is mini tangent. He kept going on and on about how great the fifty-nine is and the rich history behind it for what might as well have been hours. After a while she went back to playing her bass to tune out his painfully long rant. He didn't seem to notice at all, but Faaghira nodded every few words to make it seem like she was interested.

He stopped abruptly when he realized she hadn't been paying attention since he opened his mouth. Then he sat down quietly on a stool near Faaghira with the Les Paul. "Funny, I thought you only played the triangle and kazoo. Now about that scene upstairs; who were you talking to?" She didn't lift her eyes up from her bass as she talked to him. He knew this one was coming sooner or later. Which excuse would he use to dance his way around this one? Would he even use an excuse to get around this one? Would he tell her the ridiculously absurd truth?

"My girlfriend called me out of the blue. I saw her like three days ago but here she is checking in on me again. She doesn't usually call unless it's to confirm plans or something like that. You might've noticed that this one was a little different. She asked about our future since I moved away for college. Because she doesn't know that I'm nowhere near my college, I didn't feel the need to tell her that I'm somewhere other than where she thinks. I don't like to talk about college with anyone, not even her. I always turn into this aggressive ass-hat whenever somebody bothers me about my plans for the future."

Ah, lucky lie number five. Faaghira didn't stop playing her

bass, but she wore this mischievous smile while she listened to him talk. "So, you do have a girlfriend. I was actually going to ask about that after the jam session started. I'm glad you brought it up first, Prince Charming. What's the lucky lady's name?" I wonder how Scott will get himself out of this one. If he keeps lying it'll catch up with him eventually. Oh, but if he tells the truth now, she'll get on him for lying in the first place. Either way, this is will be extremely entertaining. "Iris; she's Czech and Danish; she's a rad chick when she wants to be."

"So, she's white. For some reason I couldn't see her being anything else."

"Yeah, she's white, but what do you mean by not seeing her as anything else?"

Faaghira put her bass on a nearby stand and turned towards Scott. "Maybe it's intuition. So, what's this chick like? Judging from your personality, something tells me that she isn't a good girl at all."

"She's a great person…most of the time. She can be really nice, but she can get bitchy just as quick. She's a sweet and polite person around most people; a princess to say the least. She's a sweetheart but it's almost like being with a different person whenever she's in her comfort zone. Curses, flips people off, drinks enough to screw her liver seven times over, does some drugs but nothing too serious. I like her though, so that's all that matters right now."

"Sounds exciting. What's she look like?"

"She has this beautiful wavy-strawberry blonde- I think is the color- yeah, strawberry blonde hair. And she has these really pretty blue eyes; you know, like a kind of icy blue. Aw man, and she's got these cute little freckles on her cheeks and-"

"Which ones?" Her expression didn't change, but her voice hinted at the question's true nature.

"Fuck you, Fae. Would it kill you to lay off the innuendos for just a second? Anyw-" "It would, believe it or not. That's why I have to keep doing it. Well I've always gotta do people like that. And I figured doing you that way would be tons of fun."

Scott rolled his eyes. "Anyway, she's got freckles on her nose too. She has these sweet sultry lips that've gotta be the softest things. And she has a really nice figure. Describing that would be extremely awkward for me, so just trust me when I say that she has a good figure. It gets me going."

"Does she have an upper lip?"

Scott put his face in his hands and laughed so hard that he snorted. He's pretty dorky. "You're killing me, woman! Yes, she has an upper lip! I never feel half an angel's kiss."

"You have any pictures? It's not that I don't believe you, I'm just curious. Except for the part with the lips; I don't believe that at all." Scott had to stretch his leg out and dig in his pocket for his phone. I don't get it; he lied about who he was talking to and he seriously has proof to back it up. If this works then he's slicker than I could ever imagine. "This first one is her on the right, her best friend behind her, and obviously that's me on the left if you couldn't already tell. Feel free to look through the rest of the gallery if you want." He handed his phone to Faaghira without the slightest bit of hesitation.

She scrolled through the pictures slowly as a way to catch every little detail in them. "She's so pretty and you two look *soooo* cute together. The lips get a pass for two reasons: they're way more visible than what I expected, and she's really pretty. If there was a third option it would be because she's your girl. I've never even had the luck of being in a relationship where everything looks okay. I know for sure that no relationship is perfect, but I know that there's something to those perfect pictures and cheesy dates. I never had a problem with not having that, but I would love to have a relationship like that at least one time. I wouldn't expect it to last long; I want one to have that experience."

"Well until I find a way back home, I'm stuck here. I guess we could try that, you know; if you want to."

"Scott, I'm positive that's a bad idea. I think we're both too different to have that kind of dynamic. I don't see anything wrong with either of us right now, so I don't see the point of trying to change who we are for the sake of an experience. Besides, it looks like you've got a pretty chill girl waiting for you at home. She may have her flaws but she sounds a lot better than me; I'm always a bitch. I'm always *that* bitch, to be exact."

There still wasn't any sign of sarcasm when she talked. Scott obviously isn't used to being around such a strong personality. She tells him what he needs to hear without a second thought. I don't think she does it the way that she should but that's just my opinion. I also think that he needs to get hit by a flying sledgehammer because he's trying to cheat on his girlfriend. Why rush to get with somebody when you'll want to be with other people too? If you can't control yourself don't go putting yourself in that situation. What a low life. "I'm not sure if I should agree with you or if I should change the subject." "It's your life boo, I'm just living in it. Make sure you choose wisely though." Faaghira picked up her bass and turned on the amplifier. She went back to idly plucking at the strings when she sat back down. "What about your love life. I don't feel it's fair to spill everything going on with mine and for you to keep yours under wraps."

"Smart choice. I suppose I have a few secrets of my own that it's time to share. Right now, I'm on a break from my…significant other. Things were just fine in the beginning, but everything's always fine in the beginning. We ran -no- we run different lives. I'm convinced that I wouldn't be the person I am today without them. I won't go saying it's good or bad until I can find out what I would've been like without them. The dude I was with before them was probably- still is a psycho. He doesn't seem like that when you talk to him, but that makes it even worse." "What makes him so crazy? Is he a thrill seeker? A daredevil? Binge drinker? Marathon cokehead? Does he binge watch mediocre adult cartoons?" Scott has a slight smirk because of how clever he felt that last one was. Faaghira, on the other hand, was unimpressed.

"You're a natural. Walter is a former leader of the resistance; he decided that they weren't going far enough to stop Atticus. Judging from the way things are now, he was right, but I don't agree with what he wanted to do to get Atticus out of power. One day when Atticus was making a speech, Walter beat some of the stage security with a nightstick. He made it to Atticus but he didn't kill him for some reason. Anyw-""Why didn't anybody shoot him? I thought that's what security gets paid to do."

"They did. He got a gun off the first guard he beat up and shot three of the guards on stage. He used bystanders as shields from their bullets. They stopped shooting at him after that. When he was on stage, he looked dead at me and said 'See you at twenty-five.' I still don't know what was meant by that. He's a little…lost. So that's Walter in a nutshell, but that's not who you were asking about. Don't worry, unless they've suddenly changed, you'll probably meeting them eventually. Maybe we should switch to a different vibe. We should be putting all these instruments to good use. Let's jam, dude." She began playing a groovy bass line before she could even finish the last sentence. She completely switched gears in the blink of an eye, as she apparently has a knack for doing. I know talking was the original intention, but I'm not sure she was ever ready for it to happen. Scott sat and listened to her play. It's partly out of admiration, but mostly because he didn't know how to play the song. "This is the song I was playing before. I'm assuming that you know how to play guitar since you picked out the sacred, sanctified, blessed by the Holy Ghost, omnipotent fifty-nine Les Paul."

"I'm no Wes Montgomery but I can play some things. I'm a fast learner so don't worry about having to teach me anything for too long. Tell me which chords to use and when; I'll have this thing down in no time!"

"Alright rock star, plug that guitar in one of amplifiers over there. They all have cables in them already so all you have to do is pick your poison. Some custom orders are the only kinds I have in here, but I'm sure you'll make due. Let's see if you're really as decent as you say you are." She said jokingly, but she wasn't totally joking. Doubting people's abilities could possibly be a character trait for this bad girl type. Scott (the apparently pretentious bastard) plugged the guitar into one of the Gibson amplifiers. It feels weird describing everything that goes on but unfortunately, I have to do it. Being the narrator means I have to do all the mundane things that move the tale along. It's unbearably awkward. Alright, let's get back on track. Scott stumbled along with the bass line until he got the hang of the song. The two ended up playing the song several times before putting the instruments back down. Scott wanted more than anything to continue the talk they were having earlier. They both had plenty to talk about. If he was hiding things there was nothing keeping her from doing the same. There were probably hopes from both sides that the other would tell the truth. Scott knows good and well that he lied about who he was talking to. It doesn't seem like she knows he lied based on where the conversation went, though I wouldn't be so quick to say that she believes him. They could both be playing a game of deception right now, but they're only fooling themselves; funny how that works. "Does it ever get lonely being here?" Scott asked while putting the guitar back on the wall, making sure not to make eye contact.

"I'm sure it does. Heck, sometimes I get lonely too."
"You never let up."

"Only as long as the blink of an eye. Being such an important, and no doubt, hated, member of society leads to that good ol' loner lifestyle. I'm the only person in the world I can trust; the world people know about, that is. That's mostly because I can't stab myself in the back even if I really want to. I don't get anything out of it if I screw myself over. That's a really weird icebreaker, but it's a pretty good one. Your turn." "Life isn't hard for me in that sense. I'm no celebrity to any degree, so my problems are a little different. I think it was around the middle of elementary that I realized I didn't fit in with everybody else."

"What do – never mind. Disregard"

"Um…okay. Everyone seemed to be living in a different world than I was. There were the nerds, the smart kids, the athletes, and the popular kids. It's kinda funny how the social structures for the next few years are laid out so early. I tried all sorts of things to try to fit in with any of them. I tried to be funny, I tried to play sports, I ended up sucking at sports; tried to get better grades, ended up quitting and staying average. I wasn't shy but I wasn't outgoing either. I was the ghost that everyone acknowledged. I had some good acquaintances scattered throughout the years but there was nobody I could really count on. The only time I got to see my best friend was whenever I took a look in the mirror. That whole thing never ended. Sure, I've had people I've had intimate conversations with over the years, but I knew there was nobody I could really count on to be there for me when I needed it. I didn't want to hold anyone to that standard because I knew nobody could reach it."

Faaghira nodded her head in approval. "And the award to saddest, suckiest school experience goes to… Scott Blue. My story is bad but it isn't sad. Like, yours is some heavy stuff. I would hate to have had that kind of thing in school. I would've turned out to be the bitterest person on the face of the Earth." "I never said that I'm not. I haven't had a chance to show it yet but I guarantee you that I'm as bitter as they come. Those years were too difficult for me to not hold any grudges. The biggest grudge I held was against myself. I still haven't forgiven myself for how my life got to be this way. The problem is that I don't know what I did wrong. I hate myself for that too."

Scott stared at the ground halfway through the conversation

and he only when Faaghira reached her hand out for his. "C'mon dude, we can't stay in here the whole time. I would love to but people will come looking for me if they don't see me at the party soon; they know I'm here by now. I can't risk somebody finding this place. I think you'll have fun up there as long as you stick with me tonight."

"Do we go out the same way? We might get seen going out that way." "Nope, I know what I said earlier, but there's a secret passage that feeds into the backyard. There's a door on the far left of the instrument wall that leads to a short hallway. Take that straight to the door that'll be directly across from you, and you'll be outside. Do you want me to go with you or do you think you got it?"

"I got it. Will you be out there too?"

Faaghira got up from the stool to turn off the amplifiers. She also took her bass and put it back on the wall. "Give me a minute. I have to clean up here but I promise I'll be out there before you know it. And don't worry about the guests, they don't bite hard." She smirked but that's the most she did because was focused on cleaning up.

Before Scott left the room, he peeked over his shoulder to check if she was doing something else. First of all: weird. Second: What did he think she would be doing instead? Even if she does something else as soon as he leaves it isn't his business. But he looked back again before closing the door behind him. He took in the sights of the dark faux wood paneled room one last time. The microphones, the keyboard, the black carpeted floor; they gave the spacious room a cooler and more intimate vibe.

"Dude, leave already." Faaghira didn't stop putting things

away to tell him that. He seriously should've left by now. Taking time out to observe the room is what he should've done in the beginning. I don't like to do the whole 'describing the setting thing because it can get painfully monotonous in a very short period of time. Luckily, I have Scott who loves to take in ~~most~~ _all_ of the sights. Why him? Why do I have to narrate for him of all people?

"I don't like you either. I didn't even ask to be here, so chill with that. Narrators are supposed to describe the environment. Since you hate your job so much why don't you just tell me how to get home and then I'll be out your hair." I thought we went over this already. I don't know why you're here and I don't care. There's a reason you're here and my job is to help you do whatever you were brought here for. I would much rather be narrating an actual children's book instead of whatever this is supposed to be. If I could leave this story right now I absolutely would. If I knew how to get you out of here, I would've told you already. It would be much appreciated if you would do what you have to in order to drive the story along instead of getting all googly eyed at every little speck of dust within a two-mile radius.

"Alright, alright, I'm going outside. I'll do my job and you do yours. Try not to criticize me if you can help it. You would be doing me a huge favor." I can't help it. Sorry not sorry. Scott rolled his eyes but he ignored me for the most part. If he argues with me for too long someone will hear him and he'll have to craft another lie about who he was talking to. He exited the hallway and emerged to the surface -no that sounds stupid. He exited the hallway and after a few steps he found himself in what must be the backyard. Oh, and before I forget, there's this incline that leads to the backyard. He had to go up on the incline to make it to the backyard, for those darlings who can't fill in the gaps. And it's also really dark on the way up there, for the other darlings starving for details.

The garden is lit with lights that rival the fireworks going off in the night sky. Of course, no part of Atticus' home would be complete without a glaring representation of him somewhere. There's a large marble statue in the middle of a brightly lit fountain. The beautiful garden in the back of the yard is flooded with people. Colorful streamers hang around the branches of the trees and in the bushes. White Christmas lights are lined up against the edges of the yard and around the flower beds in the garden. The same fireworks from before are going off right below a shining quarter-moon. It looks like something straight out of one of those cheesy romance flicks.

Behind him is the mansion itself, which is now also packed full of people. A small group of those people came to where Scott is. "Aren't you the guy Atticus shot at?" A bearded guy with clean cut, slicked back light brown hair and sunglass walked from the group to talk to Scott.

"If I'm the only one that he shot at today then I guess that would be a yes. Who's asking?"

"Some people over there wanted to take pictures with you but they had to be sure that it was you. A lot of folks here tend to be on the shy side when it comes to people like you. People around here know me as a more outgoing soul so they usually get me to do the talking. I go by Kasabian, but you can call me Kas if that's too long."

"Nice to meet you, Kas. I'm waiting for a friend; they're the only reason that I'm here in the first place. If I don't say much it's because this isn't the kind of environment that I'm used to." "I was about to make a joke about how you have a *really* long name, but that's too corny. The next thing I was going to do was ask you who your friend is; I might know them." Scott isn't in a tough situation, but he can easily make this one. Even though Faaghira is expecting some kind of fanfare when she officially gets to the party, the wrong kind of attention could be horrible. There is a chance that this Kas character knows who Faaghira is, but Scott doesn't know how. He doesn't even know this guy. Standing there and engaging in a social dance like one of those air dancers outside of a car dealership means that he'll see Faaghira anyway. She'll be looking for Scott and then...BAM! Kas will be right there. I have no idea what he'd do, but he'd be right there. What if he works for a gossip mag or something like that? "To be honest, I just met them today. They've been getting uncomfortable when I've been around other people so I'd better go somewhere that isn't so crowded. Tell those people that I might be willing to take pictures later." Scott got away as fast as he could without making it a spectacle. Scott retreated to a tree that towers over the unlit flowerbed close by. He sat down after standing for what seemed like an eternity for him. He was in the kind of place he never thought he would be, doing the thing that he knew would never change. Sitting alone somewhere. Whether he flipped a coin or thought of a way to survive a lopsided economy, he was still alone. These are the kind of thoughts that tend to stick with certain people more than anything else. That doesn't erase the fact that he's overreacting to some extent.

"What else am I supposed to do? I never chose to be here but I'm here anyway. God knows how far away my life is from here. I've been plucked from everything I knew and you expect me to shrug that off? I can't. Life sucked at home, but at least I knew what to do there." Scott, think of all the people you had in your life before now. How many of them really made anything better? "Now that I that I think about it, I had a bunch people around me every other part of the day. The problem is that they were nowhere to be found when I was having a bad time. My parents and I weren't on good terms when I moved out and my girlfriend isn't much help with emotional issues. Three people I thought I would always be able to count on couldn't do more than a grain of salt. I do have an actual best friend though, but I don't want to use him as an emotional landfill. Why do you care anyway?" Let's get one thing straight: I still don't care. I want you to get out of here so I won't have to deal with you anymore. If you find out what you're here to do now then you can just do that and get out. I personally don't think you'd get flung into a fantasy world on account of your loneliness. Do you have any other issues? "Lots of 'em. Even if you're right about the 'lesson to learn' thing, how do I know what I need to get out of all this? We can make assumptions all day, but if neither of us is right I'll be stuck here. What's the point of any of this?" That's what we're trying to find out. You don't like being lonely, right? "I'm so used to it that I might as well like it." Well now's the time to change that. Get up and take charge of your life. Change those things you don't like.

"Why do you have to be right?" He sighed and pushed himself off the ground. It feels weird announcing what he's doing when I talk to him; I digress again. When Scott went looking for Faaghira he couldn't find her. In fact, he didn't see any of the people that were by the stairs before. Everyone else in the garden is still there, but they aren't really important. Scott was slowing down the closer he got to the mansion. It was best to not try to jump into this head first. What would he even do? Anyone out there is capable of doing the same things as him. He's no superhero. And if there really was some sort of issue the people in the garden

62

would've reacted to it already.

"Something doesn't seem right about this. I'm getting some serious bad vibes. The garden isn't even that close to the house. If something bad happened they probably would've missed it." Before Scott could make another move the bullets were flying his way. Screams were coming and going with the sound of assault rifles firing. Scott dashed behind the tree to try to get clear of any stray bullets. How many times would he cross paths with the end of a barrel in one day? Can the universe not give him a break?

When the shooting stopped there were no voices to be heard. The silence could possibly be the most horrifying part of it all. It makes it almost impossible to not imagine that gruesome scene that is sitting a couple of yards away. Scott hadn't looked to see the layout of the garden before the bullets came flying. He hadn't paid attention to the number of people back there earlier, so the casualties were exponential in his head. How many people were out there with their lifeless bodies sprawled out on the ground? How much red splattered on the flowers and bushes? How many eyes are staring at everything and nothing at once? How many mothers, fathers, sisters, and brothers unknowingly walked right into the hands of death tonight? Not seeing it is possibly worse than seeing the cause of the silence. But Scott cannot gaze upon the corpses for himself at the moment. Not without joining them.

The beautiful illuminated scene now shows itself to be a major problem. Let's set up a scenario for a second. So, Scott just heard some people get gunned down. He isn't near the shooters, but if he tries to flee the scene, they'll shoot him. They'll be able to see him because of the lights that would be around him. Most of the area around the tree is dark, meaning that he would be able to hide there without being seen. But that's providing no part of him is visible from his current hiding spot. Another scenario: Let's say that Scott stays exactly where he is. There's a chance that they'll see him and shoot him immediately. Say he does hide successfully; how would he get past them? If they heard him all they would have to do is turn around and shoot. Even if he did get past them without a problem, where would he go? It's not like he has a place to go if he does escape.

He doesn't have a car to get around in and even if he did, he doesn't know how where to go. The only real way out is to find Faaghira. "You think I don't know that? I've been wondering where she was for the longest!" Wondering doesn't get anyone anywhere. "Shut up! You of all people-beings should know that I can't go looking for her now. I couldn't go back to the music room earlier because people would've seen me. She would've been beyond pissed if anyone found that room. The most I can do right now is try to stay alive and hope that she's okay. My hands are tied here and I don't know what you want me to do." Anything that'll keep you from being a sitting duck. I may not like you, but I don't want you to die.

"I guess I don't have anything to lose but my life; might as well make a move." He waited for the shooters to walk past the tree then he put the one furthest behind in a sleeper hold. The four others didn't turn around to investigate, but instead continued on to the mansion; thus we'll assume they didn't hear a sound. Scott dragged the person behind the tree and took their rifle. Leaving it could've been catastrophic, but now that he has it he'll probably have to- HE JUST SHOT THE OTHER PEOPLE!!! "In the legs; I didn't kill them. They'll live." I didn't know you knew how to use one of those things! And that speed! "Don't forget accuracy; that's the most important part." THEY CAN BLEED TO DEATH! ARE YOU REALLY GOING TO LEAVE THEM THERE?

"Looks like I'll have to work fast to get help in time. Besides, anyone can bleed to death if you give them the right injury. Why would they be any different?" Damn, that's cold man. Are you sure you've got a heart in there? "I'd like to say yes since I'm still alive, but for all I know it could be something else propping me up. I'll get help to them in time but I'm kind of hoping they won't need it." So you don't have a heart? "I guess not." Scott put each of their rifles in places around the area, making special care to put them as far away from each other as possible. Afterwards he went on his way like everything was normal.

It's time to decide the next move. Will he leave or will he stay? "Stay, of course. Like you said, I don't have anywhere else to go. If I end up dying then I dodged a metaphorical bullet that would've hit square between the eyes." Can you keep low on the dialogue for a little bit? I feel awkward switching between narrating and conversing with you. "Whatever floats your boat." So Scott was careful to be as quiet as possible as he walked up the steps. The space for the wall facing the backyard is taken up by large windows, so he's not exactly hard to see. Maybe the slow movements are for dramatic effect. The crowd of people that were outside can be seen along with the other partygoers and heavily armed strangers. Well technically they're all strangers, but these other people clearly don't belong there.

It's definitely a hostage situation, but it's a very unusual one. Nobody is tied up and nobody is on the ground. It puts on the illusion that nothing's wrong with this scene; that these dudes armed to the teeth are guests who happen to have guns. When examined closely, the partygoers are scared witless.

They're putting on a dog and pony show to make it look like they're having a grand time. It isn't fooling anybody but it keeps going anyway. Scott took a deep breath before opening the now red-stained glass door leading to the inside. The extravagant ballroom makes the sight of the terrified guests slightly more bearable. It's unsettling how terrified they look paired with their efforts to appear happy.

"Ah, my friend from earlier with the long name! You slipped away so fast I didn't even get to say goodbye. I was sure you would've been dead by now. For some reason I'm not bothered in the slightest by your continued existence. I'm not sure whether or not you're competent, but I'll assume that you are for the sake of the conversation we're about to have." This is the same guy that Scott talked to earlier. I think his name was Kasubio or something like that. I know for sure that it had a K. With a name like that I can't understand how nobody knew that he's crazy. Or maybe everyone knows he's crazy, but they had no idea he was *this* crazy.

"You? This is *your* fault? Why the heck are you doing this? Are you insane?" Kas slowly paced back and forth before answering with an awkward, creepy grin.

"I won't deny that I'm insane, but everyone else in here is far more insane than I could ever be. Unlike the other people in the universe, I'm openly crazy. Too many people do things behind closed doors. Support for heinous acts, like the ones Colonel Harland over here commits on the daily, is one of the most baffling things if you take a minute to think about it. This snobby gathering is celebrating twenty-five whole years of a paramilitary group legally terrorizing people. But hey, as long as there's money flowing to where it needs to go it's not a problem. The starving and hard-working people in this city are there because of bad choices. They were too

66

lazy; they didn't go to college; all the usual stuff. There are so many issues that are 'addressed' solely because they make it seem like we care about something more than material things. I used to buy into all of those heartless views. Now I'm much wiser; I've bought into a whole different set of heartless views."

"Is holding an entire party hostage really the answer? If you're out trying to do this to everyone, what makes you any better than Atticus?" The smile returned, this time they were paired with an unsettling but smug gaze.

"Nothing has to make me better than Atticus; I'm already better than him. For the oppressed to get the justice they deserve, they must create a system that legitimately cares about their well-being. I want such a system to be created, but it can't be done peacefully. The majority of the time, you've got to make some serious noise if you want to get anywhere. Peace has brought nothing but disillusioned people who are complacent. Those who see nothing wrong with the way things are need to be shown the truth through logic. I will show them that truth because nobody else will. You see a room full of 'innocent hostages' and I see a room chock full of the ever-oppressive bourgeoisie. All of these people have done more wrong towards humanity in a month than I could do in twenty millennia! They must be held responsible for their actions."

"Kas, listen to yourself! You sound like a maniac! You can't go around killing innocent people!"

"Did I not clarify that I am indeed a maniac? Being crazy isn't my problem, but of course someone as gullible as you would believe that. And I never said I would kill anyone…though things may have gotten a little unorganized at the door. However, I did just say that these people are not innocent. All the fathers, brothers, children, mothers, sisters, children, and spouses I often hear about are fully capable of doing horrible things. Most of them already have done horrible things. As for the rest, they are prevented from ever getting the chance. Having any kind of relationship with another human being does not take away your ability to be the scum of the Earth. Take this woman for instance; she is a mother. Of how many children I'm not sure, but that's not the point. I do know for a fact that she is cheating on her husband." Kas slowly pulled a small knife from his sleeve and is holding it in the air. Scott was about to attack, but when he considered the circumstances he quit. The chances that he would get shot an unimaginable amount of times are very high. What use would he be to anyone there if he took a dirt nap?

"She's having an affair with that man over there." Kas threw the knife so fast that it appeared to fly at the man. He was struck right below his collar bone with so much force that he was practically thrown down on the marble floor. The tiles under the man were lightly cracked after his fall. "Mr. Jesper was a philanthropist. He had multiple charities and he even gave out a significant amount of scholarships to college students and the college bound. He funded cancer research as well as research for other diseases. He gave money to hospitals, orphanages, museums, homeless shelters, and everything else under the sun. So why in the world would I throw a knife at him? Because he was a horrible human being. He beat his girlfriend and she knew nothing would happen if she told the authorities. The poor soul told me once that when she shared the news with a friend, the friend told her to try harder to please him. I then tracked down her friend and beat their face in with a lead pipe. I knew that I would have a grander stage if I waited until now to play the executioner to Mr. Jesper. However, I decided I wouldn't kill him. He isn't dead yet, but nobody should try to keep him alive. I wouldn't stop you from trying, but I implore you not to. He should be left to bleed to death."

I never thought it was possible for someone to be this cold hearted. The worst part is that I want to hate him, but I can't do it. He reminds me of someone. "I can't let you do this. Him being a horrible person isn't enough of a reason to kill him. Lives shouldn't just be thrown away like that."

Kas let out a creepy maniacal laugh in response. "You mean like the ones you left outside to bleed to death? I saw you shoot them but I did not wish to interfere. I know that it may seem harsh to say, but perhaps it would've been wiser to aim for their hearts. Getting help for them is as useful as a fire escape door in the middle of a parking lot. Nobody will help them. They will die soon if they haven't already. Have you ever toyed with the thought that everyone has someone out there who loves them? Those people out there had families. You had mothers, fathers, children, and friends out there. Have you come to terms with the fact that you are responsible for deaths, the same as I? You're no saint and you're not in a perfect world. Their deaths could've been avoided, but you were so sure that everything would go according to your plan. I purposely stalled for so long so that it would be impossible to save them. They supported me, but their violent actions were all their doing. Now they are dead, and it's all *your* doing. If we're going strictly off of body count, I'm not the bad guy here."

It still isn't easy to hate him after all of that. I'm convinced he's a horrible person, but a part of me feels guilty for thinking that. If he has one, his heart is in the right place. It's just that he has an extremely twisted way of dishing out

69

justice. "You should let these people go. If your beef is with Atticus then deal with him. Leave everyone else out of it. I'm no saint, I get it; no one is, but that doesn't mean that I can't try to make things better. If people were only allowed to help if they were perfect then nobody would make an effort. There wouldn't be a point to being a better person. A fucked-up person like you should know that; fucked up people like us should know that. This whole smart-ass business you're putting up is really cute, but nobody's got time for that bullshit when lives are on the line. Worst part is that you're the reason anybody's in danger right now. Now if your issue is really with Atticus, go terrorize him and let everyone else go. If you're as good as you say you are, you'll catch whoever goes off and does something evil or whatever you say you're fighting against."

There's no smile on Kas' face. Not a single witty remark was uttered from his mouth. It's that point between confusion and frustration when somebody hands puts your life under the spotlight. The most one can do in this situation is sit back and be upset about it. "It has come to my attention that I…may have been wrong in my approach to tonight's event. I should've got rid of at least one more person before I could be convinced to change my plans. It is not solely because of this man; certain actions have contradicted my values. Everyone can go except for Atticus. If he tries to leave I will grace any civilian still inside with a Molotov cocktail." As the crowd flooded out of the party, Atticus could be seen clearly leaning against a dining table. He didn't move, but he gave Kas a chilling stare from across the room. Faaghira was also blocked out by the crowd. She was sitting cross-legged on the floor the whole time. She was on her phone during the entire confrontation.

"Good job on calming Kas down, Scott; he's always been so difficult for some reason."

"Wait, you know him?"

"Yup, that's the ex I was telling you about in the music room, Walter. And by the way, I'm really sorry about dragging you into this mess. Even though it's not exactly my fault, I still feel sorry about it. To make up for it, I'll handle things from here." Kas' phone buzzed and he hesitantly checked. Shortly after, he put the phone back in his pocket and frowned at Faaghira. "I'm literally a few feet away from you Fae. You could've said this instead of sending me a text. You're always so perplexing. And no, I do not need to calm down; I'm in full possession of my faculties. All of this was necessary to some extent. I don't need you to be so rude when you're trying to make me sound crazy. Not that any of your rude behavior was ever warranted. However, I do appreciate your adamant protests against my bad habits. Unfortunately, I never did quit smoking; silly me, off topic again. My problem is with your tyrannical uncle, not you. I would prefer to deal with this alone, but if you truly insist on staying, I won't stop you."

Faaghira continued to play on her phone as if nothing happened. Hmm, there seems to be a whole lot of that going around here. Not the social bunch, I presume.

"Now there's a few things you need to know before you go on and give me a drawn out self-righteous speech. There are major problems in this city that can't be ignored. Yes there are people in poverty, but I didn't put them there. Whether you want to believe it or not, I made sure there's a solid amount of jobs. Now whether or not the people are qualified for those jobs is not my concern. Love it or hate it, that's the reality. There can't be a perfect world and you're a fool if you believe otherwise. The violence that you see on the news is a product of the freedom the people asked for. I think that real problem –" Atticus' smug grin cleared off his face when his tangent was cut short.

"I think that real problem is that monsters like you are in power!" Kas yelled and raised his fist, but when Faaghira shook her head he lowered his arm.

"You're so caught up with your holier than thou crusade that you can't even let me finish my damned sentence! If you had put your hatred aside for one moment that then you would've heard that I'm hardly involved with the people. What you see on the streets is their fault. In fact, if you were so concerned about them, you would've noticed that someone has been setting downtown on fire for the past half hour. I might have mentioned it earlier, but I was sure you were set on ruining my gathering." Atticus spoke in this fake innocent way that was unbearably annoying. Kas couldn't keep the irritated look off his face, but he still didn't try to hit Atticus. "Who said that I wasn't trying to ruin your pretentious little party?' Kas grunted. "You've got a point there, but if you aren't going to kill me then you don't have a point here. I suggest that you go to the city and stop that maniac if you aren't man enough to stop the one right in front of you." Atticus took pulled a flask from out of his jacket and winked at Kas before drinking. Kas clenched his fist then relaxed his hand again. It was the kind of situation most people would hate to be in; making the choice between satisfying yourself and following up on your responsibilities. As much as Kas probably detested it, Atticus was right. What's the point of getting rid of a cruel king if the kingdom will still be screwed up?

Before Kas walked out he asked where he could find the guy, to which Atticus responded "Follow the ash, you can't miss it." Kas walked out before Atticus could finish. Afterwards, Faaghira got off her phone and reached her hand out to Scott. Scott groaned and rolled his eyes but he helped her up anyway. "You're such a lazy bum."

"If I couldn't see it before, I can definitely see why you must have all girls flying your way back at...wherever you're from. So, you do know we're going to check out the situation downtown, right?" Scott was almost taken aback by the demanding question, but he quickly remembered who he was dealing with. "Actually, we're not doing that. I have a much better idea."

Faaghira was confused by his sudden leadership role because of how far out of character it seemed. Oh, but she sure wasn't complaining; she didn't do anything but give a little smile. It must've been nice to see him show some backbone. Scott took her hand and looked over his shoulder at Atticus before rushing out the door. Atticus smiled flipped him the bird while drinking from his flask. Much like the confrontation with Kas, Atticus winked at Scott which made the despot all the more unnerving. However, there isn't so much time to dwell on that because there's an idea to follow up on. Scott was expecting one of those cliché moments where Kas would be waiting for them so he could say some dramatic, love triangle building words. But nope, he was as good as gone. This is an odd one for me. Him not being there is kind of like someone walking away mid-sentence; you just don't do that, but to be fair, he totally did that earlier. It's almost like he was gone without a trace, or that he was never there in the first place. See what I did there? When Scott got over that fact, he noticed the stunning view of the lively city along with the thick clouds of smoke coming from the middle of it. Sure he was really set on seeing one of Fae's brooding ex-boyfriends (to add another dimension to the romantic interest, I'm sure), but how could anyone not notice WHEN A CITY IS ON FIRE?!?!? It doesn't even matter what you're thinking about! That's like not noticing a shooting star fall right I front of you! How can anyone do that? "I love surprises as much as the next guy, but you need to tell me where we're going. I doubt you want to walk there, and you bet your ass you're not driving my car." Fae folded her arms.

"One: it's not even your car; you stole it."

"Well do you see anyone else driving it? If I'm the only one driving it, it's mine."

"Whatever. Two: I don't think you'll like the idea of going to that place." Scott mumbled out the last words of the sentence as though he gave up on it completely. "Going to places I don't like doesn't scare me. I showed up here, didn't I?" "I know, but this place is… different." Scott walked over to the car and leaned on the passenger's side as a signal for Fae to start driving. However, Fae did the exact opposite. She sat down and turned her back to the car, refusing to even look at it until she knew where she was driving; I don't blame her.

Fae's not saying anything, and Scott, you know good and well that you're not getting anywhere without her. And don't go underestimating her; if you don't tell her anything you'll be here for an eternity. "The Fireman's house; the mansion you were talking about earlier. I know that you're scared of that place but I think that's the best place to get answers. If he, or whoever, is there is responsible then we'll be able to make sure they don't set any other places on fire. And if

74

there's nothing there then that means Kas is on the right track and we can let him handle it. And I didn't want to tell you until you started driving because I didn't want you to turn back around or go somewhere else." "I hope you realize that I can still do that. Hell, I can throw you out the car if that's what I'm in the mood for. And how did you expect us to get there if I didn't know where we were going? Gosh, you're such a dummy." She was laughing before she could finish talking. Maybe she was never in a bad mood. Maybe.

Scott laughed nervously as a way to ease his feelings and present a transition to another, less serious topic. "So how many exes do you have? You don't have to answer if you don't want to. I know romantic relationships are very personal." "I actually don't think it's that big of a deal. I never had to be with anyone, so any relationship I was in was my choice. There's hardly any optional thing I did that I won't talk about. But I think we'd better get on the road first before I revisit my past. I need to get a good rhythm going before my mind can switch gears." The path leading back to the main streets is so smooth that driving over it feels like flying. Faaghira never missed a beat with any turn. Her driving is still hectic, but it isn't reckless. It's fascinating how she's able to drive so fast but so well. It's as if she's a professional racecar driver, but even that wouldn't explain how she's able to do that on normal streets.

She was able to come to a complete stop in an unbelievably short amount of time. Apart from the fact that was a speed demon, she was a very considerate driver. After tearing through the streets at ungodly speeds, the car slowed to a halt at a red light. For the first time Scott could get a good look at the beautiful, albeit partially burning, city. He looked out the back windshield and saw lines of cars rushing out on the lanes. The mass of headlights placed a radiant glare on the glass, but the reason behind the incoming traffic wasn't any kind of pretty. Businesses and even some homes were getting torched, and while plenty of people here are well off, a hit like that is still hard to bounce back from.

Fae (I'm getting tired of saying Faaghira) checked her rear-view mirror then picked up on their conversation after seeing the wave of cars coming behind them. "Now about those exes: do you want to start from the beginning or the most recent one? I personally don't care but I figure that you might." "How about the first one? Those first relationships tend to be the lamest. "

"Yeah sure, that's a good place to start. My first relationship was in middle school with this guy named Wesley. We met in seventh grade in History. He was really shy and he and had these big glasses, oh, he was such a cutie pie! He was really sweet too. I can tell that he liked me for a while but most of the time he didn't have the guts to talk to me. I get it now though; it can be scary for some people to talk to me. I take it that he never had much luck with girls and that was his whole experience at that point. I didn't date him because I felt sorry for him though. I actually liked the guy a lot. One day after class I gave him my number and he called me that night. Oh, geez he was a nervous wreck over the phone. I tried to keep things from being awkward and I actually succeeded. It was probably the toughest thing I've ever done. With that being said, he was a gem when he was relaxed. He was really funny when he wasn't busy being so shy. I'd say he had a pretty good taste in music too. We'd been going back and forth text, calling, and hanging out sometimes for about two months when he asked what we were. Me being the smart ass that I am told him that we're human beings. He had this nervous laugh which told me that he wanted to have the whole 'are official?' discussion. As usual, I was right and

76

I told him that we've been hanging out so much that we might as well have been joined at the hip. He could call it whatever he wanted, as long as he didn't start acting weirder than he normally did. A little while later he asked if I wanted a kiss. It was and still is a really weird question, but it's one I was prepared for. I always had a bag of the minty kind of Hershey Kisses at my house. Mostly because I love them, but also for when any guy asked me for a kiss in some kind of way. Girls too, during the next year that is, but that's another story. I told him to wait for a second and I came back with that bag of Hershey Kisses. I offered him some and he took a few. Afterwards he sat there awkwardly for a little while, then he finally told me that isn't what he meant. Of course, I knew what he meant, but was indirectly teaching him a lesson. He wouldn't be getting very far if he wasn't more assertive. You've gotta be more confident in yourself if you expect to get anywhere. We had one of those weird pecks on the lips and there's a whole lot I wanted to do, but him going for a quick little kiss was a milestone. Next week I saw him at school, you know back when we couldn't drive, we mostly saw each other at school, he wanted to hold hands and shit. I was down with that because it couldn't do any harm." "So, how'd it end? It sounds like things were going smoothly."

"I broke up with him before the school year was over. It was sweet that he brought me roses and whatnot on Valentine's Day and that I was his 'date' at the dances, but I wanted more. I didn't want to push him to be someone that he wasn't but I never told him that. I never told him why I ended it because that wouldn't change anything. He probably internalized it or whatever, but at least didn't break up with him because he was weird."

"Oooh, I'm sensing some animosity here! Did some guy come along and break your heart because he thought you were too weird?"

They had driven far from the main road by this point and the crowd of cars was far behind them. The further they got from the city the easier it was to see how much damage the fire was doing to the city. The smoke was rising up to the tallest parts of the skyline. "Remind me to get back to that one. We have to get out soon; I can't drive too much further than here. Cars never work past a certain point." Fae's expression shifted to something between anger, terror and confusion for the short distance left. She was so silent that the only thing that could be heard was the car's engine which is already quiet. Scott sat and feigned interest in the dimly lit surroundings outside the window. Fae seemed to be completely disconnected from reality and it was rather frightening. She had her focus dead set on driving, even when she was supposed to stop.

The car was accelerating at speeds much faster than earlier. They passed by small groups of cars that adorned the vast and otherwise empty field. "Hey, um... Fae, aren't these those cars you were talking about?" Her expression hadn't changed. It was almost as if she was in another world entirely. "Oh no, those aren't the right abandoned cars in the middle of nowhere. I was talking a completely different set of cars." Terror and madness seem to be no obstacle for her brazen sarcasm. Her hands are clenched on the wheel and her foot is pressed hard on the gas pedal. A tear rolled down her cheek but she wiped it away before it could fall off her face. Everything outside the window turned to a blur of dark green and gray.

"Fae what's going on? You're driving like a madman! I meant to say woman! Not that women are bad drivers; I meant madwoman!" She forced a grin and responded "Don't I always?" Scott didn't have a problem with her being witty before. However, this was a different situation. Scott wasn't aware that he risked death getting in that car. There's no way he could've known it would be this bad so I can't blame him for getting a little antsy. "Now listen here lady, you're either gonna start making sense or I'm getting the fuck on up out this car. Now will you chill out or do I have to jump out of here? I don't care what you decide to do, but I'm not dying on account of you being crazy." Scott yelled at the top of his lungs.

Veins are popping from his neck and the side of his forehead. I'm sure he's red with anger, but he's not the kind of person that would show it. Fae seems to be completely unaffected by his fit of rage. She's keeping her eyes on the field but she still seems to be lost. She can obviously hear him because she gave a response earlier. Why the sudden withdraw from reality would be a fairly good question to ask. One second, she has her composure and the next she's halfway in space while still at the wheel. "I'm scared, man! I don't know if you can comprehend the terror I'm feeling right now; I'm actually facing my fears. This isn't like asking out a crush or sneaking beer out of a gas station; this is real terror! I've had nightmares my entire life about coming here and for some reason I just threw that all aside because to listen to your stupid idea! Now I'm here trying to keep my hands steady; trying to keep from going insane."

"Why don't you just stop or turn around then? You're the one driving." "You really don't get it. I'm too far to just stop and turn around. I'm scared to death but I can't quit now. I just can't bring myself to do it."

Scott took her hand and squeezed it tightly. "It's okay, it's okay; if any of that Fireman stuff us true then you've got me right by your side. Even if it isn't, I'm still right here." Fae smiled at Scott and wiped her tears on her blazer's sleeve. For a moment it seemed like everything-the entire world-froze. For that moment in time it seemed to be just the two of them. Scott started to lean in for a kiss but Fae didn't reciprocate (she was still driving). Scott was confused by this because she didn't have to keep driving. So of course, he asked about it. "Fae, you know, you can stop now." It wasn't clear why, but she was struck with fear.

"I already tried; the car's moving on its own!" The pair are panicking, but Fae is holding her composure much better than our main hero. I'll paint a picture for you.

Scott is trying in vain to open his door. He pulls the handle and pushes against the leather covered metal, but it doesn't budge. Next, he hastily unbuckles his seatbelt and repeatedly rams his shoulder against the door. The car slowly turns into a sweatbox which is made much worse by that ever so luxurious leather interior. He's sweating profusely but he retains his energy to continue ramming the door. In fact, he gained a sudden burst of energy when things got worse. He's trying even harder to open this door. If you were here, you could see the veins almost popping from his body. Okay, I admit that sounded a little disgusting. He tries with all his might but not a single one of his efforts prevailed. Now we move to the driver's seat where Fae is taking deep breaths. She's pressing down on the brakes, but it has no effect on the car. After regaining her composure, she breaks her window with a quick and powerful elbow.

She unbuckles her seatbelt and after a short moment of contemplation she jumps out of the car. Though the ground is nothing more than grass and dirt, the speed at which the car ran made the fall plenty painful. She falls on her left arm and hears a loud crack come from her shoulder. She lies on the ground and watches the car drive off deep into the field. She loses sight of it shortly after. The exhaust fumes settling in the air and tire marks are the only remnants of the wayward car. Getting up is excruciating for her because of her injured arm. Despite the pain, she's able to push herself up. Her arm is bruised but not to the extent where it would bleed. Her blazer is dusty and slightly torn near the wrists and her elbow. The only thing surrounding is nature; nothing but trees, grass, and the cold wind. There was no sound indicating a crash which is very confusing for Fae. There is no sound of an engine to indicate that the car is even still running.

So there's that picture I promised you. Fae ran as fast as she could to where the tire tracks led, but the area was empty; it's as if nothing was ever there. Minutes ago she was facing her fears with a stranger she just met that night. To think that a whirlwind semi- platonic friendship would push her to stare down her biggest fear: Nightmares of this place; nightmares of a monster in the field that would burn her alive if she couldn't escape in time. Then she ends up alone in the field that's been haunting her and just like in those nightmares, the monster with a cloth sack over its head stood across from her. All the fear she had in her nightmares seemed to dissipate in light of recent events. She lost a friend and her home is descending into chaos. Her world is tearing apart at the seams and she's been trying her hardest to ignore it. She didn't start running like she had in her nightmares. Maybe her life is the nightmare she overlooked. Maybe there is nothing left for her to fear.

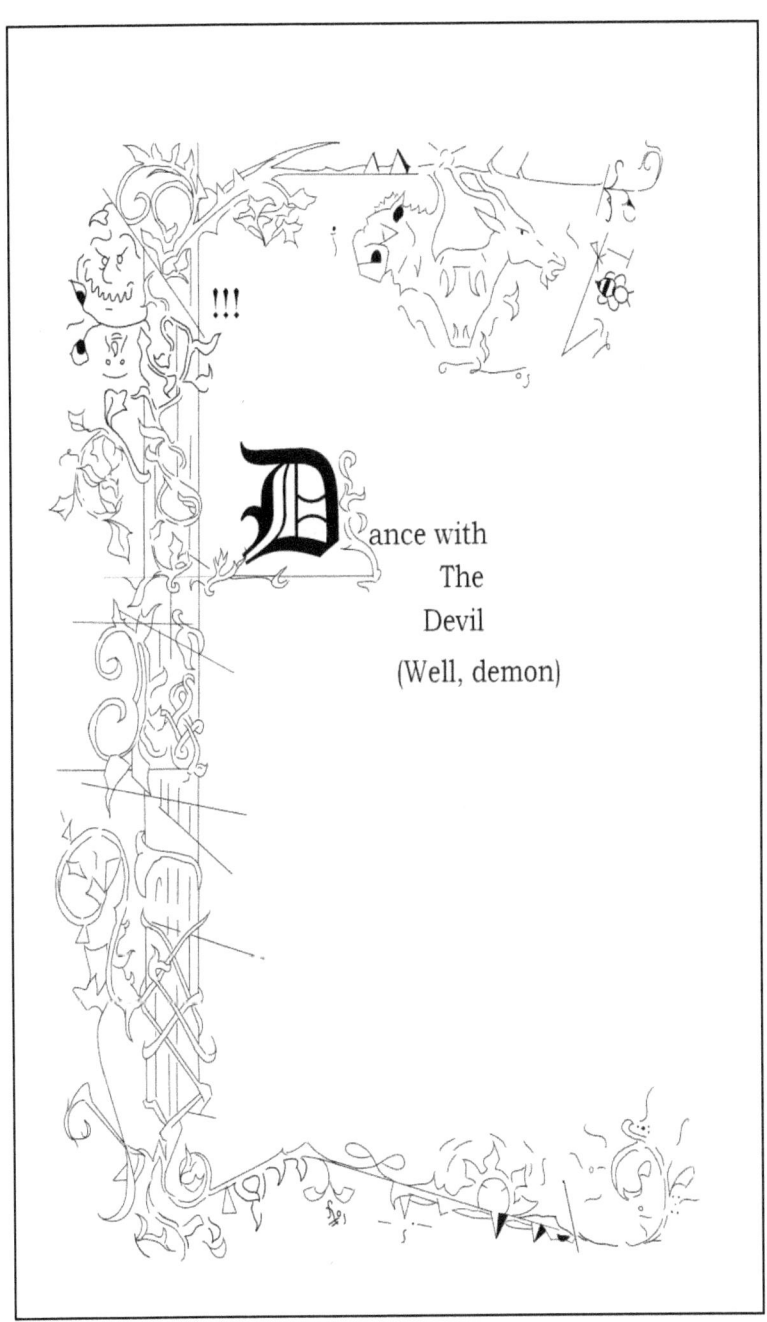

!!!

Dance with
The
Devil
(Well, demon)

CHAPTER III
DANCE WITH THE DEVIL (WELL, DEMON)

"Great. This is absolutely wonderful. I don't know where the heck I am. I'm not even sure how I got myself into this mess. But whatever I did, I hope it was worth it." "You wouldn't think so if you could remember." A young black man that looked roughly the same age as Scott, was sitting at the end of a long table and was also the only other person in the room. "Who are you?"

"Scott, my friend, I cannot tell a lie. It's wonderful to see you." The man at the table was smiling from ear to ear.

"I'm sorry, have we met?" Scott is getting aggravated. And he just made a frowny face at me. How rude.

"No, you're not, and yes, we have. The last time you saw me you were hammered in an abandoned house. Of course, I look different because I'm not hiding my true nature, but you first saw me in a can." "Hold up, are you trying to tell me that you were that crazy squirrel? "Trying implies that I'm not succeeding; anyone could see that I am. "

"I don't believe you." Scott huffed at him.

"Your cynicism is cute at best. It doesn't intimidate me. Nothing you do can intimidate me. I don't need to prove anything to you, but I would love to see the disbelief deep down in your heart turn into sheer astonishment." After uttering these words his appearance shifted into that of a squirrel. Scott cringes at the sight, but it goes so fast that there's hardly a process to cringe at; the change is short and almost seamless. Without warning, another change occurs.

84

The small animal is replaced by a young white woman with long and wavy strawberry blonde hair that looked to be close in age to Scott. She has freckles and icy blue eyes. Sound familiar? "Stop you freak!" Scott yelled at the top of his lungs but the figure changed again anyway. The blonde girl was now Faaghira, Scott's (unfairly) attractive semi-platonic friend (I think). Scott is caught between a place of fury and confusion. I don't blame him though. This is one messed up situation. "Were you them this whole time? Have you been messing with my life this whole time?"

"The answer to both of those is no; I simply wished to make your life *more* uncomfortable at this moment in time. I can pose as anyone and anything, but I rarely do; I don't see it as fair. And I haven't been messing with your life until very recently. And before you ask, I can turn into you as well."

"What kind of unholy creature are you?"
"Roswell, The Demon."

"I thought demons were those wicked looking red creatures with horns and sharp teeth. You look like a regular guy."

"Correction, I look much better than your average Joe. I'm handsome for a reason, darling. Who would do bad if it looked as ugly as it is?" "Hmm, I guess I never thought of it like that, but you're still fucking weird. So if you're supposed to entice me why aren't you a hot chick? I'm not gay." "Do you really believe that I look like this just for you? Maybe you're as egotistical as I am. This is what I normally look like. Frankly, I find those forms to be quite uncomfortable. Since no demon is limited to shape or form, you'll run across many that would love to entice you with whatever image you desire. I, however, am not one to take the appearance of worldly pleasures; I'm much too lazy for such actions. I fancy myself as the type that messes with your mind, not your head." Roswell patted himself on the back.

"Is everything that happened to me here because of you?"

"I threw you into this dimension I created; and I created this dimension, by the way; but I wouldn't give myself too much credit. All the interactions you had with people were purely your doing. They really like you there and that's actually not my fault. And just so you know, my goal is not to entice you to do anything." "Then why are you putting me through all this?" "Because I'm an asshole. I'm not like most demons, but *all* of us are assholes; if we weren't then we wouldn't be demons. And a direct answer to your question, but not really, is that we're going to have a chat over dinner. Afterwards we'll take a tour around this beautiful world I've made; there's a lot to show. But I'm going to tell you something that will make you hate the idea."

"And what would that be?" "Where is Fae?" Roswell feigned concern, looking around the room and checking under the table. "I don't know. The last time I saw her she jumped out the car. Now I'm wishing I did too. What's it to you?" "Oh…I killed her." The demon burst into laughter.

"No you didn't! You're just trying to get me riled up!"

"Yes, I'm trying to get you riled up, but I really did kill her. If you don't believe me then take a peek under the table." Roswell wore a… *sigh*… devilish smile on his face. Scott hesitated to look but he did anyway. There her body lay sprawled out on the floor. Scott rushed down to her side so fast that he hit his head on the side of the table. He lifted her wrist to check for a pulse and almost broke down when all he felt was the warmth leaving her arm. He held on just in case her heart would start beating again. He refuses to believe that she's dead even though the evidence is right in front of him. He hardly knew her but he *felt* that he knew her so well. They had a connection and Scott felt in his heart that he needed her in his life. Unfortunately, she couldn't feel anything in her heart anymore. Scott fought to hold back the tears but it worked to no avail. He sniffled and bawled then laid himself face down next to her.

"You look like you could use a tissue... box." Roswell suddenly had a tissue box in his hand which he laid down near Scott's face. Scott gathered the energy to lift his head up and look into the eyes of Fae's cold-hearted killer; Scott is positively livid. "FUCK YOU! I WILL FUCKING KILL YOU! FUCK YOU TO HELL YOU BITCH!" Scott yelled so hard that his voice cracked from being strained. He was angrier than I ever knew was possible. There was nothing but pure hatred in his eyes.

"You've got quite a mouth on you there, kidoo! And on another note, I'm positive you'd contract a disease if you did. You also can't kill me because you don't have the means. And once again; diseases." Roswell shrugged and put on a phony confused face. No doubt that he's a cold hearted freak. Even though he hasn't been around for long, any other words would seem out of character for him. "Aw shucks! You're a real sweetie pie." Scott is still furious, but he's a little confused because of how Roswell isn't making any sense. "Well I wasn't talking to Scott. I was talking to you." You can hear me? "Of course. Scott isn't the only one that can hear you. I am fully aware of your presence. A narrator has to have an audience of some kind in order to truly have a purpose. I've been listening to a good bit of this story and I must say that you're doing a bang up job. Whoever wrote this mess has got to be one special character." With the swiftness of a snake, Scott tackled Roswell and proceeded to beat his face in. Roswell's nose was broken and his eyes were surrounded by cuts and swelling dark purple circles. Blood ran from the left corner of the demon's mouth. With one right jab Roswell knocked Scott back. Roswell got on his feet but he didn't attack Scott. Scott pushed himself off the ground and punched Roswell in the jaw so hard that it cracked. Roswell retaliated by countering Scott's next punch and dislocating his shoulder. Scott grunts in agony but brushes the pain aside to try to regain his focus. Roswell goes for a right hook but Scott blocks it and follows up with a knee to the stomach. Roswell staggers but doesn't fall. He places his hands on his jaw and snaps it back into place. Scott charges at him but Roswell caught him, picked him up with one arm and slammed him through the table. The color of the room changed from a crisp bright white to a violently bright blood orange. The table, everything on it, and the chairs turned into a haunting ominous black smoke.

Scott lay between the debris of the table but he tries to get back to his feet. His injuries get the better of him and he struggles to get back up. "You've got a mean hook, my friend. How's about we call it quits for now? I can keep this up for an eternity, but you, on the other hand, you can't take too bad of a beating before your body bows out. I know you're not the happiest guy in the world right now but having your ass handed to you won't make you feel any better." Scott stared the man…demon down with a grimace, but he silently nodded in agreement.

The room was back to the white color it had before. The walls and the floor seemed to go on infinitely just as they had before. Everything was back to the way it was before but the strange part was that everything repaired itself. The table and the chairs (the only furniture in the room) are finished in a dark brown stain as they did before and they stand unbroken. Even Scott and Roswell are unscathed as if they never fought. Roswell hadn't snapped his fingers or made any effort to change revert everything back to its original state. One second Scott was battered and bruised in-between a broken table and literally the next second it's as if none of that ever happened. The two sat at opposite ends of the long table and the room seemed bare because the dozens of chairs on each side are empty. Every inch of the table's surface is engraved with a detailed scene of people in clothes from different eras looking with otherworldly looking creatures interacting with them. Other oddities such as ears bearing a knife, a giant emerging from an egg, and people being impaled on musical instruments adorned the surface.

The mix of disbelief and fear manifested itself through Scott's eyes. "How…what just happened?"

"I'm the fastest cleaner in the West… or anywhere for that matter. Perhaps now you would like to hear my proposition. You'll say yes eventually, so you might as well just say yes now." Roswell didn't need to raise his voice to be heard despite the fact that the distance between the two is unnecessarily great. From here Scott's face showed indifference. The emotional roller coaster he'd been on that night was too long for any possibility of comfort. Friendship, love, fear, death, anger, disappointment, all of these feelings struck him in rapid succession. Now he has to make a deal with the being that caused him all the pain he was feeling as well as some pain that had already passed. Love it or hate it (leaning towards hate) there's no other way to move forward.

"Alright I'll hear you out; What do you want from me?" Scott sighed bitterly. "You can barter for your friend's life; I can bring her back if it's what you choose. We're going to take a trip to various places that you may or may not be familiar with. We'll be there initially as spectators, but you're welcome to interfere if that's what you truly desire. But you should have something to eat first. A satisfied stomach eases the mind. I'll also give you the option to leave, but you'll stay to barter for her life, so I'm not sure why I made that an option." "You're saying that I can just leave right now, no strings attached?"

"Sure. Turn around and head straight and you'll be out of here. You'd never see or hear from me again and I'd leave you alone for all eternity. But we both know you won't do that, so why'd you ask?"

"Why do you know me so well? Before now I've only known you for what couldn't've been more than like two minutes, and you were a squirrel then. Yeah, I actually don't know you." Bitterness still seared in Scott's voice.

"Of this I'm well aware. It'll take a good share of time to explain but, I promise that I will. I highly suggest you get something to eat before we leave; the journey will be long and stressful. So what will you be having? Any dish you can think up is on the menu." "Any dish, you say? I've really been hankering for a freshly cooked plate of my aunt's lobster vindaloo with cocoanut rice. A side of pumpkin pie would complement it very nicely." The sarcasm rolled right off Scott's tongue. "And that's what's on your plate. I took the liberty of changing your request to sweet potato because it's better. This is a proven fact."

Scott was elated, afraid, utterly confused, but still extremely pissed. Where did this come from? How did Roswell know which aunt he was talking about? Is it poisonous? Is it real? When did it get there? How did it get there? How long has it

90

been there? Seriously, where did it come from? Scott looked across the table to read Roswell's expression for any hint of foul play, but the demon wasn't there.

"No worries darling, it's safe to eat. If I were going to kill you I wouldn't resort to something as cowardly as poison. Take your time and enjoy it, but don't take too long. And don't worry if you can't finish it now; whatever is left over will be placed in the astral refrigerator. I don't feel like explaining what that is, but you'll get to see it. Now please feel free to eat. And please never say hankering again; it sounds disgusting." Roswell sat cross-legged on a yellow pleather couch. He continuously readjusts his position to make a squeaking sounds come from the cushions. As Scott ate he would glance at the demon with disapproval. Every time Scott looked at him Roswell smiled and continued to make slight movements so much that the couch would make those annoying little squeaks. After five minutes of this Scott gently placed his fork next to the sweet potato pie (to clarify, that is an entire sweet potato pie and not a slice).

"Are you trying to make me mad?"

"I can't make you do anything; I do things and it's up to you whether or not you're mad about it. But I guess if I want to 'make' you mad, I know how. Since you're done we can leave now." "I'm not- forget it; let's get this over with." Scott angrily pushes his seat back and walks over to the couch. The couch extended horizontally and Scott sits on the opposite end of Roswell. The demon points at Scott's plate and a black portal dissolves it then disappears. "Astral refrigerator; now off we trot." The couch's legs grew longer and the piece of furniture ran past the table. It speeds through the never-ending room until it reaches another area. For the first time in a while Scott ends up somewhere new...well, sort of. The couch landed on a sidewalk across from a modest one story home. The neighborhood is dimly lit but the glow of the light posts complements the night sky beautifully. It clearly isn't the suburbs, but it has an unmistakable urban charm. The neighboring houses aren't too close like they would be in a subdivision. The street isn't very long, but it compensates by having a bodega at the end of it. The neighborhood is quiet, but because of the proximity to the city it still feels lively.

"I know this place like the back of my hand. My whole world was set around here. All my fondest memories were here: having Chinese down the street, pizza joint two blocks down; just another block to the train station. Some ways down the other side of the block are the corner stores, beauty shops and tattoo parlors. It seems like when God created the Heavens and the Earth that these shops were closed. I've always wondered why they places just sit there. They grew on me as I got older and now I can't imagine the neighborhood without them. This whole place is a part of me and I never wanted to leave. Sometimes I can't believe I left all this for college. I never even liked the idea of going through four more years of school. So why did *you* bring me here?" Scott crossed his arms as he shifted from bright reminiscence to huffing furiously.

"A coincidence, probably."
"I'm not buying it, run that one by me again."

"Okay, you got me on that one; not that I was trying. I brought you here to show you what your life was like before I had anything to do with it. Do you want to take a visit to the ol' house? We don't have to go, but whatever. I think you should go ahead and take a look."

"What did you do to my house?" Scott clenched his fists and gritted his teeth in anticipation for another fight. Just like the last time, he was sure he was too angry to lose. Roswell ignored Scott's rising temper as the demon blew smoke from out his mouth.

"Chill dude; no need to go makin' life such a drag. If it looks off to you then don't blame me; everything's the same as you left it." Roswell reclined on the couch while still blowing thin waves of smoke. Ironically, Scott is aggravated by the demon's dismissive behavior. After remembering what happened the last time he fought Roswell he decided it wasn't worth another broken limb. Scott took his time crossing the street, making sure to check for any signs that all of this is an illusion. Every little detail down to the crumpled bags of rap chips (look 'em up on the web) sitting near the storm drain is there as he remembered it. He's only seen one of his neighbors in passing so it gave him some comfort not seeing them waving or doing any kind of nice gestures. "Hey, I thought you weren't supposed to be omniscient. How do you know all of these random things about me?" Well excuse me for doing my job; this is all in the script. "I don't believe that, but whatever." Scott finally stopped postponing moving the story along when he finally crossed the street. He stopped shy of the door, probably wondering what he was even doing. This whole time has been pretty weird so I can understand why he wouldn't be jumping into things. I'm honestly not sure whether or not this is real or an illusion but I never get filled in on any of this stuff. Alright, the door is dark brown like the rest of the house but everything looks mostly gray under the night sky. He stared at the door before knocking on it, which I assume was another reassurance plan.

He knocked on the door after what I assume was realization

that he couldn't distinguish the real world from the fantasy one he's been trapped in. After waiting for an unbearably long ten seconds he began to violently slam (as if there's another way to do it) his fist on the door. Scott carried on with this until the door opened and he was greeted with a fresh backhand. The impact left a short echo in the house and one loud "clap!" that resonated through the neighborhood. Miraculously, Scott's only response was to hold his cheek and a small 'ouch'. The owner of this hand of steel is a tall-ish woman with her hair wrapped up in a multi colored satin cloth. She wears a mostly orange dashiki that she pairs with the squinting eyes of someone who's really pissed off that something had the audacity to wake them up. She isn't young but she's far from old. We've seen that Scott can be quite volatile, so it's baffling as to why he would get hit and not do anything about it.

"Scott, aren't you supposed to be at college right now? What they heck are you doing here? Did they drop you? You drink again?" The woman still appears to be half asleep but she's every bit as intimidating as a marine drill instructor. Now as to why Scott didn't do anything and why she cares so much about what he's doing? Maybe- "Mom chill for a second, alright? Can I come in? I'll tell you why I'm here and all that jazz if I can come in." Yup, that's it. His mom nodded, giving him permission to step through the doorway. However, when he did he was met with the tough expression he seemed to be so accustomed to. "Now tell me what you're doing here right now or you're your black behind is getting out my house." Damn. Hearing her makes me feel like I did something wrong and she's not even know I exist. Somehow Scott is taking this way better than he should.

"I was having a hard time adjusting at school, which I think is kinda silly, but that's what happened. I took a trip back here to have something familiar in my life again. Even though it's just for a short time, being here is giving me life. I know that I usually only come home at this time when I'm wasted but I promise that I'm not this time. You'd find out I was back in the neighborhood sooner or later and I knew you'd be ticked if I didn't come to see you. I know it's not a good time but I figured it's better for you to be mad at me for waking you up rather than being mad that I never dropped by. Leaving out the details of what I did tonight, that's what's been going on."

Does Scott always have a list of convenient lies on hand? That has to be the only way he's able to come up with these believable lies so fast. His mom seems not to be surprised by the explanation at all which means that either she bought it or she saw right through it. "Nothing familiar means you're not seeing that girl anymore?"

"I'm not talking to you about that. She has nothing to do with anything I was talking about. I'd much rather keep things peaceful between us and the way I do that is keeping my love life far away from my family." "And it's your love life that's been keeping you away from your family. We don't have to talk about it so long as you do something to fix it. You know I don't approve, but you still go an' see that girl. Now child, gowan 'an have a seat at the table. You want something to drink." She called out on her way to the kitchen as Scott closed the door behind him.

"Whatcha got?"

"Child, how many times I have to tell you to speak proper English? There's some green tea with peach, water, and ginger beer." "That's all you got?"

"You coulda told me, say you came to the neighborhood. Instead you come to my door in the middle of the night askin me why I don't have no other drink." Scott couldn't see it but she shook her head in disappointment. Scott sat at the table patiently concentrating on an intense game of tic tac toe that he started on a receipt he pulled from his wallet.

"Uh, ginger beer sounds good. And not for the reason you think, really; I know it's not alcohol. Water's too boring and I'm not in the mood for- green tea, was it? Nah, I don't like that." She returned with two ginger beers but she drank most of hers before she sat down. Scott was still heavily invested in his game of tic-tac toe. The two seemed to be in their own separate worlds. When she finished the drink he placed another pen on the table and she joined in on the game of tic-tac toe. "How're you doing in school?"

"Great grades like you like to hear about. Not like any of that really matters in college, though." After winning that game she started a new one on the other side of the receipt. "That's good. I wish you'd carry on that good performance to the rest of your life." "Look, the only reason I've ever done well in school is because it's the only thing I can do to repay you. If I wasn't broke, I'd just slide you a cool million and call it a day. And you obviously don't get how stressful it is trying to keep up with such a good academic record. My personal life is where I get to mess up, *and boy do I run with that one.* You and dad were the ones who always told me that real life isn't some fairytale where everything always works out. So why has it been so different whenever school was involved? It's always 'Take the SAT and get a perfect score so you can get a full ride scholarship and get into a good college. Take the SAT again; your score wasn't good enough. What are you majoring in? When will you get a job? All this studying will pay off when you have a six figure salary. You'll be an inspiration for the community.' Both you and dad went to college and I haven't seen any indication of a six figure salary. All my teachers went to college and they can hardly afford to pay their mortgage every month unless they're bending over on the weekends. If was thinking logically then I wouldn't have listened to any of that 'you need college' crap that everyone's been shoving…down my throat! I'm only doing this to make you happy, but that's obviously not enough for you. Of course my personal life is gonna be a wreck! Just let it be that!" After letting out his rant, he waited a moment and asked how his dad was doing. I don't even understand.

"He's doing fine but if you're really so concerned about him you should give him a call every now and then. He'd love to hear from you."

"Is he home right now?"

"He would've heard that knock and come running to the door. He's at work. I told him the hospital's never had good hours but he wanted that life anyway. I'll tell him you stopped by whenever he gets back. *Please call your father later*." She finished off with more of a demand than a request. "I promise I will. And mom, I don't think I've said it or shown it much, but I love you. I'm working on the whole 'making you guys proud' thing. I know you didn't ask for a child and even if you did, I'm the farthest thing from what you would've wanted. I know I've been tough to deal with but I want you to know that it'll only get worse. But thanks for propping me up when I stumbled at…every time of day. Thanks for the ginger beer and I'll talk to you again soon. I love you mom. But when you get mad, remember I never asked to be brought into the world, so checkmate."

97

She hugged her little boy tightly. "I love you too son. Be safe. And don't worry about how life goes sometimes, eh? You already got a full ride scholarship, so you've got plenty to be proud of." Scott begins to reach out his hand he sees her eyes are watering, but she quickly smacks it away. "Boy, I'm happy right now. Just leave it alone; people have to feel their emotions. Now it's two in the morning and I'm going back to bed. Get out my house." She turns off all the lights on her way back to bed, leaving Scott sitting alone at the table in the dark.

The faint orange glow from outside passed through the window, giving Scott a little bit of light to see. He grabbed his ginger beer, locked the front door and left through a window near the kitchen. When he was back outside he saw Roswell and the yellow couch. Scott and the demon looked directly at each other but Scott continued to walk on his side of the sidewalk. He walked down to the corner where he saw the bodega and the local deli (both closed at the moment) then stared at them as he drank. He took a seat on the curb and was unalarmed when he heard footsteps getting louder because he knew who they were from.

"I have another place to show you and my powers don't work if I get too far from that couch. Let's go back over there and we'll talk on the way to the next stop. You can stare at corner stores all you want at the next place." Roswell already started to walk back, but he turned around in anger when he saw that Scott hadn't moved at all. "Come on Scott, now's not the time to play the angsty teen; let's get moving." Roswell was trying hard to keep his composure but there's no doubt he'd snap if he didn't get his way. Scott, on the other hand, sips from his bottle without a care in the world. The demon continued get flustered and Scott's only response was to flick him off and go back to drinking.

"You have your agenda and I have mine. I've got bridges I've burned that I've gotta fix. Playing your game isn't anywhere on my list. I get that you don't understand how real life works because you're a demon, but I'm always the one who's accountable for all the stupid stuff I do. If what you've got to show me isn't right here then count me out. And listen to the words that are coming out of my mouth; I'm having a conversation with a demon. I've lost it."

"And where would you be going if you're not going with me?" Roswell folded his arms, but he didn't seem upset, just intrigued.

"There's a certain someone I've been missing out on. I have to go see them. After that I'm going back to the apartment and forgetting that any of this happened. Except for the part where you killed Fae; I'm definitely going to find a way to kill you for that. Other than that, I'm getting back to my life. I don't could care less what you do, but you're not staying here and I'm not going to wherever you're trying to take me." Scott finished the ginger beer but he kept the bottle. He crossed the street and the demon followed suit. The two walked past the houses and apartments lined up on a low incline. The character and charm of the neighborhood is undeniable even in the ominous night.

"I'm intentionally being imposing; why are you so stuck on staying in this hellhole?" Roswell had a warm smile as if he was an old friend. "Aw, a hellhole? You really mean that? That means the world coming from you. Well it's got more to do with how the place is rather than me living here my whole life. Some cars still pass through the streets this early in the morning but it's a part of the charm. I've lived here all my life and I've never been afraid of the dark. Everything is still beautiful when the lights go out. You've got people around the country and even around here who talk about this being a risky place to live. Every place is risky. Wisconsin had Dahmer and quite a few places had Bundy. Man just hearing those names makes me wish I could live in another reality." "But you can. If you-"

"Shut up, I don't want to hear it. Now where was I? Oh yeah the dangerous place thing. There's a point to everything I'm saying. There's always this quiet war against any side that's across the way. Who lives in the better city? Who has the nicer car? Who lives in the better house? Who's the better politician? Who's better looking? Why the fuck am I talking to somebody who killed one of my friends? There's this big shame game that everybody seems to be in on. Especially being black in this strange world of mine means you hear all that 'we need to do better' bull. People wanna preach but the message never goes far from the pulpit. I can't tell you how many times I've heard the whole 'this generation' shit. If you're smart you'll realize that nobody's on your side. Color never seems to be an issue when it comes to criticism. I've had White people, Asian people, Middle Eastern people, Black people, more white people, more black people, then more black people, then even more black people tell me what I'm doing wrong. The blame game's been moving for a long time and everybody playing's pointing fingers. Fingers get pointed at me all the time; I'm just too lazy to keep the line going. Fuck 'em all, that's what I say!"

"Why are you telling me all this? Don't you have a shrink?" The demon playfully egged on.

"That's a long story. The short story is no. I'm a dude; I don't need to go somewhere to cry about my feelings. I couldn't call myself a man if I couldn't handle my own problems; I'm getting off topic. So basically the point is that everything that sucks can be fixed; somebody just has to be mature enough to accept their part in the issue. You've got the old coots who tell you everything's your fault; the younger ones that bitch about you doing or saying 'the wrong thing', whatever that means. I feel like I'm rambling on, which I am, but whatever. Have you ever had to deal with any of those hacks or do you go after the greedy types?" Scott turned around to surprise Roswell with a quick right hook to the gut, but the demon dodged it and acted like nothing happened.

Roswell ran a hand through his hair as a smirk slowly grew on his face. That sly closed-mouth smile is danger in a nice frame. "Oh I've dealt with people of all kinds. If they have a heartbeat, then they're a potential client. I'm as old as hell itself but don't get me mistaken for the devil; I'm essentially the opening act that nobody wants to see that's working with an act everyone wants to see. I think the reason most people even make deals with me is because they think I'm the devil. I'm not sure I can blame them for thinking that; we have some things in common. Now being specific, I have a few stories about some interesting people that you'll probably enjoy hearing. Before I go forth with story time, I'm a little curious about you; your love life to be exact. Do you have a place in your heart for someone special?" Roswell's devilish (sorry, I had to say it) smile gave hint to some malice, but Scott didn't seem to catch it. Or maybe he just didn't seem to mind.

"I'm sure I have a hole in my heart, but I don't think it's big enough to fit a whole person in it." Technically Scott answered the question. It's not the kind of answer Roswell was looking for but apparently it's the kind that Scott gives out. "Narrator, I had you hired to read the story as you see it and *occasionally* interpret scenes. Keep in mind that Scott and I can both hear you and we both find you to be dangerously aggravating. In short, do your job right so you can live to have another one. Now Scott, you said you have a hole in your heart? What do you mean by that? I sense no internal bleeding so this must be a metaphor; but what is this a metaphor for?"

"That sounded really awkward."
"Pointing out what is perceived as wrong. When will humans learn that sometimes odd things are intentional? In layman's term: get hip to the humor, kid."

"Weird on purpose? Yeah I can roll with that."

"And you've created a perfect example. Your sentence structure usually consists of simple words weaved together to create a complex meaning. This time the words were carefully welded into small talk. You're trying to change the subject by making this one awkward and pointless. I commend you for your efforts and I truly admire the genius behind what you've done. However, I've known of this trick for generations and I'll surely never be fooled by it again. But all of this effort to dodge a question makes me want to know the answer even more. Who's this special someone you've got your heart set on, Mr. Blue?"

Scott wasn't left with many choices beyond giving a direct answer to the demon's question. Scott opted for one of those other options. "First you have to tell me why you want to know so bad. I'll tell if you go first."

The smug look quickly disappeared from Roswell's face. He really did want to know that bad. Whoops, I mean he was upset that he would have to comply to Scott's sly offer or stay unknowledgeable about Scott's love life. "Alright kid, you win. Like I already mentioned, I make deals with people.

As much as it sounds like a bad pun, I truly do play the devil's advocate. My specialty is with love and all the juicy scenes that come with it. You've heard of cupid, right?"

"Everybody has. What's that got to do with anything?"

"Well I play cupid instead of matchmaker. Just like with cupid, it's guaranteed that I can fix your relationship woes and link the hearts of any two souls. I'm not a reckless and heartless cherub, *but I am a reckless and heartless demon.* You're basically getting the same thing, but I actually come in a cool package. I've been aiding love struck and lonesome men and women and other folks of the world for as long as I've existed. Everyone wants to feel loved and some people will go the extra mile to get that feeling. Those who see all other options as undesirable turn to me to make their lives better. I oblige because it pains me to see all of these miserable people sulking about because of love. They should be sulking over more important things like the despair of all people and their inevitable deaths. So I took it upon myself to carry out their desires if they were really that stuck on the person. Everything worked well for my charity cases save for two people: a guy in the south and the worst of all, a very successful business man. Both of them have become creatures fouler than myself. Be wary of them; they roam the other dimension with the intent of setting themselves up as gods. They hate each other as much as they hate me, so you won't have to worry about dealing with them at the same time. I refuse to speak of their atrocities but I guarantee you that these vile creatures should not be trusted under any circumstance. I am interested in offering you a chance at true love. Be it distance, lack of interest, or *other complications,* I can get you all wrapped up in the arms of the one you desire in the blink of a centurion eye."

"Thanks but no thanks. I've got my own strange arrangement that I'm handling just fine. I don't need or want whatever it is you're offering. The distance part hit home but it's not enough for me to get desperate. You killed Fae and even though I seem chill about it I've been trying to think of ways to kill you this whole time. And just so you know, I will find a way to kill you. As far as my love life goes, it's not something anyone could fix and I don't want anyone to try."

"Because you think they could fix it?"

"Because I like things the way they are. The disheveled mess that happens to be my relationship is the best thing I've ever had. I don't want you or anyone else to go fucking it up. "

While it wasn't the same kind as before, a smile returned to Roswell's face. The two had walked quite a distance from where the conversation started. Because it was so early in the morning the sun hadn't risen yet. The demon was almost bursting with excitement from the progress he was making in dissecting Scott's personal life. "Oh do tell! Who's the sorry woman?"

Usually Scott can take a joke. In fact, he's usually the one making slyly distasteful jokes if you hadn't noticed already. This time Scott wasn't even slightly amused. He didn't frown; he didn't do so much as wince. Scott was more upset than I'd ever seen him. The odd thing is that he didn't blow up and get angry. Scott had the blankest expression I'd ever seen anyone have. "It's not great but it isn't sorry; she isn't sorry. My girlfriend and I love each other very much; perhaps a little too much. Our relationship is mostly stable but I don't need or want any help making things better. The two of us actually like the semi dysfunctional thing we have. But from that show you put on earlier, I'm not telling you anything you didn't already know."

"Are you both masochists and sadists simultaneously? I've never heard of both parties seeing such an unhealthy thing as desirable." Roswell feigned excitement and surprise.

"Whoa, whoa, whoa; you're crossing a line; you're making this into something it's not. The Sex is exciting but it's never sketchy or anything like that. And that's as far as I'll go talking about my sex life. Masochists and sadists at the same time" Scott laughed to himself. "I've gotta tell her about that when I see her." "When's the next time you plan on seeing her?" "That's where I'm going right now. Like I said earlier, you're welcome to hang around for a bit, but when I get close to her apartment, you're outta here. If you got any other bullshit or wanna psychoanalyze me some more, you'd better do it quick."

Roswell stopped then turned the other way. "No need, I'll be seeing you again real soon when you're back in my storybook." "I'm not going back there."

Roswell disappears but a sticky not falls from the sky onto Scott's forehead. He pulls off and examines thee note. It reads 'Later Scotty! See you soon!' with a winky face drawn before the words. Scott shook his head but he put the note in his pocket instead of throwing it away. Scott walked on and a few more cars passed through the streets. The surroundings shifted to a more luxurious kind; the apartments were more like something for the upper crust. The apartment buildings are more modern compared to the ones that Scott passed along the way. These newer buildings fall second only to the elegant high rises of Manhattan. The inner city is faintly visible from where Scott is now but the view is far from remarkable.

It's true that the city never sleeps- "Hey narrator, can you take a break for a second?" Why? Is something wrong? "Bathroom break. We'll catch up later." Oh okay. This is the first time I've narrated a story where any character took a bathroom break. I know it sounds weird, but most of the time it's either non-stop action or sleeping. I can understand though; some writers are very descriptive and they'd do a bathroom break *too* much justice.

Alright, intermission over. Scott left the side room that he went into to... so Scott walked a little bit further along his path to his girlfriend's apartment. He walked for another hour before he reached a train station. Mind you, this isn't the only one he passed. He went by at least two before getting to this one. What the reason was for him going to this specific one is beyond me. I'm positive they all could've let to wherever he's trying to go. "There's more to it than that; this is the train station I always take to Manhattan when I'm around here." It looks to be a little far from home. It also doesn't look like you're around here enough by necessity. "Whatd'ya mean? Technically nowhere is a necessity, but everywhere is a necessity if you think about it. And aren't you supposed to be gone too? I'm not in the story anymore."

I don't have an answer for that one. Back to the important things; you live pretty far from here and the train isn't even running at this early in the morning. If there are places closer to where you live then why come all the way out here? Do you even need to go to Manhattan at this hour? "I'm going to meet a friend here pretty soon and this is where we meet sometimes." What makes you so sure that this mystery person will appear this time? I didn't hear you make any calls or talk to anyone else. "That's right; you *didn't* hear me talk to anyone." Scott smiles in a way that mirrors the annoyingly smug look Roswell often wears.

This is very annoying. When he got to the station Scott walked up the stairs and waited by the top. After sitting for a while he was hugged by a beautiful young woman that had just gotten up there. She has long strawberry blonde hair and icy blue eyes. It's Scott's girlfriend; the same one that I thought he made up. "Scott, what are you doing here?" Iris (his girlfriend) was bursting with excitement when she saw her lover. Did that sound a little creepy? I think it came off that way. "I was passing through the neighborhood so I thought I'd make a quick stop at one of our old hangouts."

"It's so great to see you! What are you doing out here so early in the morning?" "For some reason I couldn't allow myself to leave here without seeing you."

"I'm so happy that you called! I rolled out of bed and got here as soon as I could because you never call unless it's for something really serious!" She paused for a moment and began to fight off the tears forming in her eyes. When she spoke again her voice was shaky but her expression yelled well- composed. "I'm sorry, I'm so sorry Scott!"

"Sorry for what? You didn't do anything yet."

"I'm sorry for whatever I did to push you away! I broke down after a month. I wanted to call you but I was convinced that I needed to get you out of my head. Just hearing your voice would've shown me why I can't live without you. I just knew that I could move on, but I realized that everything I knew was wrong!" Right now Scott looks relaxed and uncomfortable at the same exact time. Him and his girlfriend have some emotional issues that they're about to resolve, which I assume is responsible for the lack of comfort (uncomfortability isn't a word…yet). It's obvious that they care for each other on an oddly deep level. They both went out of their way to go to a specific train station at almost four in the mourning just because one called the other. There's no mistaking that the dedication is present, but something else about their meeting has Scott on guard.

"Iris, I've been missing you too… and I kind of miss where things were going. We were getting *slightly* worse, but I wanted that for some reason. Look, we can't ignore that things weren't the best. I'm a problem and you're a problem; things should've crashed and burned, but they never did. This is a sign that we can work. With that being said; I'm not sure that we should." "No, wait! Before you make up your mind about that just hear me out. I've thought a lot about what we've been like together and I figured out that I wasn't ready for what we had. I had this idea of what the perfect relationship would be like, but being with you made me realize that it's not what I need. I didn't know it at the time, but I needed you how you were. I needed you and I still need you now." Her voice is still a little shaky; probably because of the uncertainty and fear that comes with being so forward. It can be scary pouring your heart out to someone who may not care for you at all anymore.

Scott is still kind of nervous in this situation, which I find to be perplexing to the nth degree. He's not just reserved around her; he's tamed! "But I'm not good for you and you're not good for me either. You were my emotional punching bag whenever my life got stressful and I was your play thing whenever you felt like you were losing control of your life. *You lose control of your life every other day*. We're both demanding and neither of us would let up; neither of wanted to change. In fact, neither of us would admit that the relationship, our relationship, was horrible. Would it really be such a good idea for us to keep this going?"

"Yes!" Iris cried out. "We never officially broke up; we just went our separate ways for a little while. I know it sounds cliché and I know I've said it before, but this time really will be different if you just give me another chance. Nobody else can handle me the way that you do." The two sat down and Scott snuggled up in her arms. "Scott, I've gotten a lot stronger; I can take it now. I can take anything that you'd only dream of saying to me and I promise that I will. You love me and my love for you grew a lot. I can't go on without you and you need me; you depended on me for a lot and you still do. Something good can work and I know it."

Scott chuckled lightly. "Aw, that was one of our songs, but that doesn't change the fact that we're not the best fit. You shouldn't have to toughen up to love anybody; I shouldn't have to do that with you and you shouldn't have to be that way with me. But I can't deny that we had something that *felt* good. Like most things there's a chance it could work, so let's up a scenario where we try again."

"If that's what it takes. Are you starting or am I starting?"

"I'm starting. So say we get back together; you want sex, we have sex, then you have problems, what's next?"

Iris only got more emotional as the conversation carried on. "I'll tell you what's going on in my life, but only if you want to hear it. I'll listen to anything you want to say; I don't care if it stems from you getting mad at me for walking the wrong way. Sure it'll really get on my nerves, but I can take it. That's what it'll take to be with you so that's what I'm doing. I'll listen to any problem you have and I'll be there whenever you need me. It really won't be like the last times."

"Did you hear that Iris? The last times. This would be past our second chance; we've done this plenty of times already."

"Not like this! I've said I would change a bunch of times before but I wasn't serious then. I wanted to keep you around because I was afraid of being alone, but now I'm afraid of losing you. And even though you haven't said it, *I know you want me.* There's no other reason that you'd call me at three thirty, want me to meet you at one of our spots, and give a clearly flimsy argument against us being together. I know you; you weren't even trying. "She sat down next to him and leaned on his shoulder.

"I'm being as honest as I can when I say that I want to give you another chance. I just need some time to figure out if this is the best thing for us as individuals. We both want to be together but it probably isn't the healthiest choice. Look at what happened the last times; we keep trying to overpower each other and it never works."

"Well who's it supposed to work with? You knew I wouldn't change but you stayed with me anyway. And once you showed the controlling side of you, I knew that's what I would be dealing with. You're not like any other guy I've been with; you have a real backbone. For you it's not about standing up to me and trying to take charge; you're naturally aggressive and that's what I need. And I can't put enough stress on the fact that I'm the only one who can handle you. I'm trying to convince you of something that we both already know is true; we need each other. Nobody ever wanted to stay with me until you came along. I can't let you go; we have to try again. Just give me another chance, Scott. Give us another chance."

"You know what? You're right. We've both grown in our time apart so we should be stronger together now. We stayed together when we weren't used to each other and now that we are, maybe something good can work. But before that…this argument's been getting harder; I think I might need some more convincing." They hugged warmly and she kissed him on the neck… then the jaw… then the cheek… then the lips. I'll spare you the details and just sum it up with 'they kissed passionately'.

Then Iris stood up and held Scott's hand. "And I know the perfect way to start things back up again." She smiled as Scott stood up. She knew exactly what he was thinking and he knew what always came next. "You remember Ken, right? My friend from Boston?" The look on Scott's face twisted from excitement to disappointment. "Oh yeah, yeah, I remember him. What about him?"

"He's throwing a party on Monday and I would love it if you could go. You could be my plus one, you know…if you want to." She's turning out to be just as bashful as Scott. They look like they're so afraid of how the other will react. You'd think they wouldn't be so awkward give their history. Scott's expression shifts from disgust to contempt when he sees things aren't going where he thought they were. Iris blushed and started twirling her hair between her fingers when she realized why Scott was disappointed. "I think it's the best way to get to know the new us; what we're going to be. We never really did social events the last time… or the time before that… or before that… but we kind of did the first time." She went silent after that. A whopping four times that they've officially been back together, but the odd thing is that they never really broke up; apparently, things fell apart and fell back together. "Yeah, that sounds good. It'll be nice to have a change of pace. What time does it start?"

"We can go back to my place and I'll take you with me on Monday. Is that cool with you?"

Scott agreed without hesitation; the direct opposite of what he was doing earlier. Iris drove them from the station to her apartment in Manhattan. Since the city never sleeps, they took advantage of it by stopping at some parks and hidden gems along the way. The park was completely empty, though five a.m. would be a crowd at other places. Sometimes the stops were for a long walk where they could talk and take in the city's marvelous aesthetic. It's all very romantic, but there seemed to be these uncomfortable vibes hiding beneath all the good times they were having. They were out for a while doing hardly anything noteworthy. They held hands some of the time when walking through parks and through the city, but they haven't been the kind of couple who would do that everywhere they went. Sometimes they looked nervous, other times they were inseparable.

They talked about all sorts of things; weird people they've met, what they've been doing during the break (from the relationship, of course), places they traveled to, sights they saw, and they were both so excited to share their stories. It's strange seeing this thing play out; comfortable one second and awkward the next. It's like watching them switch back and forth between roles in a play. The cold and uncomfortable feelings melted away by the time the sun had risen. She drove them back her apartment in Manhattan and soon after she opened the door they were asleep on the couch. The alarm on Iris' phone went off with a song that I found to be quite annoying. She was slow to turn it off, but she began to panic when she saw the time.

"Scott wake up!"
"No."

"Come on Scott! The party's in less than three hours!" She tugged on his leg and he rolled on the floor, still wrapped up in his jacket. Iris ran to the kitchen and threw a cereal box at him. All he did in response was turn his back to her and act like he was asleep. She frowned and picked up the box of cereal from the floor. "There's no chance things will turn out good tonight if you don't get up!" He got up with his eyes barely open and trudged right past her. When Scott returned he was wrapped up in a dark green blanket. He went right past her and curled up on the couch. Before going back to sleep he told her, "You owe me a kiss."

She sighed and tugged on his leg again. "Get up, man! We have to go to this party if we're going to try this relationship a different way. You know what'll end up happening if we stay here." "Sex isn't so bad. In fact, it's great. I'll hook you up when I'm awake." Scott was trailing off and could barely finish his sentence. He was snoring just a few moments later.

However, Iris doesn't seem to be the quitting type. "Scott, Scott I know you're not really asleep. I know you don't snore." At this point she was tired of trying but she was still determined to get to this party. Scott, I really feel that you should go. Apparently this girl is trying her hardest to make things different this time, though I don't know if what she's doing is a change in any kind of way. Scott, you'll have to verify that for yourself because I don't know about what your relationship was like prior to this and I actually don't care. The friction looks to be healthy enough, as every relationship has some. In fact, it's kind of adorable seeing the way they interact with each other.

"Scott, can we please just go? At least this one time we should give this a try. If you don't like it then we don't have to do it again. I really just want to see if this will start us on a different path." Scott peeked from out of the covers and started laughing. "You didn't tell me yesterday was Sunday...and how long were we asleep? Whatever, that doesn't matter right now. Look, I hate parties so I want you to know that I'm only doing this for you. And don't worry if we're a little late; it's in three hours anyway. I actually think it would help you out a little if you learned to chill out when it comes to punctuality. Kick it back a little bit; since we're trying to compromise this time around I think you need to relax more. That's the deal; I go to this party and you gotta dial it back a little. Don't be so high strung; deal?"

Iris doesn't even think it over; she quickly said "Yes, let's go!" but it changed. "I mean; we should probably leave sometime soon. And if you say little one more time..." She had her bad habits to break; in fact, they both have bad habits to break if they want to make things different. I take it that Scott's stubbornness and Iris' demanding nature caused for some... undesirable disputes. Both of them want things their way and I can't see that not being part of their compromise. How the heck is this supposed to work?

"You still have extra clothes in that drawer? I should change my shirt...and probably find some deodorant."

"Yeah, it's in the same place it was before. Just about everything is in the same place since the last time you were here." Iris rushed over to the bathroom then back to her bedroom. She was frantically moving around, going back and forth. She showered, put on a new outfit, did her hair, did her makeup (immaculately, might I add) and then she sat on the couch. At first she was tapping her fingers on the cushion and bouncing her knee nervously. She tried to relax when Scott stopped what he was doing to give her a look of disapproval. She shot a nervous smile Scott's way then he rolled his eyes and went back to her room. She sighed and shifted positions in an effort to make herself more comfortable. She really did look awkward crossing and uncrossing her legs; leaning on one side of the couch then sitting up against the other. She continued to do awkward things until Scott was back out of the room. He just stood in the doorway and stared at her for a moment.

"Is something wrong? Did I do something wrong? Scott, did I do something wrong?" She was panicking but she tried concealed it under a flimsy coat of nonchalance.

"No, no, I was just thrown off by how uncomfortable you look. I haven't seen you like that in a long time. Would this have anything to do with you trying not to be so tense?" Scott had a bright smile on his face by the time he finished his sentence. Or would it sound more natural if it was 'when he finished talking'? As I've said before, I don't know Scott well but it seems like something that would make him happy.

When Scott sat down next to her, Iris punched his arm. "Don't do that! I hate it when you do that! Gosh you're such a jerk!" Scott laughed at her complaints knowing that that they didn't mean anything. "Love you too. Since it makes you that uncomfortable we should leave a little bit later. It's just a little over half an hour anyway; traffic can't be that bad." Iris' neutral face turned to a scowl, prompting Scott to use a new set of words. Better fix it fast, kid. If not, then I'm sure the couch will be all yours when you come back in a couple of hours. "...But we're definitely leaving soon; I just have to find my comb or something. I personally think you did a great job getting started on dropping the anxiety. I know that it must've been very- extremely stressful for you to tackle a concept that's so terrifyingly foreign to you. We *should* stay here longer to help you get over that, but you've made astounding progress; we'll handle the rest some other time. Geez, next time at least let me finish before you give me that look." She gave him a kiss on the cheek then opened the door to leave. "C'mon loser, we've got a party to get to. Get out so I can lock up." Scott was moving slowly until she gave him that angry look again. She knew he was doing it just to get under her skin. He picked up the pace when he saw that she was getting pissed. He was already heading down the stairs when she locked the door behind them. She smiled warmly for a moment before following him outside. They went on their way; Scott in the passenger seat and Iris at the wheel. The city was bursting with life as it always is. People were rushing back and forth along the streets and sidewalks. The streets were full with cars but the traffic wasn't bumper to bumper. The mass of people traveling around the city creates a sort of dance. The bright lights aren't so intimidating or flashy when you're used to seeing it. When you step back and look at it, the busy city isn't such a ruthless place. It isn't unforgiving and (as) dirty like so many people make it out to be. It's like man orchestrated its own version of what happens in nature.

The two of them, however, didn't see things the same way. The lack of appreciation for the beautiful unique surroundings is almost surprising, but when you're always surrounded by beauty it becomes normal; an expectation of sorts. As usual they had one of their regular uninteresting conversations, until Iris brought the old days out of the blue-*ahem*- out of nowhere. "Remember when we had our first argument? I never thought I'd stay with you after that. I didn't know at the time that every relationship needs a little push and shove to make it. A stagnant kind of thing where it's sunshine and roses all the time gets boring." "Uhhh, no. Arguments like that are never good for anything. Seeing something through rose colored glasses doesn't change what it is, it just changes the color. That was a shitty time and you'd understand that if you weren't trying to fool yourself into thinking everything we did was wonderful. The past sucked, the past was shit; I hated it. You didn't know that I hate arguments and you just went on and on about what's wrong and why it's wrong. You must've been able to pull that with the other guys you've been with, but I wasn't having it; that's when things really got bad. Can we just not reminisce and act like everything was perfect? Or at the very least can we see the past for what it was? Can we just do that? I, for one, love sunshine and roses."

Iris was silent for a little while and Scott simply stared out the window during the pause. The traffic was still heavy and the streets still packed with dense crowds. As soon as there was an opening Iris left the main road and pulled into a parking garage. She paid the toll and drove all the way up to the roof. They would have to walk to the party and would possibly have to talk on the way. It surely would be awkward if they didn't. We could look at it as another test; is it worth the hardships? Can they handle the responsibility that comes with a relationship? Why even test a relationship? Isn't this supposed to be for fun? When they got out the car and started walking neither one of them said a word. The structure is six floors up and they had already gone two without saying anything to each other. Scott finally broke the silence when he asked Iris how far the place was.

"It's a little bit of a walk but it's not too far." Iris spoke nervously, as though she conversed with the harbinger of death. The bouts of fear subsided but the nervousness was still present. Scott, on the other hand, was not nonchalant and well composed. As far as emotions go, he was annoyed at the very most.

"You couldn't park any closer?" Scott had his hands in his pockets and his focus was straight ahead. Not that there was anything in front of him; there was nothing noteworthy in front of him. He was drawing out long breaths to see the cold air come out and fade into the atmosphere. He pushed his hands further into his pockets to push his jacket down which I assume was a move to warm up. What may be the worst part for Iris might be that Scott isn't walking briskly or moving at a slower pace than she is. He's walking at the exact same speed; matching footsteps and the whole nine.

"Well... I could but... I wanted to talk. We don't do enough of that." "Boo, we can leave the fragile talks in the dust. Fragile is for eggs, glass, dorms, and houses without privacy. We're already back together, I know you're not like this, and I know you can't keep it up. If there's one person you can speak your mind with it's me. Not like you didn't already know that. No need to be out here playing these games. Now what's on your mind?" This time Scott actually looked at Iris. "Have I always been a problem to you?"

"Of course, that's what I love about you. What's got you thinking about that?"

"When you said the past was shitty, was I the reason?"

"Babe, my life was garbage *before* I met you. If anything, you made it a lot better; you've been a dear. I admit that things could've been better between us but, I wouldn't've stayed if I thought you weren't worth it. I could've left at any time. Since we're playing it different this time, I'm aiming for a more honest approach. Brutal as it may be, I consider it to be the greatest expression of love. But of course if you have a problem with that I guess now would be a great time to mention it." "I'm fine with you being honest, but it seems like there's some animosity behind it. It's like you're always trying to put some criticism or backhanded compliment in whatever you say. It's never *just* honesty with you." "That's part of who I am, babe. You must not have been paying any mind when I explicitly told you that this is what I'm like. All those times I poured out to you weren't for nothin'. There was a reason I did all of that. I trusted you and something told me that was a bad idea. After a while it had more to with this feeling I got around you. It was new and it felt good to have somebody there. The only problem is that you weren't there in the way that I needed you to be. I wanted to stay with you so I adapted to the way you handled things. Everything you hate about the way I tell the truth is a reflection of you. Basically, I'm your fault. Whether you love it or hate it, it's the truth."

"Um… I don't know what to say. I mean it's great that we're getting somewhere, but if that's true then I don't know to feel about that. That's a lot to take in. But if there's one thing I do know it's that all the problems we had, and probably still have, isn't all my fault. In the beginning I had no idea that you could be so bitter and harsh. You're demanding, same as I am. I like a good challenge and I'm not the kind of person that backs down from a conflict, but I automatically take the backseat whenever you get riled up. I don't want to but that's always where I end up. It's times like that where I would rather talk things out like we're doing now."

"Because it makes you feel insecure, or in other words, uncomfortable." "I…I… I'm not sure how to answer that."

"Honestly. You were uncomfortable and I already know that; now you have to be honest with yourself. What could make you insecure? First of all, you're a dime. Second: you got somebody that loves you and does you right. Though, I agree that these kind of conversations need to happen. We've got a bunch of problems we need to hash out."

"Can we talk about this later? I want to be in a different state of mind when we're at the party. No deep thoughts, just starting over and having fun." Scott shifted his focus to the world in front of him. She noticed the cold shoulder and she followed suit. They walked briskly for two more levels until Scott stopped the silence again. "Alright we can't keep doing this. Whenever something's uncomfortable for either of us we'll need to talk about it. If we both keep dodging things when they get sensitive, then we won't make it very long."

"It's not like that's exactly what I just said."

"And this time I don't feel like putting up a front to please your friends. I'm an asshole, we both know that. I don't change around your friends, I hold back. You see your friends more than I get to see mine, which is mostly my fault because I stayed with you, but that's not the point. I talk about them behind their backs and- but I want to be a much better person. I'll make fun of them behind their backs and in their faces. And before you go trying to rank on my friends, you know good and well that we hardly ever see my friends, let alone interact with them. With that being said, if you feel like talking about my friends feel free."

Iris was about to speak but she closed her mouth and continued to walk in silence. The switching back and forth from serious talks to silent walks (see what I did there?) is confusing from the outside looking in, but it makes a little bit of sense when you take a closer look at things. Even though they just got back together (officially), they didn't forget their experiences with each other; there's no need to talk the entire time if there's nothing to talk about. Small talk

120

helps move things along sometimes, but using small talk to fill in gaps between serious conversations is a silly mistake. When you don't let things run their course it always backfires. Trying to fix things too early doesn't work and sometimes that's what small talk does. They left things alone for the rest of the way there. I don't see it as a sign of weakness; it's more like a sign of understanding.

I can't be certain about why Iris cut off her response but I can make some guesses. Her decision could've been driven by fear; she didn't want to say something that would get Scott mad at her. From there two things may have happened: Scott being openly mad at her or the two of them putting on a dog and pony show for everyone at the party. Given their history, I doubt they would break up in either scenario. However, the relationship would turn back into the thing that they're trying to avoid this time around. When they were back outside the parking garage they were talking again. This time it wasn't just about issues they have with each other; too much of that doesn't solve anything. The path to a stable relationship is one that becomes narrower over time. Avoiding problems and focusing on the negatives are two extremes on opposite sides of the spectrum that can easily kill a relationship once it's off the ground.

It was when they were immersed in the world again that they got along better. The change wasn't a radical one, but when it's just the two of them things tend to get very tense and awkward when compared to how they are around others. I'm not convinced that it's a front at all; they're genuine in both situations. From what I've gathered, they've spent an awful lot of time alone. It sounds like the best thing, and it is until it isn't. When you spend a lot of time with someone you learn about a lot wonderful qualities they have. When you spend too much time with someone; the good starts to fall away while their horrible traits take center stage. It could be that they've too much of the latter.

Among the dance of the busy city, they were two of many. They weren't in their own bubble where their relationship was the center of the world. They were back in reality and it was time to live like they don't have forever; mostly because they don't. They were back to being silly and caring like they had when they reunited. The change in mood was authentic, but of course the issues from earlier didn't go away. There were times were they had the chance to carry deep conversations on different topics, but they always stopped before the topic really took off. It wasn't exactly small talk, but they made sure that the real issue wasn't pushed aside for a lighter one. From what I gather, there was a clear understanding that their problems wouldn't just up and disappear. They arrived at the party in a much better state than when they left the car. They were smiling, they were laughing (at other people); they were holding hands (on and off), and they looked like they were having a genuinely good time. The party was being held at a postmodern kind of building composed of various distorted geometric shapes. Instead of numerous lights, the majority of the light in the exterior came from a beautiful arrangement of colors emitted from glow-in-the-dark gravel. While grand in its own right, the building is miniscule when compared to the high rises and other architectural milestones that the city is known for.

People passing by also attributed to the minimizing factor (would that be the best term?) that enveloped the party. It automatically started feeling more intimate because most of the people walking in the building's direction went right past it. Each person that passed by made it seem insignificant to the point where it was no more impressive to the gazing eye than a bodega or a bus stop. When they went through the door and were met with the sight of people dancing, drinking, sitting, taking pictures, smoking (E-cigs, blunts and cigarettes), and others were just kicking back and enjoying the vibes. The main room is large with tall ceilings. It's all white with some black and red furniture. The main room isn't brightly lit but it isn't dark; more like a mixture of the two. Everything is laid in a modern fashion. The lounge area upstairs is marked by a long rectangle protruding from the wall and other various geometric shapes. There are tables covered with black cloth and they have all the fancy foods that'll make you feel like the most pretentious asshole at a pretentious asshole convention (I don't care if that was lame because it's my joke). It's not your regular old finger food or cheap stuff you might get at some regular party; they've got lobster tails, fugu, foie gras, but then there was the odd choice off pizza. However, I personally like to believe this specific pizza is also very pretentious.

Further down the table are cheese squares (with toothpicks), fruits, and three salad bowls. No drinks though; there's a bar closer to the back of the room. The spacious room makes the large party seem like an intimate gathering. Iris and Scott were back at the entrance trying to make their way through the groups of people taking up space on the floor. Iris was leading Scott past them when someone was repeatedly shouting her name (the music was loud). At first, Iris kept going, but when the person kept doing it she turned around.

"What?" Iris snapped at the person as if it were a knee-jerk reaction. "Whoa, whoa, chill out girl! No need to be so feisty, we're all here to have fun! You're getting so stressed that you can't even recognize a friend." The person in question is a slim guy with long curly hair and a disgustingly naked face. I understand that many guys don't have facial hair but you would understand that his face looks naked if

123

you could see it. He would look weird with or without facial hair. It's too hard to explain; just trust me on this one.

"Ken, I didn't know it was you. If I did I would've ignored, you longer. Hey, we can't stop to have a chat right in the center of a party. Follow me if you want to talk now or you can meet up with us before we leave, but I'm not dropping everything just to talk to you." Iris led Scott to the bar and Ken followed not too far behind. They all sat down on the stools at the counter but Ken was ignored for a while. Scott and Iris were discussing their next steps to having a more loving relationship. It wasn't an argument but it wasn't a casual conversation. They had to figure a way to make their relationship better without compromising who they are, because that won't change. After a few minutes of awkwardly sitting there, Ken squeezed his way into their conversation. "So how are you liking the party?" Ken spoke a little louder than he needed to in order to get attention.

She took her time getting back to him to avoid snapping at him, which I wouldn't blame her for doing. Even though there's no way for Ken to know exactly what's going on, it's pretty annoying to have someone barging into your conversation to get you to talk to them. I imagine that it's downright cruel to someone who's trying to keep an important bridge from burning. Of course, this is still her friend (for the time being) so entertaining his want for attention was a given. "It's great, it's great. Ken have you met my boyfriend Scott?" "So this is the Scott I keep hearing about! You're what I expected you to be like." Ken reached out his hand for a handshake. Scott looked down at Ken's hand then back at his face but he didn't move otherwise.

"And you're a lot pastier than I hoped you'd be. You appear to be completely immune to the effects of sonoluminescence; odd considering your fickle and impulsive approach to conversation. Applying just enough pressure to get a rise out of someone so that you can blow the situation out of proportion. Perhaps the phenomena will occur once the weak outer shell disintegrates to reveal... nothing." Ken put his hand down but he kept the fake smile.

"Impressive; most black people I've met aren't so articulate. I wouldn't have thought Iris would ever be with such a white black guy." Scott forced a playful smirk on his face as he clenched his fists. "You clearly haven't met most black people. In fact, I would love to talk about this topic in greater detail. And I'm sure that Iris wouldn't mind me actually talking to one of her friends." "Oh go ahead; just don't be gone too long. I'll probably be out on the balcony upstairs when you're done. Make a right as soon as you hit the top of the stairs and then a left at the end of the hall and you'll find it." She turned her attention away from them then ordered a drink and carried on as if they were never there.

Scott and Ken went outside to what would be the backyard, but you know... Manhattan. It's more concrete than grass but the city makes up for it in aesthetics. I take it that Iris is familiar with this specific place because she knew exactly where the balcony was without actually going to the second floor it's also safe to say that she is also familiar with Scott's low-key interrogations of her friends because she was there to hear that Scott doesn't like Ken, but she 'wrote it off' anyway. What Iris may not be aware of is what happens during Scott's interrogations. "I've never been a fan of Iris' friends, but you're something special; I really don't like you. Look bud, here's the deal; not only do I not like you, I also think you're a waste of oxygen and an unfortunate source of carbon-dioxide. If you call me white again, if you ever think of calling me white again, I'll either break one of your limbs

125

or one of your fingers; you don't get to choose. All that crap might fly with Iris, but I'm not having it. Being her friend doesn't mean we're cool and that you can talk to me whatever way. All it means is that I have to tolerate you when you're around us. Know your limits and stay in your lane; step out of line and I'm taking you out." He ruffled Ken's hair before telling him "Don't forget to enjoy the rest of the party" then Scott went back inside.

Scott was heading back to the bar when he remembered that Iris said she would be on the balcony. Scott also remembered what happened the last time he drank. He pushed past the people in his way (as newest Yorkers would; not polite but not rude) and made it to the balcony pretty fast. He pushed back the sliding door leading to the balcony and looked both ways to see where Iris was. She was on the far left leaning against the stainless-steel railing. She glanced at Scott then turned her gaze back to the city. Scott walked over there and stood next to her. For a moment they just watched the city together. However, the quiet moment didn't last long. Not that this is necessarily a bad thing.

Iris looked at Scott with intent and started talking, but it's debatable whether it was to him or just thinking out loud. "The world is spinning, faster and faster; unless it isn't. Recently life's been moving at such a crazy speed that it's hard to keep up. Everything's been falling away; every plan, every memory, all my inspiration. But I can't figure it out, at least not yet." Scott smiled at her with that same look she was giving him. "I dunno if you want advice or if you only need someone to listen. Regardless of which one it is, I'm ready to do it." "Scott, I love you, you know that?"

"Well obviously; how could you not? And now I'm getting more of a 'venting' vibe from this." "And that's why I love

126

you; you know me so well. There's a whole lot more that want to tell you but I just don't know if I should."

"What do ya mean, babe?"

Iris took a deep breath didn't say anything for a second. "Well you know how sometimes you want to say something but you feel that you can't." "Hmm, you know I feel that sometimes. I want to be able to tell you certain things but I don't feel that I can. You're the one person I would tell things that I wouldn't share with anyone else, but we don't have the dynamic that would make me feel comfortable doing that." "Funny, I was going to get around to saying something like that. I want that cheesy romantic relationship; laying on the grass and counting stars, talking for hours about anything at all, I want that fascination to go on forever. I'm still fascinated by you, but the sense of wonder fades whenever we're at each other's throats. I would love for it to stay there consistently but it never does."

Scott turned his head away from Iris and closed his eyes. "So is that what we're gonna do this time? You said yourself that you don't want sunshine and roses; are you sure you even know what you want, or is this just because of me?"

Iris reached her hand out to his arm but pulled back when she saw how disappointed he looked. "It's both of us, really. Maybe the potential is there for us to have that kind of relationship. We've been around each other too much and now we can't ignore our flaws. I remember when we were both on cloud nine for a while. There was nothing else in the world like that feeling. I know that people change over time and I didn't want to lose that feeling. I intentionally started pulling you away from everyone else to keep what we had from changing. So initially it was my fault, and I think I still would've done that if I knew how it would turn out. I had no idea you could be this aggressive, intimidating guy if you got mad. Even though things were working out the way I thought they would in the beginning, after a while all I did was make you mad. At some point I was getting afraid of losing you, but I was also starting to be afraid of what you would do. I never would've seen that side of you if I just let things run their course. I was in love with what we had before, but the strange thing is that I was falling in love with this volatile thing it was becoming."

"You would've seen that side of me eventually; nobody can hide who they are forever. You wouldn't've seen as much of it, but you would've seen it. When I realized what was going on I was really upset. There was a serious lack of communication on your part. You never told me that you didn't want things to change; you just started changing things in my life with no explanation. Even if those weren't your intentions, you were trapping me in. How am I supposed to believe you didn't want things to change when you literally changed everything? My life was changing so fast; how else did you expect me to react?"

"I wasn't thinking about that at the time. I know it sounds bad, and it was, but I thought you wouldn't get mad. It was a risky move for me to take but I thought it would be worth it. But like you've said a bunch of times, you could've left me. I wasn't holding you back from doing that; that was all you. You not leaving was a big part of what made me feel like it was okay, and again, it wasn't, but there was a lack of communication on your side too. So to give you a real answer, yes, it's partially your fault, but I wasn't thinking about how you felt about it. But I really am sorry about what I did and I wish I could take it back. I feel that it could've been better if I just let things run naturally. That's why I want to try again. I want to sit tight and let everything run naturally." She looked sort of apologetic when she spoke to him "I naturally need a drink." Scott walked away from the railing and closed the sliding door behind him on his way back in. Iris' guilt must've still been sitting heavy in her heart; she put her focus right back on the skyline, staring off into nothing. Meanwhile, Scott went looking for the kitchen; he really didn't feel like going through any drama just to get a drink from the bartender. The party was no less congested than it was before when Scott was trying to find his way around. However, Scott was unfazed by the amount of people he'd have to push through; he was on a mission. Apparently a little juice is what keeps him pleasant.

When he got off the main floor he saw a few people scattered around a small hallway, talking, making out, just sitting, drinking; basically the same as the people he saw earlier. Just the same as before, he kept moving as if they were never there. When he got to the kitchen there were two people talking and heating up some food in the microwave. They nodded at Scott and he nodded back, which is the most interaction he's had with any of the people there aside from Ken. He reached into the fridge and pulled out a tall bottle of wine. He pulled off the quark and drank on his way back to the hallway. When he got in the hallway he kept going down past the kitchen. I don't think he knew here he was going but he was just going. He was about half way through the bottle before he stopped and started stumbling into the walls. He dropped on the floor multiple times, but he never let the bottle drop. He would simply pick himself up and drink some more. He was stumbling around but he had unwavering determination to do… whatever it is he was trying to do. He came across a beautifully painted vase being displayed in a glass case in one of the rooms attached to the hallway. He went in the room, observed the vase; then he smashed case with his elbow and punched the vase off the display. He proceeded to laugh at it until he got bored and went back into the hallway. It turns out that this short hallway led straight into another one that was much longer. The walls were still white, just like every other place in the building. Unfortunately for the anything valuable, he ventured down there as well. He walked swaying from side to side; almost hitting the walls every time. He turned around when he was almost halfway to the end of the hall and started asking "Who's there? It's okay I'm not drunk." It was then that he noticed a trail of blood leading from the other end of the hall to where he was standing. He looked at his left hand and saw that blood was dripping from it.

In what could've secretly been an expression of pure agony, Scott was laughing hysterically at his bleeding hand. He then did a roll and just stayed on the floor. After that he sat up against the nearest wall. At this point he was unmistakably drunk. He turned his head to both sides and almost fell over when he saw Roswell sitting to his left. Roswell smiled and waved at Scott as though he was catching up with an old friend, which technically he was, but they aren't friends. Scott's response was to turn just enough so he could bang the side of his head on the wall.

"Told you I'd be seeing you soon. I may be evil, but I'm rarely wrong." Roswell was highly invested in a game of tic-tac toe on his hand but he still had that old smug look on his face. "Why are you back? I told you to go away." Scott struggled to get the words out without slurring them, but it was no use; he was piss drunk. "Me being here is your fault. I actually thought I'd be seeing you earlier, so great job on staying parched as long as you did. And hanging around your girl brought you back to the bottle just like I knew it would; even though that was also your fault. But I didn't expect you to be such a mess this time; seriously, what happened to your hand?" "It's bleeding; it got cut." Scott's response was brief, probably because that's the most logical sentence he could string together on such short notice.

"Gasp! No shit! How'd you cut it, smartass?" The sarcasm was so strong that it hit *me*. Scott laughed a little bit then took another drink after spouting out a bunch of slurred words. Roswell took the bottle and drew a tic-tac toe board on the label then gave it back to Scott along with a blue pen.

"If you win you'll never have to deal with me again. I'll be completely out of your hair for as long as you live; hell I'll even bring Faaghira back to life. But you won't win, so I'm giving you the option to go back to the other dimension with me now. You'd be sparing yourself a whole lotta disappointment. Scott stared at the bottle for what seemed like an eternity before drawing an 'x' in one of the spaces and handing it to Roswell. This went on for three minutes and nobody won. Scott was honestly trying to win but Roswell was blocking all of his moves. The vile creature didn't seem to have any intention of winning; he just didn't want Scott to win. If that isn't pure evil then I don't know what is. "Heads I win, tails you lose. Looks like it's back to adventure for ol' Scott Blue. Brace yourself kiddo." Roswell was smiling from ear to ear while Scott was lightly bumping his forehead against the wall.

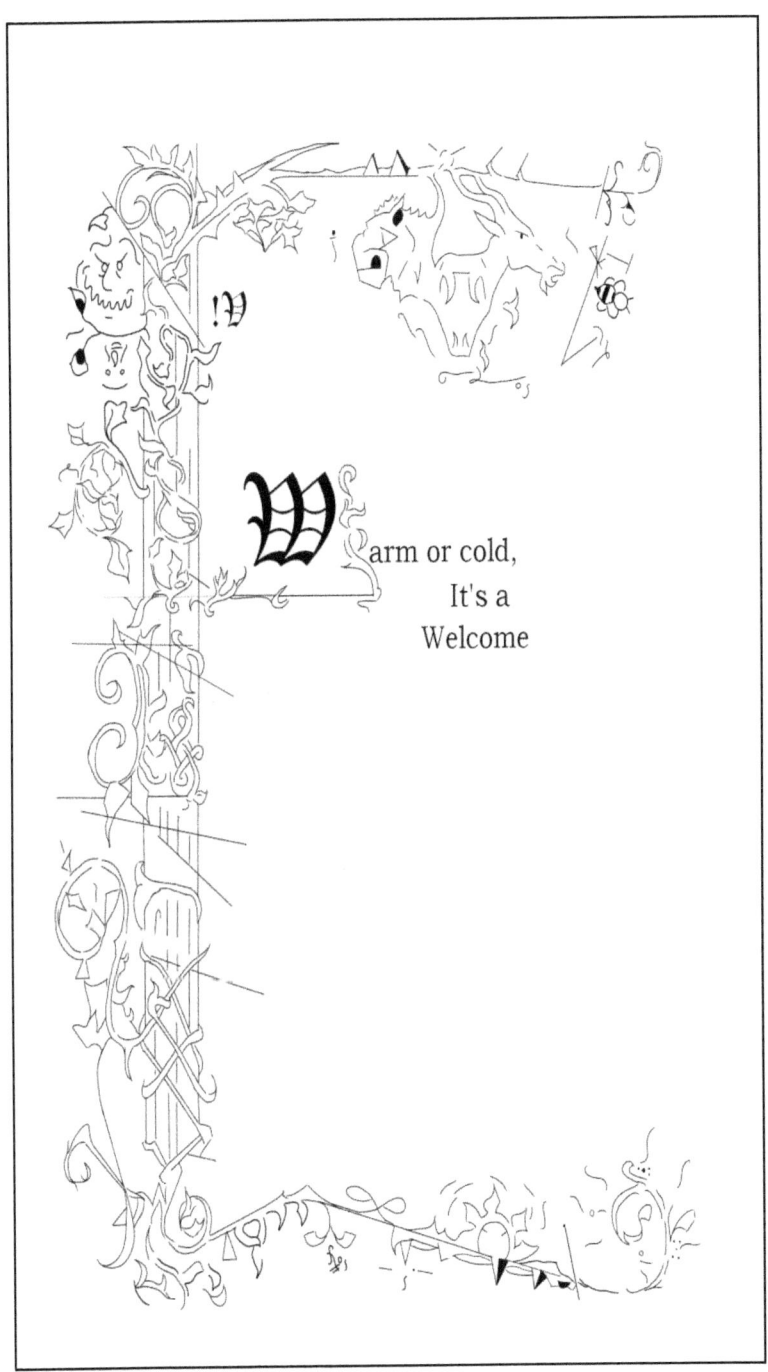

Warm or cold,
It's a
Welcome

133

CHAPTER IV
WARM OR COLD, IT'S A WELCOME

Scott falls through the wall; cold concrete pressed against his face. A light breeze blew the autumn leaves around him up in the air in a small whirlwind. He looks around him and sees that he's in an empty alleyway. This strange-

"Quick question; why isn't your narration consistent?"

What do you mean by not consistent?

"Sometimes things are in past tense and other times it's in the present. Is there something I'm not picking up on here? *What's the deal*?"

If you must know, then too bad, I'm not telling you; I probably wouldn't have to keep narrating this train wreck if you didn't get drunk. I have to keep narrating until you learn whatever you're supposed to learn from it, but I won't be done any time soon if you keep messing up. As foreign as the idea may sound to you, you have to stop screwing up. And please, try not to interrupt me if you don't have something important to share.

"NO! I can't take this shit, man! Do you even know what it feels like to be thrown into something ridiculous and everyone expects you to be okay with it? I won't sit back and just take whatever shit you're trying to give me. You've gotta deal with me the way I am. I'll play the game for a little while, but if I'm not outta here soon then I'm doing things my way. I'll play the game for now, but if you think you can go telling me to shut up, you've got another thing coming. Treat me like you're above me and you'll be sitting here a lot longer doing your job. I'd tough through all the crap that I have to for as long as I'd have to just to give you a hard time; got that?" Whatever. After that, Scott decided that this conversation was over. He wasn't up and about looking for something to tell him where he is; he just sat there. The sound of resounding cheers abruptly broke the silence and Scott almost fell over because of the sudden spike in volume. Naturally, Scott walked leisurely (he rarely rushes) to the corner to see what had people so excited.

A grand stage with screens as a backdrop towered over the crowd. Scott made his way to the crowd to get a closer look at what was going on. He was far in the back so his view wasn't the best, but he could clearly see who the speaker was when they got on stage. The tall gray-haired man in a clean white suit waved to the people as he stepped to the podium. He was followed eight security guards dressed up in riot gear and armed with an excessive amount of firepower. The screens lit up with camera angles of him at the podium, staring at audience.

The cheering died down when he raised his arms up. Overbearing tension built up among the silent crowd. When he finally spoke, his voice resounded across the streets. Scott looked around and there wasn't a single person he saw that wasn't captivated by the speaker. "It warms my heart that all of you came out here this afternoon to hear what has me so afraid. You may or may not have realized that we are in danger from threatening groups that we have let by without a second thought. Our lives are now being threatened by terrorists that we have been ignoring for the longest time. Three days ago these groups have, true to their label, terrorized innocent people and threatened the well-being of every citizen of Louisiana. They are the reason that I must have guards at a gathering where the only attendees are my loving, venerable citizens. It is not you that I fear, nor is it death; I fear for your safety. This terrorist problem has been consuming much of my time and resources, thus the economy has been in a steady decline. I sincerely wish that I could put all my attention to this issue which hurts many of your daily lives, but right now my main concern is making sure that you have lives to experience. These terrorists are internal and external; there is no one place that they can all be traced back to. However, I know of two terrorist leaders that are doing too much damage to our community to be left alive: the terrorist rebellion leaders known as Safira and Walter Kasabian. I have reason to believe that they are also responsible for the disappearance of my *dear* niece, Faaghira. Three days ago they orchestrated an attack on my estate and numerous areas around our city. It's also been three days since my niece disappeared. We must not tolerate the existence of such hateful people in our lives. They must be stopped and they must be killed! It pains me to have to take any violent action at all; all lives are valuable. However, to restore peace and order to our great nation, these people, these terrorists must be eliminated!"

The crowd cheered with thunderous applause and Scott sat bback watching everything unfold before him. Even though he didn't recognize him before, Scott realized that this 'charismatic' speaker is Atticus. Scott walked away from the crowd, leaving them to revel in their brand of justice. He kept walking but at a certain point he actually started paying attention to the neighborhood around him. This part of the city isn't so well maintained like the area that was holding the rally. There are boarding houses with broken windows and worn paint. There aren't any chain stores or fancy places around but believe it or not, they would be pretty far out of place here. The cars lined up along the sidewalks are all older models; a mix of vintage cars and some mid-eighties/ early

136

nineties stuff. Not all of them look worn out but not a single one of them is close to passing for pristine. This part of the city has that old world charm. It's colorful and inviting with that special something we simply refer to as magic. If it were taken care of like everything else, it'd be what you'd expect New Orleans to look like. The people living there were back in the streets when the rally was drawing to a close.

One of the most interesting differences between them and the folks at the rally is that these people seem to have no interest in Atticus or his war on terrorism. There's no fear in anyone's demeanor here; they're all going about their lives just the same as anyone would in any other place. As a matter of fact, this part of the city is a whole lot livelier than the so called classier one with the rally. And if anyone was wondering where all the people of color were...Seeing the vast difference in places a few feet apart is amazing at the very least. When the rally was finally over, banners dropped down from light posts and out of windows. The sounds of trumpets, drums, guitars, and instruments of different kinds filled the air. Confetti fell from the top floors of buildings; stores were opening back up; it was a festival of sorts. The further along Scott went the more exciting the surroundings were. People were smiling and waving at him as if they'd always seen him around. Not knowing what else to do, he waved back at them, then came a smile; the happiness was contagious. He kept looking around at the buildings and shops as if he'd never seen anything like them before. An older black dude (I'd say mid-fifties) left a table outside a café to ask Scott if he needed directions to get somewhere. Scott replied by- nope I'll just let him say it.

"Oh no, I'm just looking around. I've been here before but I've never seen it so festive. What's the celebration for?"

"You must not have been around here before. We have small celebrations every other day when some rally or televised speech ends. We'd do it every time he puts on one of those crapshoots, but we'd *all* get tired of partying. Atticus didn't do anything for us here and we want everyone to know it. I know they get the point by now, but we like to drive it home by celebrating every time he shuts his old bigoted aristocratic mouth." Not knowing what else to do, Scott nodded. And then he looked up at the sky and frowned; at me I presume.

The man kept talking, but he shifted the topic from Atticus to the places Scott's been in Louisiana. When Scott told him "Nowhere outside of New Orleans", the man looked at him funny. "Louisiana is a whole more than just New Orleans, you know? You're really missing out. But which places here have you been?" "I've been to the really fancy part; the real pretentious looking side."

"Pretty unusual, but who am I to judge? Man, let's stop standing in the middle of the street; it makes us look like a couple of idiots. I have a restaurant right over there by those tables I was sitting at. I promise it's not as shady as it sounds. Usually the place is pretty crowded; it's a local staple. Meal's on the house if you order something before the joint gets busy." They walked over to the other side of the street and the man propped the restaurant door open. A blue neon sign that read '*Ace N Dandy's*' sat above the doorway. Feel free to have a seat or check the place out.

"What kinda food do you make?"

"The best kind. Don't go pushing yourself to eat if you're not hungry, but I would feel bad if I didn't offer you anything." "Alright, surprise me. Gunning for something specific would make me feel like a tourist. Even though I am technically a tourist, I prefer not to come off as one. I don't want something I would usually have; that completely defeats the purpose of going somewhere different."

"You got it. Now what brings you here in the first place?"
"I'm looking for a friend."

"Well for not knowing much about Louisiana, I'd say you picked a good place to find a friend." That's when Scott realized that he picked the worst way to describe his situation. "No, no, I mean I have a friend here that I'm trying to find." "What's their name? I know most of the people around here; I'm pretty much a celebrity." Scott nodded and gave one of those blatantly fake smiles; it screamed 'I don't believe you'. He decided he'd humor the guy anyway to avoid being rude. "You wouldn't happen to know a girl named Faaghira, would you?"

"Could you describe her?"

"Long curly hair; usually has it all over on one side. I've only seen her during the span of a night, so I can't say too much about her sense of style. Oh, her hair has a silver-ish strand on the left side, I think it is. She looks a little bit taller than me under certain lighting. Um, let's see, she plays the ukulele... a lot. She's got these big brown eyes and a nice fat ass. Her body is beyond sick. Sounds familiar?"

"Oh I knew who she was from her name alone; I was just wondering how you'd describe her. By the way, you suck at descriptions. Big brown eyes and a fat ass? That really narrows it down. Is that really all you noticed?" "Um, no, I mentioned the ukulele thing, didn't I? Enough with the guilt trip, I need a cold one. You got any at that dive of yours?"

The man was clearly getting irritated, but he was trying hard not to let Scott's off kilter personality get the best of him. "It's not a dive; don't call it a dive. Do you have a favorite brand? If I don't have it here I'd be more than happy to order it for you." "You'd really do that? How about a bottle of Hen-" "Nope! Gotcha!" The man excitedly cut him off. "If it's not in the house it's not on the house." The guy went behind counter near the back of the main dining room (I'm playing it up a little bit to make up for my lack of descriptive...um...descriptions I guess would be the right word). He returned with a dark red glass bottle with two sheets of paper towel wrapped around it. "Local brew, it's some of the best stuff you'll find anywhere. A whole lot better than big brands; everything here is local and every batch gets special care. The good people over at The Magic Brew, name of the business, don't have a quota to meet; they can give quality without compromise. Now how do you know Fae?"

"You call her Fae too? I know her from an odd chain of events that ended up with me on Atticus' ferry. I'm not really sure how, but we just became friends. She's pretty great. We got split up somewhere by the outskirts of town and I haven't seen her since." "Yeah that sounds about right; she told me something along those same lines. I can call her up later if you really want to see her that bad. Now first, the meal on the house; *unfortunately, I'm a man of my word.*"

"Hey man, how about some shrimp gumbo to go along with whatever else I'm getting?" "For you, no; the first thing tourists ask for is gumbo." The man switched from a calm voice to a yell which startled Scott so much that he almost fell out his seat. "Pistolette with two banana fosters and three beignets." It's starting to get a little tedious calling the restaurant owner variations of 'the guy'; Scott should stop

140

being rude and ask his name. And *Scott* is probably wondering why I don't already know his name, and that's because he already forgot that I'm not omniscient and *I never will be*. The script makes itself up as it goes, literally.

"I just got this *nagging* feeling; I never asked your name." There! That's all you had to do. It would've been really useful if you did that from the jump, but hey, it's never too late, right? "Angelo. Hang tight I'll be right back." Angelo (thank God he has a name now) went through two swinging doors that led to the kitchen (where else would it go to?). Scott sat there awkwardly looking at different parts of the room until he took out his phone and played a knock-off version of Tetris. He lost two games in the matter of just four minutes. Scott seriously sucks at Tetris…er…fake Tetris, I mean. He kept playing to pass the time, but it didn't sound like the food was close to being finished. When people started coming in, instead of trying to talk to them he nodded at anyone that passed by and went back to playing fake Tetris. I don't understand this guy; he's bored because there's no one to talk to but when people show up he ignores them.

Two people came out of the kitchen to take orders and one of them told Scott that his food was almost ready. Afterwards another chime rang at the front; someone else walked in. There was something different about this person. She (oh yes, another lady in Scott's life) has long unkempt, thick unkempt ivory hair, beautiful amber eyes, and plump lips (sorry, I'm gushing again. Her dark lashes give her eyes a sense of mystery and warmth, as though she was a comforting specter; an odd combination that has to be seen to be understood. She isn't dressed in anything lavish, but the simple ensemble of dark washed jeans, ankle-cut leather boots, and a white floral printed sweatshirt made enough of a statement. A pair of rounded sunglasses hung from around her neck and a black wide-brim straw boater hat.

She had the look of a modern day outlaw (i.e. hipster) and she gave off that kind of energy too. Of all the places she could've sat she chose one of the stools next to Scott. After Scott lost yet another game he looked up from his phone and saw her sitting beside him. "Hi, I'm Scott; cool hair."

And now that you've seen Scott's mad flirting skills you can comprehend why he's such a hit with the ladies.

"Do you always suck this bad at Tetris or is this just for show?" Well, except for this lady. "Well you're a real confidence builder. You got a name miss sass?"

"You're only one who guessed my name's Miss Sass. I'm actually a world renowned confidence builder so you're welcome." "Hmm, how about a bet?"

"...and you're already pushing bets? Scott, you're truly a relentless businessman. Well as long as neither of the outcomes leave me without the ability to give consent, I'm down for a bet." "If you win then you won't have to listen to me talk. If I win then you have to at least tell me your name and we'll have a conversation about any topic I choose for at least five minutes." "How come I feel you're getting a lot more out of this deal than I am? I want to add to mine."

Scott thought it over, but not for too long. He had a determined look on his face; he had a plan that couldn't fail. "Alright add whatever you want to yours, but you won't get to choose what the bet is if you do." "Not a problem. Unless it's an awkward contest I have nothing to worry about. If I win then you have to tell me what you think I'm like and why. You'll get your useless conversation and I'll get mine; we'll both be happy. So what's the bet?" "I bet you can't beat me in three games of tic-tac-toe." Seriously? Tic-tac-toe again? He lost several times in a row the last time he played it. "And when you lose, do you want to try best out of three in Tetris? That'll probably go by just as fast."

Scott got a little flustered, but then he enjoyed the challenge, but then he was terrified when he remembered that Roswell is a shapeshifting demon. That instantly turned any interest into skepticism. It also made things more awkward than they already were. Nevertheless, Scott carried on with the bet. If it was Roswell, then he didn't want the demon to know he caught 'on. She set up the first game on a napkin with a pen that was on the counter. She let Scott make the first move and the game was over six moves later. Surprisingly, Scott won that time. However, he lost the next two games.

"You can still back out now. One more loss and you have to start flattering me. You might as well start talking now unless you really think you can pull through for two more games. Consecutive games, that is." She tipped the brim of her hat, put down the pen and looked at him arrogantly. Well, arrogant isn't the best way to describe it. It's more of a knowing look; the kind Gene Wilder was famous for.

"Watch me work." Scott spoke with all the confidence and finesse anyone could ever hope for. Scott knew that there was no way he could lose.

Scott lost the next game. He didn't even come close to winning. She (we'll call her the mystery woman for now) looked unsurprised, but also genuinely happy. "Even though you lost, I respect the effort. I would tell you my name since you've been such a good sport, but I'm sure I can't trust you.

But if you have to call me anything at all, just call me Mercury" "Care to explain?"

"Nope. Now for your part of the deal; I'm ready to hear it. Is it something about my eyes or is it the fact that I sat next to you that's got you so fascinated?" "It's definitely something about the way you sat next to me. But being serious, you just seem like a cool chick. You've got this cool grunge-hipster thing going on and I've never seen anything like it. It also helps that you're cute, but I don't like to put such a huge focus on that. I'm not one of those guys who throws compliments, hoping to get lucky. The compliment plus flirting equals relationship formula isn't my style."

"Never heard that version of the 'I'm not like other guys' speech. Also, I'm very gay; if we keep talking then know there's no chance of you getting with me. That being said, what's your style?" Scott covered his mouth while he cleared his throat. His voice quivered a bit. "Good question, but with a mind like mine that's wildly inappropriate; unless it isn't. I don't focus on trying to get with anyone, so all my compliments are genuine for the most part. I don't do anything I wouldn't normally do and I don't try to play up any of my good qualities. If somebody else likes it, then that's great. If they don't then that's also great; I'm not trying to please anyone." "And how far does that get you?"

"It gets me to situations some people only dream of; but some people have *really* weird dreams. As far as my love life goes, there isn't much going on. I prefer things to be on the quieter side when it comes to romance; no need to chase after leagues of women if that's not what you really want." Angelo came back out of the kitchen with a large round tray holding four plates of dessert; just what Angelo made the order for. Scott thanked him for the food to which Angelo

144

replied, "Half of this is for me; but you're welcome." Scott found it funny, but he was still a little shocked that it wasn't all for him. "For real?" "Dead ass. Why'd you think I ordered multiple dishes. That's not all for you. I'm not letting you eat that much for free."

Mercury laughed at him briefly then started talking to Angelo about something but Scott didn't want to make it obvious that he was listening in so he got around to trying his food. Between that and the growing volume of the people in the restaurant, Scott couldn't hear what they were saying. Mid conversation, Angelo gave Mercury the signal to wait then he walked back over to where he put the tray. Angelo took one of the plates of banana foster, put two beignets on it, and then went back over to Mercury.

Scott looked over at Mercury and saw her stick her tongue out at him. Her and Angelo shared the food; Scott got upset over the principle of it. Yeah, the principle; but he's fifty-something and she's like twenty- something and very gay; nothing to be jealous of. However, Scott did his thing and wedged himself into their conversation. Mind you, Mercury is sitting right next to Scott and Angelo is behind the counter in front of Mercury. He literally had to stop what he was doing so that he could butt in to their conversation. I'm not sure whether she should be flattered, disgusted or creeped out. Then again, it's a free world; Mercury can feel however she wants. "How come she gets to have some of that food?" Angelo was about to make a comment, but Mercury told him that she'd handle it. "Scott…" she called his name and gave a longing gaze. Scott's expression changed from upset to curious. Mercury put her hand out near his then took one of the beignets and ate it right in his face. "…life isn't fair; deal with it." She spoke mockingly with a mouth stuffed full of pastries. And of course, this is drastically different from any response he would've gotten from Fae. But it probably wasn't fair to expect every girl he finds attractive to be like her. It's not like he's that way with his girlfriend. It must be pretty easy to go off thinking that everything and everyone is the same as what he's familiar with. Ooh, I'm feeling a life lesson coming on!

Angelo ate half of the banana foster and left the rest for Mercury. He left from behind the counter out to the tables to take orders. The two of them sat eating in silence. At least that was the case until Scott tried to pull up the whole small talk thing. You know, it's the whole 'how's the weather, so how about NOS in the championships?' kind of jazz. As a wise person would, she ignored him and kept eating. However, Scott didn't get the message. Plagued by a severe case of 'you didn't laugh so you must not have heard my joke', Scott tried another topic in hopes to get some kind of conversation going. By this point, Mercury had enough. She put her fork down and frowned at Scott. "Okay, what is it that you're trying to get around to? What's the point if there even is one?"

Scott was at a loss for words. He obviously wasn't expecting such an aggressive response. He took a bite out of a beignet and saw her from the corner of his eye; judging harshly. There's no doubt that she noticed, but she didn't let up. Scott carefully placed the beignet back on the plate and stared at it. Then Scott stopped being so dodgy when he realized it wasn't helping. Communication is key, and yet it's usually avoided like the plague. "I like you; I may not be able to pin it down, but there's something about you that I like. It's not that you remind me of anyone; you just come off as someone who I could talk to. I tend to be innately drawn to that sort of thing. I don't know where I'd want to take things, but I feel like you'd be a cool person to have around."

"Hmm, fair enough, though, you're not taking things anywhere. If you're telling the truth, then we can talk after I finish my food. Remember, *after* I finish my food; don't try dumping any serious shit while I'm eating. Got it? Also, still gay; nothing changed from when I sat down." "Yeah, yeah, I got you." Scott sat quietly and ate his food until he broke the silence again. "That actually sounded kind of nasty; dumping serious shit on you while you're eating."

"Congratulations, you found the point. And that's why I don't want you doing it while I'm eating."

Neither of them said anything else until after they both finished eating. Mercury wrote 'Thank you' on a napkin, drew a smiley face, and put thirty dollars on top of it. Scott being the trendsetter that he is, he opted to leave a similar thank you note, but he didn't leave any money. Scott gives off a real cheapskate vibe, and no tip with a thank you note is better than a nice note with a small tip. To understand why I say this, I'll provide a little context here. So, these tips are for Angelo, who owns the restaurant. He doesn't need the tips; his business is flourishing. If you're going to give a tip in a situation like that make sure it's a good one.

When they left, Mercury was walking at a quick pace and Scott had to rush to keep up. He asked why she was walking so fast, to which she responded, "You're too slow." When Scott upped his pace and asked where they were going, she simply responded "*We're* not going anywhere; I'm going here and there." Out of other questions, he asked if she could help him find his friend, whom he didn't mention by name.

"And does this person have a name?" "Her name is Faaghira. Have you heard the name before?" Mercury froze, and her eyes instantly widened in shock, but it went away just as quick as it came. "Who are you?" she asked aggressively. Scott was confused by the swift change in tone. Why was she so flustered all of a sudden? "I'm Scott, remember?"

"How do you know her?"

"I'm a friend, honest. If you have her number, you can call her right now and see if I'm telling the truth. We were separated a few days ago and I'm trying to find her.

"Nobody's heard from her in three days; did you have something to do with that?" Mercury clenched her fist and Scott backed up a step or two. To say Mercury can be intimidating is an understatement. Not only is she much taller than Scott, but her frame is also bigger than his. To put in short, this isn't the kind of person you'd want to duke it out with. "That's not my fault. I had nothing to do with that; there's no reason to fight." Scott choked up a little, clenched his right fist, but left the other relaxed. Wind blew through the streets, pushing back Scott's jacket and blowing through Mercury's long, thick ivory hair. Even though I would hate to see either one of them get scuffed up, my money is definitely on Mercury.

"Who said we'd fight? A fight implies that you can actually hit me." "I would never hit a woman; I leave that to the weak guys." "I wasn't talking about that. The only reason it wouldn't be a fight is because you wouldn't get a single hit in. If only one person is throwing the punches then it's a beat down, not a fight." "Tempting as this sounds, I'll have to refuse. I don't have a problem with you." Aw, Scott you passed up a golden chance to get whooped by a giant woman. You confuse me more and more with each line. "Hmm, what about a proposition? if I win then you have to tell me what happened the last time you saw her."

148

"I'm *not* going to fight you. I don't want another bet, but just out of curiosity; what would happen if I won?"

"You wouldn't."

"Alright, good talk; not interested. I'm going over to her condo to see if she's there; wanna go with me?

"Hmm. Technically I'm not allowed on that side of town. How do you plan on getting there?" "Good question. I was actually gonna just walk there." Scott tried to play it off casually as if he actually knew where he was going.

Mercury laughed at him for a moment until she realized that he was actually serious. "You can't walk there and expect to get there any time today. I'd say you can take a taxi, but the ones here aren't allowed to take you all the way to that stuck up part she lives in. It's a long story, but I know another way if you don't want to go that route."

"Sure, but I'd like to hear that story. I've got stories to exchange if you tell yours." Mercury grunted. "Keep close and get your ears ready, I'm only telling this once." She took off her hat, combed through her hair back with her fingers, and put it back on. She took a breath and started walking again at a slightly slower pace. Scott kept walking up closer to her and lightly brushed his hand against hers. Mercury stopped again, tilted her hat up and looked down at Scott. "Man, I'll tell you this once: I'm *not* Faaghira. This isn't Romeo and Juliet; I don't like you. Don't try to hold my hand; don't expect me to give you a kiss just because it's what you want. I won't turn around all of a sudden and fall into your arms; I'll snap your wrist if you try that again."

Scott nodded in agreement and left more space between

them as they walked. "I have a feeling that some of that wasn't about me."

"Do you want to hear that story or not?"
"Yeah, of course."
"Then shut up and let me tell it."

Scott nodded again. "You're the boss."

Mercury rushed into an alley by a worn-down house they were passing by. She knelt in front of a wooden cellar door, wiped dust off it with two fingers and then kicked the doors in. They busted and only one of them was left hanging from the hinges. Mercury looked at Scott as a signal to follow him, which he did without questioning. When they stepped down into the cellar Mercury let out a strong sigh. The cellar is frigid, and the air is dry; essentially a giant freezer. Scott and Mercury could see their breath spread out into the air and fade up into the atmosphere.

"Somebody tried that a few years ago; taking a taxi from here straight to the other side of the city. Not even halfway there, two police cars showed up with their sirens and the car stopped. All, all of the officers came out their cars with their weapons out, shouting at the guys to get out the taxi. If my memory serves me right, the specific order was 'Get out now with your hands up and put them against the doors; no sudden movements'. So, they do what the officers say, but passenger had to scratch his nose, which he announced to make sure he didn't get shot. Guess what happened."

"He got shot." Scott sighed.

"He got shot. Both of them were shot, an excessive amount of times. The whole thing was justified in the media as self-defense. 'We felt so threatened'; that's always what they run to when they're trying to make a game out of taking lives and show the world they can get away with it. The officers involved were let off the hook and got promoted after that. *They got promoted!* They were making more money *after* they knowingly took the lives of people they were supposed to protect! It's disgusting, but that's not even the worst part. It happened multiple times after that. Now nobody even bothers trying that anymore. But I think it's disgusting that people are siding with that terror squad. Worst part is that you have a bunch of random people out here thinking that their opinion is the be all end all. Because it doesn't affect them it doesn't matter; that's their logic. Without going off topic again, that's why hailing a cab there from here is a stupid idea."

Whether it was the dry air or the heart wrenching story, Scott was choking up and was desperately trying to clear his throat. Mercury wasn't concerned at the slightest; she kept moving like she didn't hear it, or just didn't care. Miraculously, Scott's throat was cleared, leaving him free to use his voice to show how problematic he is. "Whose house is this?"

"Don't know, don't care. Did you not hear anything I said about those shootings?" "Yeah, I heard the whole thing."

"Then why is your first concern about whose house we're in?" Mercury was starting to get aggressive again. I don't blame her either; she caught Scott being unjustifiably (but unknowingly) heartless. Scott reacted with a 'why are you giving me that look? I didn't do anything' face. Mercury clenched her fists again. "It's not that I don't care; I'm terrified by the news." Suddenly, Scott felt the need to explain himself. He must have been deeply moved by

Mercury's story (and the fact her fist would be moved to his gut if he didn't give a have reasoning). "It's just that I wanted to be sure that this place is safe. If the police are that dangerous here, then we need to be sure they won't find us."

Mercury kept walking but didn't unclench her fist. Scott walked fast enough to catch up with her, but he slowed down when he was beside her. Not okay with silence for some reason, Scott brought up another topic.

"Do you think that maybe it was their fault? There's something to every argument and I don't think people would have a reason to just make up the whole 'threatened' defense. It all had to come from somewhere." Okay, joke's on me everyone, Scott's other topic was police brutality. They literally just stopped talking about that. Someone please get this man a gold star.

"Out of their asses." She didn't look at him; hardly acknowledge his presence. Quick digression: is the whole 'Not looking at the person I'm talking to' thing trending? If not, is it a disease? If it's a disease, lots of people in this story got it bad. "And what about the things we don't know? It's always one side or the other. One side is seen as more important than the other. It's never objective; it's never neutral. If it was then people would realize that we're all important as human beings."

"That all lives matter?"
"That! Exactly that!"

"You're asking me to hurt you, and as much as I'd like to, you're the last person who saw Fae. If I do look for her, I'll need to hear your part of what happened."

152

"Why are you being so hostile? Equality is a good thing. Why is it such a problem if I support all lives?"

"When you're trying to defend and justify people who couldn't care less about you, you're the problem. All lives is the socially acceptable way of saying that certain lives don't matter. Generalizations and blanket statements diminish values and only exist to make certain groups feels superior and make other groups be okay with and even adamant about things that hurt them."

"Certain lives being black, correct?"

"I'm brown skinned, but I'll say that I have a whole hell of a lot more to worry about than you do. I don't know why you're trying to justify any of it; people like us, we're in the same boat. If you need a refresher, take a good look in the mirror. Didn't think I'd have to keep telling people why they should care at this point in my life. Definitely didn't think I'd be putting up with ignorant bastards still. This concerns me; she must really be going through it these days."

Scott made the motion showing that he was about to respond, but he didn't for some reason. Thankfully, Scott didn't ask any more questions. He followed her hardly making a sound. In fact, he was so quiet that Mercury checked behind her here and then to make sure that he was still there. The cellar got darker the further they traveled, so dark that it was almost pitch black. Scott had almost stumbled over several pipes and bumped into three pillars. The only reason he had any sense of direction was because they were getting closer to a light not too far from where they were. Scott could see Mercury's outline standing out amidst the darkness.

"Where does this lead to? I mean being mysterious is cool

and all, but I don't like being left in the dark."

"Did she like your puns that much?"

"No, that wasn't- I didn't mean to make a pun. That wasn't supposed to be a pun, I swear!"

"Me too; you're not special. This is a service tunnel for an abandoned subway system. I use this to get around the city without being seen."
　"Does it move?"
　"You're an idiot."
　Scott, I think that's a no; it doesn't move. That actually sounds ridiculously stupid. How could a subway system move? I know that Fae has a room that changes levels and what not, but I just want to stress that YOU ARE NOT TALKING TO FAAGHIRA. She said that you'd be living in luxury whenever you were with HER. MERCURY IS NOT HER. Scott stopped talking and Mercury clearly didn't mind. Their only communication for a while was Mercury telling Scott "Through here" or "This way." I think it was really sinking in that she isn't Fae. The tunnels stretched pretty far, but what else would you expect from a (formerly) busy subway system? Scott's lack of complaints or corny jokes turned out to be the biggest surprise I've had since he came back.

Mercury came to a stop when they stepped into a vast room expanding for yards in every direction. Even though it wasn't in use, the station was only slightly less clean from what a well-maintained station would be like. While all the stores were obviously non-operational, they were present in their (formerly) overpriced glory. The terminal isn't extravagant like Grand Central, but it's still relatively nice. The floor is decorated with large circles composed of shapes of varying bright colors. The walls are an off white/ yellowish kind of color. They have some paintings and collages on them, but there are lighter rectangular spots showing that some pieces are missing. Sunlight is shining through a large octagonal window that takes up most of the ceiling; illuminating the polished floors. Scott gazed around the terminal looking at the sights, which surprisingly, Mercury didn't comment on. She folded her arms and looked off into space while she waited for him to finish. Scott had to call her name twice to get her attention; when he did he asked what she was thinking about. She ignored it and they moved on to another part of the station. They arrived at an area that was much smaller with staircase leading up to...um...somewhere. The stairs are barricaded by short metal barriers lined with red tape labeled 'caution'.

Mercury vaulted over it and Scott carefully put both legs over. Going up the stairs, instead of seeing light or hearing any sounds, it was dark and quiet. The stairs led into a mostly destroyed waiting area inside a warehouse.

"What is this place?" Scott was confused by the strange surroundings (and rightfully so). Everything in here seems to be backwards. What isn't golden is ruined; what isn't accepted is left to rot and die. This time I can understand Scott's curiosity; why would something that's perfectly fine be abandoned like this?

"It used to be a major transportation hub. Atticus leveled most of it then covered up the remains with a warehouse. You'd know this isn't an isolated incident if you've seen the rest of town."

"Why did he do this though? He didn't even wreck the whole station."

"The point of things like this isn't to get rid of it. For him the point is to show everyone what existed before his changed it all. The thing about Atticus is that he never completely destroys anything; he always leaves little pieces behind; he rubs it in everyone's faces. This is the most he could destroy of the station without bombing it, which I wouldn't put past him. But I'm really glad that he only covered it; I use this place all the time."

"Where do we go from here?"

"There's only one exit. Go through there and he once you're outside you'll see her building; it's a short walk from here. Before we go our own ways", she paused. "I want to hear what happened to Faaghira last time you saw her."

"We were leaving the party Atticus had, we drove to the haunted estate she was afraid of, the car lost control, she jumped out; I couldn't get out quick enough. I guess I blacked out, but I uh, didn't see her anywhere when I woke up."

"Hmm…I see."

"Aren't you coming with me?"

"I really don't feel like it."

"C'mon, you got this far already. Don't you want to see Fae?"

"I'll assume that's rhetorical. Nobody knows where she is. *Unless you do.*" Her tone was sharp; vicious.

"No, no, no, I don't know; I swear I don't know!" He took deep breaths; his heart was racing. "I-I mean what if she's there? I'm sure she'd want to see you; she's a really nice person. If she doesn't then…I don't know. You should go anyway; maybe you'll have fun."

"No." Mercury was already walking away before Scott could finish talking. Scott ran after her and tried to stop her, using himself as a blockade between her and the stairs. Mercury picked him up, put him behind her, and kept walking,

"Then can you at least tell me why you helped me out here if you don't trust me?"

"Because if I hear that other people use the tunnel then

I'll know it's your fault; and I'll kill you then find a new area."

"You asshole!"

Mercury retaliated with a faint "Birds of a feather" that faded away fast. Scott decided that going after her again would amount to nothing. Why didn't Mercury want to see Faaghira? That's what had them going on this trip in the first place; why would Mercury turn away at the last second? They obviously have a history, but maybe it's not a good one. A mutual disagreement, maybe? Who was she anyway? I don't know.

When Scott left through the one door leading outside, he eyes were momentarily stunned by the bright sunlight. He was in a park full of trees, sidewalks and benches. People were out, walking and talking, having picnics, parents spending time with their kids. Scott looked at all of that with a bit of longing, and I'm on his side this time. I've seen firsthand how craptastic his life can be. His relationship with his parents is shoddy at best and his love life is anything but smooth…but that's totally his fault. He could just leave his girlfriend. Scott, why won't you break things off with your girlfriend?

"Not here" Scott whispered "I don't want all these people to think I'm crazy. I'll go somewhere a bit off the path so we can talk."

Why not just go back in the warehouse?

"Because I have somewhere to be and I'm not postponing that just to humor you. And could you please stop doing that? It's really annoying."

How about this; act like you're talking to someone on the phone then you won't look like you're crazy when you're talking to me. And stop doing what? My job? Bud, remember that if I stop doing my job then everything falls apart. That means you won't be able to get back home to your crappy life. Like I said before, deal with it.

157

Scott took my advice and acted like he was talking over the phone and he finally had the chance to call me anything but a son of God without having to wait to get to a good hiding spot. He was aggravated by my constant narration of his actions. He certainly took that opportunity and called me every word he knew. Was all that worth it? No because I'll still be here getting on his nerves no matter what he says. He brought a tiny bit of attention to himself with the excessive swearing, but most people didn't even care. At the most he got some salty looks from a few parents that had to cover their kids' ears. Scott, being the darling that he is, completely disregarded the feelings of everyone else in the park; he didn't care.

"I'd be an idiot if I cared; screw them."

I'm not sure if they'd like that; and why the bitterness all of a sudden? Maybe it's not sudden and I just didn't care enough to notice it the first time, but you're still being a buttface.

"Is that in the script?"

Call it the unabridged version. That doesn't sound like an 'evil' lack of concern for human life. Roswell has pure evil behind everything that he says; no matter how good natured or horrible he makes things sound. What happened? Did someone break your heart and turn you into a sourpuss?

"I'm not talking about that with you and *never* compare me to Roswell again."

Come on Scott, I'll keep bothering you until you tell me why you're like this. You've been a mess, Faaghira's been a mess, Mercury is a mess, Kasabian is a mess; again, you're a mess. However, the only one I can actually talk to so you're getting all the heart to hearts. I have all the time in the world and it technically, you do too.

Scott shifted his eyes to check if anyone was listening in and lowered his voice when he (acted) like he was back on the phone. "Life; life makes me sour. I've had to care about people that couldn't give less of a shit about me for my entire life. That's the story in a nutshell. Now I don't mind you asking me about stuff, but do yourself a favor and stay away from that conversation. Anyway, you said Fae has problems; do you know something that I don't?"

Scott, I know a bunch of things that you don't. "But I thought you weren't omniscient." I'm not, but I have notes on everyone you've met so far. I'm technically not allowed to share anything on these notes, but I'll tell you some stuff because I've been probing your private life a little too much; I feel a little guilty. I'll give you until you get to Fae's condo; her floor, to be clear. Once you're there I shut up and this talk never happened. And don't walk slower than you are right now or I pull my offer.

"Say no more. Alright, first thing; does she have feelings for me?" And of course that's the first thing that Scott asks about. He has a girlfriend and he's worried about other chicks catching feelings for him. Since I'm a person of my word, I reluctantly, *reluctantly*, comply. It says here that she has a soft spot for you. She was being honest when she said that you're the nicest guy she met, but did you notice how she said that you'd be horrible for each other?

"Clear as day; why asking?"

From what I gather, she was trying to get you to stop pursuing her romantically. I know I just said that she likes you somewhat, but just hear me out. She *probably* thinks you'd play her heart strings then pull them right out if you got too close. "Why would she think that?" She would think that because you're not shy about the fact that you have a girlfriend but you're still trying your hardest to get with her. She's tough but she's also a total softie on the inside. She doesn't want her heart torn to shreds; plain and simple; nobody does, if we're being honest. You can't fault her for thinking that. Also, with you as the standard for nice guys, she must've had a horrible experience with dudes. Bottom

159

line, she said you're horrible for each other because of you. She was too good for you and she knew it.

"Yeah, can't argue with that. I'll be the first to admit that I'm not the greatest person, but I would never hurt her on purpose, but she doesn't know me well enough to know that. I wish I could just tell her; but Roswell killed her; that fucking asshole!" Don't get me wrong, I never mistook you for a great person, but you never struck me as a hedonist. "I hate you. Now tell me more stuff." She likes romantic dynamics that are more casual than anything. This is why she'd hold your hand and kiss you but doesn't have any kind of talks about what you guys are. She likes keeping things at a place where they're romantic but have no chance of getting messy. Even though that's unavoidable, it's admirable. What you two have is cute at times and you should see where it goes; she definitely wants to. As much as I hate to tell you this, keep giving her that kind of relationship she longs for and she'll eventually get to the point where she'd bring you twenty moons if you asked her to.

"That's a lot of power, too much even, but if that's what'll make her happy then I'll run with it. Hopefully those notes are wrong about how far she'd go just for me. What if I ruin her? I don't always have the best self-control. If she's really that vulnerable, then I might just end up taking advantage of that somewhere down the line." Your problem, not mine. And one more thing: she's got a heart of gold, but she's definitely not someone I'd try to take advantage of. But like I said, she'd do about anything for you if you gave her that casual romantic thing she wants so bad. She can be a doormat sometimes once she actually gets the kind of relationship she wants because she'll do about anything to keep from losing it; it being the relationship, not the person she's with. Now you're slowing down Scott, I need you to keep a regular pace. Her complex isn't more than a block from where you are. The streets and sidewalks are crowded but they aren't so bad that they'll keep you from getting to her. Hurry up, Buttercup.

"What about Mercury?" Not only does she not like you; she openly dislikes you. Do us all a favor and spare us the pain of having to see you hit on her. She would probably pummel you for even asking about her. Stay away from her. Don't even poke her with a fifty-foot pole; she will put the hurt on you. She's off limits; steer clear. And that's a demand, not a request. Also, she's a lesbian, seriously; that's a thing women can be. Not everyone you like is a love interest. Anyone else on your mind?

"Roswell, what's his deal?" Funny, there's nothing here in the author's notes except for a smiley face. I've got some opinions on him if that's any consolation. "So do I; what's your take?" Firstly, while I make fun of you and tease you about being a horrible person, Roswell is legit evil. The stuff he pulls isn't an act; he's actually that horrible. I get the chills whenever he's around. There's something so unsettling about him. Second, he's a demon; he's literally a demon. He may not be the devil himself, but he's damn close. Alright, can we please talk about someone else?

"Okay, okay. Atticus?" Oh that's easy! It says here that he's self-centered bigoted, rich, stupid, unabashedly racist, but he's filthy rich. People love him, and even more people hate him. The general consensus here is that he's better than the other option, which nobody talks about for some reason. Sometimes I wonder if there's an actual alternative. "Well you know certain kinds of people talk about law and order or anarchy. Even if the current people in charge suck they say it's always better than anarchy. I think it's all an excuse to keep people from having to come up with new ideas. Every system is flawed and the 'by the books' law and order thing doesn't always work. But hey, as long as it's what the powerful people want then it's what they'll get."

You're a little smarter than I thought you were, Scott. I

love having conversations like this; stuff with substance, but unfortunately we don't have a whole lot of time left. You're almost where you wanted to be, and I don't feel like picking any of this back up later. Alright, one topic left; choose wisely. "I know you're just the narrator, but do you know what the rest of this dimension is like? And also, what happened to Fae when I disappeared?" Easy on the questions; I'll get to the second one if I have time. Her building is only a few feet away from you so I'd suggest taking the stairs if you want to get your answers.

Scott walked through the automatic doors but before he could go into the lobby he was confronted by a tall dark-skinned man dressed in black suit. He has a thick beard, but his head is shaved clean.

"Are you Scott?" The man didn't have a scowl or anything like that, but his resting face is just as intimidating as anything else. Scott tried to look tough in a similar nonchalant way, but it just didn't work out. The man raised an eyebrow at Scott; an indirect way of saying 'I hope you know that's not doing anything.'

"Yeah that's me." Scott said confidently. The man pulled a photo from his jacket pocket, looked at it then let Scott pass. The man disappeared into a room behind the concierge desk and Scott hesitantly opened the door to the stairwell.

"I don't remember any security being at the desk." It would make sense that there's some kind of security here because it's a high class joint. You probably didn't see security because you were with Faaghira the last time you stepped through those doors. They wouldn't have any reason to come out if you were okay with her. Now about the whole other dimension business. I think it's very confusing but I can try to explain it the best way that I can. This is an alternate version of what you know as the United States. Basically, everything is based around what you're familiar with. I don't know much about you, but apparently the author knows you pretty well. The notes here are pretty vague. All it says is 'Continuity, will explain later.' Sorry I can't shed any more light on that. As far as your other question goes, I think Faaghira can answer that. "That definitely wasn't worth taking the stairs. I didn't even reach the second floor yet." Sorry that it wasn't worth the wait, but you're the one that chose the questions. It's your fault once again Scott.

"I don't have to put up with this shit. I'm taking the elevator." Scott turned back out of the stairwell and went back into the lobby to call an elevator. Scott stood awkwardly waiting for the elevator and when the doors slid open he (and I) was startled when they revealed Roswell standing behind them. He had his inviting but unsettling smile draped across his face. This time he had a golf sweater on with black joggers and black track shoes.

"What are you doing here Roswell? "

"I'm just stopping by to check in on one of my favorite people, but I see you're here too. I feel we got off on the wrong foot a couple times. How about we take the time for you to really get to know me? It may or may not help you understand anything, *but I really like talking about myself.*"

"Fine; say whatever it is then leave me alone."

"You are pretty ungrateful, Blue. You're so enamored with this life I made for you, but yet you condemn me. You're the bratty, overly sensitive, problematic child I never got to have. Look Scott, I know you don't like me, but I want you to know that deep down in my black, nearly non-existent heart, I don't like you either."

"And what was the point of that?"

"Hush up; don't interrupt me. Now, where was I? Right; I don't like you, but I'm the more important one out of the two of us. With that being said, I clearly have the most influence on your life. And before you go protesting that in any way, think about it. And when you're done I'll be waiting for my accolades on my doorstep."

"Shut up."

"You're a mess with me and you're probably an even bigger mess without me. But I do think you're right about me beating around the bush. Since I'm the only one that can actually tell you what's going on, I'll have mercy and learn you some knowledge. This world you're in is centered around you, but nobody else knows that, so you're not the center of this world, technically speaking."

"So then what's the point of me being here?"

"Hold on, hold on, I'm getting to that part. When I first saw you, you were in a relationship that was bound to fail and fail miserably at that. Miraculously, you're still in it. As you know, I'm a demon, and I probably already explained the whole 'making deals' situation already. What I haven't mentioned is that my entire job is to ruin people's lives and leave them to pick up the pieces if there's any left; that's right, I lied in the beginning. However, you're a special case. I find you to be so fascinating because you never *needed* me to ruin your life; you were already taking care of that yourself. I usually have to push and pry to get people to the point that you were at, but you were there all on your own. You were outdoing me and you inspired me to up my game. I've rarely ever seen a human put themselves on such a destructive path without any promises of fame, fortune, or fantasy. I knew that if I were going to mess things up for you, I needed to do something bigger than anything I've ever done before. I felt proud and deeply hurt at the same time when I saw your potential to ruin lives. It's unfortunate that you were so focused on messing with only yours, but luckily you caught some other people in the crossfire. Not as many as I would've hoped, but you did pretty damn great for it not being your actual job."

Scott pressed the button to go up to the eighth floor then leaned against the wall of the elevator. When the door closed

Roswell stepped up to the keypad, pressed the buttons for every floor below the eighth, then leaned against the opposite wall.

"Spoiler alert: We might be seeing some delays on the way to your side chick's pad. The elevator will be making a stop or two and I heard through the grapevine that there might be a power outage somewhere between floors one and eight."

"Can you just leave me alone?"

"Of course I can, I just don't feel like it. That was a waste of a question. But to be fair, I can totally understand why you'd be so upset. I pretty much threw you on a moving train and everyone on the train is looking at you like you're crazy. The thing is that everyone else could be the crazy ones. Another wonderful part is that your awkward interactions and erratic emotions make you seem so much stranger than you really are. I know the truth and so do you; nobody else does. Not even your narrator friend really gets it. All they do is read some words and make comments." Hey, I do more than that! "Darling, interrupt me again and I'll come up there and beat your face in. Pardon, their manners, Scott. Some people just love to talk, especially when they know they'll get in trouble for it. I want you to understand that you really don't belong here. It doesn't matter if you change and all of a sudden are more 'natural'; you'll always be an outcast. This whole setup I made for you is to make you realize your potential; rather, lack of it. You can be so much more than human once you let go of your humanity. I personally believe that's what's holding you back from accomplishing all the goals you have for yourself."

"I don't know what you're trying to do but it won't work. I don't care what you offer me; you could promise me the galaxy and I still wouldn't side with you."

The elevator doors slid open when it stopped at the second floor. Roswell grinned at Scott the whole time that the doors were open. Scott started to play the fake Tetris game he has on his phone and looked up every few seconds to see if Roswell was still looking at him. There's no doubt that Roswell gives Scott the creeps.

"I give everyone the creeps; I'm a demon; I'm not afraid to make people extremely uncomfortable. Believe it or not, that's one of my favorite hobbies. Swinging back around to what you were saying about taking sides; this isn't about good and evil. I'm not a villain if you're not a hero."

"But you are a villain; you're a demon. You kill people, you trick people, you make people suffer; sounds like a villain to me."

"There are good guys that do all of those things. You shouldn't go around calling me a villain unless you can prove that you're a hero. If I am a villain, I'm *your* villain."

"If you need an example, I saved the people at Atticus' uppity party the other day. Lots of innocent people would've died without me."

"Don't act delusional, I'm obviously not getting fooled by that lie and neither are you. You hurt more than you helped. You're rushing out to save lives when you don't even know whose lives you're saving. Do you think all those people were upstanding citizens who got money from being hard scrabble Americans? They got their money from cheating people, extortion, bribery, trafficking; humans and drugs; embezzlement; that's how they got all the money they can use for charities and making the community a better place. You saved some rotten ones from getting their just desserts. Now that you mention it, you might be a hero after all. But whose hero are you? If all the people who've been fucked over to kingdom come by the upper crust find out that you're the reason those cats are still swinging...."

"You're a demon; I'd be stupid take in everything you say as truth. Even if you were right about them being bad, it's not right for me to get flak for trying to do things the right way. Killing them isn't gonna magically solve all these people's problems!"

"Haven't you heard? Enablers are just as guilty as the actors. But don't sweat it, we can always spin the story around so that you're still the hero. That's all you want, right? To be the hero? Well I gave you the opportunity and right now you're doing a real shitty job."

"You're trying to paint me as some weird dude having delusions of grandeur; I didn't show up here to be bullied or ridiculed. Hell, you know better than anyone that I didn't ask for this shit. I didn't ask to be anyone's savior so what else do you think I would do being forced into that role?"

"Scott I gotta hand it to ya, you're pretty smart. Third floor." The doors opened and stayed open for a while as if someone was going to walk in. Roswell stared at Scott until it closed. To pass the time (and avoid Roswell's unnerving stare) Scott picked back up on that game of fake Tetris he was playing earlier.

"Why do you keep staring at me?"

"Because I know it really gets under your skin."

"Why do you always go quiet whenever the doors open?" Scott was starting to mess up in his game.

"Because I know how much it gets under your skin."

"Can you not? I'd love that."

"You waste your questions; such a shame. And if I could be made uncomfortable by anything then your horribly concise answers and awkward conversation skills would have me shuddering. I could, and should be asking you why you're doing that, but frankly, I don't care. But let's talk about what your role is in this world of mine. Maybe you didn't notice, but a good number of the people you've seen around are black. A few black aristocrats, fledgling black middle class, mostly black in poverty. I'm interested in showing you exactly how you view other black people. Could you sit well in a predominantly black world? I know it seems silly and the question should have an obvious answer, but I know you'd have problems coming to any conclusions on that. You see, another one of the things that makes you so interesting is that you don't have any strong opinions regarding your own race. A conscientious objector can't be a hero; they don't believe in fighting for anything. This is definitely gonna sound really creepy, but I've been watching you for a long time. I've noticed that you're the in-between. I won't bother telling you more things you already know, of course, but I want you to keep our conversation in mind when you travel around."

"I believe in a lot of things, but I know what you're talking about. The whole average Joe story; not rich but not dirt poor, not prejudiced- "

"Scott" Roswell laughed "You know you're lying. You're prejudiced as fuck."

Scott brushed his comment aside and continued. "Alright, fine. I may have a little prejudice, but that's not the point. There are all these stigmas that come with being black that I just don't feel like dealing with right now. That's it. Quit prying and leave me alone!"

"We both know there's more to it. It's definitely about race, but it's also got something to do with perception. I know how this plays out, but I won't spoil the ending for you. But one last bit of advice, don't try to salvage things after dinner, you should've fixed this years ago. Advice given. Fourth floor; this is my stop. Don't get got." The elevator doors and a crowd of journalists and people excitedly holding papers out were cheering as soon as Roswell stepped out. "I'll sign autographs and take pictures, but please, no interviews."

When the doors closed all the other buttons Roswell pressed stopped glowing. The elevator suddenly sped up and the force threw Scott to the floor. "The fuck did he do?" The elevator came to an abrupt stop, hurling Scott against the ceiling then back down to the floor. "Damn it! I hate him!" Like him or not, he does follow through on his word. He said that the elevator would stop somewhere between the first and eighth floor.

"Next time I see him I'll kill him!"

"And no you won't either." Roswell was sitting on the floor next to Scott like he never left. Scott jumped up in shock, but he hit his head on a handrail and it broke and fell on him. Roswell laughed hysterically but Scott didn't find it so funny. He lunged at Roswell, but the demon blocked it effortlessly by hitting Scott's ribcage with his knee. "You can't kill me! And even if you could, you don't have the guts. And even if all you wanna do is beat me in a fight, you'll have to be more creative than aggressive. Man, I've seen every trick in the book. I'm not afraid of you like some of the people you've roughed up over the years. I'm not intimidated by you; I can be one scary muthafucka."

Roswell smashed an acoustic guitar over Scott's back. Wait, he smashed an acoustic guitar over Scott's back? Where the heck did that come from? Roswell- "Call me Roswell, the demon this time. I feel like being a little more official." Okay, Roswell, the demon, where the hell did you get a guitar? "I'm a demon; I do what I want. Logic doesn't apply to me; learn that lesson and learn it good. By the way, this isn't just any ol' acoustic, it's a thirty-eight Gibson ES one fifty. Can't go wrong with a classic!" The guitar repaired itself and Roswell...the demon, continuously broke the instrument on Scott. Roswell eventually stopped and left the guitar shattered to pieces. Scott picked himself up and punched Roswell so hard that it cracked the demon's jaw. Scott carried on with a flurry of jabs and hooks, but his stamina was declining rapidly due to his injuries.

Roswell held his chin and instead of moving his jaw back into place he aligned the rest of his head with his jaw. After mending his injury Roswell hardly had a scratch on him while Scott looked like he'd been taking daily trips to Hell for the last five years. He had gashes on his face and on his back, blood dripping from everywhere, and scars for miles. "You had to hit me when I was already down and you had to use a weapon to do it. Who's the bitch now, huh?! C'mon and fight me like a man! I can take you on just like this! I don't need any of that magic shit you got up your sleeves!" Yet his injuries can't hold him down.

Roswell grinned but didn't make any moves. Scott grew tired of waiting and punched Roswell repeatedly. The hits were having an impact, or at least I think they were; it's hard to tell. During that time Roswell didn't do anything, but when he fought it was devastating. He plunged his fist into Scott's abdomen, lifted him up with that same fist then slammed him into the floor. Miraculously (but oddly), Scott was in much better shape than before. He actually appeared to be untouched.

"I want our last fight to be fair, so I'm showing you the ropes. Also, you never ask for me to show up, except for when you did, but that was indirect; you didn't actually think I'd show up. So I didn't think it would be right to beat you up then leave you all battered and bloody. And as for you, narrator: stop switching between past and present tense before someone catches on. Oooo and before I forget there's something I was supposed to mention earlier." Roswell pointed at him while looking the other way "Oh yeah, just the tip: don't play fair; there are no rules." The doors opened and Scott checked the keypad to see if the nightmare was over. Yup, it's the eighth floor; crisis averted. Scott got up and dusted off his clothes (there wasn't any dust on his clothes) then flipped off the demon (well if you can't fight him and win...). Roswell smiled and waved as he disappeared.

That was really weird. "Huh, you're telling me. I can't stand that freakshow." I hope I'm not overstepping my boundaries, but was he right about the whole race thing? "It's complicated; that's all the time I have for that. If you'll excuse me I'm going to look for Fae now." He left the elevator and immediately started trying to guess which unit Faaghira *would've* been in; she's dead and he's in denial. "Yo, chill dude; I got this. I think she said that her favorite unit was six, so this one might be open." Scott checked unit number six and BAM! It was locked. She probably locked all her doors, even if she was in them. Well duh, who wouldn't? "She didn't unlock the door the last time I was here. I'm guessing there's a lot of security around here, but I just didn't see them because I was with her before and she....if I was some random dude I'm pretty sure I would've been escorted off the lot before I could even get anywhere near the lobby."

Scott tried door after door but none of the ones he checked were open. There were a few more doors to check and he would've kept going but Faaghira finally opened the sixth door which (he skipped over the second time) and told him to chill out.

"Oh my god! Fae! I thought you were dead!" Scott ran to Faaghira and embraced her, but the hug she gave in return was lackluster. She had that morning squint, the crusty eyes, that dry 'I just woke up voice', and her hair is a little messy (but it still looks beautiful).

"Scott, what are you doing here so early in the morning? It's great to see you, but a lady needs her sleep."

Scott chuckled after checking his phone. "Fae, it's almost four in the afternoon. When did you go to sleep?"

"Bullshit, let me see your phone." Scott was trying to keep a straight face when he gave her the phone but he couldn't contain his smile. Fae covered her face with her hand and groaned. "Ugh! What is the meaning of this?!" She said dramatically.

"A lot happened since we...since then!" Scott talked like

Faaghira was fully paying attention. When she only responded with 'Same', he realized that small talk wouldn't work with her when she was tired. He either needed substance or he needed to wait until she was legitimately awake before trying to strike up a conversation. "I also have a confession to make." Her eyes didn't widen or anything like that, but she opened the door, signaling for Scott to go in.

This condo looks a lot bigger than the other, but that's probably because there's not nearly as much furniture in it. There's two chairs and a small coffee table, all silver and in the futuristic sixties design. The only other piece of furniture on the lower level is a very comfortable looking orange sofa that also has the futuristic sixties aesthetic. The room is a solid light grey color which contrasts beautifully with the sunlight shining in. Just like the other unit, the large windows facing towards the city take place of an actual wall.

"So why'd you think I was dead?" Her words definitely sound demanding, but she's too groggy to have any force behind them. Scott slowly pulled a chair from under the table and it made a low screeching sound against the floor. Faaghira is in the other seat rapidly tapping her fingers on the table. "Today, Scott." He quickly sat down and apologized in hopes that she'd be less grumpy. Turns out that compliance and an apology isn't the magic cure for sleepiness.

"Okay so I'll get right to it; that time when you asked me who I was talking to, I wasn't talking to my girlfriend."

Faaghira looked a little concerned but she didn't look totally surprised. "But you do have a girlfriend, right?"

"Yeah that really was my girlfriend; everything I said about her was true."

"So who were you talking to?" Her voice hadn't cleared up at all, but she was listening intently.

Scott let out a deep breath puffing his cheeks and looking

down at the table. "I'm not sure how to explain this..."

"Just go for it dude."

"I was... there's a... I have a narrator."

"Like for a documentary?"

"Actually, they're for a book. They're really annoying and they don't help most of the time."

Fae nodded then just looked at him for a moment. "How much acid have you been dropping? You can tell me, I do it too sometimes."

Scott sighed in frustration. "I've never done acid. I'm completely sober right now. It's hard to prove that they're real but I can try." Scott drummed his hands on the table until he came up with an idea. "You're a total softie on the inside and you're a hopeless romantic. You like laid back relationships so that's why you hold my hand and kiss me, but never define what we are. You were kind of pushing me away because I have a girlfriend, but the only reason that's an issue for you is because you don't want your heart broken. It makes sense; if I'm not faithful to my girlfriend then what would stop me from being unfaithful to you? Also, when you really like someone, you'd bend over backwards for them. As long as they don't seriously hurt your feelings then they can't do any wrong in your eyes. And don't worry" Scott rested his hand on hers; "I'd never do anything to hurt you."

Fae looks to be in a state somewhere between confusion and fright. The shock expressed in her eyes is genuine. "Did the narrator tell you that?"

"Now do you believe me?"

"You just said some really personal stuff that only me and one other person would know. You don't know them and I know I didn't tell you" She pulled her hand from under Scott's and put both her arms under the table. "So how long have you had this narrator?"

"They were there the day we met but I know for sure that I had them before I ever saw you. There's a lot more to it if

173

you'll give me the chance to explain it all."

"I would say that I need some time to process this, but I doubt any amount of thought will lead to this making sense."

"It won't make sense; I just need you to listen." Scott paused and took another breath. "I was out drinking with some friends one night and then I blacked out. When I woke up I was in an abandoned house then a squirrel jumped out of a can and started talking to me. The house caught on fire and whenever I walked glass broke. A wall got angry at me and it grew arms and legs and tried to kill me, then I jumped out a window. I downed a bottle of Sazerac and blacked out again. This time when I woke up I was on a pile of leaves and the narrator told me that I'm in a children's book and I have to try to ignore them. I was confused and I still am and I'm freaking out! I don't know what to do; I'm just trying to get back home!" Scott gradually sounded more distressed as he spoke.

"So all of this that you're telling me…is real?"

"I swear I'm not making this up. I wouldn't be telling you this if it wasn't real."

"Looks like this is wearing on you; but if it's not too much to ask, I'd like to know what happened to you that night we went to the field."

"I was actually gonna ask you the same thing! So, you probably already know this, but the car never crashed. I have no idea how it happened, but I was transported to this white room with a huge table in the middle of it. There was this guy there named Roswell, but he's an actual demon."

"Would that also happen to be the name of the squirrel you mentioned earlier?"

"Yeah, how'd you know that?"

"Remind me to tell you later; continue."

"Huh, odd. So he's the most evil dude I've ever seen. He has powers that are hard to explain, but I remember him clearly saying that he's a shapeshifter. I'm also pretty sure he knows everything about me. He said he killed you and you were there; you were dead under the table"

"Umm…okay. Is he omniscient?"

"I think he might be. I won't spend too much time thinking about that because the only thing I'm concerned with is getting back home. For me that happens to be another dimension that I don't know how to get back to. Is this making sense?"

"Not one bit."

"Okay so he said he wanted to take me on this trip through different parts of this dimension, but the first place he took me was back home. I didn't want to, but he said if I did it then he'd bring you back to life, I didn't want to chance it. I know it sounds ridiculous, but everything was real; I didn't really know you were alive till just now!" Scott was panicking so much that words were starting to get mashed together.

"…Right. Then why'd you end up back here?"

"Well that might be might my fault, but I can't say for sure."

"You wanted to get home, then you did, then you're back here again and it's possibly your fault? Excuse me?" Faaghira looked really stressed out trying to make sense of Scott's explanation and rightfully so; it's a tough act to understand.

"Hold up, let me explain. We were back in my old neighborhood, Roswell and I, which I was really skeptical of. I didn't know if it really was home, but after I went to visit my mom I understood that I actually was back in the real world."

"Did you come back because it was too boring for you there?"

"No…I ended up back here because I got drunk and lost a game of tic-tac-toe with a demon! The getting drunk part was my fault, but I was at a party with my girlfriend and we

175

had a… disagreement so I drank it off. I was having a real good time; then out of nowhere Roswell shows up. I hate that guy. He makes an offer; if I didn't win in a game of tic-tac-toe then I'd have to show up back here. If I won then he'd leave me alone forever. Technically I didn't lose because he wasn't trying to win; he was just trying to keep me from winning. I didn't get it at first, but he basically fixed it so that I'd be back in his…um…I guess dimension would still be the best word. If only I won; I'd never have to see or hear from him ever again."

"But then you never would've seen me again. Wouldn't you be sad?"

"Yeah but you'd be alright. I mean sure you might be a little down about it for a minute, but it would pass; you'd forget about me. Plus there's the whole thing about me thinking you were dead this whole time."

"It would probably would take more than a minute, and I'd get over you for sure, but what makes you think I forget you? Not saying that you're wrong; just want to know why you think that."

"Uh…we're getting off topic. To sum it all up, I just want to get back home and stay there. I told you all of this because…well…I don't know; I was hoping someone here could help me get back home."

Faaghira rubbed her chin and appeared to be staring off into space. "I might know someone that can help, but I need some coffee first. Do you want some?"

Scott tried to utter words but he choked up and gave a thumbs up instead. Faaghira started brewing some coffee while Scott drummed lightly drummed on the table. "Well this is awkward." Scott tried to spark up a conversation but it quickly fell flat. Maybe he didn't think coffee actually meant coffee. She ignored him and Scott went back to drumming on the table. When the coffee finished brewing she poured two mugs full and brought one over to the table.

"Thanks a million Fae."

"This is mine."

"What about mine?"

"You have legs." She shooed him away then loudly drank from her mug. Scott cringed when he got up from his seat and gave her the side eye.

"Can you drink that any louder?" Scott sassed at her, but to his surprise (and annoyance) she drank louder. "I was being sarcastic." Scott sighed. She placed the mug down the table then picked it back up and sipped even louder than before. Scott shook his fist at her when he went to go the other mug.

"That story of yours sounds like it's missing a few parts, but something told me that would happen. But I can't say I blame you, it sounds like things are moving at light speed. I know I wouldn't handle it well either if my whole life was being thrown around in such a crazy way."

"Who said I can't handle it?" Scott snapped back at her. Faaghira laughed and held arms in the air.

"Yo, chill dude. It's ok to be overwhelmed sometimes; what's your issue with that anyway?"

"Fae, you're wonderful, but please leave it alone."

Fae shook her head at him with a playful look on her face. She got up from the table and waved at Scott to signal him to follow her. They went upstairs to the second floor and oh if only you could see Scott's face. He looked so excited, so giddy, he tried to hide it but it didn't work. She opened the door to a room that would've been empty if not for a mattress on the floor with two pillows and a cover thrown over it. He grinned of course, surely expecting some kind of event, but his disappointment was the most beautiful part of all. Faaghira pulled back the covers and Scott jumped back so far that he fell on the floor. Fae laughed hysterically, but what made Scott react (or overreact) like that was genuinely startling.

A charred skeleton covered in a cloak was sprawled out on the bed. It propped itself up, pulled a cloth sack over its head and tied the bottom with short rope. It put on a pair of boots then stood up. Flames engulfed the skeleton, but they went away as quickly as it came. When the fire dissipated, new markings that resembled a face were on the cloth. The scene was very frightening, so much so that Faaghira was a little stirred by it, even though she must've seen it before. She wasn't stunned like he was, but there was definitely some serious fear. While it was pretty unsettling, the funny thing about it is how silly the markings on the cloth are. All of that suspense ended in the cloth having eyes, a nose, a mouth, and smile lines, all painted in a laughably goofy way. One eye is clearly bigger than the other and the expression is a mix of 'I have no idea what's going on', 'I don't actually care about anything', and 'shit happens'.

Under normal circumstances I'm sure they both would've laughed, but it was still an unsettling sight. "Do you remember when we were separated a couple days ago? This is who I met that night." Still frightened, Faaghira still introduced the fire skeleton thing. "This is also the fire monster that I was telling you about. His name is Baron Sugar and he's actually a super nice guy."

Scott hesitantly reaches his hand out to shake Baron Sugar's hand, but Sugar just stood there. I imagine he was making some kind of face at Scott but it's impossible to tell. This annoys me.

"Hello, Scott. And hello to you, narrator. I would highly appreciate a lack of comments on my traits, if you would not mind; if you would, then please stop now." Sugar still didn't reciprocate so Scott gave up and put his hand down. It's obvious that Scott was uneasy with not having any expressions to read. And apparently he can hear me too. What the heck is going on here?

"Do not fret; I will ignore you most of the time. Now

Faaghira, Scott, I understand that my appearance is off-putting. However, I can guarantee that my appearance is far more terrifying than the man behind it, or in my case, the shell of a man behind it. Neither of you have anything to fear. I have already explained things to Faaghira, but you, Scott, have no idea who or what I am. Faaghira brought me here because she thought I could help you, and I would suggest that you listen. She waited days for you; I did not just show up today; I have been here for a while. She convinced me to stay and wait with her even though there was no way for her to know when you would come back. She would wait for as long as it took for you to come back."

"And what if I never came back?"

"I asked the same question when we were discussing this. She asked me to wait for a month; even tried to barter with me so I would stay."

"So what made you wait?"

"I explained to her that there was nothing anyone in this world could offer me to have me act in their favor. I usually dismiss the affairs of people, but when she explained the situation it intrigued me. Being pulled around at rapid speeds and not knowing what do; being lost in the broadest terms; I identify with this. I was in a similar predicament *many* years ago."

Faaghira whispered to Scott "Sorry if you got the idea we were gonna have sex; I should've specified what was up here. Anyway, I think he can help you get back home."

"But he's really creepy. I'll be able to get back home without his help." Scott whispered back discretely.

"Yes, I am very creepy, but you do not know how to get back home. I highly doubt that you could get back without my help." Sugar whispered in Scott's ear. Scott didn't jump back this time; instead he was frozen in disbelief. Him and Faaghira hadn't taken their eyes off of Baron Sugar for a second, and there he was standing next to Scott. Weird stuff's been going on throughout this book, so that's probably not the part that's got Scott so freaked out. It's probably just because Baron Sugar seems hella creepy.

"How did you- never mind. What is it that you have to tell me?"

"Being sent to a strange world, a world where you have no place, where there seems to be no meaning. You did not ask for this; no sane man ever would. As bad as things have been for you, I want you to understand that they can be much worse, and they will be if we do not get you back to where you are supposed to be. It would take some time to explain, but you do not want to stay here much longer than you already have. I know it seems quite contradictory; Faaghira was hoping you'd come back so she could tell you to leave. However, getting you to leave was not her original intent. After she told me your story I took it upon myself to make sure you returned to your life and never found your way here again."

"What are you talking about?"

"I have lived this story the whole way through; as you can see, it does not end well. This must all be very confusing, I am sure."

"You're telling me I'll be a flaming abomination if I don't get back home soon?"

Fae nudged Scott with her elbow and apologized for Scott's less than charming nature. "Scott isn't always aware that he has a filter *that he should totally be using more.*"

"Do not apologize; he is not sorry, and I take no offence to being called a creature, as it is true. Yes Scott, you may share the same fate as me if you lose sight of what should matter to you. You too will be reduced to a shell of a man; to a creature. If what I believe is true, then I must warn you that the evil that is responsible all for this is not easy to avoid."

"Let me guess, Roswell the demon is the evil you're

talking about."

"The one to whom I can attribute a portion of my pain. But beware Scott; the work of this demon is founded on personal flaws. For many years I blamed that creature for all of my struggles, but after some time passed I came to understand that I am a large factor in my grief."

Scott asked rather rudely (that doesn't sound right), "What's the point, Shakespeare?" This Baron Sugar dude seriously bothers me; it's literally impossible to describe his expression! Okay for future reference, any time that someone talks to him we'll just assume that he's responding in some kind of way. Okay, so where'd we leave off? Oh yeah, so Scott's being an ass and then Sugar's face emits a red glow. Beads of sweat rolled down from Scott's forehead, but his expression hadn't changed a bit. I'm sure he's actually terrified; heck, I would be too! Good job on the resilience Scott!

"Shut up! Can you just stop with the jokes for just one second? It's always goddamned jokes with you!"

"Calm yourself Scott; anger will reduce you to nothing. I do not believe you are equipped to handle a serious conversation at the moment. To lighten the mood both of you are welcome to ask me any question you have; I have an extensive knowledge of the world."

Scott was only able to say the words "Why are you-" before Faaghira cut him off.

"Are there really other dimensions out there?"

"Do not underestimate yourself; you may already know the answer. However, I can give you my experience of the Netherplains. In my youth, after I had gained the horrible gift of power, I sought refuge in unfamiliar places. It is possible that I was hiding from my own shadow or from the sun that would show it to me. I have seen good and evil abound; the worst and best of humanity, but more often than not, I witnessed the ugly side of nature. But of course, this is not to take away from the beauty of these foreign lands. The earth and its creations have no quarrel with man, therefore any existence without a society holds no hatred towards you. The first and last lands that I journeyed to are the most memorable. The first was simply a field of sunflowers. No trees, no buildings, no people, no animals, no other forms of life. The only other thing was a river that stretched as far as the eye could see. The water shimmered in the sunlight and did the same in the moonlight. It was undeniably beautiful. It was absolute torture. I had never been in a place where there was nothing else but nature and myself. I tried to drown myself in the river many times but nothing could end the suffering I was experiencing. Oddly enough, the final reality that I found myself in was almost exactly the same. This time the only difference was that the flowers were roses instead of sunflowers."

"What made that time different if it was basically the same place?"

"I changed. The sun and moon showed me my shadow and I awaited the sight instead of avoiding it. The waters could never take my life, despite the fact that I became a fire. Logic became irrelevant when I came to terms with the fact that I no longer was a logical being, nor would I ever be again, assuming that I ever was. Since the waters could never take my life, I had no choice but to observe their beauty. The time I spent there grew shorter; the sun had risen and set at the pace of a year instead of a month. In my solitude my weakness turned to strength, but I came to understand that my humanity, a significant feature, had shriveled down to a horribly frail frame. I could not starve, I did not thirst, I sought no gains, I had no fear, my feelings had been worn thin. I understood that I was so far removed from the world that I could never go back. Though I loved the peace in solidarity, I desired an environment where I could attempt to maintain the qualities that made me human. Whether or not it was a mistake, I returned to a familiar place."

"I don't mean to sound rude" Faaghira said bashfully "but that didn't answer my question."

"A question for show is noble to an audience, and an audience there is. However, the truth lies behind it, this wall of answers and curiosity. I have already answered your question, but you never specified the kind of answer you sought."

"I wanted to-" Faaghira tried to clarify but she was sharply interrupted by Sugar.

"But do not waste precious life attempting to explain. I answered it and now I am tired of the question. I would be delighted to answer something that is generally unknown. But be warned, if it is unknown, there is the chance that I may not have a sufficient answer."

Scott nudged Faaghira and winked. "You said you've been in my shoes before; how would you get home if you were me right now?"

"I fear that I am happy to announce that it is both fortunate and unfortunate that I have a sufficient answer. You and I should discuss this in detail on a later date, but I can promise you that there is a way for you to get home."

"If you don't want Fae to hear it then I won't listen. And all this from someone who doesn't even know what solidarity means. It's solitude, you freak."

"It appears that you will not be hearing it today, but when I tell you will understand why I requested a private audience. From what I understand, you and Faaghira have plenty to discuss. I have wares of my own; call out to me and I will return if you require my aid. Until that time, farewell." Baron Sugar unlocked the latches on the nearest window and tossed himself out of it. It's no less of an off-putting sight, but the way Sugar flopped over the window was almost in slapstick territory. Scott held back an outburst of laughter which Fae noticed; she playfully pushed his shoulder.

"Fae, where'd you find that creep?" Scott said laughing. Faaghira nervously laughed along but it was definitely far from genuine. It was more of a 'I don't want to make this awkward' kind of laugh.

"Scott" She said nervously, "you just met the Fireman. I still think it's a stupid name so I'm not calling him that anymore, but yeah, that's him."

"That's the fire monster you were afraid of? He's hella weird and creepy but he doesn't seem scary."

"Maybe he doesn't seem so bad to you, but I've been afraid of him for as long as I can remember."

"Hard to tell; you had it living with you for a few days. It looks to me like you're pretty chill with this 'monster'."

"When I jumped out the car and it disappeared I started to panic like crazy. On top of that, that he was standing there in the field. He was looking right at me; the nightmare I've had night after night was happening. I was frozen; I couldn't move no matter how hard I tried. I thought I was going to die that night, but he held out his hand to help me up. I thought he would torch me if I took his hand, but I took it anyway. I figured that if he was going to kill me then nothing I did or didn't do would change that. He asked me if anyone else was still in the car and I mentioned you. He told me that we needed to find you immediately then he walked me over to where it looked like the car went. It's safe to say that we were both freaking out when we saw that it wasn't there. At least I think he was freaking out; maybe he was mildly surprised at the most; it's hard to tell with him. After that I didn't feel so helpless anymore; he could be worried just like I was. But that doesn't change the fact that was terrifying. I know this makes me sound crazy, but I think he could sense my fear."

"Don't worry; I don't think you're any crazier than before."

"Gee thanks." Faaghira took a moment to get back in her

train of thought. "I had this uneasy feeling; like I was gonna get sick. There's no way that he couldn't see it. He would randomly stop when we went looking for you, but he would just keep walking after that. I was scared every time he turned around, but I couldn't just quit."

"Because you wanted to find me."

"I didn't have the strength to walk all the way back home. Besides, the monst- I mean Baron Sugar was already looking for you and since I couldn't go anywhere else I just said fuck it and I joined in."

"I'm so glad I was at the front of your thoughts."

"Always, babe." She winked at him, but he didn't find it so amusing. He gave this clearly fake, weird half smile thing. She doesn't seem to pay it any mind; picking back up where she left off. "He carried me around everywhere on his back. He walked around the woods and the bayou, but he flew around the city. Being carried around like that made me feel like I was a kid again. I wanted to talk to him about something to break the ice, but I was still afraid because no matter how nice he is, he's still the thing that gave me nightmares all my life. He asked me where I wanted to be dropped off, but I didn't answer at first. A small part of me had this fear that if he knew where I lived he would burn the entire place down when I went to sleep. After playing the thought over a few times in my head I realized that my fear wasn't rational anymore. I met the person I'd been so afraid of all my life and other than looking creepy, there was nothing scary about him. Part of me was always so stuck in the past while every other part moved on. I told him, he brought me here, then he was going to leave. I was so afraid, and he didn't seem to care at all. I felt so insignificant; then I realized that I was to him. I had this whole idea in my head of what he was like and that he was out to get me, but I was just a random person to him. I asked him to tell me about himself. I felt like it was time that I put my fears behind me for good. You know most of the important parts that come after that."

"Now that I'm here what's next?"

"Getting you back home, dummy."

"No, I mean for us. Correct me if I'm wrong, but I don't think you want me to leave."

"Scott" she sighed, "Why do you keep doing this? It's not about what I want and it's not about what you want either. It's about doing what's best if getting you home is what's best for you, then that's my main concern right now. I know that I'm great, and I know I seem really into you, but this how I am. Some people stay on my mind for a while, but it's not even love adjacent. Can't say it's lust, but it's never been love."

Scott stepped up close to Faaghira and lightly brushed a loose strand of hair hanging over the side of her face. "You care so much, but who's looking out for you? Let me make you my main concern."

"You're so corny." She laughed nervously then gulped and cleared her throat.

Scott lightly tilted her chin up and kissed from her collarbone up to the top of her neck. She wrapped her arms around his shoulders and smiled slyly. He slowly moved his hands down to her hips as he gave her a small peck on the side of her neck. She let out a light breath then leaned his head forward and planted a soft kiss on his lips. She moved her arms off of his shoulders and slowly slid down to the mattress. She reached out her hand and Scott placed his palm in hers; leading him down to the covers with her.

"COUCH! COUCH! BARON SUGAR WAS JUST HERE AND IT'S STILL HELLA CREEPY!" Scott didn't shout, but he wasn't calm enough for his volume to be considered normal.

"Oh, um, sorry" she said shyly. "I wasn't thinking about that. I don't mind going to the couch."

186

"Fae, I'm so sorry about that. I should've just let go; we were having a moment."

"Scott it's fine, really. I know I would've done the same thing if I was thinking about Baron Sugar having been there."

"Really?"

"Absolutely not; if I'm in the mood I don't give a damn. Dude, you totally messed with the moment."

"And I'll make up for it." Scott knelt down and raised his hand out to her. "M'lady."

"Such a gentleman. I bet you do that to all the chicks you're trying to smash. Lucky for you, I have a soft spot for that romantic junk."

"If there's one thing I have, it's romantic junk." Scott smiled slyly.

Faaghira smiled, showing her beautiful shining white teeth. "Please, *please* stop talking."

Scott stood up and this time it was him that led the way. They held hands going down the stairs. She whispered something to Scott that made him smile from ear to ear. Scott cupped his hands at the base of her jaw and kissed her passionately. She draped her arms over his shoulders and he ran his fingers slowly down her thighs. She wraps one leg around his waist and he lightly strokes it while their lips lock. He holds that leg to his side and lifts the other. They hadn't even gotten halfway down the stairs yet. She leaned against him and flung her hair tie out, letting her hair cascade down to her back. She came up for air, but she rushed her head down to the side of his neck, kissing it; using her breath to make a light breeze graze over his skin.

Scott quickly carried her over to the couch and sat down with her straddling him. She rushed to pull her shirt off, tossing it to the floor. Scott pulled off his shirt from the side to keep from accidentally hitting her in the face; he wasn't gonna mess up *this* time.

"Fae, you're a goddess; your body is unreal!"

"And keys open doors. Go crazy; I fucking dare you."

Scott kissed right below her chest then kept going down until he was close to her navel.

"Is this okay?"

"Yes!" she sighed. "I would've told you to stop if I didn't like it. Now goddammit will you just get back down there already?" Scott laid on his back, kissing past her navel, down to the waistline of her shorts. She's about to pull them down lower when Scott interrupts.

"Quick question"

"It better be."

"Do you know someone named Mercury?"

Faaghira sighs then gets off him. She lifts up one of the cushions, picking up a black box from underneath. She opened the box and took out a small velvet pouch with a cap at the end. She carefully emptied some contents of the pouch in her hand; about a matchbox by the looks of it. She carefully placed it on a gold rolling paper; rolling it all into a thin joint and lights it with a chrome lighter in the shape of a small flask. After blowing out thin cloud of smoke she got up from the couch, box in hand, and went out to the balcony on the other side of the room.

Scott tried to get up…but I can totally see why it wouldn't be comfortable. He took his phone out of his pocket and immediately went to the gallery. He frantically swiped until he got to a picture of John Quincy Adams, which he stared at for a while. "This is by far the ugliest person I've ever seen. If anyone can still want sex right after seeing this guy, there's no hope for them." Okay, so this is really awkward… but Scott's totally chill now. Tmi; I never want to read this again.

Faaghira was looking out on the city but the sliding door to the balcony was open so he let himself through. "Fae I'm sorry about that. I shouldn't have mentioned Mercury until after we had sex."

"That would've went over a lot worse." She took another puff, blowing out the smoke with a faint whistle.

"What about that made you so upset?"

"Scott, I like you, but I don't think you understand how much of your business this isn't. If I want sex, I want sex. If you want to have sex with me and I'm in the mood, you better not ruin it for me; don't be that guy. I do this for me, not you or anyone else. If you're down with that then cool, if not, don't try in the first place. You had one job! You're stressing me out, man; don't make me regret trying to look out for you." She sighed and took another puff. "In short, we used to be together, but things took a turn. Why'd you even bring it up?"

"Yeah, I saw her earlier today. What happened between you two?"

"I talked about her before; I just didn't mention her name. If you can remember what I said about my exes earlier then you'll be able to put two and two together. If not; I don't feel like repeating myself, especially not now."

"Okay." He leaned on the railing and watched the city with her. "Fae?"

"What else is on your mind, babe?"

"Can I have some weed?" Scott had this childlike quality in his voice when he asked which made Faaghira chuckle.

"This is my stress weed; I usually don't let anyone use it, but I'll share this once since I'm feeling generous. Weed's in the pouch and rolling papers are in that long case right there. Just don't take too much; the plug is out of town till next week." She passed the box to Scott and watched as he excitedly rolled a joint with the gold paper. "It's edible gold. It's dirt cheap, for me anyway."

"You wouldn't happen to have one of those fancy cigarette holders, would you?"

"Not for you. C'mon, let's watch a movie or something

since that doesn't rely on you not ruining everything. Let's just chill for a minute. I'll go find something; I'm in the mood for a corny movie." She turned back around when she was about to step inside. "Ooh I almost forgot; don't smoke inside. I don't want the whole place smelling like weed."

"Fae, the door's open."

"It'll smell a *little* like weed but that's part of the charm. As long as it's not the whole place I'm good." They spent a few minutes smoking out, not saying anything. They leaned against the railing, watching the city while enjoying each other's company. "I've got a clip so you can get the roach too if you want. I hardly bother anymore 'cause it always makes me feel like I'm trying too hard. Defeats the purpose of trying to relax, you know?"

Scott nodded his head but then he told her that he was good enough with what he already had. Fae lightly tapped her cigarette holder on the railing, making the roach fall out. They went back inside after Scott tossed his over. Fae closed the door behind them, but she hardly got the chance to with Scott kissing her again. "Scott, you're too much. You're lucky you're cute, you bad little boy."

"I may be bad but I'm not little." Scott said slyly.

Faaghira rolled her eyes and smiled. "A *big* let down, Mr. Bad Boy. You had exactly one job and you blew it. Kinda funny; wouldn't'na meant a thing, but boy it coulda felt great. No matter how smooth you think you are, the plans aren't changing. We're watching something and that's that. I'm not changing my mind just because I'm high."

"Alright, alright, you're the boss."

"You're damn right I am." They slouched on the couch while they watched a knock off version of *A Cat In Paris* called *The Badger on Portland*. They didn't cuddle or anything like they probably would've earlier. They were just vegging out on the couch, laughing at the odd animation and cheesy lines. Maybe it's the weed or maybe the movie is really that much of a gem. Of course, it wasn't very long until Scott and Faaghira were hungry.

"It's cool, I got this huge tin of kettle corn that has a shit ton of flavors. Sit tight, I'll be right back." Faaghira's first attempt of getting off the couch ended with her sitting back down before she could even get her butt off the cushion. This happened two more times until she was finally able to get up.

"First try! One hundred percent!" Scott threw a fist up in the air while he laughed at her.

"You know something, Scott-." Are you wondering why she stopped? Because she just walked off mid-sentence. And she looked really serious too; like she was about to drop some serious wisdom. She just left. She later returned with a large tin of kettle corn and it really does have a bunch of flavors!

"Hell yeah, kettle corn!" Scott grabbed a handful of caramel ones and popped them in his mouth. "So what were you going to say earlier?"

"When?"

"Before you got the kettle corn. You said, 'You know something, Scott-' but you never finished; you just left."

"Huh, I guess it wasn't important. Maybe I was thinking of saying something insightful, but I must've forgot what it was when I was gonna say it."

"Hey Fae?"

"Right here, babe."

"Let's do something super lame."

"Way ahead of you; we're watching a corny movie."

"No, I mean lamer."

"Is that even a real word?"

Scott's face is building with excitement as if he's about to tell you the most earth-shattering news anyone would ever hear in their whole entire lives. "Let's watch the news!"

Faaghira was idly taking pieces of kettle corn and stuffing

them in her mouth. "M'kay."

Faaghira turned on the news but judging by the look on her face she probably wished she didn't listen to him.

A PSA was on the news station…and every other channel they flipped to. Atticus was on the screen, smoking a cigarette with a holder similar to the one Scott saw on Fae's balcony. He had a smug look on his face (it seems like everyone in this place does) which made both Scott and Faaghira scowl. "Tonight I'd like to show you, my beautiful people of Louisiana, that the system works! I have with me a special guest this afternoon" he paused "but they're not in this room. With the efforts of our brave men and women who serve the state; all colors and creeds, I have apprehended the founder of the terrorist group that has been trying to undermine the authority for quite some time now. The terrorist leader known as Safira is currently staying at City Hall; she will be rightfully be sent to the gallows tomorrow afternoon at three. As I mentioned before, I alone can restore law and order and I intend on following up on that promise. The attacks on our police, the crime, the treason, will all be eradicated once we get rid of the heart of the problem. Without these terrorists in our midst, I will be able to focus government funding on raising up each economic class. I will be able to usher in a new age of prosperity for all. Thank you." He puffed on the pipe one more time before the broadcast reverted to the cartoon.

Fae put the tin on the floor then curled up on the couch. "He's gonna kill her." There was a wave of apprehensiveness in her voice. Scott caressed her shoulders and held her in his arms in an effort to comfort her. "Aw shucks, shoulders again." She laughed faintly, but it evaporated quickly. "He's gonna kill her unless I do something about it. No time to mope around; time to do some work." Her anxiety grew into a sense of urgency. It wasn't a drastic change, as she wasn't exactly sad before; she looked

192

to be in emotional limbo.

Scott looked genuinely surprised when he saw determination instead of tears. "How would you rescue her? Atticus has the police and probably enough firepower to tear a city to shreds. The chances of getting within even a mile of her are slim to none."

"Hell hath no fury." She walked briskly out the condo and Scott chased after her.

"I get that you want to save her, but you need to be smart about this. At least take some time to come up with a plan!"

"I have a plan: fight fire with fire." She rushed into her seventh unit and stormed upstairs. Scott ran after her again but he slowed down a bit after nearly tripping over a step.

"If you fight fire with fire then everyone burns!"

"It's about time we all burned anyway." She opened a dresser drawer and took out a patag along with a kasuyu. She went to her closet and put on a dark blue jumpsuit, a black bomber jacket, and black suede Chelsea boots, and since she's never one to fully take herself seriously, fuzzy black socks with smiley faces on each side (a joke for her personally since they were covered by her pants and boots).

"Fae, they have guns, lots of guns. How far do you expect to get with a throwing axe and a short sword?"

"Them having guns just means that I don't have to bring my own; I'll use theirs if it comes to that."

"Fae I'm worried about you! Look, I don't want to lose you over something that you can avoid."

She smiled devilishly. "So you'd be totally chill with losing me over something that I can't avoid?"

"No, no that's not what I meant! You know what I meant. I don't want to lose you at all. Ever."

"You know it, they know it, we all know it. You sound tense Boobear, have a lollipop." She takes a lollipop out of the mason jar on the top of the dresser and puts it in his hand, then gets ready to leave.

"You're going without me?" He looked puzzled.

"With all that work you did trying to talk me out of it I didn't think you'd even want to help me. Besides, I don't need your help. The real important question here is whether or not you can fight."

"I can hold my own if that's what you're asking. I think I could keep up with you."

"That's *exactly* what I was asking. If you're coming with then grab a shirt from my closet. And don't worry, *everybody's* wanting to raid my wardrobe. I don't know if they'll fit, but you can probably find something your size; I've been down with the whole oversize thing for a minute."

Scott gently shuffled through the clothes and found a black velvet sweater that fit well enough. "How do I look?"

"Are you kidding me? My clothes can make anyone look good; they're mine! No more time to waste; I'm out."

Faaghira grabbed his hand and rushed him down the stairs then to the elevator. When they got to the lobby the serious dude from before (not a concierge, apparently) wished Faaghira luck with a smile, but when Scott made eye contact he was serious again. Scott waved but the guy threw up a peace sign real quick then disappeared into a back room behind the front desk.

Scott took a few steps back but he stopped before he left the lobby. One of the chairs…winked at him. Yes. The chair was normal…but then it had an eye, just one, and it winked at him. It was just as creepy as it sounds. Scott shuddered for a moment but he seemed to be fine as soon as Faaghira called out to him. He looked back one more time before leaving. This time it gave him two thumbs up. The even stranger part is that the arms were formed from the two back legs; not the front. "The Epitome; I'll see you there, Scott Blue" it whispered to Scott in a monotone voice. Scott shook his head, probably in disbelief, and then went outside to Faaghira.

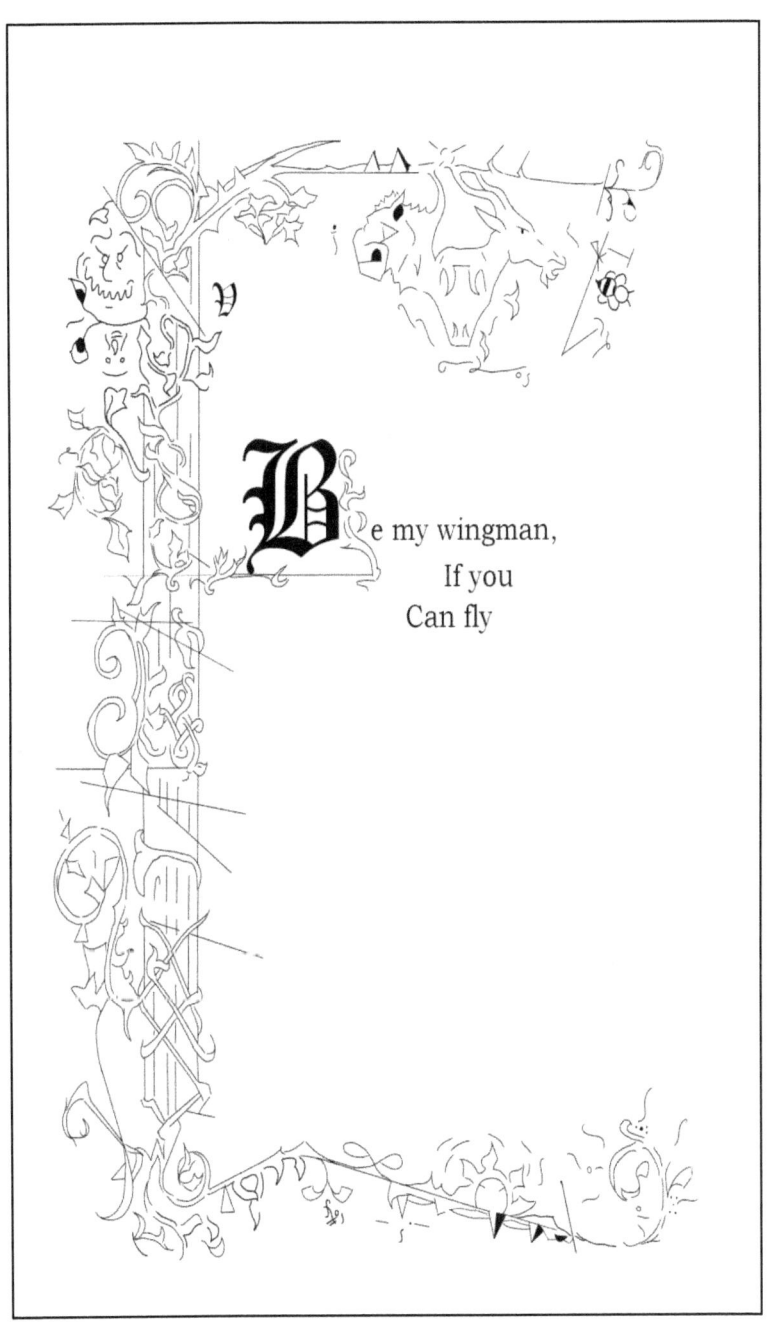

Be my wingman,
If you
Can fly

CHAPTER V
BE MY WINGMAN, IF YOU CAN FLY

"Whose car are we stealing this time?"

"I'm not stealing a car this time; this is too serious for that!"

"Forreal? I-"

"Nah, I'm just messing with you. I found this totally sick seventy-eight Trans Am that I promised myself I'd drive at least once. It's got this iridescent blue paint job that's been calling my name." Faaghira's smile was absolutely gorgeous.

"Which one is it?"

"Oh, you know; the only iridescent blue car here."

Scott scanned the parking lot until he saw it; an iridescent Firebird sticking out like a sore thumb. Faaghira placed a black box on the hood then pointed a remote at it. The doors unlocked and Faaghira signaled him to get in the car. He went without protest; rightfully so. Faaghira isn't the kind of person that you keep waiting. "I thought you would've broken through one of the windows. You're just full of surprises."

"The heck would I do that? I would have to get it fixed and I really don't feel like going through all that trouble. There's no need to wreck it if I can get around that."

"You mean like last time?"

"Too soon. "She opens the glove compartment to take out Queen's Jazz cd and puts it into the receiver. She skips to the sixth track and floors it as soon as Freddie starts singing. The tires screech against the pavement and sparks fly out when she makes the first turn. Scott holds on tightly to the seatbelt and the bottom of his seat, but the force is still enough to push him around.

"Fae, why do you always drive so fast?"

"To get to the other side." She seemed to be more serious

196

when she drove, but you'd be hard pressed to find her without at least of pinch of dry humor.

"Were you high the last time too?"

"Believe it or not, weed doesn't affect my driving at all; I'm always reckless. The best part is that I'm always 'wreckless'. Honestly, I don't even know how it's even possible for me to be so amazing." She slowed down when they got closer to the heart of the city (but not too much). She parked in front of a museum then got out the car.

"Won't you get a fine for doing that?"

"I personally won't, but that doesn't mean that other people won't. Aristocratic rules; call it privilege if that's your cup of barley. Besides, I don't have the time to go find an actual spot, and it doesn't make sense to follow one rule so I can commit *at least* five other crimes." She gently closed the door behind her and suggested Scott do the same. Scott slammed it out of spite, earning him a side eye. Scott smiled but it went away when she kept giving him that look. Scott held out his hand for Faaghira to hold it but she lowered a switchblade to her hand.

"Ooops." She shrugged her shoulders then pushed the blade back up her sleeve. He followed her down to a restaurant close to City Hall.

"Hold up" she paused. "This'll be dangerous; are you sure you can handle it?"

"Yeah, I got this. Like I said, I'm as tough as they come."

"I don't remember you saying that."

"You must be turning into an old woman."

"And that must be why you want to sleep with me so bad. Let's get something to eat real quick; I need a second to come up with a plan." They walked into the restaurant and just chilled out. They had some small talk and desert; afterwards they walked out to City Hall.

"Fae, why are we going through the front entrance?"

"Because that's the easiest way in. I'm not afraid of

anything. I'm going to rescue Safira and I dare *anyone* to fight me on that."

But of course, the guards at the entrance did just that. Try, that is; nobody had a hairs chance of stopping her. They didn't have any guns on them but they did have shock batons.

"Madam-"

"Just call me Faaghira; I'm not a fortune teller."

"Faaghira, we have orders to keep everyone off the premises until the terrorist is executed; even you."

"Get out my way." She casually brushed past the guard, but he struck her with the baton. Sparks shot off her arm where the baton hit. She shouted in pain but retaliated by elbowing him in the chest. Scott grabbed the guard and choked him out. The other guard shot at them, but Scott used the guard he was holding to shield him and Faaghira. Faaghira threw the kasuyu at the other guard with it landing in his abdomen. She cringed as the blood spilled out from his wound. She cleared her throat and went up to the top of the steps to sit down.

"I don't kill people, Scott. What did I just do?"

"Looks like you may have just possibly killed somebody. If it makes you feel any better I'll probably end up killing somebody too." He patted her on the back as a ~~really awkward~~ form of comfort. "He was probably an asshat too!"

"Damn it, Scott, stop trying to make me feel better about murder!"

"But is it making you feel better?"

"Have I ever told you that you're the worst? Because you're the worst. Let's keep going, there's a lot more where they came from." She got back to her feet and kicked the doors open. She left the kusuyu in the guard's body, instead opting for the gun she pried from his lifeless hands. She gently brushed her hand over the dead guard's eyes to close them. Scott grabbed a baton then ran after her. Faaghira looked around the room, seeing that the main hall was unguarded.

"Do you think this is a trap?"

"No, it feels more like a safety precaution."

"Are you being sarcastic or serious?"

"Yes. I don't know exactly where she'd be but I have an idea of where to find her. I was never aware there was ever a gallows here. Keep an eye out for where you see the most guards. Knowing Atticus he'll want to make this huge show out of cutting down the resistance."

"Is this all just for show then?"

"It's political, but it's real. That's why I have to get her out of here!" She whispered loudly to be stern but not loud enough to where it would alert anyone else that might be around. She peered closely at the ground; taking note of the faint boot and skid marks on the floor. "Let's go the other way."

"But why? Didn't you see those marks on the ground? How could this not be the way?"

"If this is the right way then we'll come back as soon as I'm sure this other side isn't right."

"Tell you what; I'll go the right way and you can come around when you find out that I was right." Scott spoke proudly.

She jokingly said to Scott, "Alright Power Man, just make sure you don't get yourself into any trouble that you can't get out of", then walked off to the opposite hall.

"I don't know what she's thinking, but this isn't a rabbit trail. And when I find Safira I'll try not to say I told you so."

She already left. "Shut up, nobody asked you." Asked me what? "Just shut up." Why you mad, bro? Scott went off being all standoffish and weird. He was hopping across the tiles on one foot to pass the time. He tripped on- nothing; maybe he slipped? He kind of looked around to make sure nobody (Faaghira) was watching then kept going like nothing happened. Well guess what Scott; something did happen and I know about it! And I would tell all your friends if they could hear me. "You don't even know my friends." Yet. I don't know your friends, yet. "Get back to doing your job, will ya?"

Ok I see how it is; so after sassing at me Scott went back to looking for Safira. He came across a guard (which he should've expected) that was patrolling the corridors. Not properly equipped for the situation, Scott did the sensible thing and- talked to them? Scott, wtf bro?

"Hey, you're not supposed to be here; are you?" the guard asked quietly.

"No, are you supposed to be here?"

"Yeah I work here; what are you doing here?"

"I've never been to City Hall and this is as good a night as any to go for it." He closed his eyes and paused abruptly; it was too awkward for words. It was borderline cringe-worthy. "Hey, do you want to sit down and talk or something?"

The guard was seriously confused. "I'm really not supposed to."

"Be honest with yourself; do you have something better to do?"

"Not really. I've been patrolling for hours and it's getting really boring. I'm supposed to making sure that nobody is on the premises except from Atticus and other guards. Right now I'm failing at my job.

"I wasn't asking all that; I just wanted to know if you were down for a conversation."

"Uh, I guess I have time, but you should leave immediately after that."

There was yet *another* awkward pause courtesy of Scott. He closed his eyes again and took a breath; the same awkward way that he did before. "Do you guys have any drinks around here?"

"There's orange juice in the conference room."

"No alcohol?"

"I'm not giving you alcohol."

"Fair enough." Scott sighed as they sat down.

"Have we met before?"

"Not before today; I don't think."

"Quick question: where's the conference room?"

"I'll tell you if you come back tomorrow."

"Good deal." He paused, again, then did this awkward clap thing. "This is awkward."

"Really? I don't think it was awkward until you started clapping. So what's your name.

"Scott."

"You're not going to tell me your name?" Scott looked hopeful.

"Nope. Okay well I'm going to get back to my job. Do I have to escort you out?"

"No, I know the way. Before you go, do you know where Safira is?"

"I need you to vacate the premises immediately before I have to take you in for questioning."

"Oh, my bad, I meant to say Safari. But I take it that's a no then?"

The guard took out a pair of handcuffs and tried to cuff Scott. Scott grabbed their shock baton and pressed it on them until they passed out. He walked down the hall where the guard came from earlier. He moved quietly through the halls, avoiding other guards while he searched for the conference room. Unlike that guard he so abruptly ended that conversation with, these ones have guns. These aren't your "good ol' American dream" guns; these are war kinds of weapons. These are the kinds that show exactly how out-gunned you are. These are the kind of guns that make some people want to get of rid of guns, period. These aren't the kind of guns that you try to be a hero around. Technically, he trying to be a hero around them. Keyword "around."

Scot carefully shifted around the corner to a door labeled 'conference'. He quietly opened it then closed it before anyone would notice.

The strange part was that there was nothing on the inside. It was pitch black and Scott was falling but there was literally no end in sight.

"Nice one." Chill with the sarcasm, fam. Aren't you worried at all? "Who? Me? Of course I'm worried" You don't seem to be panicking or anything. "Correction; I'm not screaming. I could die at any moment and I can't see shit; this is hella scary."

There was a muffled 'thud' that broke the fall. Scott stopped falling; he landed on- Hey Scott. "Yeah?" What broke the fall? "Something really soft; might be a mattress or a quilt. I can't tell; it's pitch dark in here." Don't you mean pitch dark? "No. Hey, is there anything about a light switch in the script?" No but it's for the best; I don't want to get turned on when I'm reading.

"I hate you." Scott couldn't walk on the 'something really soft; it might be a mattress or a quilt' without tripping.

"Damn it, I need a light!"

The lights turn on; the room is very reminiscent of a discotheque. But like a pre-school discotheque. I know that doesn't make sense, but hear me out on this one. It has a line of those adorable little basketball hoops, and adorable little plastic tables with those cute little blue chairs; and an adorable little...bar...with adorable little juice boxes on the shelf behind it.

"This is weird." Sure is. Is there is anyone at the bar? "Honestly I hope not." Go over there and find out. You know, what do you have to lose?

"I hate you even more." After professing his hate for me (how sweet), Scott took a seat on a stool at the counter. "Anybody home?" No response. He helped himself to whatever was behind the counter; in this case it was one of the many juice boxes. Um… baiiu juice boxes? Scott is lighting up like a soccer mom seeing the sales of the week at a local grocery store (hate welcomed). He put another one on the counter and slowly rested his head down.

"You're not one of the Authority Men! I don't recognize you; I vote you out!" a dry, quite annoying voice yelled at Scott. Scott picked his head up and gave the yeller a nice and slow side eye. The short man who the voice belongs to grimaced (bigly).

"Veto" Scott tipped the opened juice box forward and sipped loudly.

"No, no, my turn! Watch this; override!"

"Super Veto"

"Super override." The short man said in an annoying, childish voice.

"Super duper un-veto."

"Super duper un-override! Bing!"

"Thank you." Scott said in a whiny voice before taking another sip from the (alcohol filled) juice box.

The little man throws a stool then flips another one other. "You can't do this, it's not fair!"

"Ooo baby don't tell me I rigged the system; I might admit to it."

"Look, you can't be here; I won't stand for it!"

"Well I'll sit for it; feel free to pop a squat." Scott had a smug look while he sipped from the straw.

"That's it! You're outta here!" The little man yelled at him.

"No, that's' not it; I'm still here last time I checked."

"AUTHORITY MEN HEARING!" The little man clapped his hands and other child-sized men, or simply children with old faces, came riding in on tricycles; honking little horns mounted on the handlebars. They formed a half circle around the bar and honked their horns in rapid succession.

"I've been wondering where all the weird went. Part of me was actually starting to miss it a little; back when Roswell was a squirrel and the walls came to life to try to kill me. Now if I knew baby men would be riding trikes, I wouldn't've wanted that weirdness back. Seriously, this is too much; all their faces look like wilting sacks of potatoes. What makes it even worse is that it's those faces on toddler bodies. This is so repulsive that I literally can't vomit; I literally can't even vomit."

"Authority Men, there has been a problem of state emergency!" The main toddler-man combo deal, let's call him Newt, barked at his fellow toddler-men. "This boy" he pointed a grubby finger at Scott "has violated federal laws and infringed upon our natural rights by drinking *two* of our juice boxes!"

"For Christ's sake, I didn't even drink the other one; the fuck you mean?"

"That's the kind- that's the kind of vulgar language we've been trying to keep out of here! He's a common thug!" All the toddler-men combo deals _nearly_ spoke in unison, but they were slightly off which made it less creepy and a tad sillier.

"Even if I was a thug, the last thing I'd be is common. Take another shot, shortstacks."

Newt, clearly furious, threw his (small) fist up in the air. "I'll make sure you never see the outside of a cell!"

Scott calmly tore open the top of his juice box and tossed it in Newt's face. The toddler-man yelled (awkwardly) while covering his eyes. Newt's skin turned to a dusty orange tint. "Look! Look at what you did!"

"I can't _not_ see it. But if it's any consolation, you can always open conversations with 'Orange you glad to see me?' Heck, you could even make it a statement instead of a question. Forreal, use that."

204

"Get him to the courtroom NOW!"

Some of the toddler-men started to run into Scott's stool with their trikes but he kicked them over. "Don't touch me, creepy man children! I'll go to your stupid courtroom, but if any of you do so much as lay one finger on me, one finger, I will break all your arms with your trikes and stick you in the basketball hoops. So I leave you with two choices: You either keep those small, heathenous hands to yourselves; or you come and test me. I dare you, I fucking dare you."

"Follow us." The small men said (almost) in unison as they rode their tricycles away from the bar. Scott complied, but before he left he grabbed the other juice box then winked at Newt.

Scott walked alongside the convoy of tricycles to the courtroom which isn't a separate room. He slowed down when he saw the ones at the front slow down. He knelt down slightly and stuck out the baton at a wheel of one of the tricycles and the toddler-man on it was flung forward. The others ignored it so maybe this kind of thing was normal. The toddler-men got off their trikes and did this adorable little dance where they twirled around and kicked out their stubby legs. However, the cuteness factor shot down when taking into account their big old man faces.

They sat down in a large circle around Scott which is admittedly really creepy. Newt teabags one of the men to get inside the circle (he could've asked one of them to move) then does a split while scowling at Scott. Newts face was orange with anger which made the visual that much more cringe worthy.

"This super-predator proves us right in our safety initiatives. I don't even know how he got in here; this is our private room! Nobody else is supposed to be in here but us!"

Scott laughed at the toddler-man's tantrum. "What?! Look, you guys probably have more of a clue than I do. Seriously, I have no idea what life is anymore at this point.

Oh and props on the super-predator thing; it's been a minute since I heard that one. And as far as the juice box thing goes, you don't need the extra alcohol. Granted, I don't either, but that's not relevant. The point is that you've got more than enough so it shouldn't be a problem if I shave a bit off the top. Call me a freeloader if you want, but if you do that you might as well call me the n-word since you're going all out."

"There you go; all of them pull the race card! We're dealing with a real issue here, not some social crusade! The fact is that you committed a serious crime and you need to face the repercussions of it. Why do you people always have to make it about race? It's about upholding law and order!"

Scott's expression went through multiple stages. First he was confused; then in disbelief; then unamused. "The race card? *You* people? Social Crusade? Law and order? Goodbye; all of you are cancelled." Scott punt kicks Newt out of the circle, sending the other toddler-men into a flurry. They jumped on him, furiously kicking and punching Scott. He flung them off one by one until he was rid of them all.

"I didn't think you could do it, but somehow you managed to make this sound weirder than it actually was." Okay, geez man, I'm just trying to make it a little more interesting. "You don't have to go further than the fact that I'm fighting off toddler-men. Again, toddler-men. Don't make this any weirder than it is." Okay, whatever. So Scott walked off from the fray, but he made a quick stop back to steal some of their money and put their wallets in places that are too high for them to reach.

One of the toddler-men demanded that Scott to come back, but another one interrupted him saying that they shouldn't try and stop Scott. His argument was that they didn't have the resources to give them even a slight chance of winning. Another agreed with the first and made a little speech for it. After that a bunch of them were going to the center of the circle, rambling on about nothing in particular.

Scott got bored and left. And rightfully so, but he totally should've left earlier.

By now he was much further from where the arguing men were but they could still be heard. A very normal looking door was a few feet away from where he stood. What do you say Scott, are you going to take a chance with that door? "Probably; I don't really care at this point. But I guess I don't have another option, do I?" I don't see anything else in the script or the notes. Just press your luck and see where it takes you.

"I've been meaning to ask you about the script thing; how does it work? Can't you just tell me what happens next?" I wish I could but I can't read ahead. I can only read what's happening and what already happened. The story itself works like a page coming out of a typewriter; you don't see the entire thing until the writing is done. But unlike a typewriter, the desk the paper comes out of doesn't put words on anything. I think the whole thing was already written; I'm not sure. Instead of multiple papers it's just one increasingly long one; it's like a receipt. I already tried tearing it to see if it would stop, but a new paper picked up where the other one left off. And whenever you're not doing anything, like now, the story doesn't actually continue. Time passes but that's it.

"Hmm, any idea who the author is?" Not a clue. If I had any communication with them then I would've asked if there's any other way to get you back home. "Didn't Roswell mention something about hiring you?" Okay, about that; Roswell did hire me to narrate a children's book, but I didn't know he was a demon. He seemed like a normal guy to me. I never met the author but that wasn't anything special. When you're a narrator you don't usually meet the person who wrote the material; or at least I never do. "Is Roswell forcing you to do this?" Believe it or not, he isn't. If you remember, he said that he doesn't want me to go off script.

He doesn't care about me specifically; he just wants someone to finish the story. I can leave at any time but you're stuck here. I'm probably just as tired of this as you are but I refuse to leave until you get home. From what I've seen, you've got a lot of issues without all this extra crazy stuff. I think you should at least have the chance to fix that other stuff just the same as everyone else does. Though, whether or not you bother to fix anything is all up to you.

"I know there's one thing I've been avoiding that I need to handle, but I'll cross that bridge when I get there." And what would that be? "I'll check out where this door leads." Oh so we're playing that game? Scott obviously feels that I'm prying too much so he changed the subject by going through the door. On the other side of it was something that actually resembles a conference room. It's same kind of deal you'd see in the movies; long table in the center, chairs all around, the screen across from one end of the table; the whole nine. Someone had their head down on the table, snoring obnoxiously. Scott shook his head but otherwise ignored them. The screen is way more interesting. Way more; I'm saying that as if someone snoring is captivating. Displayed on the screen are live feeds from all the cameras in City Hall. Fae was on a few of them, which understandably worried Scott. Was she planning on getting seen? Did she care?

Scott quietly sat in one of the chairs and glued his eyes to the screen. Faaghira didn't look like she was trying to avoid the cameras. It looked like she was actually going out of her way to be in the range of every camera she was near. With that being said, she miraculously wasn't seen by any of the guards. She knocked out the guards she couldn't sneak around with the blunt of the kasuyu and avoided the rest. She tucked the unconscious guards away in corners, closets, and elevators. She was right about not needing Scott's help. Looks like she was also right about where Safira is being held. She's running into all the guards and Scott happened to be in the wrong place at the wrong time. As for the other one- people tend not to be so threatening when they're asleep.

"Shut up for a second, I think I see something." You think you see something? How are you not sure? Sight is something you have or you don't; there's not a gray area. "I was right; there's someone sneaking up on her. Quick, what's fastest way to where she is?" I don't know; didn't I tell you that I'm not omniscient? For the last time, I know just as much as you do. "Is there anything in the author's notes that can help me out?" Oh right, I know a little bit more than you do. Let's see, which chapter is this? "How am I supposed to know?" Right, sorry. You already saw Atticus on tv so that would make this *'Be my wingman, if you can fly'*. It says here that there's a hitman; public corridor, elevator. Does that make any sense? "Believe it or not, it kinda does. The person sneaking up on her is a hit man; they're in the public co- wait, I don't have time for this! I have to warn Fae!"

Scott whipped out his phone but he purposely dropped it after looking through his contacts. "I never got her number. Of course I wouldn't have a girl's number when I actually need it." Whoa, you doing alright there? "I-I don't know; that's not important right now. I have to help Fae in time." Scott threw the sleeping guard off his chair and threw it at the large set of windows. The glass didn't even bear a scratch. I get the whole thing with this being an emergency, but did you really need to throw the guard out of the chair? That was a little extra. "He's out cold. If he didn't wake up by now then it's obvious he was drugged. I just got an idea about how I'm going to get to her; give me a second." Scott picked up his phone and the guard's handgun then shot at the glass. There was definitely an impact, but the glass still didn't break.

"I didn't know this glass was so thick! Regardless, this is the fastest way out." He fired a large rectangle into the window then threw the chair at it again. It finally shattered, but it Scott grunted at the sound. Trigger from earlier? "You don't remember the shattering glass sounds from the abandoned house?" Doesn't ring a bell. "You seriously don't remember that? It wasn't that long ago." You must've been high when you heard whatever you did. "Never mind, I don't have time for this."

Scott carefully steps out of the window to avoid getting cut by the glass. To give an idea of what it probably feels like; this type of glass is essentially the super version of clamshell packaging. Despite his efforts, part of the bottom of his pants was torn. He rolled on the ground but he was quick to bounce back up. Now really isn't the time to play around or waste any time; he's got a friend to save. "Damn right." I forgot to ask, is my narrating getting in the way of your mojo or whatever? "No, it's actually got me feeling like a badass over here. Keep that going dude, I dig it!"

Scott scaled up to the second floor using the outer wall's mega pretentious architecture to his advantage. He's no Spider-Man, but he was quick enough to get the job done. He was holding on to a ledge when he realized that he didn't have a plan to get inside. "Okay, you can shut up now." No thanks. So about Scott not having a plan; he must be freaking out on the inside. It's a pretty high stakes game and he's not doing too hot right now. "I said you can shut up now." He can't hold himself up there forever; he has to think of something quick if he wants to save Faaghira and not break his legs. "Break my legs? I could die if I fall from here!" No, I'm pretty sure you would only break your legs from that height. But Faaghira could still totally die. "I SAID SHUT UP!" Scott uses his fist to break to punch right through that glass just like an action hero! That's some flimsy glass. "Damn it; that hurt a lot more than I thought it would!" And his hand is bleeding profusely like a mere mortal's. What did you think would happen you idiot? Well the window is broken so ignore that bloody hand and save your friend or else you would've busted up your hand for nothing.

"Yeah, getting to that part." Scott pulled himself through the window and he landed hard on broken glass. He shrugged it off (it'll be back later) and went rushed down a short set of stairs to find Faaghira. Sure enough, that sneaky guy from before is there in the hall but he's much closer to the staircase than he is to Faaghira. It doesn't look like she even noticed him. and Scott used that to his advantage. He rammed the guy into a storage closet before the dude had a chance to...um...do whatever he was planning on doing before. I don't even know if he was actually going to do anything bad. But on the other hand, he did look pretty suspicious. You know what, I'll go ahead and say this is justified.

The dude pulled a knife from his boot and stabs at Scott. It slashes the sweater, but the knife doesn't go deep enough to actually do any real damage. The attacker (don't know what else to call him) slashed at him again, but this time Scott was ready. He kicked the assailant (variety is the spice of life) in the shin then hit him with a strong jab to the chest. After knocking the wind out of him, Scott peeked out the door to see if Faaghira heard any of what just happened.

However, he only caught a glimpse of her before he was forced to the ground with an armbar. She looked highly invested in checking doors to notice anything else. I don't know whether or not this is good, but Scott was totally getting butt handed to him.

"What are you doing?" Scott whispered forcefully at the attacker.

"What am I doing? Why did you stop me from doing it?" The attacker said in the same hushed tone. Wait, why are they whisper-yelling?

"Why are you trying to kill Fae?"

"I'm not trying to kill Faaghira. By the way, aren't you Scott?"

"Yeah, who the hell are you?" Scott asked aggressively.

"Someone who's seen you around before. We have a common interest"

"I don't think you understand how this works; you're supposed to make yourself seem *less* suspicious. Sorry to say, but you're not doing such a good job."

The currently nameless guy was about to say something, serious or witty; I don't know; but he stopped for some reason. Maybe it clicked that disagreements aren't the best way to see your side of things. Scott shot Mr. No-name a suspicious look while he wasn't paying attention. Yeah, I'm not too sure of this guy either.

"So uh, mystery guy, I didn't catch your name? I think we should be on a mutual first name basis; mostly because it's pretty creepy that you know me and I have absolutely no idea who you are." Scott's still looking a little leery but it's not yelling 'you look suspicious'. The dark-skinned stranger stood still, deeply contemplating something, it seems. Scott took a moment to take some mental notes on the guy (I promise I'm not omniscient; this was legit in the script). He had rounded red sunglasses, a low fade, and a grizzly stubble. Scott's face grew sour for a moment after looking at it for too long.

"I can see your concern. Call me Donovan." Scott snapped back to reality as soon as Donovan (thank the goodness he has a name now) started talking.

"Donovan; got it. So remind me why you're here. I think I forgot somewhere after the part where you tried to kill me but before the part where you actually got shadier. Oh, and letting me go would be nice."

"So around the part where I asked you why you were trying to stop me." Donovan let go of Scott's arm, dropping him on the floor.

"One hundred percent. That's the one." Scott stood up and dusted off the sweater.

"I'm here to help the rebellion. Faaghira doesn't support us anymore and I don't want her to swoop in and take credit for what we did. I know she's only here to rescue the commander, which I have no problems with; but she doesn't care about everyone else here. That's why I couldn't let myself stay home tonight. So are you with me or not?"

Scott had an uncertain face; the kind you might get when someone pushes an ultimatum on you. "I'll shadow you and I'll figure out if I'm down with that." Oh, that's actually not what I was expecting. Okay, cool; that's cool.

They passed right over Faaghira before she disappeared into the next hall. Scott looked down from the walkway at where Faaghira had passed through with a sense of longing. The moment was brief, but after getting to know Scott, I wouldn't expect any kind of reflection to last more than a couple of seconds. On the other end of the walkway was a rather dull room with light gray walls and no furniture to speak of. It's way out of place with the extravagant, quite gaudy aesthetic of the rest of City Hall. In this gray room are five cells; each at the moment with its own prisoner.

Donovan took a ring of keys from the side of his belt and tried to unlock one of the cells. Oh, but guess what; nothing happened! It didn't work! Scott could help laughing a little; he didn't even flinch when Donovan got pissed. Scott actually started laughing harder, this time with an obnoxiously hearty voice; probably out of spite. Donovan clenched his fist while looking for another way to open the cells; a surefire way to keep your cool. Scott walked over to a corner, sat down, and played two drawn out games of tic tac toe on a napkin he got from out his pocket while Donovan kept looking for ways to open the cells. After about five minutes of trying, Donovan slips into the next room over and three cells slide open with a loud click.

Scott looks up to see the prisoners after finishing his matches; and what he saw next was shocking! Jk, I hate seeing clickbait articles like that. But it was strange that Donovan hadn't come back yet. It was also strange that the prisoners looked like they were on some serious crystals. They were akin to walking corpses; dry, fading skin; just enough muscle to still be alive. Their clothes are worn and tattered; adding to how uncomfortable this makes this scene (at least for me). They sat in the corners of their cells; staring at Scott with their harsh eyes. They were unnerving, but perhaps the most terrifying part is that they aren't soulless; there's a person trapped somewhere under all that madness. Horror pulled down on Scott's face, but neither him, nor the prisoners budged. Scott slowly stood up, but both exits closed off and locked shut. He slowly sat back down while keeping a close eye on the sickly prisoners. Their stares could make just about anyone shiver and I'm positive that they did that to Scott too.

"Hey, what's up guys? You doing alright?" But of course Scott wouldn't let on something as stupid as fear… or logic. All the prisoners got up and shuffled towards Scott. It's apparent that they're not friendly, I repeat, they're not friendly. "You're looking a little lean there. Sorry, I ran out of snacks but I do have some food for thought left over. Just give me a second." He emptied his back pockets and small pieces of lint fell out. "Damn, I left the rest of it outside. I don't mean to be rude; uno momento por favor." He pushed down on the door handle to see if it was still locked (surprise, it was) and gave up afterwards. "Do you like games? We can play tic-tac toe or something else if you want. I've got a few more napkins if you've got another game in mind. What's that? No? Okay, can you help me get out of here?" The prisoners went from frail, sickly people to angry, frail, and sickly people. They attacked him with furious punches, but Scott was able to dodge a few of them so he doesn't look nearly as bad as he could've looked.

He punched one of them in the face, but after hearing a loud crack during the impact he backed away from them. The sight of those people; standing, unflinching, unreasonable, unnerving; but somewhere in there is a person that was probably just like anyone else. Blood is running out of the gash Scott put in that person's face but they didn't even bat an eye. They don't care; they don't care that they're hurt. A tortured soul full of directionless anger is a heartbreaking sight; so much so that it's probably why Scott backed off.

Scott frantically tried to open the door to the next room where Donovan disappeared to, but unlike the other handle, this one broke off. "Donovan, you little bitch! I swear when I get my hands on that guy…I'll probably throw him out a window or something!" It was then that Scott had a eureka moment. There's a window in the room, albeit smaller than the other ones he passed (through) earlier. He tapped on the glass and came to the conclusion that the different sound he heard meant that this isn't plexiglass. "Ok so before I go I've gotta ask; why are you trying to fight me? I don't have any beef with you."

One of the prisoners finally spoke; sounding far more regular than they looked. "You and the rest of the bastards that put us here think you can do anything and get away with it. We may not be able to do much anymore, but we'll be damned; all of us; if we have the chance to do something, anything to fight back!"

Scott looks really stressed out right now. I can't blame him for it either; he just walked into a room and some sick angry people are telling him that everything wrong is his fault. "Thanks for backing me on this one. Look guys, I'll tell you this exactly one time: I have nothing to do with these people. I'm sorry that you got screwed over but don't pin that on me. That guy in the other room turned on me, but I actually saw that coming; that guy was sus like no other. If you're gonna go after anyone, go after him. Also, I punched a window and my hand kinda still hurts. And my legs are *maybe* hurting the *tiniest* bit."

However, none of them stopped attacking him. Scott backed into the window and waited for another punch to be thrown his way. Oh I see where this is going.

"Dammit!" one of the prisoners yelled in frustration after their fist hit the glass. Another prisoner charged at Scott but Scott (barely) dodged the hit. The impact shattered just enough of the glass for Scott to jump through without getting cut (too much). He dropped on an awning, but it broke as soon as he landed. Scott quickly grabbed on to a ledge to keep from falling on the solid concrete below. The ledge extended over to another window which could possibly be for the next room. "Will you shut up already?" Oh well excuse me for doing my job.

After giving me an unnecessary amount of sass (which is any amount of sass to be honest), he carefully made his way over to the next window. Peeking in, he saw Donovan poking away at a tablet of sorts. He knocked on the window and it startled Donovan (obviously) and fired a shotgun at Scott. Wait, so where did the shotgun come from? "I guess that serves me right for being obnoxious, this time anyway. It works every other time." Yeah, I think your definition of 'works' is way different from the rest of the world. "Hey, shut it bookworm! I'm trying not to die over here." Ooo, bookworm! Is that what you call the nerds when you're at the playground sipping on juiceboxes? " Hey, I'm just trying to do my job. I can't concentrate with you running your mouth every ten seconds!" Freaking hypocrite.

The bullets shattered the glass (how much shattered glass is in this chapter alone?) and after three more relentless bursts, the shooting stopped. Donovan stepped close to the window and aimed the shotgun over the ledge. Scott tugged on the shotgun, causing Donovan to drop it.

"Come on dude, why do you wanna kill me so bad? Do you really wanna add to those black on black crime statistics?"

"God, why are you so annoying?" Donovan sighed.

"Gasp! Don't tell me you're *a coon?*" Scott said sarcastically (read obnoxiously). He pulled himself up but his hands got smacked before he could pull himself through the window. Donovan tried to punt kick Scott but it failed miserably. Scott pulled his leg and Donovan slammed against the concrete ledge.

"God what the fuck, man?" Donovan yelled.

"Oh ok, so you can pull a shotgun on me and that's totally chill, but I make you fall on your back and I'm the problem. Now tell me; how much sense does that make?"

Instead of giving any sort of rational response, he kicked at Scott again, but this time Scott stomped on Donovan's knee. Donovan yelled in pain, but Scott didn't much of a reaction at all. "You know, I won't kill you; I don't kill people, at least not intentionally. What you really need to know is that I'm the dude that fights to send people to the hospital; I'm not out to teach anybody a lesson. I really want to hurt you, but I'm a pretty nice guy so I'll give you a warning; turn yourself in to whoever you'd have to turn yourself into and keep yourself from getting any broken bones. If you don't then I'll hurt you. It'll suck, trust me.

And of course Donovan didn't listen. And of course Donovan got that beatdown he was promised.

"You people don't understand; I want a future for Louisiana. The rest of the states are collapsing because they don't have a serious leader. I don't want my home to fall like the rest of them. I don't agree with everything he says but Atticus is our only hope for keeping things the way they are. That's why I can't let anyone in the resistance get any of their plans off the ground. If they kill him then they'll be able to pat themselves on the back while the rest of us burn in the chaos!" And of course Donovan had something else to add.

"First off, I'm not even part of the resistance. Second-" Donovan cut in with more ranting, but Scott had enough.

"Yo, look at me. Look at me. Shut up, okay? Nobody told you to interrupt me; and if they did then tell them that they can come get this beating too. Now, second; if the way things are is what you're trying to keep then it looks like you've got nothing to lose. This place is a shit-storm, Atticus is a dick; from what Fae told me, the majority of people here are poor. Racism, classism, *and* an aristocracy? This doesn't sound so great to me. Back home I only have to deal with two of those…I think. My girlfriend knows more about this than I do; I only pick up some things she mentions."

"This isn't about race, this is about security! Everyone knows that Louisiana means business because Atticus is the real deal!"

"Bud, when's the last time you looked in the mirror? We're both black; it's always about race. And I've been hearing a lot about this Atticus character, but nobody told me exactly what it is he's even trying to do. He doesn't strike me as the kind of guy that has a plan other than being in power. And while I'm not the blackest person you'd ever meet, even I can tell you're a sellout. A coon, for better words."

Scott left Donovan there, bruised and battered but not close to the hands of death. Even after the beating, Donovan had the nerve to keep talking. "You're making a mistake!"

"Coon." Scott uttered while walking away. Donovan tried to stand up, but his legs gave out on him. Scott went back and kicked him in the shin then went back through the window and on to the next room. He shut the door behind him, shutting out the sound of Donovan's pain-induced yelling.

This next room is fully furnished with a small coffee table and a couple of chairs. There's a window (why are there so many windows?) covered by velvet curtains. Light shone through slits in the curtain and spread through on the table and the floor. The has a renaissance style aesthetic to it; a visual that's totally out of place with the rest of City Hall. There is no point to this room. There's nothing noteworthy in here; teapots in a cabinet along with china sets, a stack of newspapers, a small green vase with flowers; why is this room even here?

"I don't even know. I'll just leave. This is stupid." So we agree on something. There's another door through here so see where that leads. "Yeah alright. Not like I have anything else to do. Captain coon is one room down and the three stooges are just two rooms over. Can't go anywhere but forward; not that I'd want to go anywhere but forward."

Scott opened the door and it led back into the series of hallways. He stopped to look down at the floor of the entrance... like a weirdo. Yeah, I get it, it's fancy and shiny. You don't see floors like this every day; what's the big deal? "I like being weird sometimes, you know?" Knowing you, I can believe that. "Partially. Partially knowing me; we're not friends." Hmm, I wonder why.

Scott put his middle finger up at the ceiling (at me) and went down a set of stairs at the end of the hallway (The architect that designed this place needs to unlearn how to do architecture. Seriously, this place is a maze more than a City Hall!). He found his way back to the main entrance and after standing and waiting for Faaghira for a minute or so; he went outside and sat on the steps.

He was on his phone playing more faux Tetris to pass the time when a gigantic banner draped over a building across the street. At first he didn't notice it, but when he did... he shrugged and went back to his (apparently very intense) game of fake Tetris (Fetris?). Another banner rolled down over that one, but this one pushed a gust of wind all the way to Scott. He just turned on his side and went back to his game. Another banner dropped over that one and a stronger gust of wind blew at Scott. He ignored this one too, but another banner dropped down and the wind smacked the phone out of his hand. Scott finally acknowledges the banner. It reads:

'You were supposed to look at the first banner and so now you're getting all this other crap. So I want you to know that you can't change those people. Oh and things are about to get really weird. Really weird. I've been slacking all this time. Sorry about that; I was busy setting up the next surprise. There probably won't be any more after that. I've got a lot going on. Love you and hate you- Scott'

"Wait, Me? I didn't write that? And what surprise?" You don't get banners like that at home? "If I did then I never noticed it." Well maybe this is for some other guy named Scott. It's a common name, dude. "You got me on that one. One of my best friends' names is Scott." Really? "Nope, gotcha! I'm the only Scott I know." You're a bitch, you know that? "I'm cool but even I don't think I'm that great. But on a serious note; do you know what that other surprise is Roswell was talking about?" What makes you think it was him? "There's a poorly drawn smiley face on the bottom of the banner. Besides, who else would do something like that?"

Faaghira walked out of City Hall with Safira beside her. The tall, celestial, now champagne-haired woman was unharmed and she's still just as threatening as before. I feel I'm doing something wrong just look at her. She displays a type of steely aggression that isn't exactly threatening, but it's far from inviting. Her bulky figure made her that much more intimidating, but surprisingly none of that undermines her beauty at all. In fact, it adds to it. She has her hair in a high pony tail and the way her messy, wavy voluminous hair

220

just flows and gosh I better stop because I'm gushing. Someone please help.

"Some help you were." Faaghira said (somewhat) jokingly to Scott. She sat next to him and motioned for Safira to do the same, but Safira crossed her arms and gave Scott a judging look.

"What? I didn't even do anything."

"Precisely." Safira was condescending in her response but she wasn't fully focused, as the banners caught her attention.

"Don't mind Safira; she's always edgy. But what *were* you doing all this time? Normally I don't care, but this time it actually *is* my business. And what happened to your clothes? What happened to my sweater?"

"I got lost and ran into a hitman, I think. Then there were some really messed up people that attacked me; prisoners, they said. When I found my way back to the entrance I figured I'd just sit out here and wait for you to come out."

Faaghira glanced at Safira and Safira grunted and rolled her eyes. "You've never been here before so you-" Faaghira gave Safira a piercing glance, then Safira cleared her throat and continued. "Are pardoned. You are pardoned."

Faaghira gave a nod of approval before taking over the conversation. "Alright, tell me exactly what happened when we get back to my place, but right now I'm curious about those banners. Who put them there?"

Scott picked up his phone and checked to see if the screen was cracked. "Great, no cracks. I was worried for a second." He unlocked his phone and went straight to that stupid fake Tetris game but it crashed then uninstalled. He furrowed his brow and stared at the screen in disbelief.

"Earth to Scott; I asked about the banners." Faaghira said while she nudged him in the shoulder.

"Banners, right. Those are all from Roswell. I didn't see him put them there but I don't know who else would. It's also addressed to me, so there's that. If you wanna know why he did it then you're outta luck on that one. That dude doesn't make any sense."

"You two have a lot in common." Safira spoke in the same condescending way, leading Faaghira to give yet another scolding look. "Why are you looking at me like that? That wasn't mean, it was just an observation."

"Come on, let's get out of here." Faaghira walked off to her car and the others followed. Scott's eyes were drawn to the city for the entire walk. And no, it wasn't a long walk, but his eyes were captivated by the colors and the smells and sounds. It was one of the other parts; one of the ones that's *not* Bourbon Street. The cars riding past; the lights and the colorful buildings; the wonderful food; the wonderful people; all of it transcends the chaotic infrastructure of the government and the economy. Scott lit up with glee and excitedly took Faaghira by the hand.

"Can we go and see the city? You haven't taken me out yet and this place looks super dope!" Scott spoke with childlike glee and Faaghira looked flattered. He was like a kid begging their mom to take them to a theme park. However, whatever feeling was ruined by the seemingly sudden appearance of Atticus (He was actually there the entire time. There were no words exchanged for what appeared to be ages.) Safira stretched her arms out and cracked her knuckles while staring Atticus dead in the eyes with an unblinking; piercing gaze. Atticus looked down then turned his attention to Faaghira and cleared his throat.

"The barrier between order and what is natural has been broken and rebuilt over and over again. The law has always been unacceptable in our inherent nature, but it's the only thing that keeps us grounded. But I wasn't surprised when I heard that my iniquitous niece was rescuing the freakish leader of the immoral rebellion. I understand that freedom takes opposition, but when responsibility is beaten to death, freedom is in danger. A rebellion is a danger to an established democracy; *especially when such a thing is led by a freak.* A mistake simply makes more mistakes. The rebellion doomed itself for failure the moment it began. Such a disgusting, incompetent, overall nasty leader could never help the people who were asking for their help. The lazy and greedy people of any society always rely on the weak-minded to represent them. And luckily, they've found a snake rise from the ashes and they took it as their own." He then turned back to Safira. This time he had confidence that was lacking before; marked by a proud smirk on his off-putting, partially wrinkled face. His old beady eyes appeared to have a brand new spark of life.

Safira stood with her arms crossed, giving the same look as before. She was unafraid of whatever Atticus would do next, but she was also calm. Don't get me wrong, she still looks intimidating, but she doesn't look close to pissed, well kind of. She doesn't look any more pissed than normal.

"But much to my surprise, this is no garden snake. Their poison is fatal, but fortunately for the people, I have the cure." After finishing his clearly antagonizing speech, Atticus quickly pulled a shotgun from his pant leg. The spectacle caused everyone to step back in fear; everyone except for Safira. She still stood with her arms crossed; unflinching and unamused.

First Atticus aimed the gun directly at her, but when he didn't get a reaction he pressed the barrel directly on her forehead. Faaghira began to reach her hand out to her, but when Safira gave her a cold glance Faaghira rested her arm and buried her head into Scott's shoulder. Scott clenched his fist but he soon relaxed it when Faaghira rested her hand on it. Scott looked angry, but this appeared to be a different kind of anger. This is the anger of inaction; the anger of helplessness.

Safira's reaction was more terrifying than that gun on her

forehead.

She blinked slowly, exactly one time. Then she spoke in a calm yet forceful way.

"I can kill you. You already know that. A crutch by your leg couldn't stop me if I wanted you dead right now." She walked away from the gun and leaned against the Faaghira's car. "Come on you two, we're leaving." Faaghira raised her head from Scott's shoulder and looked at Safira with disbelief. She looked back and forth between Safira and Atticus with an expression that could easily be described as flabbergasted. Atticus is just as stunned as Faaghira is. It took him a while to put the shotgun down after she stepped away from him.

"Come on Scott, I'll take you to go see the city another time." Scott reached out his arm just a little as he usually did when they held hands. She would normally grab hold of it and sometimes even interlace fingers, but this time she went to the car and got in the driver's seat as if Scott was completely invisible. Atticus snickered and Safira immediately shut him down before Scott even had the chance to react.

"I'm still here. Shut up if you want me to stay over here and keep your arms working so you can put that oversized slingshot back in its holster." Scott thanked Safira, but she ignored it, got in the backseat and gently closed the door. Scott sighed as he got in the passenger's seat. Faaghira adjusted the rear view mirror then sped off from City Hall. She took a glance in the mirror before the building was completely out of sight and saw Atticus put the shotgun back into his pant leg. She smiled briefly but it faded into a serious face. Scott gazed out the window after seeing the rather uninviting expressions of the other two people in the car.

Scott awkwardly bobbed his head to the silence that was blasting in the car. He looked at Safira and opened his mouth to say something but she cut him off before he had the chance.

"You have a problem."

"No, I'm fine. I don't want to start anything with you."

"That didn't even sound like a question; what made you think it was a question?" She reclined in her seat then stretched her left arm and folded her arms again.

"Hey I'm just trying to be nice. Me and Fae communicate with each other and that's why we get along so well. But you; you're always mean for no reason. That's probably why you and Fae couldn't last. You don't care about anyone do you?"

The car began to slow down but there were no stop signs or traffic lights. They weren't near the complex either.

"Scott, please stop." Faaghira said shyly. It's odd seeing her like this; worried and silently panicking.

The car started back at its previous speed and everyone was silent again.

"No, this is something you need to hear. Things suck right now, I get that. But there's no reason to be a bitch about it. We all deal with tough times and I can guarantee that someone's got it worse than you. You can't just push away people that are trying to help and expect everything to turn up."

Safira kept looking ahead as she had for the whole ride. She muttered "Pull over", with all the calmness and force she normally exuded.

The car slowed down but it quickly sped up again. "No. We're almost at my place so I'm not pulling over. I know you're both hard headed and you'll settle things however you will, but just don't come to my condo without getting all of that negativity out. I'll leave the door open so you know which one it is." Everyone was quiet for the rest of the ride. When they arrived in the parking lot Fae shut off the engine and left the car. Scott and Safira got out and shut their doors but they didn't follow the gorgeous dark-skinned woman inside.

The scene is tense; the mildly ignorant black guy and the intimidating, seemingly titanic, and far stronger woman with brown terra-cotta colored skin. She was only a head taller, but she appeared to tower over him. Still, he didn't wince or shudder.

"Every time I see Fae anywhere near you she's always different. She becomes a shell of the person that I know. What happened between you two? What did you do to her? I swear if you hurt her I'll-"

"You'll keep talking at me until it makes you feel better. That's the most you'll do. You don't understand and you wouldn't even if I dumbed it down for you. You don't know her nearly as well as I do, so don't come at me with that 'she's different when she's around you' crap. She's showing you exactly what she wants you to see. And for the record, this is the first time you've even seen us anywhere near each other. That Fae you saw back there, the one that buried her head into your shoulder, that's a real part of her that she was trying to keep you from seeing. She had no reason to show you; she's vulnerable. You don't know what she's like; you don't know anything about her."

"That's not true."

"Yeah? So you know her last name?"

"Working on that one."

"Her favorite color?"

"Something on the spectrum between very dark and extremely light."

"Sexuality."

"Easy. Fae's bisexual." He's confident and bold, but...

"Wow" she said as Scott smiled proudly. "That couldn't be further from the truth. She's asexual but she's bi-_romantic_. There's a big difference between the two."

"She seems pretty sexual to me. Maybe she lied to you."

"Most people love sex. They love it so much that they see

it as necessary for stability in a relationship. And what does someone do if they don't like sex but want an intimate relationship? They either give in or they let their partner get their jump in other people's pants. But the problem with that is that their partner could end up liking sex more than their own relationship. Tell me, when did you start 'falling for her'?"

"It's a little tough to explain. I liked her when I first saw her but when I spent more time with her the more I was attracted to her."

"And you were hoping that this time would lead to…"

"I didn't know where it would lead, but I was hoping that we would have a stronger bond."

"Sex. If she wouldn't have sex then you would've seen her as a waste of a beautiful body. You're not the first person she put on a pedestal. But the other ones made sex more important than emotions. She wouldn't want me to tell you any of this because she wouldn't want to drive you away. The only reason she has so much sex is because that's what everyone seems to want. She cares about people and their feelings. She hates feeling lonely, so she'll put up with things so she can have someone to love at the end of the day. She's stupid like that, but I digress."

"She didn't seem sex repulsed to me. Not too long ago she initiated-"

"Tmi. Did she even want to or was she trying to get something out of the way?"

"Well she obviously wanted to."

"You don't know shit, do you? I've been trying to protect her from people like you, but it never works. I guess I'm the stupid one for trying. She always falls for it."

"Maybe she's not falling for anything. Maybe she's dealing with one thing to get to what she wants."

"Really? Thanks for clearing that up because I didn't *just* say that. The point is that she's not getting one over on anyone. All they have to do is cuddle up and send her flowers to get all the sex they want. She'll never admit it because she's getting her emotional needs met."

"You can't generalize me off of what other people did. I'm not them; I actually give a damn about her."

"If you knew how many times I heard that you'd quit trying to convince me. When every person that comes along says that they're different, she believes it. And another thing; there's nothing wrong with me because I don't fit your model of a person. I'm serious; I hardly smile; but I'm doing more than you ever have. Now with that being said, don't step out of line." Scott was about to speak but Safira cut him off sharply. "Cross me in any way shape or form and I guarantee that you'll get messed up. As for Fae, she's grown; she can handle herself. Just don't take advantage; it's a shitty way to treat anyone."

Safira walked past him without bumping into him or brushing his side. She walked past him as if he wasn't even there. Scott looked focused as she took each step. Heck, I can't blame him, I did too. But Scott, she pretty much hates your guts. "Doesn't mean I don't like watching her leave." You can't see it but I'm shaking my head at you. (But I'm low key congratulating you for having exquisite taste.)

"Thanks bud, I should go and catch up with Safira. I know it's complicated, but I have to go see Fae anyway. And I don't want it to be awkward between me and Safira if we're gonna be working together." Scott, I hate to be the one to break it to you but it's too late to keep things from getting awkward. "No sweat, I got this." With that he went on his way to catch up with her.

"Hey Safira, wait up!" She wasn't walking fast, nor was she far ahead of him but he still yelled out to her. She stopped but she didn't say anything or even look at Scott. She waited for him but when he was close enough she kept moving. When the entered through the revolving doors they were

228

greeted by the same black dude that served as the security(/concierge?). He came really close to almost smiling, and he's seen Scott before, so that one must've been for Safira.

Scott naturally turned to the stairwell but Safira stopped him in his tracks with a condescending "No." She kept walking down the lobby and he followed suit. She stopped at a part of the wall that didn't look different from any other. She ran her hand down the side of it then knocked on the wall. The wall slid back to reveal the interior of an elevator. Ok, so it was really an elevator and not a wall? What is this, the Batcave?

Safira got in the elevator first, and after just standing there stupidly for a moment, Scott went in too. As for the interaction between the pair; awkward is an understatement. There's no doubt that it was Scott's fault. He acted like he was looking around and checking out the elevator he went on his phone a couple of times, but it was one of those weird 'checking the time/ secretly seeing if anyone texted me' things.

"So why *didn't* you kill Atticus? I mean you had the chance. He was right there. If he's the only person in your way then why didn't you just kill him?" But then he did that.

"You don't get it. He's a problem; I want him out, but I can't do anything about it yet. If he dies another Atticus, or possibly someone else that's worse somehow would step up. If I kill him and I take his place then I'd become him. Believe when I say that this isn't the first time I could've killed him. If the systems he made stay in place then everyone, no matter how well-meaning, will be horrible at the very least. He's been in power so long that it's about taking down an entire government rather than just one person. Pretty much everybody would have to be with me on this one for it to work. That didn't happen and I doubt that it ever will in my lifetime."

"Then Saff, what's the point of all this if you know it won't work?"

"Okay, let's get this straightened out; my name is Safira. You will call me Safira and nothing else. Next; this is an uphill battle that no one can win alone. I started it and I know I won't finish it. Soon enough it'll be time to pass the torch. Until then I have to make sure there's something to pass on."

Safira was silent again.

"Yeah. So where'd you get your jacket? It's pretty dope." But Scott kept talking. The guy is allergic to shutting up.

She didn't answer until the elevator doors slid open. Scott kept doing that awkward head nod that he's been doing every time he gets uncomfortable. She had a puzzled look when she saw the act, but she quickly disregarded it and returned to looking ahead with her arms crossed; quietly judging Scott.

"Radius. It's a local clothing store." She left the elevator so fast that for a moment, Scott hadn't even realized that she wasn't still there. When he snapped back to reality he rushed out to catch up with her.

"Huh, I'm surprised you're warming up to me so fast." Scott carried on in his slightly annoying but sort of charming way.

"Don't get it twisted; I still don't like you. You asked me a question and I answered it. Be that as it may, I won't deprive a community owned business of more profit." But none of that charm seemed to work on her.

"So what's the big deal with community owned stuff anyway?" But he kept trying anyway.

She walked on with determination in her step; seemingly ignoring Scott's constant tries to…to…wait a second, what is he even trying to do? She doesn't like him!

"The more you open your mouth the harder it is to understand why she likes you."

"Jealous?"

230

"You actually wouldn't be too bad if you weren't so annoying." She stopped abruptly then continued. "And if you were someone else."

Scott was squaring up, but he was walking behind her and she didn't care enough to pay him any mind. But he kept talking anyway, because of course he would.

"You know what? I would fight you if you weren't a girl." But then he mumbled under his breath "And if you weren't buff."

"And you still wouldn't stand a chance." I'd say she shot him down pretty good. She also still doesn't care. The rest of their walk through the corridors were silent, as Scott was too distracted by the ice he'd need for his burn.

"Shut up."

"Come again?"

"I was just thinking out loud. Disregard. But you have pretty hair. I like the new color; it looks good on you." Scott mumbled loudly enough to be heard but quietly enough to show how scared he was.

The tension was brief because they arrived at a unit with an open door. Faaghira came out to meet them at the doorway. She was wearing a black sweatshirt with "Amadeus" in bold comic sans font and plaid boxers in lieu of pants. Scott was staring and it was so obvious. Everyone could see that he was staring. But nobody said anything about it. Yet another awkward moment.

"Did you get it all out?" But luckily Faaghira cut the moment short before it got too weird.

"Yeah. What was is it I was supposed to get out?" But Scott comes in with the rebound! Will Faaghira still be able to pull through?

"Did you and Saff air out all your issues?" She was caught between a smirk and a frown, resulting in an emotionally ambiguous expression. "I'm not letting you in if you didn't chill out."

Safira rolled her eyes and brushed past Faaghira, who didn't seem the least bit surprised.

"Okay, yeah. Feel free to walk into my home; that's cool too."

Scott took Faaghira by the hand and reassured her that there wouldn't be any problems.

"There's still some left, but hey, we can ignore that for now."

"But we're picking it back up later." Safira called out while she was at the fridge pouring a tall glass of strawberry milk.

"Absolutely." Scott shouted back to her with a smile, but it disappeared when he saw Faaghira facepalm.

"You two...you two are so stressful."

"That's why you love us." Scott and Safira spoke at the same time, as if one was trying to beat the other to the punch. Safira closed the fridge and sat down at a small round table at the back of the room. Faaghira left the doorway went to fridge and Scott followed suit. She already let go of his hand but he was still just as close to her, so not much of a change on his part.

"By the way I forgot to mention, but I love your aesthetic. Your buns are always cute." Scott was trying to pour on the wit while sitting on the countertop, waiting for Faaghira to get whatever she was looking for from the fridge. See, she has her hair in a bun right now; same as she did last time. I think that's her 'home' look.

"Make more of those corny puns and you'll be getting exactly as much sex as you did last time."

"And I'll shut up now." Finally! Finally somebody got him to shut his mouth!

Faaghira bent down and leaned further into the fridge; a movement that peaked Scott's interest, no doubt. She snapped back up with an ice-cold beer bottle wrapped in a paper towel. "Got it. Beer's a guilty pleasure."

Scott blinked a few times and rubbed his eyes. "Oh yeah,

I drink a little bit every now and then. Not too much though; too much juice can mess you up real good." And Scott's pants should catch on fire any minute now. With all the alcohol he downs, he might as well be a liquor bottle.

Faaghira went to the table at the far corner of the room, pulled out the chair, turned it around and sat down. She looked at Scott and patted the seat next to her. He was there in the blink of an eye. He might as well have teleported across the room.

"Beer is nasty; you still have poor taste. Okay, so the elephant in the room; Atticus could've stopped us. He had the chance to cut all the opposition down right there. Plus he was alone. He's stepping up his game for something. Sending me to the gallows was a bold move. That's not the kind of thing you do without a bigger plan. This is especially weird because as strong as I am, he proved that he could've pressed this kind of stint at any point in time. So why now?" Safira took a sip from her glass of strawberry milk and gestured to Faaghira to carry on the conversation. She opened her mouth and-

"You sure you didn't overhear anything that could help us figure this out?" Scott stole the mic; again.

"That wasn't an invitation, but since we're on the same side I'll humor you for now. They intentionally didn't say anything to me when I was there. I don't think the guards thought I wouldn't go to the gallows, but Atticus runs a tight ship; he rules by fear. I wouldn't put it past him to kill anyone that even looked at me for too long. But if it's any consolation to me, the place they were keeping me in was pretty nice. It was basically a ballroom. And since I have to say it out loud; Faaghira, what do you think about this situation?" Safira gave Scott a quick but intense side eye then continued drinking from her glass.

Faaghira twisted off the cap of her beer then flicked it on the table. She cleared her throat and leaned forward; draping

her body over the back rest. "Then we'll have to stop him from making his next move; whatever it is. I have an idea of how to get him out of office, but I can't do it by myself."

Safira put the glass down, crossed her arms and leaned back in her chair. She sighed and bowed her head. "Look, I owe my life to you; you know that. But the rebellion isn't taking your help anymore."

Scott gave Safira a steely look and pounded his fist on the table to get everyone's attention. "Now correct me if I'm wrong; but aren't you the one who just told me that the rebellion can't do anything on its own?"

"You wouldn't understand. The rebellion is more symbolic than active. For a lot of people it's the spec of sunlight that pierces through a gray sky. Who would want to know that one of the clouds is thing that'll help save them?"

Faaghira took in some more beer and pressed it back down to the table with enough force that the sound echoed through the open room. "And your freedom fighters sure have been doing a bang-up job of stopping The Junta. We have our own issues, sure, but this isn't about us. If you want to make this about us, then fine. I would rather try and fail miserably than watch people suffer when I know I can help. I have the chance to do something and I'll be damned if I let your petty shit stop me!"

Safira finally looked up at Faaghira but still looked closed off. "You're filthy stinkin' rich! I'm not stopping you from helping anybody! You've got me fucked up if you think I'll let you use me as your scapegoat." She seemed to have calmed down a little but Faaghira was pissed and it looked like it was just getting started.

"Scapegoat? You literally bar me from helping people. Almost everyone in this whole fucking state thinks I'm the spawn of the devil. But you know what? I still fund businesses; housing; schools; social security; health care; you fucking name it Saff. You. Fucking. Name. It."

"I didn't tell anyone you're the spawn of the devil."

"And who did you tell that I wasn't? Nobody. None of the stuff I just said is news to you. You know good and well everything that I do and you let them think I'm not on their side!"

At this point Scott sat back and watched. I don't blame you bud, this would literally be the worst time for you to say anything.

Safira got up to get some more milk but the argument still didn't let up for a second. "I have an entire movement to lead. People need me so I need to focus on my duties as a leader. I can't give you a signal boost every time you're a Good Samaritan."

"Gah! You're so infuriating! I don't need people to know everything I'm doing; I just don't want to be hated by the people I'm helping! Is that too much to ask?"

"I can't control people's perception of you. I admit that I haven't been doing a good job on making sure you don't get a bad rap. I'll do what I can but I'm not making any promises." While still physically intimidating, Safira was getting a verbal smackdown from Fae.

"Tell me something Saff; what kind of leader can't accept help?"

"One that has things figured out."

"And you know that's not you so what are you even doing? Another thing; what always happens to movements led by one person?"

The room grew silent. The two exchanged cold looks but not another word was said.

Scott took this as his que to put himself back in the conversation. He'd been on the sidelines for a while. Maybe this was his cry for relevancy. "When the leader dies the movement goes down with them."

Faaghira put the cap back on the bottle and pressed her hands against her face. Scott's eyes widened in panic but he took a sigh of relief when she spoke. "At least someone's making sense around here."

Safira's expression was stone cold, but for some reason she didn't seem nearly as intimidating. "Okay, so what would you like me to do?"

"Saff, let me help you. Atticus' administration has been blowing out of proportion since before I was even born and we have the chance to end it. Let's get this done. I don't care if we don't work together after this or if we never speak again. We're closer to getting rid of him than we'll be for a really long time. There won't have to be a rebellion anymore; we can finally have a real community. I would like for you to put aside any disdain you have for the way I handle things and just work with me."

Safira nodded in agreement. I guess Fae knew that this was close enough to an 'okay' because she went on explaining how things would have to work.

"First we'll have to cripple him." Fae's words brought a slight smile to Safira's face but when Fae saw it she had to clear up that they wouldn't be physically crippling him. "His main resources need to be cut off. From there we'll have a kind of proxy boxing match. I'm not saying that this'll even the playing field, but it'll give us all the advantage we need."

Safira nodded again but any hint of happiness she had after hearing Fae's plan disappeared when she looked at Scott. "You got any ideas?"

"Me? I'm not one of the players; I'm just a spectator.

"I get that Fae likes you but I don't think you'd have a seat at this table if you didn't have anything to offer. So whatcha got?"

Fae immediately jumped In to defend Scott. "Give him a second. It's hard to come up with something good when you're put on the spot."

Scott rested his chin on his fist and looked at Fae with a raised eyebrow. "Um, girl what are you talking about? You don't know that."

She mirrored his gesture with a smug look on her face. "We both know how I know that. Don't worry babe, I still love you. In the meantime I'll draw up some detailed plans with Saffie."

"Please don't call me that in front of him."

Scott started chuckling, but he fixed his face when Safira grunted at him. "And I'll go get my creative juices flowing."

Faaghira smiled knowingly. "Dude, that sounds crazy nasty coming from you, but…go get those juices flowing, I guess." She winked at him then went in the kitchen to put her beer back in the fridge.

"Seriously Fae? I didn't even mean that as an innuendo! I'm gonna step out to the balcony and get some air."

"Need some time to clear your head?"

"Good. Bye. Can you get me some food from the fridge?"

"Sure." She took a brown recyclable take-out box and put it on the counter by the stove. "I'll love you forever if you heat that up for me." She said as she went back to the fridge.

"Yeah babe, how long?"

"forty-three seconds in the microwave, but take it out after forty seconds; I don't like odd numbers."

"Don't sweat it, I got you. Anything else?"

"No I'm just getting some water and that's all. I have to stay sober if I'm going to come up with anything useful for this plan Saffie and I are cooking up."

"But you already had most of that beer"

"Shhhh! That doesn't count."

Scott microwaved it exactly how she requested while she got a ninja mug from one of the cabinets. She scooped in some ice from the freezer then poured in some water from a bottle on the door of the fridge. "Hey Fae."

"Yeah Scott?"

"Thanks for the food. You're always spoiling me."

"Aww, you're so sweet. But this is mine so I don't know

what you're thanking me for. You're grown; you can get your own food. There's some more stuff in the fridge so have at it." She took the container from Scott's hand and took the mug along with her back to the table.

"I'm stealing some of the food in here." Scott called out to her, but all she did was smile.

"You're not even stealing anything; I told you to have at it. You frustrate me."

He smiled but she wasn't looking so that was for him more than anything. He takes out a compostable tray with vegetable pulao and fried shrimp and brings a can of ginger ale along with him. He walks past the table to open the sliding door to the balcony and overhears Safira tell Fae "You two are disgusting" before stepping out and closing the door behind him.

He chuckled at Safira's playful jab at them. She seems to be lightening up in her own special way. He opened the container when he realized that he didn't have a fork. Smart move.

"Chill, it was a spur of the moment thing. Sometimes how I exit is more important than having everything. You gotta look cool when you leave; it leaves a good impression. "Well I hope you look as cool going back in and getting a fork. "Nah, I'll chill out here for a bit and I'll slide back in after a few minutes. You gotta play it off." Scott, you're literally a dummy.

"You do not need to go back inside if it is that big of a deal to you. Here is a fork."

Scott casually turned to where the voice was coming from and reached out his hand. "Oh thanks y-" His eyes widened in horror. "God! Can you not? Sneaking up on people is creepy!" In all his fright he almost dropped his food. The figure standing in front of him has a brown knit cloth sack with cartoonish painted eyes (one is bigger than the other); a nose (basically a teardrop colored blue); and a mouth (basically a banana with a diagonal line at each end); over its head and one of those douche-tastic shoulder capes. Underneath it is a singed dark brown cloak.

But we've seen this guy before. It's Baron Sugar, the creepy fire creature man-thing from before. He's also The Fireman; the urban legend that had Faaghira so spooked. But I guess he's not an urban legend because he's real; he was literally right there.

Baron holds out a fork with the hand that's not covered with the cape and Scott takes it.

"While I do not associate myself with that demon, I can see why he loves to appear in this way. Your reaction, or overreaction, is entertaining."

Scott is obviously flustered by the comment but he tries to play it off. "What do you want?"

"Much appreciated if you would stop being an ignoramus."

"Always semantics, huh." Scott snatched the fork from Baron Sugar's hand.

"Correct. I see an opportunity to eradicate the demon. I want the universe to be rid of him and you want to get home."

"Home? Uh…"

"You are going back home."

"I've been thinking; what if I stay here? I get more love here than I do back home. Everybody needs love so that's a plus. But most importantly, I'm part of something bigger than myself here. I can really make a difference.

"But yet, you do not. Everything else you said may be true, but what troubles do you avoid by reveling in lackluster heroics? Though it may not be apparent, there is nothing for you here. The life you are living, while alluring, is not for you. If it had been then it would have been yours from the beginning. Engulfing yourself in a world that is not your own is a surefire path to misery."

"You're telling me all this as if it's supposed to change my mind. I'm happy here and that's what matters to me right now."

"Contentment or conceit?" Baron stood idly.

"Even if it's not forever, can I get to enjoy something finally going right?"

Roswell climbed over the railing. Scott flipped out and dropped the food. Roswell caught it then leaned on the railing and winked at Scott.

"What the literal hell?" Yeah Scott, I hear you on that one, but that was in the script. It's not my fault; blame him.

"Ew, this isn't even warm! Who the heck eats cold rice and shrimp?" Roswell complained but he kept eating anyway.

Baron Sugar braced himself to fight but he didn't attack Roswell. The demon shot him a quick smile then went back to eating.

"You know Scott, as much as I hate Firepit's guts, or at least I would if he had guts; or any organs; he's got a point. You should really think about what you're staying for. After that you'll realize that I'm the real reason then you'll be like 'Oh crap!' and I'll probably still be eating this because it shouldn't take you that long to realize it. And this pulao is dope; would be even better if you heated it up. Doesn't Fae have a microwave?"

"Yeah, but…NO! What are you doing here? Go away! Actually, both of you; both of you go away. Shoo. Leave me be."

Baron Sugar relaxed but his presence still gave off uneasiness. "I would also like to know why you are here, demon."

"Hey Sugar. Oooo I like that! Narrator, call him Sugar from now on. The audience should know who he is by now and I think it's absolutely adorable. So Scott, I showed up here tonight because you need help. Well you need help in pretty much every aspect of your life, because you're a mess; but your current dilemma is one I want to help you with. I'm great at finding solutions and you're horrible at coming up with solutions; it's a match made in heaven. "

"What?" This isn't making any sense to Scott or me.

"You'll want my help. You actually need it to be of any use to this revolution that's so important to Fae. So what would you want to bring to the conversation?

"Leave him, demon!" Sugar yelled but the aggression was betrayed by the silly face painted on the cloth.

"Wait, I wanna hear him out." Scott took a deep breath.

"Thanks a million; one hundred percent. Now I want you to think. How do you hurt someone who stands on money?"

"Pull it from under their feet.?" Scott shrugged.

"Precisely. And how do we do that?" Roswell gave a tight-lipped smile, covering the mouthful of rice.

"Well Fae's plan is to cut off Atticus' resources, but I don't know what that entails. But I don't want to propose something that she already plans on doing."

Sugar stepped forward to physically insert himself back into the conversation. "Why is contributing your concern? You were not worried about this before, were you?"

"The reason doesn't matter. Now something that she probably hasn't found a way to implement is mass civil disobedience." Roswell spoke as he pulled open the refrigerator portal and placed the compostable tray in.

"Do not buy into it." Sugar implored Scott but the painted face makes it harder to take his urgency seriously.

"Listen to him as soon as he offers an alternative." Roswell mocked Sugar dry voice.

"Heathen." Sugar's hands curled into fists.

"Aww, stop it Sugar; you're making me blush."

The banter between the two supernatural beings ended up working Scott out of his own conversation. "So how would this civil disobedience thing supposed to work?" He had to

241

center it back to him. In this case it's warranted.

Roswell looked delighted to see the conversation shift away from an argument. "Mass civil obedience works best by presenting facts to the largest population. Find a way to let the people know that Atticus isn't afraid to wipe most of them off the map."

"For a demon, you give some decent advice. Do you really think this'll work?"

"Nope, but you can try it. But let me toss another idea out there before you do that."

"Shoot." Scott nodded, listening intently.

"How about after you put your idea out there, you go back home to see how it compares to your far more glamourous life here?"

"I don't know whether or not to answer that. What's your game?"

"I can't say. I'm not all that good at games. I actually suck at games. Like basketball and football; I suck at those. Hockey too; and table tennis."

"What about golf?" Scott squinted at the demon.

"Oh, golf isn't a real sport." Roswell smirked.

"What do you mean? A lot of people golf."

"Well a lot of people talk; is that suddenly a sport now?" Roswell laughed.

"We're getting way off topic." Scott shook his head and sighed.

"But we're picking this back up later. I am <u>not</u> letting this go."

"Okay, so get to the point. What's your angle?"

"Right, or obtuse. Maybe I have an acute one. It might be a hypothetical angle, so I can't really see it. But if it isn't hypothetical then I guess it would be a straight angle. But to answer your question, kind of, I just want to make sure you make the right decision. There's only one decision, and my goals are completely selfish. And I want you to know that you're going regardless of how you feel about it, so you might as well say yes."

"Sure. Why not? I have to go talk to Fae about that plan real quick. She's probably wondering what's taking me so long."

"She is not." Roswell and Sugar said simultaneously then stared each other down. I'm sure that Sugar was also angry to some degree but again, that painted face.

Scott slid the door open just enough to squeeze his upper body through. Fae gave a quizzical yet warm look. But Safira, on the other hand, she looked pissed off again. Though I can't blame either of them; Scott's a weird dude.

"So I came up with something. Get this: mass civil disobedience. Did you guys already think of that?" he looked a little worried.

Faaghira caught it and reassured him with a smile. "Oh yeah, yeah, we can do that. We have to figure out a way to do that. We definitely need to do that. And I'm not just saying it to make you feel better, I really mean it."

Scott lets out a sigh of relief that is quickly overturned when he sees Safira's enduring scowl.

"Ok so I'll leave you to figure out how to put that together. I'll be outside if you need me; or if you just wanna talk then that's cool too." He quickly slid the door closed and tucked himself away in corner where there was no way Fae and Safira could see him.

"So Roswell, about that offer…"

𝔍f that's
What you
Wanted

CHAPTER VI
IF THAT'S WHAT YOU WANTED

Roswell smiled while he opened a portal and looked at Sugar with a sly glance. "Don't take it personally. I usually win and it doesn't help you that you've been pretty boring. You didn't even say anything most of the time. No need for the long face."

I'm sure Baron Sugar is giving him a grimace or a scowl, or some disapproving look, but he basically has a scarecrow's head with a face too silly to take seriously.

"Tell ya what-", Roswell said, "you can come along if you feel like playing guardian angel for Blue. I know why you're really here, but I don't have a problem with that because you turned out pretty cool. Oh and sorry about the face…and everything else. I actually meant to apologize for that a couple years ago but it kept slipping my mind. You know, I'm a busy demon; there's always just a storm of everything brewing. But if it makes you feel better-"

"It does not." Sugar growled.

"But if it makes you feel better I can never remember the day I consider to be my birthday. Either that or I never know what I want to do when that day comes up. It's tough, but it's not necessarily both of them at the same time. It's one of them, but I keep forgetting which one it is. I digress; I'm a mess." Roswell's laugh lingered for way too long.

"I will go. Before we leave I would like to know why the sudden change of heart. You have never let me near your space, and I have done my very best to keep you as far away from me as possible." As usual, Baron Sugar's expression of emotion was lackluster.

"The old one was acting up and the warranty ran out, so I couldn't return it. In short, a change of heart was long past due. Now shall we be off?"

Sugar nodded but didn't budge. "You first."

"You got me." He smiled and put his hand through the portal. It passed through the other side as if it wasn't even there. "Okay real portal this time. And to be fair to you, I'll go first." Roswell let himself drop through the portal and nothing came out on the other side. After a bout of hesitation, Scott leapt off the balcony and went into the portal.

He was falling slowly through a void of pure black. He looked around and saw Roswell waving at him from every direction. The demon sported a fairly weak smile that paired well with the lazy gesture that passed for a wave.

Scott shook his head then looked below him.

The darkness under him was torn by the lights and sounds of the city below. He looked up again and caught one last glimpse of the demons waving at him before the portal dissipated. Scott fell much faster now. The wind buzzed past his ears and blew against his clothes. Sugar jumped off the balcony and swooped down at breakneck speed and caught Scott.

SNAP!

When Sugar stopped it was too sudden. He had Scott under one arm and used the other to clench his fingers into the building. Fire engulfed his feet and the flames climbed up Baron Sugar's body, but miraculously the man(?) didn't falter. The fire propelled him up at the same speed as when he was trying to catch up to Scott. When Baron Sugar was back on the balcony he saw that Scott wasn't moving. Sugar gently placed him on the ground.

"Kudos. You killed him. I already know you didn't mean to, but that was still pretty harsh. I didn't expect him to live very long anyway. I was always saving him from alcohol poisoning; the guy couldn't go a few hours without drinking. And he would've smelled like it too if it weren't for me. But of course, I'm me so I felt weird doing too much justifiable good deeds." Roswell literally appeared out of nowhere, but

Sugar wasn't even the least bit surprised.

"This is your fault. If you did not pull that trick then I would not have had to save him."

"You know he would've already been dead if that's what I wanted. He still would've been alive if you'd just trust me and let me catch him. I had a plan, but noooo, you just had to step in and be the savior. And if this is how you save people then you should really consider being a contractor. Not that you need the money, or could use it."

"Roswell, fix this mess."

"Seems like I'm always cleaning up other people's messes. I'll do it but I need a favor in return."

"I will not do you any favors."

"You're a goody two shoes so I know you can't have this sitting on your conscience. Just agree. It's just one tiny little favor."

"Fine. What is your request?"

"Don't be so quick to save someone if you're not considering what saving them will do. You'll always end up pulling a Gwen Stacy that way."

"And your request?"

"That was my request." Roswell lightly tapped Scott on the forehead and he sprung up like a kid that just had a nightmare.

Scott gasped for air but neither Sugar or Roswell had much of a reaction to it. "What just happened?"

"Oh, you died, again. Fireface saved you, Gwen Stacy style. Your neck snapped and he asked me to save you, so I did. But before you go thinking he did something for you, I was going to save you anyway. Your life is bad enough, so I really don't want you missing out on that." Roswell spoke casually with just enough calmness and clarity to be painfully annoying and comforting at the same time.

"Good thing you reminded me. So now that we brought that back to the surface, can you kill me again? I really don't want to go back to college. Or see my parents. Or my girlfriend."

"I thought you liked your girlfriend."

"I do...it's complicated." Scott ran his fingers through his course hair and tilted his head down to the floor. (So it's been a while since he combed his hair. Not everybody's got the time.)

With the bat of an eye, Roswell opened another portal. Unlike the other, this was wider and isn't dark void. Instead it's more like a clear window to another world. It was a street in a neighborhood much like Scott's. Cars are parked along the sidewalks, but unlike Scott's neighborhood, this one was all apartments. They all walked through at the same time (to make sure Roswell didn't cheat them again).

The portal immediately evaporated 8-bit style with the first blow of the winter breeze. The three of them stood on the snow covered sidewalk just looking straight ahead. Scott's attention turned from the scenery to Baron Sugar whose 'face' burned off, revealing an old charred skull. The rest of his clothes stayed completely intact with every pinch of ash and soot on them. The wind started to get more intense but the fire on Sugar's skull grew.

"You did this on purpose." Sugar's voice changed from the muffled adenoidal voice he had before to an outright husky sound. Of course since we have context we know he's talking to Roswell. Plus, Scott's been getting pushed out the spotlight pretty often. Some main character he is.

"Hey, I heard that!"

"So did I." Both Sugar and Roswell spoke at the same time and both of them immediately went into an abrupt silence.

"Jinx, you owe me an apology." Both of them spoke at the same time again, but they still seemed to be ignoring each other. If you could see it you'd swear it's an anime. You two are so tense for no reason.

"Fun fact: I never blink. This whole shindig is a lot more like a anime than you think." Roswell said lou- "AND-and Sugar and I can see the words the other one is about to say. The other guy can do it too, but I'm not talking about them so don't bother asking." Roswell sai- "OH OH OH OH, AND- and Sugar and I have a lot more in common but he doesn't like to talk about why, but this'll probably spark Scott's curiosity and Sugar will do almost anything to make sure Scott doesn't end up like him. And another thing; I promise that this might be the last one; the three of us can hear you. That's all. Carry on." Roswell said to the- Hey, I'm not saying that! "Oh but you are, you remember your job when you explained it to Scott? You said the story can't move along without you and I'll hold you to it. I refuse to even consider thinking about wanting to take another step until you read your lines. Read them exactly how they are in the manuscript." You're an asshole, Roswell. "Come on now, you should know that compliments won't get you out of this." Ugh, fine! "From the top: The three of us can hear you. That's all. Carry on." *sighs*Roswell said to the unsurprisingly negligent narrator.

"Can we go now? I love New York and I love being outside, but during winter I don't love them at the same time." Scott whined.

"Don't want to catch a bad case of the sniffles? I hear ya on that one. But I honestly think that's the greatest of your worries. Even if someone around finds three black guys outside in the streets in the dead of night utterly suspicious, the weather's too bad for them to do anything but keep their doors locked and hope we don't notice them."

"Wait a second, Baron Sugar isn't black. He's a fire-man, creature."

"Ah, but don't be fooled, Sugar is probably the blackest one out of all of us. I thought you already told him the story."

"I do not need to tell the story. However, I will share the

relevant parts with Scott if it will help him understand that you are dangerous and he needs to be as far away from anything you are responsible for."

"A hypocrite of the same thread. I swear, we might as well be two sides of the same person. Tell ya what; I'll let you say whatever you want and I won't interrupt you. Matter of fact, we can tell this story together. I can fill in whatever gaps there are so Scott can get a clear picture of what happened. But most importantly he'll get to see how much better my version of life is and he'll make the right choice." Roswell walked up the sidewalk and the other two followed close by.

Scott took brisk paces with his hands curled up deep inside his pockets. He tilted his head down and puffed up his shoulders in an effort to shield his neck from the cold. He was still wearing Faaghira's sweater and it's more of a fashion statement than something you'd hike out for a snow day (and it still has cuts). "So do I get a say in any of this or am I just going to keep getting dragged around like a bitch?"

"Hey, what's so bad about being a bitch? And nobody glued your lips shut; you can talk whenever you want to. So however you feel you're being treated right now, well that's all on you. It's on you. So whatcha gonna do?" Roswell was grooving to an imaginary beat.

"Can you prove to me that you're not a meme? Because all this time you've basically been a living meme mixed in with a YouTube comment section." Scott blew out a puff of cold air.

"No I can't, and if I could I still wouldn't. And a fair word of warning: don't use any references that might be outdated. Remember that there was a time that people thought hair metal bands would never go out of style." Roswell said smugly.

Completely removed from the conversation, Baron Sugar walked in silence, but not without the ominous presence

251

that's always paired with him. This is creeping Scott out big time, but of course since he's him he tries to ignore it and hope no one notices. But you're not fooling anyone Scott; we can all see it.

"I apologize if my appearance makes you uncomfortable. I am unable to remedy this. Get used to this because I will not disappear. I can promise that you will see things that will make you far more uncomfortable than you are now. With a fowl creature like Roswell in such close proximity, you are bound to see something much far more terrifying."

"Trust me, I've had a sample. But if there's really something worse, then it can't faze me. I'm in the streets of New York during a blizzard and I'm casually talking to two, count it, two demons. Nothing can shock me anymore; I've gone nuts." Scott covered his eyes with his hands and took a deep breath. His words don't look to be true to his heart but this isn't anything out of the ordinary by now. His words are hollow and his actions reveal a more vulnerable person than we see at other spots. Could this be the real Scott Blue?

"I don't know if this is the *real* him but it's definitely genuine at the moment, probably. But I think this has been a pretty confusing emotional roller coaster for all of us except for me because I've never been on the same ride as everyone else. This is technically my ride, after all; I can't be surprised by the twists and turns I put on the track. However, I'll be the first to say that this is probably really stressful for everyone else and we're all still wondering what the point is behind all of this. Fortunately, I'll give you a direct answer…kind of. We just got to our first stop, so I'll take a moment to put some things out in the open, and hopefully make things more confusing than they already are." Roswell spoke in a kind of condescending fashion.

"This is an extension of the path we had been traveling on. What is this destination you speak of?" Sugar's voice was growing to a point so ferocious that it even made

Roswell take a step back.

"The journey is the destination sometimes. In this case the journey is Imaginary Park. We were supposed to go to an actual park but walking a few more blocks without any explanation wouldn't have left you guys willing to listen to what I want to say. And I totally get that; I wouldn't listen to me either. That's why we're stopping here. And we were also supposed to go back to another place after this, but both of you've already been there so there's no point in going right now." Roswell sat down in the snow with his legs crossed and closed his eyes, giving the appearance of a meditative pose.

"What other place have I been?" Scott is *definitely* getting more agitated.

"I should clarify: You've been there before but you had no idea where it was."

"That really helps. Was it the abandoned house?"

"Liar, it totally helped. It wasn't the house; it was the other part after you jumped out the window."

"Does it have a name?" Scott's answers are sounding far briefer than before.

"The Orange Triangle Of Regret. It is the vilest dwelling this side of Hell." Sugar cut off Roswell before he could utter another word.

"Aww, thanks so much! But you're really building me up to something way better than I am. The Orange Triangle is nowhere close to Hell; it's actually my house and it's pretty cozy. "

"It is too empty to be a house." Baron Sugar sounds like he's starting to calm down but there's no doubt that he's still irritated. His forceful presence is still intimidating, even to Roswell.

"Is a model house not a house if there's nothing in it?"

"Model home?" It's another one of those cases where Sugar is probably confused but he doesn't have an actual face to show it.

Roswell let out a deep breath and motioned for the other two to sit down with him. They reluctantly comply and the three of them sat in uninterrupted silence. A silence that only lasts for a fleeting moment in time because of-

"I'm tired of all this waiting and riddles. What is this? Seriously, what is all of this? I'm not here to entertain you! Do I look like a clown, huh? Do I look like some stinkin' clown that's here to amuse you?" Scott. Because of Scott.

Scott yelled at the demon, but his fury bore no fruit. The wind was whistling intensely through the streets; its force similar to that of pounding thunder. The cold breeze caused Sugar's flame to go through a cycle of flickering on and off. He pushed back his cloak and revealed a small assortment of knit tan sacks tucked behind his belt. Sugar takes one and sits it on top of his 'neck' and it slowly inflates until it looks exactly the same as the one he was wearing before (hope he doesn't burn this one too). He turned his head towards Roswell and while looking at the demon the face on the tan cloth changed from a oddly painted smiley face to an oddly painted frown. "I hate you" Sugar said in his horribly imposing (but low key captivating) voice.

Roswell put on fake but momentary smile then opened his eyes. "And now that you're both officially tired of me we can begin." Roswell uncrossed his legs, turned over, then planked with his face pressing into the snow. "First off, Scott, you really shouldn't be so mad at me. Let me learn you some knowledge: I've been saving your black behind from the most dangerous person in your life; you." Oddly enough, the snow didn't muffle Roswell's voice.

"Saving me from myself? Sure; that's not cliché at all."

"And this cliché is correct. You ever stopped to think why I'd do enough damage to kill you and always make sure you're all clean without a scratch when the scrap is over? Have you thought about why I won't kill you or leave any permanent damage whenever we cross paths? Have you thought about why neither of you are trying to kill me right now? Both of you hate me and make no mistake, I don't like you either, but there's an unmentioned respect. See, your situation isn't exactly unique, and this isn't the kind of talk I'd normally have but I think this is something that needs to be brought to your attention. Do you by chance know the amount of alcohol you consume on a regular basis? I'll tell you. You drink enough to kill a grizzly. Do you know why you don't die? Because I save you; you don't die because I save you. Granted, I'm a sorry excuse for a savior. All I do is trade out your alcohol for my imagination. Not exactly the kind of thing you'd consider help."

"And your 'help' has proven to literally be one of the least helpful things. You stress me out!" He paused to catch his breath. "This entire world is stressing me out." Believe me when I say that Scott is nowhere near as dramatic as he comes off here. He's actually kind of calm.

Baron Sugar lifted up his cloth 'face' just a little and an unholy wail belted out followed by a dashing bolt of fire. The burning shot torched a nearby car on the other end of the street. "I second that notion." He pulled the cloth back down and looked forward; completely ignoring what just happened. Roswell sprung up.

Scott and Roswell both leaned in to look at the car, but their reactions are complete opposites. Scott looks absolutely mortified. "What in the name of logic? What was that?"

"A sneeze." Sugar kept his posture facing forward, making the matter seem insignificant.

Roswell, on the other hand, he's giddy with excitement. His hands are pressed against his cheeks and he's grinning from ear to ear. "You have the most adorable sneeze. You sound like a demonic whale on shrooms and you always torch stuff! But my favorite part is that you're so chill about it. You know good and well that this isn't normal! Nobody sneezes like that! Boy, if that ever stops putting a smile on my face then I'll have to die."

"Quick, Baron keep sneezing so he can get bored of it so he can die" Scott gestured as though he was going to whisper to him but instead he practically yelled at Sugar.

"Quick, somebody call Scott's girlfriend so they can try to outdo each other in a brutal season of '*So You Think You Can Be More Emotionally Abusive*'. Afterwards Scott can go hang out with his horrible friends and down himself in enough liquor to fill up all the pots in a soup kitchen." Roswell looked Scott dead in the eyes; unflinching and unwavering. The cold stare shook Scott but he tried to hide it. Didn't work this time. All it took was one look and Scott was wavering between confidence and insecurity.

"Weren't you going to tell us the reason you dragged us out here? And I mean the real reason; not that bull you come up with." Scott sounded confident, but his words were about as strong as a toothpick.

Roswell laughed in a hilariously dorky way and playfully slapped his knee. "'Bout as strong as a toothpick! Wonderful! Now I'll tell you this: Imagination Park isn't the place you go to for explanation. This is the place you go to learn. This is where you see the world around you for what it is and you make your judgements from there. But before I go on my spiel, I think it would be nice if Sugar told you the story of how we first met."

Baron Sugar's painted face quickly changed to a menacing scowl (that in all reality still looks whimsical). "Those days must not be romanticized. This was no romantic outing. This was a gruesome time that ruined my life beyond repair. It took me from a man to a monster. I can never regain what I lost. I will never be able to rediscover that person I was all that time ago. They are but a dream that slips through my fingers any time I feel it within my grasp. I was once a human like you, Scott. I was once someone that hoped for the future. In one swift move I have become a shell of that person. I live on today only because I have been given the curse of life eternal. As I walk the earth I make it my mission to prevent your liveliest self from becoming a distant memory. It is not too late for you, so I implore you to stay away from this demon and know that his promises will lead to nothing but the ultimate misery."

Scott looked over at Roswell for some sort of response. "I dunno, he's got a point" the demon shrugged.

Scott stood up and brushed as much snow off of his clothes as he could. He started to walk off but a chilling breeze made him try to bury himself in his clothes in a frantic attempt to be shielded from the cold. He tried to keep moving but the harsh winds were too much for him to bear. "I hate this stupid wind. Stupid weather. And I hate the stupid demon that put me here!" Scott shivered so much that he had a hard time getting the words out. He stumbled twice and tried his hardest to force himself to push on, but he stopped after seeing the lack of distance he had from where he just was. "What's the point?" he sighed heavily.

"You cold, bud?" Roswell was being oddly sympathetic. Scott shook his head from side to side; unintentionally displaying his man-baby tendencies. Roswell reached behind him and tore a thin line into the air. He pulls a blanket out of the line and hands it to Scott.

"I said I wasn't cold." Scott tried to act tough but neither of the supernatural beings bought the act. "But thanks anyway."

"You definitely live up to the whole man-baby legacy" Roswell said as he laid back in the snow with a face so smug that it's arguably the most punchable thing with a nine-mile radius.

"And Roswell, one more thing."

"Shoot."

257

"What's that line for?" Scott watched as Roswell slowly scanned the area; looking under his arms; under his legs; on the front and back of his hands; he even took off his shoes and patted them down to see if anything came out. "The one right behind you" Scott had an annoyed look which Roswell countered with a phony surprised look.

"Oh *this* line! I can't pull things out of thin air. I have to create portals out of thin air so I can pull things out of them. I thought we just went over the no portal, no powers thing."

"You know I don't pay attention to people. I take that back; there are some people I pay attention to. But you're also not one of those people."

"Then you're in luck; neither me or Sugar are people, so you can listen to us. Case closed. Next order of business: story time. Since I already have a portal open, let's tune in to the news. News in real time!"

Baron Sugar stands up with his arms crossed, looking down on the demon. "Real time news? I am not certain that this will be as pleasant as you are making this sound."

"Oh, loosen up, Fireface" Roswell reaches his hand into the portal and widens it. The line is stretched into a large trapezoid and it holds an image of a snow filled park at night."

"Two questions; what are we looking at and why is this a trapezoid?"

"Two; because I don't cut corners; circles are for squares. For the first one, it would be easier if I set the scene for you. A young thirty something year old woman is out for a walk in Central Park. It's two in the morning; there shouldn't be any problem. The streets are full of snow, and again, it's only the second hour of the day. Hardly anyone would be around, if anyone at all. She's minding her own business; that shouldn't be bothering anyone."

Line posts line the partially cleared walkway; lighting the way for her to go further down her path. She whistles monotonously, shuffling along with her hands buried in the pockets of her dartmouth green puffer coat. She walks solemnly with her head down low. She stops to sit down on a nearby bench. The glow from one of the light posts shines down on her, giving her an almost ethereal quality. She sits peacefully. She sits so peacefully that she's so far out of place in an area like New York. She begins talking not long after.

Her phone isn't out; has no Bluetooth in her ear; but she speaks knowing that whoever she's talking to can hear her. She speaks intently on things that plague her; unsupportive family; being ostracized by loved ones; problems at work; being afraid to be a black Muslim woman in a place where that seems to be an unholy trinity. It's not everyone, sure, but even one is far more than too much.

A lonely space for a lonely face.

But this silence; this safe space; this solemn time, was infringed on by a loud siren and the flashing red and white lights that tail close behind. She sees this and is unalarmed. She didn't pay it much mind. Shootings, public executions, whatever they call them; they've been in the news but that doesn't mean that fear is rational. Those horrible scenes; they're something to be aware of at the most. It happened to others, but it doesn't happen to everyone.

It happened to others, but it won't happen to her.

She carries on her conversation. The siren cuts off, but the lights still flash in the distance. She hears a car door slam, but she doesn't move a muscle. There was nothing to fear. She hadn't done anything wrong. There was nothing to be afraid of.

But if she hadn't done anything wrong then why would a police officer be coming her way?

She clears her throat, but otherwise composes herself in the same way she had before.

She is calm. She is graceful. She is brave.

The officer approaches her at the bench. A clean cut black man, maybe somewhere around her age, maybe a little older. He isn't a large figure by any stretch of the imagination, but he's not a frail guy by any means. He's got one hand firmly on his belt but the other is relaxed.

"How are we doing this morning?"

"*I'm* doing fine."

"Any particular reason why you're wandering around Central Park at two a.m.?"

"I'm sitting."

"Girl, I don't recall asking for an attitude. I just got sent down to investigate a complaint about a potentially dangerous person walking around here every week, and right now you're the only person I see. So I'll ask again; is there any reason why you're here?"

"Honestly, I was coming out here to get some fresh air. I do this all the time. Am I being detained?"

"No but I want to check you for anything suspicious."

"You don't have my permission for a search. If I'm not being detained then I'll be leaving now."

She walks away from the bench and puts her hands in her pocket. She begins to pull her right hand out of her pocket.

The shouts of rolling thunder; that dreaded sound.

Three bullets fly forward. Chunks of lead run through the air like freight trains crashing through a meadow. The time that elapsed, it was forever; it was faster than a blink of the eye.

Somewhere, it *is* forever.

Three shots rang out. She didn't stand a chance. Three holes are in the back of her puffer coat with small puddles of red flowing out of them. Half her hand was still in her pocket, but it was far out enough that it was clear what she had been reaching for.

It was her phone. The last thing she would ever do is press

that power button. The portion of the screen that lay outside her pocket reads the time of two-twelve a.m.

The portal goes dark then becomes completely transparent, revealing the rest of the neighborhood on the other side of it. Scott was frantically still; a result of overwhelming stress. He was shaking; frozen to a standstill. His fists curled up, but his face hadn't moved to anger. Instead it was fear that took center stage. "What did we just watch?" Scott's voice was getting shaky.

"Bud, you just got an insider look into the news."

"Did that just happen? Like, was that just now?"

"It's real as the days that pass."

"You could've stopped it right? You could've stopped it! Why didn't you stop it?!" Scott was still frozen in disbelief. His face was tense, his shoulders were locked, and his fists were clenched. It's strange seeing him like this. The egotistical, defensive, rude, awkward Scott Blue is was so vulnerable, so hurt by something that didn't affect him.

Roswell clasped (correct, not clapped) his hands together but no sly grin or remark followed. He had more of a blank expression than anything else. "If I did then what if it happened again? Would it be my fault if she was murdered then? And who's the one to blame; the one who watched the shot or the one who pulled the trigger? And if you're so concerned about her death why didn't *you* do something, huh? Any of us could've done something, but my portal, my problem, right? And let's say for a second that I do stop her from being murdered; what about everyone else I don't save? I'm not God and I'm not the Devil; I can't be everywhere at once. Not to mention that I'd have to be watching situations like this all around, but I still couldn't save them all. Some of those tries would be met with failure, and failure means watching countless people meet a gruesome demise. I may be a demon, but torture porn isn't down my alley. And all of that would be implying that I want to save all of these people. I have no incentive to save anyone. I'll let you in on a not-so-secret; people will die because of other people. From what I've seen here, that knowledge gets used as a talking point to say why things made for killing aren't dangerous. There's still a large swatch of people that yell 'no' when someone else says that something needs to change. And why would *I* stop it? Seriously, why would I stop it? I'm a demon; I'm still evil."

Scott's eyes began to water but he rubbed them before any tears could flow down. "You don't have to be evil!" He was almost at a yelling point, but he calmed himself when he saw Roswell furrow his brow.

"Not a soul stopped you from acting." Sugar cut in, which surprised Roswell, but Scott was too riled up to care.

"How was I supposed to know she would get shot?! Roswell is the one who pulled up this shit in the first place! He knew this would happen! He knew this would happen and he put it on display! He's so sick!" At this point Scott stopped caring about Roswell's dirty looks and he yelled like crazy.

"It is true that you did not know. I admit that I was aware because I have seen situations like this many times before. Roswell knew because he is a demon; forever linked to misfortune." Baron Sugar shook his head in disappointment.

"Wait, *you* knew too? Why didn't you do anything?" Scott shouted; his voice shivering in sadness.

"It pains me to say, but the demon is correct. We could have stopped it, but we are not the ones who caused it." Sugar hung his head down.

"You see Scott" Roswell cut back in the mix but he still didn't have that smug face like he normally would. "I may be the demon, but I'm not always the problem. It appears the reality of Imaginary Park is too much for you to handle. You're denying yourself the truth that you're a spectator at best. Things like this happen all the time, but you never seemed to care. But this time it's pushed right in your face and you criticize me for not lifting a finger. But you were here at that same moment where something could've been done. A valuable lesson for you; you were right here with us. You did exactly what you would've done if you were there in Central Park; absolutely *nothing*. What a hypocrite. Very sad."

"Take me to the next place and get this stupid tour over with." Scott huffed in a fit.

"Then off we trot" Roswell flicked his finger at the sky and an octagonal portal opened. The inside of it is blank.

Scott looked at it oddly, but he was still pissed off. "I guess there's a reason behind the octagon too?"

"Because pentagrams are overrated" Roswell spoke in what's probably one of the douchiest ways possible.

"That doesn't even make sense." Scott squinted, adding confusion to the mix of his muddled emotions.

"It will never make sense; just go with it." Sugar (technically?) reassured Scott before stepping through the portal. Roswell followed suit, but he jumped back out immediately with a long rope and ties it around his waist.

"If you don't trust me you can hold on to this" He held out the rope to Scott. "But, if you do you might get duped anyway. Just throwing that out there."

Scott hesitantly grabbed on to the rope. Sugar peeks his head out and his face changes to one of disappointment.

"What are you looking at? You got a problem with me?" Scott began to get riled up again.

"I am trying hard to convince myself that you don't deserve what's coming to you." Sugar falls back into the portal, leaving Scott with a cryptic (but not so cryptic) message. Roswell smiles in the most devious, devilish way then goes back into the portal Scott tightens his grip and is yanked through.

The inside of the octagon is a tunnel that has a galactic-like interior. Lights of various colors are scattered across the darkness. They glow ominously and seem so radiant that anyone could reach out and touch them. But the sheer number contained in the astral canvas brings out their true distance from where Scott is speeding through. For a time, he held the rope with a steel grip and dashed through what appeared to be an infinite stretch of empty space. It got colder the further he went. Ice started to build up on his end of the rope and his hands started turning blue. Every breath he took came out as a slow-moving uniform puff of air. Scott watched each one flow away into the atmosphere.

But there was something far above it that caught his eye. Two large spheres of malachite were commanding his attention with their presence. He looked up them and they seemed to be looking down at him. He wasn't slowing down, but the spheres were always at the same distance. They were traveling at the same speed as him, so everything seemed motionless except for the 'stars' (still not sure if this is actually space) they were flying past. The rigid spheres of malachite hung over Scott the entire way to the end of the tunnel, where a hole colored in different hues of blue opened up to him.

Scott was pulled through the opening and he emerged alone. He looked ahead to see the other end of the rope, but he couldn't see that far ahead. He looked down and saw Roswell waving at him.

"You played yourself!" the demon called out to Scott. Roswell went on his way, sipping tea from a mug with his face printed all over it. He stood in an open field of healthy green grass with patches of dills, nasturtiums, willows, zinnias, and one lone tansy.

"Then who's pulling the rope?" Scott was utterly terrified.

The opposite end of the rope turned slightly, and it's tied to...to...a cartoon anvil? What? It has eyes and a mouth and-this is just weird! Who wrote this? Who wrote this in here? It winked at him. It for real just winked at Scott! Who? Who did this? Okay so now it's dropping; it's plummeting. It's yanking the rope down. I- this is- intense!

"Oh hell no, I'm out!" Scott let go of the rope and dropped down from the sky at a rapid speed. "Ha! You have to save me if you don't want me to die!" He yelled at Roswell, doing his own take on the demon's annoying grin. But Roswell didn't look concerned at the slightest. He simply looked up and had another sip of tea.

"It's chamomile with orange blossom honey. Scott, I do want you die, but just not right now. But that doesn't mean I'll go up there and save you. You've gotta hit the floor just like everyone else." Roswell kept walking and sipping from his mug. Scott closed his eyes and put his arms out as if it would stop him from falling.

And miraculously, it did.

Just kidding, he hit the ground hard. So hard, in fact, that he crashed right through it. A small crater was left by the impact. Scott...bounced out of it? What's going on? What pushed him back up?

"A bounce house. They're underground so he wouldn't die if he let go of the rope. And why do so many people in this book barrage everyone with questions? I mean seriously, nobody can get the chance to answer the first one; it never ends. If I took a shot for every time people did that I would've- taken a lot of shots by now. I dunno, I'm not a drinker. But Scott, on the other hand..."

"I hate you." Scott was struggling to get up, but he quit after falling a bunch of times. He crawled over to Rowell and punched him in the shin. Roswell looked down, tilted Scott's head up and poured the rest of the tea on Scott's face.

"Get up, buttercup; there's a world to see. A word of wisdom before you go: don't ever hit me without expecting to get something right back."

"Okay, noted. So where are we exactly?"

Roswell scans the area and facepalmed so hard that his hand slammed right through his head. "My bad, we weren't supposed to go here. His arm breaks off and it's pulled through his head with his left hand. "Here, hold this. Thanks bud." He gives the bloody arm to Scott which makes Scott freak out like crazy. Scott dropped it like a hot potato the second it fell in his hands.

"A hot potato? Don't compare this to a hot potato! This is gross! This is a bloody *fucking arm*!"

"Hey watch it, that's not my fucking arm. I left my fucking arm back at my place, but I do agree that that arm you were just holding was definitely bloody. Anyway, we were supposed to visit your mom's house. Actually, *you* were supposed to visit your mom's house."

"You're really doubling down here aren't you?"

"Oh definitely. You have a bunch of things in your life that I can pick from to make you feel like shit. I don't actually have to do anything to ruin for life and it's one of the most fascinating and depressing things. I just can't stop bragging about it!" Roswell was smiling from ear to ear.

A shadow forming over them steals their attention and wipes the smile clean off of Roswell's face. "Show off" Roswell grunts under his breath.

A cloud of smoke materializes up above. It blocks out the sunlight before forming into the fire fueled (literally) man, Baron Sugar. He floated down, descending like the general idea of a deity. "I assumed that you were much smarter than that. And yet, here you are drenched in tea. I am completely unsurprised."

"Yeah, well I don't like you either" Scott said aggressively. Now we're starting to get back to the Scott we know and… tolerate.

Sugar offered to help Scott up but pushed his hand away and got upon his own. Roswell threw the mug away into a

266

bush and intentionally bumped Scott's shoulder when he passed by. Scott's eyes were immediately drawn to the hole in Roswell's face. He watched in a mix of horror and awe watching the hole in his head refill itself.

"Dude, that's sick! Why do you do stuff like this?" Scott quickly covered his eyes with his arms. Roswell laughed so hard at Scott's fidgeting that tears were rolling out of his eyes. When Scott put his arms down he was sporting a sour look on his face. He raised his fist to hit Roswell, but he backed down when Roswell looked like he was squaring up. Scott clears his throat and looks away in an effort to make himself seem tougher. It obviously didn't work. I don't get the point of the tough guy act when all of us can see through it.

"So I won't be out of practice when I'm around normal people." Scott's face turned to a sour smile that came out so weird that both Roswell and Sugar shuddered at the act.

"Chill man, just- man, just get this over with."

Roswell punched a hole into the air and it grew into a trapezoid that grew larger than any of the three. "Okay then, on with the ride then. And Sugar, you either have right now or immediately after we get back to tell Scott your story. You have a few seconds so make your choice now."

"My parents were freed slaves long before the Civil War. I disregarded them and made foolish decisions, one of them being a deal with Roswell, which cost me my humanity. I urge you not to take any deal he offers to you, no matter how alluring they may be. Everyone I knew is dead. Everyone I ever loved is dead. My life is gone but I am cursed to never die. I make this effort to prevent you from becoming a monster as I already have. Go with Roswell on this journey he has crafted. As you already know, he will send you to these places with or without your agreement. Therefore, it is best to go without protest. Remember to never let any pleasures of this world; any promises of wealth or wisdom, lead you to this demon's desired path."

"He's so long winded. You'd think almost two hundred years is enough to be casual with the English language. And don't believe him, because we're both liars. Your choice is your choice, but I hope you listen to me because I'm correct. But I do hope, for some strange reason, that his story resonated with you to some degree. I know it was brief; he's not much of a talker. But to be fair, I didn't give him enough time to explain in greater detail but more on that later. He's probably pissed off that I gave him such a short amount of time and that he could've actually had more because we're still here. And now we're leaving. See ya, Sugar." Roswell vaulted into the portal, but Scott didn't follow after him.

"I guess I gotta, you know, leave. So..um…"

"Yes."

"Yeah, I'll see you later then." Scott had this really awkward goodbye that he wouldn't quite get to finish because Roswell cut him off.

"Dude, let's go! Sugar, just go find some business to mind. Things could be getting crazy nasty over in New Orleans. Faaghira's at a pretty bad disadvantage here. She might need some help if she wants a chance of winning. I would say 'or if she wants a chance at living' but we already know nobody there would kill her. She's Switzerland and nobody messes with Switzerland. Thems the brakes. Don't worry, I'll catch up with you real soon. Scott and I have some catching up to do. Don't worry, I won't hurt the guy. If I was going to then- whoops, I already forgot about those last few times." Roswell pondered for a moment before going back into the portal.

"Yeah, we already fought, like, twice."

"But if we do fight again then I'll wait until we're all in the same place so that he can stand a chance. I wouldn't want it to be unfair. But spoiler alert: I'll still win." Roswell's voice echoed out of the portal.

"Don't worry about me" Scott reassured Sugar, "I'll try not to get into any trouble. I probably will anyway. Just don't sweat any of that though, I'll be fine."

Sugar stands for a moment; he looks like he's about to say something. "..." But he doesn't. A heart (anatomical) shaped portal opens behind him. It blows wind out in a furious storm, violently rustling Baron Sugar's robes. He looked to Roswell then disappeared into the portal. When no one is left, Scott goes into Roswell's portal. Both of those gateways close when he makes his choice. Scott and Roswell arrive at the same neighborhood as before. This is where Scott used to live and its' als-

"Actually I still kind of live here. I come back over break and I don't have my own place yet, so I still have a few reasons to stop by. But aside from that part you're doing just fine; you can keep going." Ahem, like I was saying, it's also where his parents currently live. It's actually a pretty nice place.

"It is pretty nice, isn't it? But could you just run over me with a semi instead of have me go back there?" Scott sounds like he's joking but I'm pretty sure some part of him is dead serious.

"I could but this is obviously much worse than anything I could come up with at the moment."

"My parents and I have nothing to talk about right now, so you'd better be taking me back to my old neighborhood to get me some Chinese from up the block."

"Incorrect; there's a few elephants in the room. There's so many elephants that you and your parents can hardly even fit in the room."

"And it's the conversations we didn't have that keeps us on speaking terms."

Roswell crouched down and took out a breakfast sandwich from the front pocket of his hoodie. Wait a second, were you wearing a hoodie the whole time? "Sure. And before you ask, I have an astral fridge in all of my pockets. I never eat enough so now I always have food on hand, or would 'on pocket' be the right term? Back to Scott; this talk might just be the thing you need to make seriously reconsider my offer for smooth sailing in the other dimension."

"Is that a pancake, ham, egg and cheese sandwich?"

"Turkey; I low key like it better in sandwiches but don't tell anyone."

"Really? Huh. Damn, I'm getting off topic. The life you're trying to push on me is one that won't last."

"But it's better than what you have now." Roswell took a bite from his sandwich then meticulously patted his mouth with a napkin.

Scott sighed out of frustration then dragged his hands down his face. "It's too early; we'll have to come back later."

"What time?" Roswell stuffed another bite of his sandwich before trying to get up...and falling over. He held the sandwich in the air the entire time so that it wouldn't drop. "Got it, crisis averted!" He's so excited that he didn't drop his sandwich. I don't understand; I've never seen anyone so happy about a sandwich. "Of course you wouldn't get it; you never had a sandwich this good in your whole entire life."

"I think ten or eleven would be better than freakin' two in the morning again! Seriously, why is it always two?"

"Got it" Roswell opens a portal and pushes Scott through it. When he pulls Scott back out the sunlight is out, taking the place of the dark morning sky. "It's eleven seventeen; go on ahead so we can see how bad this gets."

"You don't know how much I hate you" Scott didn't have any kind of special expression, he just looked upset.

"I'm not completely sure but I'm in the ballpark. I've set the time so now you set up the conversation. And if you don't do it then I'll keep putting you back here until you do."

"Fine" Scott whines. He starts to walk towards the house,

270

but he quickly paces in the other direction. When he gets around the corner he's back on the street as before. "You've got to be kidding me."

"Now that we've got that out of the way you can go have that falling out with your mum." Roswell didn't look surprised that Scott tried to walk off. He wasn't smiling but he had a hint of a smirk, kind of.

"Okay for real this time. I'll go but I better be getting something real good for this."

"For you, the best thing to wish for is the sweet release of death. But if you're looking for a reward, try hope." Roswell gestures towards the house with a firm gaze. Scott gets as far as the porch steps before he jets down the block. He turns the corner but, he stops as soon as her realizes that he's back on the same block again.

"Hi again" Roswell waved at him excitedly with wide smile.

"I forgot you *could* actually do stuff like this."

"But...how?" Roswell feigned confusion but didn't even bother hiding his smile.

"Just- whatever. If I go this time will you leave me alone?"

"If you go then I'll stop putting you back in this spot if you leave again. That's good enough for you."

Scott sighs then reluctantly goes back over to the house, but he stops and turns back around. "Oh, so now you're deciding my feelings for me too?"

"Yup. Now quit stalling. Any relationship that's hanging by a thread needs to get put out of its misery. Either you handle it now or it'll come back to get you later. Take your pick."

"I'm not going to cut my mom out of my life. After all she's done for me, why would I do that?"

"And she treats you like..."

"She's a little cold but that she cares." Scott's voice

271

started to lower but he still tried to make his words sound firm.

"And she treats you like…"

"Look, I get that she's tough; that builds resilience. I wouldn't be the same person if she was your stereotypical mom."

"You wouldn't be the person you are now; you say that like you're a great person. But what I really want you to do is finish the following statement: She treats you like…"

"I'll go talk to her, but just so you know, this won't prove anything."

"It's the fact that you say it won't prove anything that proves everything."

"No it doesn't!" Scott shouted at the demon. Afterward, he stormed over to the house, but he gently knocked on the door. Showing his anger anywhere near his mother wouldn't lead to anything but trouble. He took some time to catch his composure while he waited for her to answer. He didn't have any mantras, but he did have to take a few deep breaths.

"Hello Scott." Her words seemed kind enough, but the ice-cold delivery invalidated any kind of comfort that was thrown out there. Scott had a subtle shift from anger to anxiety when he looked her in the eyes. It was apparent that he felt that something was wrong, but fear wasn't the driving force behind it. The odd, or maybe not so odd, thing is that he isn't surprised by her tone at all.

"Hey mom."

"What are you doing back here?"

"Mom" he took another deep breath and mustered up the courage to continue. "Mom, we need to talk."

"Alright, what do you need to talk about?"

"Mom, I get that you want the best for me but sometimes, you're too harsh." He winced when he finished. He cleared his throat and shifted his eyes to the side before looking straight at her again. She didn't look entertained at the least.

She was displaying unrequited disapproval with the most piercing gaze anyone in this story had so far. Those eyes were sharp enough to slice right through concrete.

"Just because I don't live in la la land and I'm trying to get you to wake up and see your own potential, that doesn't mean you suddenly have the right to be ungrateful. I'm sorry the real world hurts your feelings and that you need me to coddle them along with putting a roof over your shoulder; food on the table; and a bed for you to sleep in."

"Gee, thanks for doing your job."

"I know you didn't just say that to me. What kind of devil got a hold of you thinking that you could disrespect me like that?"

"The devil of this reality everyone keeps telling me to wake up to. You're getting back what you put in."

"I know I raised you better than that!"

"See, I may not be acting like the son you wanted, but I'm acting like the one you raised. It's not just about what you said, it's what you did. How am I supposed to be virtuous or respectable or whatever when you aren't? And why do you expect so much out of me and refuse to help me get anywhere I want to be?"

"Because you won't listen; you're busy chasing dreams that don't make sense. You can't seem to get it through your thick skull that the real world is not easy. Bills have to be paid; you need to eat; you need a roof over your head. *Come on*, do you really think, do you really think you can pay for that with dreams?"

"If I had support then maybe they wouldn't still be dreams!" It escalated to the point where he was shouting at her with all the strength his voice would allow. To say his mom wasn't happy about it would be an understatement. She was fuming.

"Don't blame me for you not getting anywhere by now."

"Too late, I'm already bitter. No thanks to you." He didn't

sound as aggressive as before but what he said was the most aggressive thing to part from his lips so far. His mom had a look of pure rage in her eyes that could put a gaping hole straight through someone's heart.

"Get. Off. My. Porch. Don't bother coming back when you're out of school. I don't care if it's after graduation and you're broke with no place to stay or just if school let out for break. I'll tell your father to get you your things. You two can handle that since you seem to know it all. I hope your little girlfriend can take care of you."

"I love you too." Scott forced out all the bitterness he could give (I'm just assuming here but it sounds about right). He watches his mother turn her back on him and close the door. Tears run down from his eyes. He moves his arm up to his cheek to wipe them away, but he lowered it. "No, I've earned these. I'll let them stay, just this once. The tears roll all the way down and drop down onto the floor. He walks away from the house and doesn't look back. He sees Roswell waiting for him around the corner, but Scott goes the other way. The sad young black man walked away from the home he knew and he walked away from an uncertain future. He walked past the cars lined up next to the sidewalks and the modest houses their owners reside in. He walks in silence for an entire two blocks before Roswell reappears.

"Tough crowd?" Roswell sounded partially sympathetic but his all too eager smile ruined any sense of humanity he might've been showing. Scott just looked at him with his teary red eyes without saying a word, and he really didn't have to. His eyes alone are speaking volumes. The first time he's shown this much vulnerability since he ended up in this story and it stronger than any time he's been angry. There's no telling whether or not it struck a chord with Roswell, but the smile disappeared from the demon's face.

"It actually didn't strike a chord with me; my nature is a far cry from empathy. Scott, no matter how much you hate

274

me for it, this needed to happen." When Roswell said his name, Scott laid down on the sidewalk, crying and sniffling away. Roswell took a deep breath then sat down next to him, but it took him forever to sit because this was one of those cases where he would move as fast a very frail hundred and ten-year-old man. "Your reality is an unfortunate one, but why are you crying?"

"What do you mean 'why am I crying'? My mom just officially kicked me out. Oh, but not only that; she's cutting me out of her life! I'm not her child anymore!" Scott raised his voice, but he was choking up so much that his words didn't come out clearly. It sounded a lot more like a slurred drunken banter. Roswell didn't respond in any particular way, he just sat there. "What's wrong with you? Do you even have emotions?"

The question pushed Roswell into a deep train of thought. "Hmm, I don't think so. At least not the ones most people refer to when they say 'emotions'. I won't say no but I can't jump out and say yes."

"How does someone get like that; being completely devoid of emotions? 'Cause I wanna be like that too."

"Again, I'm not a human. Second, being like me is pretty great. Put it on your wish list, kid. But another thing that helps me out is having a lot of work to do. Speaking of, the reason I'm not as smug as I should be right now is because it dawned on me not too long ago that I have some business to take care of so the tour will have to be cut short. Until next week; same time, same channel; mostly avoiding copyright infringement." Roswell winked at him with the old smug look he usually wears.

A hole opens up in the ground under Scott, pulling him from the sidewalk and plunging him into...into... "What's the problem?" I don't know what you're falling into. Obviously, Roswell knows but he's not here, so I have no idea what to say next. "Does it say anything in the author's

275

notes?" Nothing helpful; it says, 'the narrator has no idea what to do'. "But doesn't progression of the story depend on you reading the script?" Yeah but there's nothing else at this part so keep falling, I guess. "Okay, not like I can actually stop."

Scott is falling through another astral tunnel and that same creepy eye is there. Whenever it moves it makes this disgusting swishing sound. To give you an idea, it's pretty much sounds like pasta being mixed around in a pot. Something about the way that sounds is just so...ugh. Anyway, Scott floats through the void, taking in the sights of the stars, the comets, and the other astral sights. Before exiting the surreal space, the eye winked at him. "Dude, this place is weird." He comes across an encompassing gas cloud giving off a glow of various iridescent colours. "Yeah, it looks pretty dope. Is it symbolic or something?" Maybe, symbolism isn't my area of expertise, so I truly don't have a single clue. But you're heading right for it so I hope for your sake that it isn't toxic. "Right now I honestly wouldn't mind if it killed me off."

So it ends up not doing anything when he passes through. It stays in place and carries on the same way it had before. "Damn it, can something here just legit kill me? And I don't want to be brought back either." Um...sorry to hear that. Look, just hold out, alright? This book has to be ending soon; there's no way bull like this could keep going on much longer. "Leave it up to Roswell and this'll keep running for another ten years."

But fortunately Scott wouldn't be stuck in the depths of the astral plane for much longer. A spiral of glass formed in the abyss, encasing Scott in its uneven shell. "Eh, whatever. I hope they actually come through this time." The surroundings of the astral plane fade away into nothing

Scott jumps up and hits his head on a hard surface above him. His bruised head falls back on the soft couch cushion below him. "Damn it, who did that?" He looked up and his eyes were met by a wooden tray attached to a stool-like maple box.

"Safira, I told you he might hit his head!" Faaghira's voice came from the other side of the room, but Scott didn't dare look up. With his luck he'd just hit his head again. He settled for lightly tapping against the tray instead of getting up. As soon as he heard footsteps rush over to him he rose yet again...and hit his head...yet again. He tries to play it off when Faaghira comes around the corner but, nah, not even close.

"Scott, are you alright?" Faaghira pushed the tray up and sat down on Scott's legs. He frantically tried to readjust himself but just grabbed a pillow and put it in his lap then sat up.

"Me? Pfft, I'm fine! Are you okay?" He's trying hard to look calm but it's not fooling anyone. He's too frantic...and excitable.

She shook her head and did a quick eye roll. His efforts aren't landing well but he always seems to have some kind of charm when he's around her. How she sees any charm in his antics is beyond me. "That tray really must've done a number on your head; you're acting weirder than normal. What happened out there?"

"Out where? Who said I was anywhere? I mean, I left but that's all there is to it."

"I already know you went back home; Baron Sugar told me. I'm just curious as to why you came back. Don't get me wrong, I'm happy to see you, but why didn't you stay back there? That was where you were trying so hard to get to, after all."

"I knew you'd miss me...and some other stuff but who cares? I don't care. I also don't like leaving jobs unfinished. I wanted to help sort out this whole Atticus situation, so I came back for that too." He kept repositioning himself on the couch while he talked, so now he's smiling in an effort to make it less awkward. It's really not working, buddy. Faaghira definitely isn't buying it.

"Thanks for thinking about me, but-"

"But what?" Scott interrupted frantically.

"I think you should've stayed home. Look, it's great to see you; it really is, but I'm about to be bogged down in the worst fight this place has ever seen. I don't want you anywhere near me right now. Tell Baron Sugar to take you back."

"No. I'm here now, so you'll just have to deal."

"I won't argue with you, so looks like I'll just have to get you up to speed." She got off his legs and sat on the floor, resting her back against the couch. "Safira and I came up with a main plan and a contingency just in case things go sour. The main gist is that we cut off resources like I was saying before. Some of the places we'll hit will be dummy targets so when he won't know what our plan is when he retaliates. If he can't find a pattern then he can't pin us down so we have to keep him from catching on."

"Looks like you've got the game on lock. What do you think would make this go bad?" Scott's chilling out a little but he's still looking a little antsy. (Side note: he's really annoyed by all my comments but he knows I'm doing it to antagonize him. The best part is that he can't fire back at me without sounding crazy because most of the time he's the only one around that can hear me)

"Well for one I'm making this sound way easier than it actually will be. Atticus may be the scum off the Earth but he's not an idiot; at least not in the traditional sense."

"He's also your uncle."

"Don't remind me." She let out a deep breath before she continued. "There won't be a large window of time where this could work. We'll have to work fast and effectively but I'm sure we can pull it off. We're also doing the mass disobedience thing, so I thought you'd be happy about that if you got to hear it, but you did, and you weren't supposed to since you're not supposed to be here."

"Right on!" He got so excited and it's just so precious.

"You're too much; it's adorable." She giggled and kissed him on the cheek.

"So when is all this supposed to start off?"

"Tomorrow, probably. Saffie has to call up her troops or whatever it is she does. They'll start with their real targets then switch over to dummy ones. Civil disobedience will start in two or three days depending on how fast I can organize it. Unfortunately it can't be a rapid fire thing because he'll know everything is tied together."

"But won't he know they're tied together anyway because of how close they'll be?"

"Probably, but he won't be prepared for it. I can't say that the plan will go by without a hitch, but I'm confident that we can make it with the city intact." Faaghira had some faint traces of regret in her voice but she was doing her best to mask it with her beautiful smile.

"That's great! Any other news?" Scott appeared to be genuinely excited which means he couldn't see through her smile. He looked at her with glowing intent; with hope; she just couldn't let him down.

"Yeah, Saffie wanted to talk to you about something. I'm sure it's not anything bad, but you should still go."

"Okay, no prob, bob."

"One more thing…"

"You name it."

"Don't call her Saff."

"I won't."

"Or Saffie."

"I'll see you in a few." Scott sprung up from the couch with all the exhilaration of a really, *really* annoying dog.

"Scott, I'm serious!" She sounded playful, of course, but

she probably isn't joking.

"Love you too." Scott walks out, disregarding Faaghira's words with playful banter. He goes to the table where Safira had been when he went outside earlier. She was still there after all this time; scanning over some pages and writing on a scattered pile of papers in front of her. There's a small tower of papers in front of her. Scott pulls out the chair on her left, but he hesitates when she a gives brief but chilling look of disapproval. I'm sure he got the message, but he still sat down anyway.

"Hey Saffie, I heard you were looking for me."

"Call me Saffie again and see how fast I fling you off the balcony." She didn't even care enough to look up from her papers. I'm glad she didn't; her eyes would've gave me the chills. Scott cleared his throat with a fake cough.

"So what did you need me for?"

"I didn't need you for anything."

"Did you want to apologize for earlier?"

"I would love to if I did anything wrong. I wanted to talk to you about society as a general measure. I understand that we've had different experiences, but it takes different looks for adequate discussions and solutions. If the revolution turns out to be a success, a properly functioning society needs to be implemented in order for it to have longevity. Things certainly can't stay where they are but some flaws are so deeply rooted in social norms that they cannot be undone without some sort of miracle. In short, I want the perfect achievable balance and I'd like your help to create that. "

"Putting all that jumbo aside; you care about what I think?" He's getting hopeful; proud, even. Something about his excited face makes him so punchable.

"I trust Fae's judgement-" She paused; abruptly cutting off the remainder of the thought before it could come to fruition. "I trust Fae's judgement, but I'm baffled; what would have her enamored with someone so dense?"

"I'm not dense; I'm a realist!"

"Call it whatever you want, but you're dense. Regardless, I want to implement a standard out there for acceptance. It'll take some time for it to work well enough, but without any effort to combat the current systems and beliefs then another Atticus could easily come into power."

"So you expect the abused and their abusers to hold hands and sing kumbaya just because their old government was overthrown?"

"Did you understand *anything* that I just said?"

"And you're also not considering that there'll be another you if there's ever another him. It may not seem like it sometimes, but everything balances itself out."

"And to believe you actually call yourself a realist. That's not how the real world works. Just because one thing happens it doesn't mean that the opposite takes place the next day. Do poor people get rich a year after the wealthy get their profits?"

"No, but when would it work like that?"

"It's what you're implying. I want to fix things; that means not having the same societal struggle we do now. Wars were never meant to last forever. Hell, they don't even have to happen."

"Who said this was a war?"

"I don't understand what she sees in you! I'm more intelligent; better looking; far more aware of important issues; and I'm stronger than you!"

"You forgot to put *jealous* somewhere in there."

"You're nothing short of annoying. Putting that aside, I would still appreciate your help. Race relations among other issues will plague any efforts of significant beneficial change if there isn't preparation."

"You sound a lot like someone I know. I personally never believed the whole 'nation to fix' thing that everybody's crying about. Race isn't as big of an issue as it seems. Hell, my girlfriend is white. Some of the old stuff is still around and always will be. You don't need to put a plan in place to 'fix' anything, especially if you know nothing can be fixed. You can't make some kindergarten 'How I stopped racism kind of thing. Some things are the way they are."

"And that's how you really feel about it?"

"Um, yeah. Do we have a problem?" Scott instantly put his guard up.

"We don't have a problem; *you* have problems." She was steadily getting more intense. It's easy to see from her strained eyes that she's exhausted, but the bloodshot gaze makes her so much more intimidating. The best part (or worst; I don't know) is that she isn't giving him her full attention. She's deeply focused on her papers.

"So the only reason I'm over here is to be ridiculed by you?" Scott's tone has a lot more sass than anger right now. In fact, it's more sass than anything.

"Leave, I'll handle this myself. You two must get along so well because neither of you make sense." She's aggravated and there's no doubt about it. However, it's not any brash actions that give it away; she's cool and collected. It's those cold eyes that give the illusion of indifference. Combined with her naturally commanding voice, it's a dangerous combination. It's one that could easily give anyone without a keen eye a sign of acceptance or even tolerance.

"Later Saffie" he ushered slyly before getting up from his eat and walking away. Whether it was because of sheer annoyance or because of the case load; she didn't retaliate. The most she did was shoo him away with her free hand as she wrote furiously with the other.

Scott looks at Fae for approval on his way back to the couch, but he gets shut down when she didn't even do so much as smirk. Her expression isn't nearly as cold as

Safira's, but the usual warmth is definitely missing. No nervous smile or awkward laughter; instead it's some degree of disapproval. He seemed to have taken notice but rather than address it, he set up a joke that ultimately fell flat. Afterwards, she went from disapproval to concern, and after seeing the fruits of his failed efforts, he cleared his throat a little louder than normal.

"So Fae, I didn't get to ask you, so rude of me; how was your day?"

"Scott, you haven't been gone for a day."

"Well what about the time I was gone? How was that?"

"Just fine. Scott, what is this?"

"Oh good; I was meaning to ask you about this thing we have going on between us but I'm glad you brought it up first."

"No, not that; we'll get to that later. What I wanted to know is why in the frump you're acting like such a douche."

"Why in the... *frump?*" Scott was holding in a fit of laughter which in turn started to crack Fae's straight face. She fixed it real quick and furrowed her brow to make herself seem more serious.

"Yes Scott, frump; I'm trying to get around cursing for the next four days because I made a bet with Safira. I'm probably gonna lose, but that's not the point. Why are you acting so douche all of a sudden?"

"All of a sudden? I'm always a douche, if you haven't already noticed. So about our dynamic; relationship status if you will."

"Nope, you're not dodging this time. What happened back home that made you... this?"

"Nothing bad enough for you to be in my business about. In fact, everything was how it normally is. If you don't believe me; well I don't know what else to tell you."

"I *don't* believe you. Call me out if I'm wrong, but would you come back here if everything was really the same as when you left it? You were willing to fight to get back to your shitty love life, so something must have really been bad for you to *want* to get away from it. With that being said; what was it that changed when you went back?"

"Me, I changed. I wasn't the same after I met you and I couldn't cut this place out before giving us a try. I wasn't even fighting before."

"You fracking liar! I know you're lying because you never just suddenly feel a burst of emotions. I know you like me and I like you; we've been past that part. You were still trying to get with me after you told me you have a girlfriend and I was okay with that. Maybe I shouldn't have been, but it didn't seem to matter to you. It didn't seem like you would even care to try and hide anything from your girlfriend. From the way you were carrying on, she must not care either. But don't you dare try to tell me that *I'm* the reason you're back here!" She hasn't come close to yelling so far but the sheer intensity in her voice more than makes up for it.

For Scott, there's no smile or snide remark to show. He's stuck in the truth of the matter; the truth of raw emotion. He begrudgingly sat down on the couch and patted the cushion next to his; signaling for Faaghira to sit down. She did, but on the floor and not the couch. Unlike pretty much everyone that's talked to Scott so far, she looked him dead in the eyes.

"Fae, love makes people crazy things; you should know that."

"I should know that? You're trying to call me the crazy one?"

"No, Fae you know that's not what I meant!" He quickly propped himself up to get closer to Faaghira, but the proximity didn't do any good. The air between them is cold. The two warm hearts crafted an iceberg from one's negligence. This is different from Safira's intimidating eyes or the piercing disapproval of Scott's own mother. This is distance; worlds apart from the tender care that was still living just moments ago.

"This better be swinging in a different direction real soon or else I'm out." She leaned forward with her hands resting on her knees; a final hearing for Scott's plea. He cleared his throat once more and ran his fingers through his coarse hair before saying another word.

"Fae, I love you; isn't that enough for you?"

"Nope; come and get me when you're ready to cut the bullshit. And if you still want to know what we have, what's going on between us; there's officially nothing until further notice. I'm still holding out for you, but from what I've seen you've got some big problems and I'm not trying to solve them. I'm not your mom."

Scott started to go into a squint, presumably to mask the buildup of water in his eyes. "I'll go and...um; just tell Baron Sugar if you need me for anything." They both part from the couch; Faaghira goes to the table and Scott heads to the front door. Neither one looked backed at the other as they left. Scott quietly shut the door behind him.

He walked down the hallway and stopped when he passed a mirror hanging over a desk. He took a few steps back to look at himself. His eyes were strained, his face was solemn; he looked exhausted. It's not the sleepy kind of tired; it's the type that spurs from a manic time. "God, what did they do to you?" He laughed slightly but it faded away before he moved away from the mirror. He went to the elevator, rapidly pressed the button to call, then waited impatiently for it to come up. As soon as it opened he paced inside and leaned against the back wall. "Well this is shit." Maybe it wouldn't be this bad if you did some things differently. "Like you would've done any better. I did what I know works so you can chill with that. Everything turned out the way it turned out and nothing can change that. It's also safe to say that about eighty percent of what I've had to deal with in the past few days isn't even real. New Orleans, Faaghira, a demon that follows me around, you, another dimension that's apparently in a children's book; none of this shit matters because it's not real."

"I'll have you know that I'm very real. If I wasn't then you would've already died from alcohol poisoning." Roswell was next to Scott; deeply focused on writing in a composition book.

Scott pursed his lips, shut his eyes, and tilted his head up to the ceiling. "Go away. Please go away. I didn't want to be bothered before, but I definitely don't want to be bothered now."

"Alright, alright, say no more." Roswell is gone without a trace.

Scott opens his left eye to check if Roswell is still there even though I just said he disappeared. "I don't have time for your crap either." Um, actually, you do. I'm still the narrator of the story you're in so deal with it. "So when is this gonna be over anyway?" Why the rush? It's not like you have a home to go back to. "Nooooooo! Too soon, man; way too soon." Scott's weak, raspy exclamation- "Can you stop? For like, one minute? I'm not in the zone right now; I'm sure whoever's reading this crap gets the point."

"Say no more." As soon as the elevator doors opened, Roswell paced through leaving Scott in solitude again? When did he come back? This script makes no sense! Scott, you might've been right in calling this a crapshoot.

"You doubted my futuristic prowess? Why am I not surprised?" Maybe because there's no prowess to speak of. "Yeah, whatever. Hey, you wouldn't happen to know any good eats around here, would you?" No, but you could ask Roswell if there's any spots nearby. I'm sure he'll do that weird reappearing thing if you call him out. "I don't think you understand; I'm trying to get away from him. I'm not calling him here. He left already and he's leaving me alone right now, so I'll pass on bringing him back." Are you

286

hungry or not? "Funny thing, I'm not really so much as I'm sad. I'm embracing my feminine side and indulging in some beautiful but clearly unhealthy food." Is that what you think women do when they're sad? "No, that's what *I* do when *I'm* sad. I'm embracing my feminine side by talking about my feelings; those were two separate statements."

Scott walked out of the lobby much slower than he had anywhere else at the moment. He was still trudging along even when he passed by the (intimidating) concierge (? Still not sure if that's what he is). He walked on, pushed the entrance doors open and didn't look back.

But then he ruined it all by going back inside the lobby. He slammed his hand down on the concierge desk then- "If it wouldn't be any inconvenience for you; would you mind telling me if there's any good restaurants around the area?" -gently requested information on nearby restaurants in the most gentle way possible. This is weird, even for you.

"You're Scott, correct?" The concierge, guard- person put a note on the desk and slid it over to Scott. He doesn't smile or anything of the sort; his unwavering, serious face stays.

"Thanks. You're a very scary man, keep it up." Scott leans in to pat him on the shoulder but man grabs Scott's arm and slams it on the desk.

"Don't touch me." The concierge let go then vanished to a room behind the desk. Scott was only able utter the first sound of another word before the concierge shut the door and locked it. Scott shrugged and took the list with him as he walked out of the lobby.

Scott stood for a while, admiring the sights of the buildings, streets, and cars all around. Everything is posh and high end, from the people and the streetlights all the way down to the fire hydrants (don't ask). While nothing is gold plated (it would look too cheap), it's all the highest quality materials you could only find in some of the wealthiest places in the world. Most of the skyline is modular instead of the traditional geometric designs. It wasn't futuristic per se, it's mostly post-modern (there's a difference, I promise). Everything was bright; everything was overly bright. It wasn't blinding but it was just a little, just a little much. Scott briefly covered his eyes, but he adjusted real quick. He had to get over it to be able to see all the sights, of course.

"Okay, so this is pretty boring; I'm gonna check this note to see if there's any good eats in town." I'm pretty sure there are. I mean, there has to be; look at this place! The only problem might be getting you something you can afford. "Hey, I have a couple dollars in my pocket; I can get something if I want it." I'm getting a vibe that you wouldn't want it if it's not on the dollar menu. "Back it up; I bet you I can walk into any one of these places on this list and buy something." Alright, but just so you know, water and complementary bread don't count. "Okay, I see how it is. Let's check this first place on here: *Rocco, West 18th and Dagget.* Dagget; that's a weird name for a street; I hope it's not far. What does it say in the author's notes?" No more. "So you're just going to quit on me now? Figures." Calm down; the author's notes say 'no more'. Like I said before, there's no way I can read far ahead of where you are. Also, the notes aren't always that specific. Remember that I'm a narrator and not a strategy guide. "That's cool and all, but where do I go?"

After much deliberation with an outside force, Scott was left to face the situation on his own. "Fine, I'll go look for it. Just so you know; it's your fault if I get lost." But of course, he's enjoying a nice match of the blame game before setting off to find the first restaurant. "I don't need your help; I'm can find it on my own."

After going through a cycle of going in circles, getting lost, and looking for city maps for the better half of twenty minutes; Scott found a small park and rested in an area far from everyone else. He picked a stray Queen Anne's Lace stem from the fresh, evenly cut, lush green grass. He held it up in the center of the moon and idly twirled it around. "I don't suppose you know where Rocco is." Scott went into an abrupt silence. "Right now all I really want is something to get my spirits up; the good kind." He put the flower down gently by his knee then laid back on the grass.

"Didn't think I'd see someone like you around here." An airy voice flowed over to his ears, causing him to rise up and trace the source. I bet you can't guess who- well actually you can't guess who it is because this isn't someone he's come across before, but it shouldn't come as a surprise that the person in question is a beautiful woman. Her figure differs from Faaghira's, very slim, but from what I've gathered; to Scott, a body is a body. Her skin is lighter than Faaghira's but it still worlds away from fair. Her hair is a long, ravenous black stream. Her eyes are a vibrant reddish-brown; accentuated by a harsh, black liner. Those doe eyes are big enough to get lost in, but yet a mere glance would be insufficient for taking in the beauty. Her lips are colored with glistening in black lip gloss. She's donned in a red flannel shirt, black skinny jeans and hi tops of the same color; laces and all. But before we go any further, well... let's just see how this goes.

"You're not getting a pass just because you're hot; what do you mean 'someone like me'?"

"Relax, I didn't mean to come off the wrong way. I meant I didn't think I'd see someone who has time to chill out. Everyone in this city is always working hard at something; it's usually just part of one big rat race."

"Speaking of race, which I usually don't; your opening was pretty racist."

"Well it doesn't *have* to be."

"No, not that one, but I'm definitely thinking. But before

this carries on, I need to know something."

"If you need it that bad then you'll *have* to say please."

"Are you racist?"

She tilted her head to the side and made an inquisitive face, which soon turned into a playful smile. "That's not something I get asked every day. Hmm, let's see…I consider myself to be pretty racist, but I don't always do a good job of keeping up with it."

"Are you being serious?"

"Is it a deal breaker?"

"Deal breaker? You move pretty fast; what's your angle?"

"Acute, but I'm a lot more than just a pretty angle. I have a name too; it's Daphne."

"Well, Daphne, I have a favor to ask."

Her face lit with a sultry grin. "Already? You didn't even buy me dinner yet."

"Actually, that's *exactly* what this is about."

𝔙!!

𝕿he Best
Things In
Life...

CHAPTER VII
THE BEST THINGS IN LIFE...

"So let me get this straight; you're actually going to take me to dinner and all I have to do is show you where the place is?"

"Yeah. If you'd rather stay here in the park, then I'd totally understand; it's a beautiful place. The only thing is that I'll have to find someone else that'll take me there, but they won't be as good of companions as you." Scott had that smug smile on his face.

"Ooo, companion; you're really sweet talking me...um...what's your name again?"

"My bad, I didn't tell you already. I'm Scott, your favorite person for tonight." He threw his fist up into the air, but it fell down just as fast.

Daphne smiled at the silly gesture, but otherwise, it fell flat. "Which place is it?"

"I overheard some people talking about this place called Rocco. Do you know how to get there or am I on my own?" Scott sat up to look her in the eyes.

"It's a cool place if you don't have a certain food in mind. You get whatever they put on the menu, but they'd go through hell and high water to make sure you like it. I definitely know where it is but we'd better hurry before it closes." Daphne went to a tree a few yards behind them before the last words part from her lips. She returned with a longboard with blatant knock off versions of popular characters painted all over. The board has duct tape covering a few spots but the vibrant colors (along with the knock offs themselves) make it look edgy and worn in rather than old and worn out. "Earth to Scott. You can check it out after dinner; let's get a move on." She put one foot on the board and was ready to push forward, but she relaxed when she saw Scott reaching his hand out. She looked back at him for a little bit, but she started coasting immediately after.

Scott hurried to catch up when he realized that she wasn't stopping. "Hey Daph, wait up!"

"There's a deadline, kid. It's a little ways off from here but we can make it in time. We can't stop till we get there."

"Can we talk on the way?"

"I can; can you?" She kicked back, pushing her board with enough force to blow air in Scott's face.

Scott rushes to catch up with the new girl that has him interested.

He can't catch up with her at walking speed but as we know, Scott is quite lazy. The streets are still busy at this time of night; as real cities never die out. Cars were still out on the street, but Daphne didn't seem to care at all. One of them was about six seconds from a new color splash on the windshield but the car stopped just in time. She has an annoyingly smug smirk as she continued to cross the street. Scott mouthed 'sorry' to the car then ran to catch up to Daphne.

"You're insane! You could've got hit! You could've gotten yourself killed!" He didn't yell or shout, but he did sound pretty excitable. It was more of a 'Wow, you almost got yourself killed! You're so cool; marry me' kind of thing. Put someone pretty in front of him and he's about as resilient as a bed sheet.

"But I didn't so no biggie." She had a laser focus on her path; wherever it was to. She didn't bother telling Scott which way they were going. This didn't last for long; she slowed down just enough for their paces to be pretty close (slow for her considering she was on a longboard). "But what was it you were so anxious to talk about?"

"You never talk just to talk?"

"I'm not trying to stall anyone; why would I do that?" She gave another strong kick back and zipped past Scott.

"Wait!" He rushed after her, going a much faster pace than before. He was finally going a speed that people would use when they actually have somewhere to be. He pushed through people in his effort to get to her, but he wasn't moving any faster. It was one of those rude and completely unnecessary shoves people do on the streets sometimes. Daphne, however, was no better. She was basically plowing over anyone that didn't clear out of her path (which wasn't apparent at all).

After a gently chaotic mix of sharp turns, angry people swearing, and cars honking their horns in frustration, Scott found himself at another large and utterly pretentious looking building. It looks like an office building more than anything else, but it doesn't *feel* like one. There was no name on the building, which in the wake of Atticus' governing, is a rare and valuable sight.

Daphne sat on her longboard, waiting at the chrome-covered revolving doors. "Took you long enough."

"Give me a break; you have a skateboard."

Daphne picked up the longboard and tucked it underneath her shoulder before pushing through the chrome doors. She muttered "longboard" under her breath before disappearing inside the building. He was just about to follow, but he froze before the door handlebar was in his reach.

"Do you have business in there?" A medium height, middle aged man with a scratchy stubble called out to Scott in a harsh tone. His shape is odd; it imitates a bulging sack of potatoes with a rope tied tightly at the bottom end. Or better yet, from a farther angle, the entire shape could easily be compared to a bowling pin. It may be more accurate to say that it is the mirror image of a Hershey Kiss with two toothpicks sticking out of the bottom. But enough about the shape or his crusty face and lack of lips; he's has to be some kind of important for Scott to freeze up like he did. The (misshapen) guy is decked out in riot gear, with his hand in

294

his holster (okay I need to stop joking; this is getting serious). His fingers are close enough to the trigger to pull in the blink of an eye. The words 'Justice and Peace Authority' are printed on his armored vest

Scott took a deep breath but otherwise, his body was motionless. "No matter what, don't turn around. The only way he's looking you in the eyes is if he turns over your dead body" Scott advised himself in a hushed voice.

"Boy, I'm speaking to you. What's the matter, you don't have a voice?" The officer's boots made loud clicking noises that steadily got louder along with his voice.

"My business is none of yours. I didn't do anything so leave me alone and go find something else to do." Scott's eyes were shut and he hadn't turned around; just like he said. He didn't raise his voice, but in his bold words were hints of shakiness. However, these were fading drops in tone that easily be missed because of how brief they were.

But then it happened; that sound. The gun had been drawn from its holster. Next was the infamous 'click'.

Scott is already pushing through the revolving doors like planned on doing earlier. The movement is very slow; a sluggish anticipation.

The air thins out as the next sound follows. Next comes shock; not from the sound that came, but for the one that didn't. The officer was called over the radio and he responded immediately.

"Lewis, what are you doing?" The grating voice on the other end was unmistakable and the sudden shift in the officer, apparent. He looked to have true fear struck into him; the officer was frozen still.

"I'm- someone is going into the Houston building. They're unauthorized and they could possibly be a terrorist; I don't want to take any chances. This is standard pr-"

"You are operating under old orders. There's been a change in procedure and I know that you were briefed on this. So tell me, and I need a *good* reason; what are you doing?"

"It's a suspicious person; it's defying an officer's orders, and I have reason to believe that this could be a potential threat to this area."

"As I thought. You will report to City Hall within the hour. If you don't then I'll have to meet you where you are. There 'll be quick work, understand?"

"Yes sir, Mr. Bellamy." The officer holstered his gun and began walking away from the scene. Before leaving he said "you're real lucky this time!" in a... rather indiscrete way. Scott finally pushed through the revolving doors, but the sound of the officer's radio going back on reached Scott's ears before he got in the lobby.

Daphne was sitting with her legs crossed, in a chair between an elevator and a magazine rack. She was smoking a worn cigarette.

"Some help *you* were."

"Easy, politics aren't my thing."

"I literally could've died."

"And I'm happy you didn't." She blew a puff of smoke into the lobby's clean air and followed up with a flirtatious smile. Despite the invitation, Scott appeared to be unamused.

"You're lucky you're hot."

"It's not luck. Face it, I hit the genetic jackpot. But you've got me wondering; what would you do if I was *different*?"

"It depends..." Daphne got up from her seat and called an elevator while Scott was stuck in his thoughts. When the elevator opened and Daphne pressed the button for the twelfth floor, Scott nodded his head... for whatever reason. "If by different you mean ugly, then I definitely would've went somewhere else. To be honest, I probably wouldn't show up here with you. And if you mean *not a jerk*, then I'd ask you to marry me a month or two. You should be excited; it's a pretty big deal if I'd wanna marry anyone."

"In that case, I'm honored. This restaurant should make up for *whatever* it is that has your legs all tied up in a knot. It's a swanky joint; great for someone with pockets."

The elevator doors slid open to reveal the clean, large, and luxurious twelfth floor. Jazz (the kind usually made out to be elevator music) is being played live, but the musicians are nowhere to be seen (from the entrance, at least). The grandiose is fairly unnecessary, but it falls in line with the intense competition that seems to be happening between each square inch of the city. Everything, from the chairs to the floors, has gold lining. Excessive is an understatement, but that's fitting being that so far the city comes off as one big, glaring overstatement. The entire floor is a lounge area with furniture has all the curves, shine, and glamour of the future of yesteryear. Not a single patron is dressed in anything remotely casual, which makes Daphne and Scott look like a sixty-four pack of crayons at a funeral.

The two were met with judging stares when people started taking notice of them. Nobody actually said anything; they simply looked at Scott and Daphne with the subtlest form of disgust. The duo strolled past the onlookers; Daphne was unfazed, but Scott was a different story. His breathing was quietly released but rapid in pace. His right hand was varying from having the slightest bit of shakiness to closely resembling a tremor. He wasn't displaying any other unusual traits, but when put side by side with Daphne, he was an avalanche of uneasiness. She was a stone fortress and he was a clay house made on sand by the ocean.

"I get it" Scott spoke angrily, but as softly as he could.

"Get what?"

"I get that we don't look like all the other stiffs in here but damn, do they have to look at us like *that*?" Scott, I give you props on that one; but remember what I said about talking to me around other people.

When the duo made their way to a diner near the outer

297

rim of the lounge area, the judging patrons turned their attention back to whatever it is they were doing earlier. The diner isn't tiny, but it appears modest relative to the rest of the room. It is separated from the lounge by sliding doors with beige screens that take in light but keep out prying eyes. Above sliding doors are two cursive 'R's; one for each entrance.

"Rocco's?" Scott asked in a way that feigned certainty but still managed to have some confidence.

"What gave it away?"

"Lucky guess. Luck only swings around when I'm guessing."

"Also, it's Rocco; singular and it doesn't own anything." Daphne was quick to light the fire under Scott.

They stood at the sliding door for the front entrance for a brief moment, which was really only brief because Daphne got tired of standing there and doing nothing. She opened the door and closed it behind her, which seemed to be just what was needed to pull Scott back to reality. Well, I guess it counts as reality. He hastily opened the door, but he closed it gently when the host standing behind the bar stopped what they was doing and looked at Scott with a cold, but blank expression. They didn't say anything; instead they immediately went back to their business.

"Two" the host spoke in a gentle voice that had a base of firmness.

"It's his bill; just so you know." Daphne made sure to clear up any confusion; she wasn't paying for whatever they were having. But Scott is? Yeah, let's see how that one plays out.

Scott went to go pull out the chair next to Daphne, but it moved outwards on its own. He flinched at the movement, though it wasn't exactly sudden. He cleared his throat then sat down when he noticed Daphne snickering at him. The host returned with three menus; two for Scott and Daphne, and the third was placed at the last seat at the far end of the counter (the counter isn't that long). Daphne and Scott looked through their menus simultaneously, but only one was surprised by the 'minimalist' options.

"Hey Daphne, did you know that this menu only has two choices on it?"

"I mean, yeah; we're looking at the same menu."

"But I thought there would be more than 'seafood with rice' and 'landfood with rice'. I know high end restaurants tend to be more conservative in their number of choices, but I never thought I'd see something like this! And who calls it 'landfood'? It's just food!"

The host's face was unchanging and as cold as it was, no anger or disappointment was displayed. "If you don't like that I'd recommend seafood with rice."

"Is there any chance I can get it without rice?"

"We don't have that on the menu."

"But you'd literally be saving rice if you just kept it off my plate."

"I can guarantee that we have more than enough rice for each guest. Also, let me point out that 'no rice' is not an option on our menu."

"That's stupid. I'll have the seafood, I guess." Scott grudgingly put the menu down and handed to the host.

Daphne beamed with a wide eyed smile and rested her cheek in her palm, watching Scott run on. "And I'll have some of that lovely landfood, with rice, of course." However, her smile started to dull out a little when the host didn't laugh. The host's face hadn't changed at all; it remained generally emotionless. Scott started laughing at her but when host looked at him the same way, the laughter hushed itself out of existence. The host then went into the kitchen, leaving the two of them alone.

"Daphne-" but that didn't last long because someone else came in sitting down at the opposite end of the counter. The man that came in was young; he looked to be around his early twenties. His nappy hair is sponged into faint coils and the sides are cut down to a skin fade. He has a weak moustache and bushy eyebrows but no other facial hair. Hold up, this sounds familiar. "That can't be him."

"What happened, you know that guy?" Daphne perked up and leaned forward.

"No, my bad; he just kinda looks like this other black dude I know." Scott began to trail off as Daphne lost interest. However, Scott's eyes still lingered on that guy for a little longer. "It's not a gay thing, I swear!" Scott cleared his throat again then readjusted in his seat...again.

The host emerged from the kitchen and a chef passed by on the way to the counter. The chef placed a wooden box down in a slightly lower area behind the counter. The small prepping station isn't obstructed from where Scott and Daphne were seated. The chef masterfully crafted a meal of shrimp, scallop, and lobster vindaloo; it was placed over a plate of steaming coconut rice. She gently put the plate down in front of Daphne, wiped the area down, and then started preparing more food. This time it was freshly cooked tortellini that the chef covered with various cheeses and spices in one swift motion. Afterwards she seared chicken cutlets, mixed vegetables and white rice in peanut sauce.

"Oh, landfood. You could've just said it was chicken." Scott looked down at the plate in front of him with a mix of content and confusion. But when the chef crossed her arms and turned her back, Scott started scarfing down the food. He slowed down to a complete stop when he noticed the host looking at him with that uneasy stare. "The food is good, just in case you were wondering." The host almost smiled but never fully got there. Actually, it wasn't really that close to a smile; it just wasn't a frown. Scott and Daphne dined on more of their respective meals after finishing their first plates (everything else is in relatively small portions). The chef beamed proudly at the work she had done, then she vanished into kitchen. The host went over to the other end of the counter where that guy was sitting, but they returned almost to Scott immediately.

"Your bill was paid by that gentleman over there. I assume you know each other but as long as the bill is paid then your business is none of my business. Enjoy the rest of your night." The host went back to the other end of the counter, but the patron that paid the bill was already leaving. Scott carefully followed after him, keeping a good bit of distance from the guy. Daphne was puzzled by the strange behavior but she didn't say anything; she followed to see where he was going with this. They followed him through the flurry of patrons all the way back to the elevator. The man stopped at the elevator doors and-

"I'll take it from here."

"Who's he talking to?" Daphne must be pretty weirded out right now. I totally understand though; this is weird.

"First off I'm not weird. Scratch that; I'm *extremely* weird. I'm weird but I did pay for your food, and you're already going downstairs, so we should talk for a minute."

"Um... no thanks; we were about to do something else, but you go ahead and have fun with whatever it is you're doing." Daphne faked a smile then started walking away. She would've walked off, but Scott's immobility had her tied on a short leash. "Oh yeah, I forgot; thanks for paying the bill. Scott, I thanked guy; we can leave now and go play pool like you said we would."

"You can chill; Scott sucks at pool. My name is Roswell, by the way. It's nice to meet you Daphne. You're wondering who I am, but you also probably don't care. No worries though, I don't care about you either; I'm here for Scott but he's not leaving without you so looks like we'll get to know each other anyway."

"Can you just leave me alone?" Scott groaned at the sight

of the man; unsurprised but begrudging, nonetheless. He rubbed his eyes with his palms then peeked out one to see if the guy was still there.

"What are you, a toddler? I won't vanish just because you cover your eyes it doesn't mean I'll magically disappear from existence. I mean, I could, but I don't use my power for show. But, before we continue; are you crazy kids going in the elevator right now or are you leaving later? There's not that much to do up here and you definitely wouldn't fit in with anything anyone's doing. Daphne, I'm talking to you too."

"Not trying to be rude, but who the fuck are you anyway?" Daphne tensed up, but she was more defensive than angry.

"Babe, you're not even that tough, so don't try me. Scott, are you bringing your new girlfriend or not?"

"I'm not going in the elevator with you; like Daphne said, we have things to do."

"Alright, and which one of you was going to pay for those things?"

"You know what? This place does seem really boring and the only plan we actually had was to eat at that restaurant, which we already did; now's a pretty good time to call it a night."

"I thought you had money!" She whispered angrily in Scott's ear before nudging him in elbow.

"I have money but I not that much money. Did you notice that the menu didn't have any prices? I can't afford a place like that!"

"Neither of you could pay for it. You showed up to get time away from your not-girlfriend and this chick comes along for free food at a pretentious dive. There's no telling which one of you is more full of shit."

"You mean, which one of us is full of more shit." Daphne smiled in a way almost as smug as Roswell's signature look.

"Yup, it's definitely you, darling" Roswell's arm inverted, leading him to call the elevator in the most disgusting, absolutely unsettling way. "Believe it kid; I haven't been playing up on the whole demon shtick in a while."

Daphne reluctantly got in the elevator when it opened, but as Roswell pointed out; there wasn't much of a choice. Roswell's arm turned itself back around after he pressed the panel for the first floor. Daphne cringed at the sight while Scott, on the other hand, actually looked somewhat relieved (weirdo). Daphne quietly made her way to the back wall and wasted no time getting on her phone.

"I've gotta hand it to you; out of all the people around, you always find the girls that are basically you. I knew you were a narcissist, but I didn't know it was so serious; this is great!" Roswell threw his fist up in the air in what has to be the most dramatic way possible. Scott responded to the demon with a weak smile and thumbs up.

There was silence for a short time, but the small space made every second stretch out for an unbearable amount of time. Daphne would look up from her phone momentarily to shoot quick glances at Scott.

"So is this a normal thing for you or do you actually think this is weird too?"

"Trust me, he thinks this is weird, but this definitely isn't even close to the weirdest thing he's dealt with in the past two days; and I'm Roswell, by the way. So were you two planning on going somewhere special or even not so special after dinner? Call me nosy, but I just love a good story about other people's relationships."

"Alright, Nosy" Daphne put her attention back on her phone; she tilted it up slightly then took an inconspicuous picture of the demon. There was no flash or sound from the camera, but a knowing smile cracked itself out on Roswell's face. When the elevator door (just one) opened, it revealed...

a strange, poorly drawn forest. Okay, this is weird, even for you; the heck is this?

"Oops, my bad; that place shows up out of the bl... um... it appears at random times. Just ignore that; act like you didn't see it." The demon manually shut the elevator door then reopened it. This time the lobby from earlier was there, but it was filled with dead security and patrons. Scott and Daphne were petrified by the morbid sight, but Roswell looked at the scene with squinted eyes whilst rubbing his chin. "Hmm, this wasn't supposed to happen." Daphne's eyes looked vacant, as her soul up and left. Before he closed the door, he caught a glimpse of a bloody red tiger with elongated vulture wings. It was still faced forward with its back turned to the elevator; tearing at the remains of multiple corpses simultaneously. "Damn it, not him again!" he slammed the door closed.

"What the fuck was that?" Scott was terrified by the sight and Daphne was struck by a panic attack. There was a violent pounding on the door that was so loud it cut off whatever Roswell was about to say next. Roswell waited for the sound to subside, but he was agitated when it persisted. He opened the door and backhanded the creature.

"Fuck off, I'm busy"; Roswell's discontent led to a rather underwhelming display of emotions. The creature let out a disorienting, heavily distorted howl right in Roswell's face. Whatever bit of his trademark smile that was there was replaced by anger. He hit the creature with a hard right hook to the jaw, leaving a cracked bone and a mouth hanging sideways. "Never minds his own business" Roswell slammed the door and when he reopened it there was a completely different lobby. The lobby was clean just as it was before, but it was clearly a different lobby. There was a different concierge, different art; different colored walls; different furniture; it was really, really weird. "Yeah, I had to make a quick change of plans. That 'thing' messed everything up."

"What. The. Ever. Loving. Fuck? What did you do?" Daphne was freaking out like crazy.

Roswell walked out, muttering under his breath; "Motherfuckers never happy." Scott and Daphne hesitantly followed him outside back on the sidewalk. "Hey so don't plan on following me around all night because that creep just gave me more work to do. I was actually supposed to be around the whole time so I could troll you on your...um...date? Outing? Whatever the hell people call it these days."

Daphne shyly raised her hand and Roswell excitedly called on her; "Yes, you with the long hair!"

"What's going on?"

"Excellent question. Hey, how about we go shopping or something; you know, walk off all that seafood and landfood you had. Don't worry about paying for anything; we already established that you're both broke in this part of town, so I'll cover it. Just don't go wild."

"Define wild" Daphne sounded odd; she was caught between interest and utter terror.

"Something the average Joe couldn't afford without bending over on the weekends. But if that's your deal then I heard there's a lot of people with 'good morals' who'd be very generous under the right lighting, or lack of."

"I'll pass."

"But they'd still probably try to smash. Alright let's go hit the stores."

"Do we have to do this, or do we have an actual say?" Scott finally chimed in after taking a backseat to the main conversation for so long. Sometimes I feel like this story is named for the wrong person.

"Well it's either shopping; a threesome; or going to a park and stargazing. Also, I know you won't go for it, but we could totally do a jazzy dance number. It's a lovely night;

we're in a beautiful city with decent public transit; most importantly, there's no smog." Roswell fought to contain his excitement, but it was no use; after a few seconds he was smiling from ear to ear.

"Suddenly, I have this strange urge to buy some stuff" Scott playfully scratched his head, faking coyness.

"Shopping doesn't sound too bad right about now."

"What turned you off; was it the threesome?" Roswell faked a gasp and covered his mouth with his hand.

"That actually wouldn't be that bad. I'm opting out because of the dance number; I hate musicals." Daphne crossed her arms and tried to smile but was still (understandably) freaked out.

"Well don't worry because *this is the start of something new-*" Roswell excitedly snapped his fingers to a beat.

"Cut it out."

"But Daphne… *it feels so right to avoid copyright infringement.*" Roswell held his hand out to her; making an extra effort to feign longing.

"Stop it now; *this isn't funny!*" Daphne's anger was building up fast.

"If it really bothers you that much. Okay so did you have anywhere in particular that you wanted to spend my money or is anywhere good?"

"Well I don't know the city at all so anywhere is fine with me." Scott physically wedged himself between Daphne and Roswell, but she was the only one irritated by the act. Roswell smirked proudly and closed his eyes to savor the moment.

"I love the part where you thought I was talking to you. Since I have to spell it out for you to get, I won't; I'm not doing you any favors. Now Daphne, is there anywhere that you're banking on?"

"I don't want to go to a clothing store; that's way too cliché. Also, no food because we just ate. Wait a second; did you eat?"

"I carry around a fridge with some leftovers everywhere I go, and I also have very particular tastes, so most joints aren't on my radar."

"Are you being sarcastic?"

"What's your guess? Whatever you think is right, so long as you think that I'm being dead serious. It's real, but before you ask, this is legit a real fridge and no you can't see it. Down to real business; where you wanna to go?"

"Let's keep walking and I'll point it out if I see something interesting. Remember that I'm not taking any suggestions; I still think you're a creep."

"Seeing that you're here with Scott, I don't trust your discretion at the slightest." Roswell pointed directly at Scott, but when Scott didn't react, Roswell continuously poked him until Scott yelled at him to stop. "Oh, you're so much fun."

They kept walking for a few blocks passing a few restaurants, jewelry stores, cafés, clothing stores and car shops. A quick side note: the car shops here are stores where you can buy cars as well as have them serviced. However, only one of the places they came across caught her eye: a modest looking jewelry store (well, modest when compared to all the places around it; the sign says 'jewelry' instead of an actual name).

"That's the place; I don't know if it's still in there but there's something I saw last time I was here that I wanted to get, but there was no way I could afford it. Luckily you can, so if you wouldn't mind then that's what I want."

"And what did you say this was?" Roswell was strolling past the store where Scott and Daphne already stopped.

"Wait!" She called out to the demon, "It's this really fancy looking silver necklace that has red agate stones in it. People say it belonged to The Fireman at some point and I think it would be pretty rad to have that." She reached out

307

for his arm, but Scott's knee-jerk reaction was to hold back her wrist. "Jealous already?"

"I'm not jealous but he's a dangerous guy. Don't touch him; he's not the kind of guy you'd want to try and hit on." Scott looked slightly worried, but he fixed his face when she looked back at him.

"Scott's going out of his way to protect someone? Am I the one that was put in another dimension? Hmm, water under the bridge. Tell you what; I'll go ahead and get you that necklace. I'm low key a huge fan of myths and legend, especially anything about *The Fireman* and other supernatural baddies." Roswell smiled in her direction, but some part of it seemed to fly past her and go directly to Scott. The demon illuminated with an aura of brooding red, but Daphne didn't see it; just Scott. Like so many things, it wasn't real; unless she was the one seeing an illusion. There was no prolonged stare or awkward silence; that moment passed so fast that it seems like it never happened at all. When Scott blinked Daphne had a small, rectangular velvet case in her hand and the three of them were walking into a bar.

"This seems like the perfect setup for a really bad joke. It must be true; life imitates art. Oh and Daphne, darling, you forgot your longboard at the lobby of the place we left. Don't worry, I'll buy you a new one." Roswell held open the door for Daphne, and the demon winked at Scott as he walked through. "Take a dive in the water and you'll still come out on fire. Come on down and have a drink, it's on me."

"Drinks? Uh...no drinks for me right now. I should go and see how Fae's doing." Scott hadn't even went two feet into the bar before turning the other way to leave. However, he was stopped cold when he heard what was playing on the bar's surprisingly underwhelming television.

"Hey folks, it's Atticus here with some important news to share. As you may already be aware, the terrorists that call themselves the rebellion are a very imminent threat, but recently there has been a violent attack on our economy that is causing the market to go below equilibrium. Due to this imbalance there would be no way to maintain stability and our economy would crash. I will have to raise the government's spending to account for the upcoming loss of revenue and stimulate the economy. However, along with that I will have to implement new taxes on the areas that are unfairly benefitting from this economic imbalance. I guarantee you that everything will return to normal *very* soon. There may even be a shift to an increase in revenue for our industrial sector. This means that we'll be expecting more millionaires in the next few months. If there's another issue then we'll handle that as we get to that point. God bless you all." Atticus smiled and waved before the program ends and the television reverts back to a baseball match.

"Fae must be freaking out right now. I have to get back to her and see how she's doing." Scott whispered to himself, or technically me.

Before leaving the bar, he heard someone say that they were "Happy to have a man of God in office." Scott heard Roswell's voice quietly call out "amen to that" before stepping back out into the streets.

"I could almost feel how smug he was. I mean, he always is, but there was something about this time that made me really uncomfortable." Doesn't he always make you uncomfortable? "Well yeah, but this time was different; worst part is that he hardly said anything. Anyway, I'm putting that aside for now; Fae might need my help." You helping her is the same as her wheeling around a broken carriage full of bricks. I'm sure she could do it, but it would hold her back more than anything. "But I can't- hold that thought for a second" Scott pulled his phone from his pocket and put it up to his ear. "Okay, so I can't keep letting that happen; I need to get some weight in this situation so I can pull it. She does so much and it makes me look like I'm not doing anything at all." Maybe because you're not. "Hush, I can help and I will. First order of business is to tell her about what Atticus just said." She probably already knows, but whatever helps you sleep at night. "But maybe I can do something to help, you don't know!"

With those words spoken, Scott hurried to Faaghira's complex…walking, of course. Also, he got lost a few times on his way there. He didn't how to get there but he knew where he was headed. It took him somewhere around twenty minutes of perseverance, but when he went straight for the stairs as soon as he got in the building. He ran all the way up to the eighth floor as fast as he could (which actually wasn't very fast) and frantically pushed at every door until one of them finally opened.

"Fae! You have to watch out for Atticus; he's trying to make-." He paused when he saw Faaghira at the table marking in a book while a little girl in the chair beside her did the same. Both of them looked at Scott; the little girl with a blasé expression and Faaghira with excitement.

Scott couldn't help but smile at Faaghira; her melanin blessed skin, her vibrant (slightly) different colored eyes, her illuminating grin, and her glistening kinky tresses are part of nature's most captivating composition.

"Was that in the script?" Umm…yeah. So, Faaghira's radiance was there in its wondrous display, while the little girl was giving off the complete opposite. The little girl was clearly not amused in any stretch of the imagination, and for some reason, this made Scott quite nervous.

V!!!

It Wasn't Awkward Until You Made It

CHAPTER VIII
IT WASN'T AWKWARD UNTIL YOU MADE IT

"Scott, this is my little sister Larimar."

"Oh, you have a little sister? You never said you had any siblings."

"She probably thought I wouldn't like you. You should know that she's almost never wrong." Larimar went back to marking in the book instead of engaging in a hostile stare-down. Scott was hesitant to join them at the table despite Faaghira's insistence, but he still went to take a seat. He was about to walk around Faaghira to sit next to her, but Safira was still there. To make things clear, Scott already saw her sitting with the two sisters, but he was hoping the rebel leader would give up her seat. Safira's eyes narrowed instead of a giving a scowl, but Scott still managed to get the picture. Scott was careful not to get too close to Larimar; he risked irritating her when moving the chair out to sit. "So what are you working on?" Scott peeked over Larimar's arm, taking note of a tin of colored pencils. The little girl almost completely ignored him; her first response was to lift her arm up so he could see the book clearly.

"We're coloring; this is what Fae and me do during family time. Do you want to color too?" Larimar gathered up a bundle of colored pencils and offered it up to him.

Scott looked at Faaghira from the corner of his eye. She nodded and mouthed "say yes" to him with a beaming smile. She also gave him two thumbs up to accompany her cute smile.

"Yes of course, I'd be delighted!" Scott smiled as he gently took them from her hand and Faaghira was looked excited to see Larimar smiling back. "So do I just reach over and color anywhere?"

312

"Yup. I don't say this to everyone, but you can even color outside the lines." Larimar spoke as if she was letting Scott in on the biggest secret this side of the universe. She flipped to a whole new page leaving her and Fae's work unfinished. Fae carried out a playful groan for a few seconds before getting over her sister's *harsh* decision. The three of them began coloring on the new page; an image of swan printed in a minimalist style with bold lines.

"Hey Saff, you want in on this?" Fae nudged Safira in the arm, but the woman of intimidating stature shook her head and resumed her work. "Just so you know, you're really missing out on the best time of the week. Plus, this is one of the few times Elle allowed other people to be present during family bonding. Well, at least you'll be here to witness it."

Scott, Fae and Larimar got to work making the bland page into a colorful wonderland, complete with drawn in sunflowers, fearsome monsters, and what could only be described as obtuse potato people (Larimar stressed that this was her favorite part). They were all sharing laughs and teasing each other's use of colors and additions to the page. It looked like a lot of fun.

"Is Scott one of your night friends?" Larimar casually went on coloring just the same as if she hadn't dropped that line. Fae sunk in her chair but she didn't stop coloring. Scott eyes widened and his grip loosened so much that the pencil slipped out of his hand and dropped on the coloring book. However, he picked it back up after seeing that Fae was still going, though not unfazed. "It's okay, your night friends are pretty nice most of the time. You didn't tell me anything about him so you must think he's pretty special. You tell me a lot about how nice they are most of the time. The second reason I know you think he's special is because it's family bonding time and he's still here. I was mad when he showed up but you always tell me to be nice. I thinked about it and he's gotta be special if you didn't tell him to leave so I'm okay with him if you are."

Safira was smiling from ear to ear during the ordeal, but she still hadn't budged from drafting plans. "Elle, I need you to know that you're my favorite."

"Why wouldn't I be? Who else would it be? Bun Butt?"

Safira busted out laughing. She buried her face in the stacks of papers and pounded her fist on the table. "Oh my god; Fae, does Elle call you Bun Butt? Your nickname is Bun Butt? And on top of that, night friends?! You weren't joking when you said family bonding would be fun! This little girl is the gem this world desperately needs!"

"I don't get what's so funny; she has friends that she only sees at night. There's nothing wrong with having friends for different times."

"Elle, please be quiet. And again, it's not thinked or thunk, it's thought." Fae looked exhausted, but she continued to color, albeit grudgingly."

"Bun Butt, are you angry at me?" Elle pouted.

"Oh no, no I'm not angry at you, I'm just tired. I'm sorry if I made you feel like it's your fault."

"That's okay", Larimar looked up from the page and smiled at her sister, "I know you didn't mean it."

"Aww, you're so sweet."

"I was talking about the apology." Elle put her head down to hide her smile.

"See, this is why you're not my favorite sister; you're always playing around."

"I'm your only sister, Bun; I'll always be your favorite." Larimar was chuckling while Fae lit up and ruffled her little sister's long, black curly hair. Everyone at the table was laughing; even Safira was laughing along with the rest of them. The atmosphere in the room was light, but it there was a subtle change when Baron Sugar materialized on the couch. Fae's laughter died down when she noticed the figure in his cloak and the brown knitted cloth that serves as his head. Sugar was sitting faced forward with his back to everyone else. He didn't do or say anything; he just sat there, existing. Fae was getting uneasy and everyone was able to see it, but nobody said anything about it. Scott looked at Fae with longing, but he didn't dare to act on it. Safira glanced over briefly, but she went right back to her work."

"Larimar, it's time to go to bed, alright kid?" Faaghira put down her colored pencils and put them back in the tin box.

"Okay, I guess I'm tired. Can I sleep with you tonight?" Larimar raised her arms for Fae to pick her up and her big sister reluctantly knelt down to let Larimar latch around her back.

"You get the bed to yourself tonight; I've gotta get back to work now. I'll see you tomorrow, Lumpy." Fae playfully slung Larimar around.

"Bun, you said you'd stop calling me Lumpy!" Larimar pouted.

"I'll drop that as soon as you stop calling me Bun Butt." Faaghira was grinning but tried to hide it when Larimar was starting to catch a glimpse of it.

"Nuh uh, no way." Larimar giggled at Fae's horrible effort to hide the smile. The little girl gave her sister a kiss on the cheek which turned into a sloppy buzz of her lips.

"Okay, g'night Lumpy." Fae left the table with Larimar gripping over her shoulders; much akin to a backpack. She carried her sister upstairs then returned after a few minutes. She took her seat at the table; the happiness she just had wiped itself away in the blink of an eye. "You're back early."

"Misfortune schedules no appointments. It seems that with your actions there are strong efforts to undo them all. The first school you built; laid to waste. Scorched earth accounts for the majority of the remains."

The room was silenced by a cloud of emotions; discontent, hatred, anger, sadness, disbelief; it brewed a heinous storm. Scott's eyes widened in shock; Safira pushed her chair back, making it drag hard against the floor. She stormed to the kitchen and returned with three beers that she slammed on the table. "This is bullshit! We need to take that asshole down right now!"

Fae placed her palm on her forehead and slowly dragged it down until it shielded her eyes. "He said he wouldn't," the usual strength in her voice began to waver, "he hit Switzerland; he crossed the line. Tell me what it looked like; tell me what happened in detail."

"The school and all of its grounds were decimated. There were corpses scattered in some places, however, they were few, as school was not in session. The victims; their bodies were scorched, but along with the remaining flesh was rubberized and some of them…some of them saw it coming; their impending doom. Everything was ruined; a small apocalypse. Part of the playground is standing; the swing sets to be specific. Though, from the brutality of the event, I do not believe that a fire could have caused all of this. A few bricks from the foundation of the-"

"That's more than enough, thank you. We had an agreement; neither of us would attack the other's structures directly. The line was crossed, and regardless of whether or not he's the one who carried this out, he'll pay for it. I let a lot of his bullshit slide but I'll be damned if I let him get away with this. Scott, is this what you came to tell me about?" Fae moved her hand briefly and slim streams of tears rolled down her face. They stained the thin pages of the coloring book, making the areas hit become brittle. She wiped her tears with the back of her hand then placed it back over her eyes. "Saff, change up the schedules; I've been putting this off for too long."

"I haven't finished drafting up the plans yet, but I can get something set up in two days at the most. I can't expedite this any more than that. If you want to try a direct attack then I can pull something together sooner if you want." Safira didn't look nearly as upset as Fae did; probably because this was a chance to get back at Atticus on her terms. That's not what this was about, of course, but Atticus betraying the 'Switzerland Agreement' would be a turning point that could go in the favor of the rebellion. Even if she didn't agree with it, there was still the chance that she would. But maybe, maybe it's simply an act of caring. Persistent as she may be, I haven't seen her display any manipulative tendencies or be underhanded in that way.

"Not so soon, we all need some rest. Things are only going downhill from here; we're getting to the point where we have to decide if things will ever be coming back up. Give yourselves some time, and Baron, you do…whatever it is that you normally do when you're not being scary." Fae grabbed one of the beers left in the fridge and downed a quarter before Safira tugged it away from her. "Good night Saff; thanks again. I'll see you tomorrow, or actually I guess it would be a few hours. Just call me if you need me for anything."

"Gotcha, I'll see you around." She headed for the door, but before she left, she motioned the tip of a hat to Scott "See ya, fellow night friend." Scott cleared his throat…again. He did this really awkward pacing around that made him look like a kid left in line at a grocery store while their mom went to 'go get one more thing'. A big blinding spotlight may as well been shining down right on him.

"Sooo…night friends?"

"We spend a lot of time together and you know, kids are curious. If there's something she catches on to that I don't want to explain yet, then I just reword it. Sorry you had to hear that."

"No, that's not a problem. I was actually wondering if we could arrange something like that; I think it sounds pretty sexy, or…friendly."

"You're digging a hole, man. Plus, you're grown; you can

just say you wanna smash. What's been up with you anyway? You've been moody like crazy lately."

"How do you know that this isn't how I normally am?"

"Because I wouldn't let you anywhere near where I live if that was the case. I don't know everything about you, but I know you well enough for me to see that you're acting stranger than normal. Something about you just seems unusually awkward and I can't put my finger on it, but frankly, I wouldn't want to." Faaghira reclined, propping her feet up on another chair. "Scott, seriously chill out for a second; I thought we were past that stage. We've been over this."

"I could've sworn I've heard that one before" Scott smiled; snuggled up in his wit.

"Save your jokes; save the world."

"It's not you, well, it's not *just* you. I have some…things that I've been trying to sort out, but that's not the main thing bothering me right now. I came back to tell you about Atticus."

"He did something else? If it's not important then you don't have to tell me; I'll just wait till tomorrow and find out then."

"But this is something you should know now." Scott held Fae in his arms, but he still made sure to keep some distance between them. "Basically, Atticus said he's gonna start raising taxes for the people you've been helping that aren't rich."

"Great, that's almost everyone in the city. What makes this worse is that the tax goes to the rest of the state. I can't do it all and he knows it. He's cutting me down all across the board; he's taking me out of favor from people that already don't like me *and* people outside of the city that I never even got the chance to help." She stopped abruptly; zoning out after the words left her lips.

"What's wrong?"

"Everything, everything is wrong. You wanna sit down on the couch? These seats aren't comfortable enough for me right now." She went to the back of the couch then threw herself over it. Her legs were sticking up from her shins being propped up on the back cushion. She basically looked like a plank on an incline. Scott didn't hesitate to sit by her; he even laughed a bit on account of her being so silly. Baron Sugar on the other hand, he didn't seem to enjoy it in any way. He scooted over to make room for her then re-crossed his legs. "Baron, I don't want to be rude, but could you step out for a little?"

"If you need me then call for me again; I will reappear shortly after." Sugar took off his cloak and with one swing of the black cloth, it covered him. In the same brief moment in time, the cloak and the man vanished without leaving even much as a light breeze (you know, because the cloak- never mind).

"He still kind of gives me the creeps, but that's besides the point ; he's a great guy if you get to know him. But enough about him, enough about all this serious crap; I need a break."

"Hey babe, you sure you don't want to sit down instead of...planking or whatever it is you're doing?"

"I'm not babe right now, I'm not anybody's anything; right now I'm just Faaghira."

"Okay, gotcha." Scott was slow to say anything else. He looked on as Fae sank down in her mood and he must not have been sure what to say. I don't know if there was anything that could be said that would be right. "So...would sex make you feel better?" Leave it to Scott to find one of the worst things you could possibly say at a time like this.

"My sister's upstairs, plus...Scott, sometimes I wonder why I even like you."

"How about some basic questions to jog your memory."

"Is this still Scott I'm talking to or is this a cooler, less douchey clone?"

"Ha ha, very funny. I've never done this kind of thing before so forgive me if I'm not all that great at-"

"At getting to know people? Are you telling me that you didn't get to know your girlfriend?"

"We know each other very well, actually. Iris and I have a different kind of relationship than what a lot of people are used to. Trust me when I say that we know each other very well. You know something, that doesn't really matter right now. Do you mind if I ask you just anything or are there limits on what we can talk about?"

"It depends, but I wanna see where you're taking this first. I'll probably regret saying this, but ask me anything."

"How did you get to be so rich?" Scott didn't make an effort to move in any closer.

"This actually didn't start out bad. Actually, nobody asks me the story behind my money. Most people don't care and those that do tend to think I'm some sort of criminal. Technically, I am a criminal by old law but things were amended a long time before I was born. My family got rich because of charm, political influence, and helping Atticus start up his 'defense against terrorism' initiative. I'm not saying what they did was justified, but there was no way they would've even considered it if they knew how things would end up." Fae didn't sound sad, but her voice did have a sort of lowly dragging in it.

"How can you be so sure?"

"Because I wouldn't have to fill their role if they didn't go with it. Larimar would have her parents taking care of her instead of her flaky, passive aggressive sister."

"You're not any of those things!" He began to raise his voice, but it didn't go on long since he remembered Fae's little sister was upstairs, presumably asleep. "You're this beautiful, wonderful leader that already showed the world she has nothing to prove."

"Smooth, but not totally smooth; maybe like a two-hundred grit compliment. While I appreciate the thought, you can't tell me what I'm not and what I am; you're not me. Even the people who know me like that can't tell me that *my* own perception of *myself* is wrong, so there's not a single way that you can."

"Easy, easy, I didn't mean it like that; I was just trying to cheer you up."

"But when did you hear me ask for that? If I really wanted to laugh that bad then I would've turned on a cartoon or something."

"Is it that time of month? You're being really moody all of a sudden."

"I must be a masochist; it's the only logical explanation."

"The only logical explanation for what?"

Fae sighed under her breath. "The aside, regarding earlier." She paused for so long that Scott thought that she was asleep. He hesitantly poked her stomach a few times, but he stopped when she hissed at him for it. "It was me and my baby sis; poor girl hardly got to spend any time with 'em. I wasn't supposed to have access to any of the 'family jewels' until I turned eighteen, but Atticus was quick to make me the exception for that rule. He didn't do it out of kindness and I knew that back then. When you give a kid a pile of millions you don't expect them to last that long with it. He wanted me to be broke and out of his way; he told me that to my face recently. I cheated him out of a lot of deals, I blackmailed him, and I got started making some businesses with friends then I made some bank. Millions turned into billions, empty land turned into complexes, but a lot of people were getting poorer. I didn't care as much at that point, but I started to open my eyes to it when I was traveling around the state. It wasn't a culture shock thing; it was more of a 'shit' moment. That's when I realized that the world was different; that my world was different. If only you could see what it's like the further out you go from the city. The towns out there, they're ruined. This is way below any acceptable standard of living for any person in the entire world. But here's the thing, this wasn't some far away land I was trying to save; this was right here in my home! There was no way I would let this go, especially since I had the money and power to fix it. So this is where I got my start with everything I'm a part of and most of the things I believe in. The top tier schools, the thriving communities, the black owned businesses branching out across the state; I believed in all of it before I put my first dollar down. The point of what I'm saying is that I wasn't always the magnificent bombshell you're sitting by; before all that work, I was just a bombshell. Also, I've still got some ways to go as a human being, but most importantly, I have to do a lot better before I could even consider myself a good sister. So um…yeah, that's the short version of how I got my money."

"That's the short version? I'd hate to sit through the unabridged edition."

"There he is! I was starting to get worried for a minute there; I thought you were replaced by some handsome guy that isn't an asshole. Anyway, since you asked me about my money and it ended up leading up to my parents, you should tell me about yours. I want details too; don't give me any of that 'it's bad' bull. I put myself out there, so time to step up and do the same.

"Okay, fine. Now about my folks…I'm not sure exactly where to start so this might turn out being all over the place. My relationship with them is…a little complicated. They can be vile at times, but they're great overall. We're on a break right now because of disagreements about college and my life in general. We would go through these cycles of being hostile then being warm; drastic differences that would change our relationship forever. I had a falling out with my mom recently and it was a really bad one to say the least.

You know, I really don't like saying a whole lot about them because it paints them in a bad light, but I'll try to tell you everything because you're you." He took a deep breath before going on. "We were just fine when I was a kid, but when it came time for college; that's when everything went south."

"Time for college? Like there's an actual age where college is an involuntary part of the human experience? Were they making you go or was that all your decision?"

"No one can 'make' me do anything, but I had a lot of opposition coming my way if I didn't fall in line. I thought that choosing to go would be the end of it but there was always another demand waiting at the after. I was banking on something I didn't think would be available to me anytime soon. The way people've been talking about it all this time, I thought it was just about going and having a graduation where everybody throws their caps in the air. Then the closer I got the more it turned into 'What are you majoring in? You need to go after something that'll get you a lot of money.' It stopped being 'You can be anything you want.' Reality was setting in; a reality I should've gotten years ago. After a while, all I was hearing was that I need to get an education; fuck, they could never even be upfront that there was no way I could afford it. I ended up getting to go anyway on the scholarship of Iris' dime."

"That's your girlfriend, right?"

"Yeah that's the same Iris. I mentioned it to her once, but I said I was going to take out some loans for it. She said she wouldn't let me take out loans as long as she could do something about it."

"Did she pry it out of you or did you bring it up out of the blue?"

"She was concerned. She's really a caring person. It's safe to say that she's...aggressively helpful. She's a special kind of girl that I'm really lucky to have. Mom doesn't like her at all, but she also doesn't seem to like me much either. Still, even with her kindness, I don't want to take advantage, so I picked out a school in Manhattan that was really cheap by college standards. She wanted to pay for my room and board too but I told her I'd be fine. I told her I'd live with my best friend till I could pay for my own place. She reluctantly agreed but she agreed, nonetheless. I got rent money by writing articles and doing some freelance book editing but she still wanted me to stay with her at least twice a month. I wasn't obligated to, but she's *very* persuasive. It also helps that the sex is always bomb. I honestly thought she would be more demanding at that point but she was surprisingly really chill about the whole thing. One of those nights she asked me why I didn't want to dorm and I just told her the truth; I don't want to have to go back home when the semester is over. In fact, I didn't really have a home anymore; I was resting my head wherever I could until I was good on my own two."

"Do your parents know how you feel?"

"Roswell brought me back there, back where I'm supposed to be. I went back to their house and ended up getting in a spat with mom and long story short, I'm not welcome back there. I 've been disowned but I already saw it coming for months, and so did that bastard Roswell. He brought me back there just so that could happen, but it's hardly his fault. Like I said before, no one can make me do anything; I could've went somewhere else when he put me in front of that house but where what would that do in the grand scheme of things? I was going to be disowned at some point; why not just get it over with now? It was a tough decision but it's something I had to do. Maybe it wouldn't't've happened if I kept my mouth closed like I usually do, maybe there'd be something left for me to fix."

"Maybe she was caught up in the moment. I remember my mom telling me to take angry words with a grain of salt.

I know it seems backwards, but give her another chance"

"While I hate that it had to happen this way; there has to be consequences for what they say. Again, the love's still there. I love them so much that I won't try to change how they are; from here we'll be going our separate ways. That's basically everything with my parents. Is there anything else you want to know?"

"Yeah, I really want to know more about your girlfriend but I'm tired right now. I'm gonna go hit the hay but you're free to crash here if you want." Faaghira let herself fall on the floor then proceeded to grudgingly carry herself up to the staircase.

"Yeah" Scott laughed nervously, "it's not like I have anywhere else to go."

"Yeah…uh…so if you need anything then I'm in the room with the big stainless-steel doors; you can't miss it. Otherwise, if everything goes alright then I'll see you in a few hours." Scott was left alone once more, but before he could go into a soliloquy on his current state, the cushion next to the one he was resting on ventured into a monologue of its own. Yup, it's getting weird again.

"The company, the inclusion, the feeling of acceptance; it's all fleeting, is it not? As soon as everyone disappears, you're all alone again. You know that, but you're looking for something. My favorite part is that you don't know what it is and that you acknowledge it. You fill in that search with what you heard was important but you've experienced that need in yourself. You try and fail, but you always know you're going fail *every single time*." The cushion spoke in smooth whisper, but its words kept the voice from being calming.

"What in the actual fuck?" Scott's reaction is perfectly understandable being that a *couch cushion* was giving his life a grim philosophical analysis of his own life. Scott kept his voice low as well, but it was probably because he didn't want Faaghira back down and see him yelling at her couch.

"It's funny how, and not 'ha ha' funny, that even after explaining what's no doubt the strangest experience you've ever had, you're afraid of her judging you. Maybe now you'll see that it's always been…just you and me."

"Roswell?"

"Alive and in the couch. Or rather, I am the couch cushion. Don't you remember? Don't you remember when I told you I could be anything? I can be anything at any given time if that's what I want to be. Now that it's just us, you can ask me anything at all. The two of us, we're the only ones who are living in the same world. You're being pushed out of your own much faster than a snail's pace and I wasn't a part of it to begin with. Even if you don't want to admit it: by now there's a serious disconnect between your reality and your fantasy. But knowing what you've had to put up with, what is reality?"

"If you're trying to confuse me or something then you're out of luck. There's no way in hell that I'm falling for that shit."

"Hell, yeah, reppin' the hometown! I'm pretty sure that I don't have any tricks up my sleeve; my sleeves are too tight for that. I'm just here to talk; disappointment to disappointment. Consider this an amnesty period. We don't have to have any animosity towards each other right now, but if that's what you want then more power to you. I wanted to wait until you were alone to tell you that you haven't been getting that many lines. I'll let you in on a little secret: I don't write anybody's lines. What's been getting you down to the point where you're taking a backseat to your own story? If you wouldn't mind shedding some light on that then that would be great. I can kind of read your mind but I don't get that part."

"How can you only partially read people's minds?"

"Like, why would anyone get stainless-steel doors? My

powers are complicated. Sometimes they suck, but enough about me." "Yeah, enough about you. Look, I'm tired and there's probably some stuff I'll have to do tomorrow so I'm gonna go to sleep. Don't wake me up to bother me; I'll be pissed if you take me away from a good dream." Scott bunched up close to his end of the couch, distancing himself from Roswell, the cushion; however, he wasn't able to rest for more than a second or two. There were hands pinching and poking Scott's face as soon as he closed his eyes. Being that he jumped up and cursed at the couch, it's safe to say that he was frightened by it. "Damn! Hey man, fuck you and that creepy shit you're always pulling!" Scott moved a few feet from the couch then sat on the floor with his back against the wall. "And give me a blanket or something; it's cold."

Roswell (still a cushion) grew stubby legs and extremely long and flimsy arms it slapped Scott with a purple blanket then sat upright on the couch where he was sitting before. "See ya real soon." Roswell's voice echoed with a sound of heavily distorted reverberation. It was a truly ungodly sound; like a demonic ocean level in a poorly programmed game. It was this sound, this flux of chaos that weighed in Scott's head like a wheelbarrow overflowing with concrete. Scott's eyes were straining; he was struggling to stay awake, but the sound fought him to sleep.

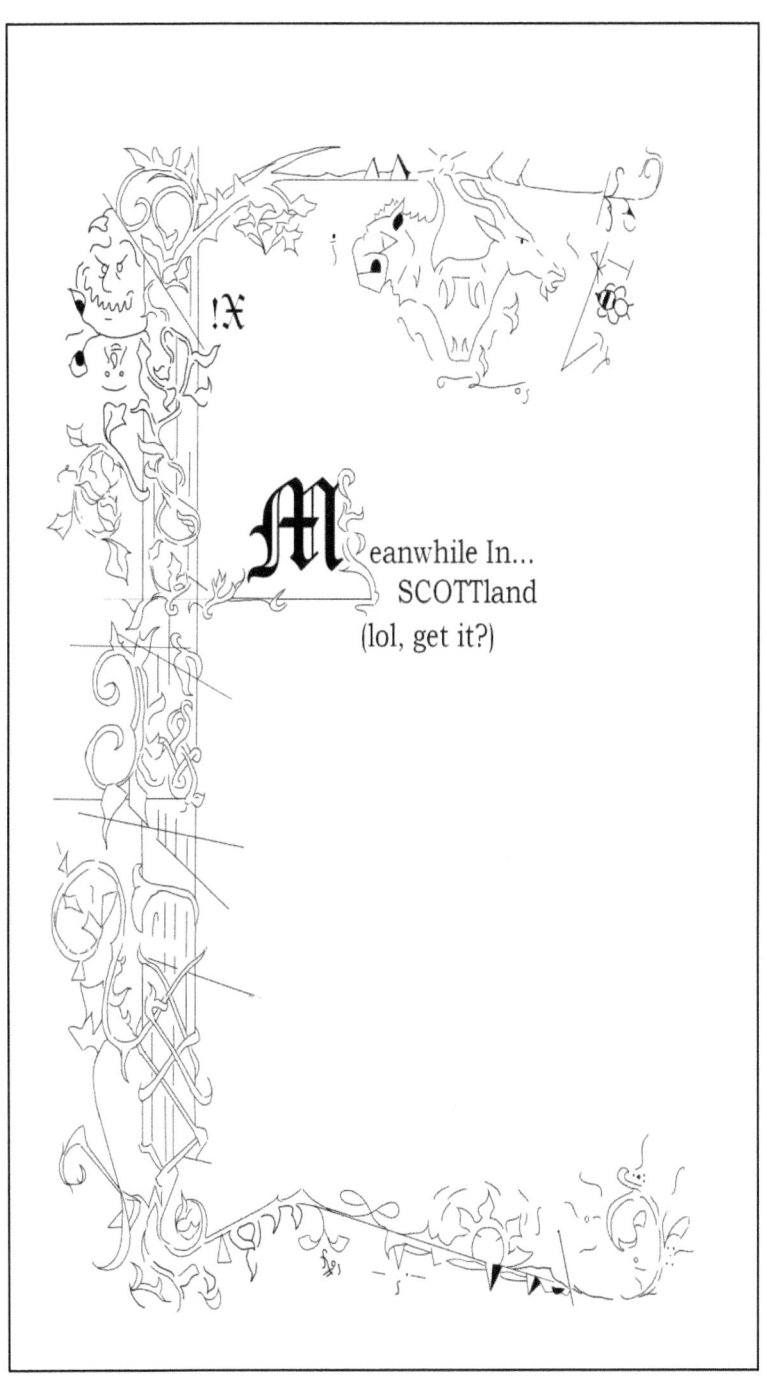

Meanwhile In...
SCOTTland
(lol, get it?)

CHAPTER IX
MEANWHILE IN... SCOTTLAND
(LOL, GET IT?)

I'm back home again? This is weird, no big move or scene or hoopla bringing me here. I guess weird is the new normal for me. But if turning out back here means I'm out of that astral dimensional shit then I'm down. Speaking of down, where am I anyway?

"Told you I'd see ya *real* soon."

Fuck, it's Roswell! Am I stuck in another one of his illusions?

"It was real as the dickens all the other times too, and if you're wondering what's going on right now then I can clear that up for you."

Really? That's oddly nice of you, thanks.

"What are you thanking me for? I never said I'd tell you anything, all I said is that I *can* clear things up for you."

Figures; I can't believe I fell for that.

"I can."

Cut the shit, what's going on? Seriously what's going on with my life? What the fuck happened to my life?

"You're back home like you wanted. Here, I'll set the scene for you: you're in a church, a small one; the one close by your girlfriend's apartment. She doesn't know you're here, your parents don't know you're here, your friends don't know you're here; nobody knows that you're here right now. You could walk away from it all and start over somewhere else but we all know you won't, so don't act like you'll even consider it. By the way, you're the guest narrator of this chapter so you'll essentially be thinking out loud the entire time; no pressure."

Um...okay. So uh hi everybody, I'm Scott. Right now I-

"They already know who you are; they've been following

up for a few chapters now. Just get on with it."

Okay, sorry. Quick recap: Iris is my girlfriend of a few years. Right now I might call her up, but I'll go see a friend first. I love her with all my heart, but she takes up a lot of room in my life so I'll take a little break before she finds out that there's space she isn't taking up.

"I can see why you love her so much; she's a real catch."

Alright, so do I talk in past or present tense? I'm not sure how to do this narrator thing and I'm pretty sure it's the case that I can't get rid of you if I don't do this.

"Whichever one is the one you're more comfortable with. Now unlike with the narrator, you don't have to act like I'm not here; you can yell at me to your heart's content. With that being said, go forth and mess things up like you always do. I'll be right here giving you shit about it the whole time."

Figures, I can't wait to get this fuckery out of my hair. Okay, so I left the church and I was gonna keep walking out to a friend's house but Iris was waiting for me like she always does. She'll get pissed at me for a little bit, but then we'll be back where we normally are. But on the other hand, I don't have to go back to her right now. I can go somewhere else for a bit so long as none of her friends tell her that I'm around. Okay, so I kept walking-

"WE kept walking. That or 'Roswell and I' would be acceptable. If you keep forgetting to include me then I'll be very indifferent, and you don't want that, do you?

Whatever. Look, I decided that I should go see a friend for now even though a big part of me will regret it later. It feels weird talking to…well…nobody, but it's kinda therapeutic, I guess. I don't talk about my personal life all that much, but I might as well be okay with it since I'll have to do at least a little bit of that for however long I'm narrating. My best friend lives in The Bronx is a call and a little bit of a drive out to his pad. I figured I'd leave before there's even a chance that she'd know I'm there, so I called a car around and I was on my way to Pelham Bay. I didn't mean to rhyme; that was lame.

Traffic wasn't bad so far and the driver didn't give me any problems, but I got this urge to call Iris a couple times along the way. I played Block Match Slide instead, also known as the fake Tetris game I've been playing. I like to play it whenever I think about her and she's not there.

"Aww, Scott's all soft and mushy on the inside! I already knew that, but I can't pass up the chance to tease you for it."

Shut up, asshole.

"You've got some nerve." My driver was pissed! She's an older Indian lady; thick accent that makes her English sound a little choppy. I had to tell her that I was texting someone and they were starting to piss me off. She brushed it off but I doubt she bought it. I looked out the window for the rest of the ride; partly to take in the old sights, but mostly to try ignoring Roswell.

"And you suck at that too, by the way."

Whatever, so I got out of the car and paid the driver. I was walking around my friend's neighborhood for a bit and he actually called me before I could call him. I had it in my mind to be petty and miss the call then call him back in ten minutes but I answered in a split second.

"Kid, Shawn told me your black ass was wandering around my block. Why are you showing up by my house without telling me? You always gotta call me before so I can buy some snacks and stuff. Damn man, you already know keep those pantries clean!" My best friend Charlie is the kind of guy that'll come through for you, but not without giving you a bunch of shit first. He's the guy I've always wanted to be but life dealt us different hands. He got the supportive parents, the cool instruments and he turned out with a lot of money and he bought his own house cash in New York. He's what a lot of people around would call a real black person. The rest would say 'he doesn't respect himself', whatever that's supposed to mean. Most of the people in high school liked him and I got…everyone else. Well at least I have Iris.

Charlie, man, I didn't want to make you show out for me; you always do that and it makes me feel bad.

"Feel bad? Makes you feel bad? Either you've been hanging around Iris too much or you haven't been seeing her enough. You've always been two things as long as we've known each other: petty and upset. It's common knowledge so I don't know why you feel you have to point it out. Yo, so I don't want you just walking around my block lookin' like a dope. Go chill in my house till I get back; I'll be there in like fifteen. I had a party couple days ago and somebody put some bologna and welfare bread in the fridge, so you can make yourself a sandwich. You can make as many as you want cause I only mess with artisan bread and they didn't even get the good bologna. I got cheese too. I bought that cheese though, so you know it's good." He ended the call right there. I remember him telling me before that he never said goodbye because communication is one long conversation. Now that I think about it, he hardly says hello either, he always just jumps right into a conversation.

I went in his house like he said (I have two keys), turned off his alarm, and made a real nice fried bologna and cheese sandwich. I went in his room (mostly neat but there's no mistaking that it's lived in) where he has an N-64 and I was playing Smash Brothers to pass the time, but I got really into it when I started losing the first match. I used Link that first time around and he used to be my best person, but I guess that somewhere down the line I lost it. Well, I lost it but not too much because I was back to whooping behind in the next fight. I got comfy in his rolling office chair, and before I knew it half an hour had passed and Charlie was there; turns out he was there for a while but I was too focused to notice.

"You spent all this time playing and you not even good. Put down that controller and let a real man play." Charlie got up from the floor (which he'd been sitting on for like, a quarter-hour) and unrolled the cord around one of the controllers under the tv. He ruffled my hair then sat on his bed, leaning forward to make sure I saw him taunt me with his conniving smile. At that point I knew I had to win! "Yeah, dig in baby! You thought didn't, you? I'm the king at this man; this is my kingdom! Nobody schools me in my house, especially not when I use Donkey Kong!" But then at the next point I knew I lost. I lost bad, like, first person out. But you know, I'm cool with losing as long as it's against someone I know I can't beat. "Ight, so what's got you down this time?"

What's got me down? What makes you think something's gotta be wrong for me to want to come see you?

"Because nothing's ever right when *you* make an effort to physically come out and see somebody."

That's not true for Iris.

"The devil is a lie; things are definitely wrong whenever you go out to see your girl."

Step off, alright? Things are bad with mom and I've been having…life is just a mess right now. Iris is a constant and she's the only reason I'm even in school right now. She really cares about me, so try not to talk bad about her.

"She's the girl you picked and you've been together for a while. Plus, you're grown so I can't knock you for that. Only advice I have for you on that is to ask yourself if your relationship is still working at the end of each day. There's no use keeping an old method if it's not helping you anymore, and you've definitely gotta drop it if it's holding you back. As for your mom…well…how bad did things get?"

Thank God for real friends! Sure I'm shit with them, but I wouldn't be shit without 'em.

*It's midnight. It was one minute till but it's finally

334

midnight.*

"She kicked you out?! Damn, man I'm sorry to hear it, but it's definitely no surprise. Things weren't looking up and every time- my bad, I'll stop there. You're not alone in this; I've got your back. Come on man, bring it in." Charlie and I both got up and made the biggest bear hug this side of the milky way. He even gave me some of those huge pats on the back, so I did the same, then it turned into a competition to see who could pat the other's back the fastest. He won by default but there's no doubt that I would've won if I was in a better mood. "I need to go buy some groceries for whenever you decide to crash here. Come on and help me pick out some snacks and stuff."

He drove us down a few blocks to the little grocery store he usually shops from. It's nothing special or anything; just a local place. Walking through those doors was breath of fresh air. Pizza and what have to be the greatest sandwiches in the world were being made right there at the front and the beautiful smells...I'm in Heaven. Alright, that's enough prose for now. On to the ever glorious grocery shopping in the small, nearly empty store, filled to the brim with anything and everything you could possibly need; including all those delicious foods that are so good that they have to be bad for you.

"We're going with the usual routine: we each get a basket and stock it with whatever you want, but if the pile gets even a centimeter taller than the basket then something's going back. I'm not putting up with that stunt you pulled last time."

Stunt? Why are you so serious? Dude, they're just groceries.

"Dude, it's just money that you don't have to pay for these miniscule groceries."

Always attacking my wallet! One day you won't be able to make fun of me for being broke.

"I'm pushing you to it. I believe you'll get to that point,

but I see it as my job to make you uncomfortable with where you're at so you'll actually want to move forward. There's all the advice I'm giving for the day, so any more problems will have to wait till tomorrow. One last thing: don't buy too much junk food because you won't eat all of it and I'll hardly have any. I don't waste food in my house so don't over pack. With that being said, let the shopping commence!"

We were quick to go to opposite ends of the store while being equally careful not to hit any shelves (the place is crowded with items, not people). I slowed down when it got to the point where neither of us could see each other. This wasn't a race and even if it was, I'd rather lose than just throw a bunch of random stuff in my basket just so I could get to the checkout lane first. Plus, there's the whole money thing; I'm not rushing to pay for something if I don't have the cash on me. Also, heeding his warning I decided I'd lay off the sweets. My basket was looking a little skimpy by the time I was done. I met up with Charlie in such a short time that he worried about me. We skimmed over what could've been a really deep conversation and went through checkout. He patted me on the back but didn't say a word; he knows I'm not some type of pansy that needs to be coddled. He doesn't like when I say this kind of stuff so I'm careful not to say it around him. He added my items on to his bill at checkout, and I felt a little...weird. He had salad, fruits, and water; that was all followed by a family size bag of chips and a chocolate bar. I eat healthy, just not now. Hey, I've had a bunch bad stuff happen so cut me some slack. I'll fix everything later.

We went back to his place and just sat and ate our snacks. I don't know how he eats so little. We talked about random things, but as it always does; things got personal.

"You don't seem like yourself these days. You're still a freeloader and you make horrible choices, but you're never so...removed. Is this still about your mom or is this

336

something else?"

He's one of the only people allowed to pry like that. I was going to say 'in this world' but...you know, she's technically not in this world. I'm still not completely sure how that works, but okay.

You remember all those times when you said I could tell you anything?

"I've been waiting for this one."

Hold up, what do you think I'm gonna say? I'm not gay or anything, you know?

"Nigga, that ain't no problem. Nobody with a even a grain of sense would give a damn if you're gay. I've been waiting for the day when you'd let me know what's bothering you without having to fuss and fight to get it out of you. Goddamn, you've got a lot of problems! Since I'm your friend, your best friend at that, I'm here for you to tell me what's going on. So, what's going on?"

I've been having these dreams...well, they're kind of one dream. I'm not even sure if they're dreams; they feel real; they feel as real as you and me. And there's this girl...there's this girl in my dreams and she's...complicated. She's the most amazing person I've ever met and she does so much; I just can't measure up. Meeting her changed my whole life, but it also made me realize something: I couldn't be with someone like her. Life never lines up for me and...I wouldn't want to hold anyone back.

"You hold me back all the time; I'm not doing anything right now because of you. By the way, *she's* the best person you've ever met? I am *deeply* offended."

Well you're my best friend, meaning you decided to put up with me for however long, so you're used to me holding you back. By the way, offense intended; mission accomplished. You're welcome.

"Your parents?"

*They're obligated to care...or at least provide...in a

financial kind of way, methinks. And before you ask, don't ask about Iris.*

"Wasn't going to. What else happens in those dreams?"

There's this guy...he's...I actually don't know what he is. We talk sometimes; he pisses me off but he also makes a lot of sense. Right now he's one of the people that makes the most sense.

"So in the dreams, is this guy always there? Does he happen to be everywhere you go or is he just in random places?"

Um...yes? I think he's always there; he might be. He's a tough guy to explain. He might be bad, but I just don't know. When I'm there...in the dreams, I feel like I'm somebody, but I feel like everyone else is so much more. I feel like I need to do more, but I don't know what to do. Another weird thing, and this has nothing to do with what I was talking about, but America was disbanded somehow and It's really weird.

"America disbanded? You sure this was a dream? Maybe God's been sending you to the future."

I don't know!

"Chill, man! All I'm saying is that I it doesn't sound far off from what could end up happening. How often do you get these kinds of dreams?"

It feels like I'm never out of it. Things are better there, for me at least. And sometimes I feel like there's a right thing to say, but it's never one of my options; sometimes the only things for me to choose from are bad and worse.

"Uh...wow. It shouldn't surprise you, but I'm not sure what to tell you. It sounds like you've some things that are too complicated for my advice. Listen man; just try to take it easy, alright? Try to get out more and try new things. You have a bad habit of locking yourself away somewhere and making an echo chamber consisting of your girlfriend and bad ideas. If you give your senses some new surroundings

then your brain will have more things to form dreams from.
"

Charlie is the best friend I could've asked for; good thing I didn't have to ask for him. *Charlie, you're the best. I need to go. I'm gonna go; I have to spend some time with my girlfriend before she finds out that I'm back in the area.*

"Man, nobody should be afraid of their partner. Do you really think she'd know where you are right now?"

I've been with her for a while now; I know what she's capable of. I better head out so I can get somewhere that's not too close before the odd hours hit.

"I'll drive you to wherever you're going and you can call her up on the way if you want."

Charlie, you really are the best friend I've got.

"Sometimes..." Charlie just up and stopped out of nowhere. He sighed and went to his room to get the keys. There was this really awkward silence that lasted until we were in the car. "Sometimes I worry that I'm the only friend you've got."

Silence again. I told him about this record store about fifteen out. If he could drop me there, that'd be nice. We said our goodbyes; it was bittersweet but this is the way things are right now. I called Iris and she answered immediately; her excitement overtook my effort to tell her where I was. She was happy to see- er-hear for me. She didn't even bother asking where I've been all this time. Hell, I don't know how much time passed since we were at that party.

"That means no sex since the party either; I wonder how you made it through. "

Fuck off! 'Kay, back to what I was saying. There weren't any talks of love or the future, just bullshit with her friends and some silly shit she's been seeing in Times Square over the past few days. It was a nice feeling; we haven't done that in a long time. I deliberately didn't want Charlie to drop me off at a café or anything like that because I've been hoping we could reconnect over a nice afternoon out like we used to. We have the best times when she's driving us around and I'm hoping we get that chance today. She's always been something special to me.

I walked around the store, checking my phone every once in a while and checking out some albums, and this lady was trying to act slick while she stocked cd's in the same place for a whole ten minutes. Some other people passed through and she asked them if they needed help with anything, then she went back to acting like she was really into stocking cd's while she watched to make sure I wasn't trying to 'pocket any merchandise'. I moved to another part of the store and, long and behold, she made her way over there. Iris called and I answered but I hung up as soon as I saw that she was in the store.

Oppai!

She smiled and put her phone in her pocket when she looked in my direction. We ran to each other and embraced with the biggest, coziest hug, right there in the middle of the store. I spun her around while still holding her tight. Then as per our tradition, we whispered sweet nothings to each other.

That lady back there with the glasses is hella racist. She's been watching me like a hawk and following me around the store. She was stocking cd's for as long as I was by them and she just happened to be done when I went somewhere else. Coincidentally, she had work to do in that part of the store too

"Beat her ass or get her fired; which one do I need to do?" Iris beamed and kissed me on the side of my neck.

Babe, don't go so far; people are watching!

"Ok, fine" she giggled quietly, "I'll hold back if you really want me to. Say, let's get out of this piece."

Yeah, you can choose the venue this time.

"Venue?" she giggled a little louder this time. "You're making this sound like we're performing at a concert or something."

And the world is our stage!

"Actually, the burrows to upstate is our stage; you still have college." She took my hand and led me out to her car. I never seen anything like it before; it looked like a Trans-Am, but there were some changes here and there that set it apart. The sleek design is complemented by the gorgeous candy-apple red finish; I could die for this thing. "I just got this one last week. I could never find the kind of car I wanted in the color I wanted so I had this custom made. Sure it cost a few dollars, but it was totally worth it. And of course, I'm choosing the place; it's my car *and* you can't drive." She keyed the ignition and off we went.

Hey Iris, it's been a while since I asked you how you've been.

"I know."

So how've you been?

"If I said great then I'd definitely be lying, but I've never had much of a problem with lying if it's for the right reasons. Though, since you already know it's not great, I take it that you want to hear the truth."

The truth; that would be nice.

"Let's see; I got a new job as an editor for a big publishing house, my parents-"

*What's bad about being an editor? What happened? Not enough eye candy there for you?"

"It pays well but it's beating me up, taking my soul and spitting me back out on the daily. And no there aren't any guys there better looking than you, and you haven't seen any girls that are more attractive than me."

What makes you so sure?

"Um...look at me; I'm fucking beautiful. Like I was saying, my job sucks, my parents are still racist-"

Apple trees don't make pears; I might as well be racist too! Hell, we're all racist!

"Scott Blues, you are absolute trash, absolute trash."

And that's why you love me.

"And that's why I love you." She grinned so hard that her eyes scrunched up and her dimples were showing. "I just remembered somethin'; loverboy, could you start up the cd player? There's this band I wanted you to hear."

I did as she said and I ended up getting a pretty odd surprise. It was some alternative rock band; indie for sure; I didn't think she listened to this kind of stuff. It meant something to her, so I sat back and listened to it.

"Do you know who this is?"

Because I can tell indie bands apart.

"North By North; I love them!"

North By North...oh, I remember Charlie talking about them before.

"Oh...well...Charlie's the one who introduced me to their music." She was looking a little nervous, but she wasn't overpowered by it, or at least she shouldn't've been; she was the one driving.

Charlie? When'd you see him? What day did you see him, Iris?

"It was like a month ago; we didn't do anything; I swear! He-he just wanted to get to know me; he didn't mean anything by hanging out with me! You were out somewhere and you weren't answering your phone and he called me up and asked if I could meet him at the park closest to my apartment. He-he- well don't you want your friends to know the kind of person you're dating?"

Charlie could've asked me anything he wanted to know about you! I have nothing but good things to say to him about you! I defend you any time he talks shit about you; anytime anybody does! You could've told him you were busy or you could've waited until I got back and we could've all hung out together! I trust Charlie with all my life, but you can't go doing stuff like this! Stop going behind my back!

342

"I'm sorry, okay?!" She took a breather; some time to compose herself, and rightfully so. "Scott, I'm sorry, I wasn't thinking. I promise I'll make it up to you; I'll do whatever you want."

Well…really, all I want is to catch up. I've been going through some things and I'm sure you have too. I know so, since that's one of the things you did tell me. We should talk about it. Changes are normal and maybe we should see if we still fit together.

"We will; somehow we always do." She didn't seem the least bit worried that we'd be breaking up. We've been through so much that we always just…adapt.

So where are we going?

"Down into the subway; I like the ambience. There's some pretty good restaurants down there too. We're not going into the city though; just hanging out underground."

Cool, underneath the streets. Now that I think about it, I've never taken the time to check out any of those places.

She didn't say anything else; all she did was smile. She drove us to the train station we made into our little spot and we went upstairs to get our tickets and wait for our train. We're already used the sporadic nature of our conversations, so we sent each other memes the whole time. We didn't say a word to each other on the train ride, but that actually isn't out of the ordinary because we like to talk shit about some of the people we see and it's not something you do out loud. We'd text each other things like "the guy in the shirt" or "hat at 3 o'clock" ad we'd always understand what those meant. It's the little things that show me why I fell in love in the first place. When we got off that train…something about it…New York is just magical for me. I haven't been out this far without a plan or agenda, so it felt freeing. I know it sounds silly, but freedom feels good.

I took her by the hand and she laced her fingers in with mine. That's about all the leading I got to do because she took over from there. She took me to a small bakery; a nice little hole in the wall. Technically, they're all small holes in the wall. We took a seat at the table at the front, apparently so we could watch all the people pass by (her idea, not mine). She bought us three raspberry-filled crepes in a small, thin corrugated box. She placed them on the table, but I was confused when she stood with her arms crossed instead of sitting down and enjoying a crepe.

"Is this fine or do you want something else?" She didn't look upset, just...meh; beautiful as always, but very meh.

I thought my girlfriend would make sure I like what she's getting before she gets it.

"Funny, I thought my boyfriend would like a good surprise, especially since he surprises me all the time."

Funny, I thought you liked adventure.

"I *love* adventure, but not knowing where you are some of the time is *really* annoying."

You don't need to know where I am all the time. Nobody needs to know where I every single day of my fucking miserable life! I didn't yell or raise my voice, it was just more intense. This isn't new or anything.

"Why would I get in a relationship with someone and not want to know where they are? I'm not even trying to control anything. I'm interested in your life; I'm interested in our life together. We can't have a life together if you're not there." She looked a little down, but I guess she wasn't really sad or anything like that.

I get it, but- look, like I've said; we need to reconvene since I've been through some changes...again. I don't know if we could work the same way that we have before. I definitely don't want to break up; I don't think there's anyone better for me.

"Okay, so if you don't want to break up then what are you trying to say?"

*We need to get to know each other, and I mean really

know each other. We've been past the 'favorite color' stage, but even after all this time, there's a lot we don't know that we really should.*

"Um…uh…you're actually serious? Um…okay, where do we start?"

What do you expect out of me? Out of us?

"Something nice- are you feeling okay? You've brought this up at least seven times in the past two months. You're sounding like a broken record right now."

Nope…do you still want to hear about it? Apparently, I haven't been keeping up. According to you, I keep repeating myself and time is flying past me. I swear it was only maybe three days. I can't believe it's been seven months! And seven times? Christ!

"Yeah, definitely. I don't recall anything that could make you so…out of it. I genuinely want to know what the problem is; maybe I can fix it." Controlling as it sounds, she'll never let any of my problems go without trying to fix it first. She's also scary good at fixing my problems in particular. I'm not complaining or anything; she's a dope girlfriend.

*Here it goes: my mom kicked me out, I'm losing touch with reality, I'm broke, my life is a mess, and, *and* I have to do these really weird things to keep my liver from failing; do you think you could fix that?!* That sounded more intense than I thought it would; let's tweak that a little bit. *You can ignore the last part.* Nice! Nah, who am I kidding?

"What?! Your mom kicked you out?! Like for good?"

Yeah, we're done.

"Uh…uh…um…was it because of me?"

No, no, baby it's not you! This was going to happen at some point; I was expecting this.

"You can live with me again…well…only if you want to. We could find a place, but if you don't want to do that then I could help you look for a place. As far as jobs go I know

345

some people I can link you up with. I'm not familiar with the whole reality thing-I mean-no, that didn't come out right. I don't understand what you're talking about, but I want to. There's a lot that I don't know that I want to learn about, which, and I know this probably isn't a good time, but like with social issues and stuff; I know a lot more than I did before, but there's still so much I don't know. Is it okay if I talk about that with you?"

She cares more about other people a hell of a lot more than I do; gotta love her. After my nod of approval, she went on about how she saw a different world once after we met. I love listening to this story! She's so passionate, and...I'm not really, but that's not the point. Once again, I sat back and let her take the lead, only this time I'd get to have a crepe...or two; I don't know why she bought three.

"I was living in this bubble all my life; and I know this sounds bad, but I knew about things that were going on but I just didn't care. Other people's issues weren't my problem. It sounds kinda cheesy, but when I first saw you I knew I wanted you in my life for something."

The 'something' being sex.

"...Yeah, but I started thinking about all those things I was trying to ignore. You could've been one of those people that got gunned down." She cleared her throat and took a bite from one of the crepes. "That could've been you I'd be hearing about in the morning. I went to this party-"; she stopped to finish chewing her food; she's the only person I can tolerate talking with their mouth full. "I went to this party, the one we met at; I went there looking to have a good time then go home. When I saw you, I had a few thoughts about what you might be like; how you might perceive me. When you came up and talked to me, I felt like I'd known you forever. The problem was that I'd already seen and heard about things you could've dealt with all this time before we met. When you smiled...when you smiled I

346

thought of someone I saw on the news when I was seventeen; someone who'd never get to smile again. I felt so guilty; I've never felt so guilty before, but that's not why I kept talking to you. It's the fact that I liked you and if I decided to take anything anywhere then I'd have to stop ignoring a bunch of things that made me uncomfortable. Love would never be 'just love' again; it would be a statement. Good intentions would mean anything unless there were good results that followed."

Wow…uh, Iris I've never heard you say something so…profound.

"Only because I know you don't like to hear it. You don't seem to care about most things going on and I can only say so much until I'm overstepping my boundaries. Really, if you don't say anything then I can't do anything other than hope that you will eventually, because leaving you isn't an option."

Shit, I am I still in the other dimension? What the fuck was that? What the fuck is this? I was hoping I'd try to make things less volatile between us, but I didn't expect her to say something like that! It seems like *I* don't care?! Just because I'm not out at every single protest and calling out everything wrong with the whole goddam world, doesn't mean I don't care! And she thinks she can try and drag me for 'not being black enough'. I can't believe the nerve! This bitch…

Hey babe, I'm gonna run up to the bathroom real quick; I'll be right back. Of course I couldn't say it to her; not now; we're in public. Also, I'm trying this thing where I'm less of a shitty person sometimes. Maybe a little bit of time to regain my composure and I'll be better off.

"There's actually something else I wanted to talk to you about."

Won't be as quick as the bathroom. I left the table and went back out into the main crowd so I could find a spot to take a breather; figured the actual bathroom would be best.

347

The restroom sign overhead was a little ways from the bakery, or maybe it seemed that way because of all the people that I had to push past. There's other people there, but there are always other people there; it's a bathroom. I would've preferred to be alone, but rinsing my face should be just as good.

"Sup kid?" No! Why are you back?! "I'm the reason you're here in the first place, so you shouldn't be complaining. Anyway, that's not why I'm here."

*So why are you here…and where did everyone go? *

"It's like there's a disease everyone's getting where they can't ask one question at a time. Not to mention that you're asking a really stupid question; I made an entire dimension, what makes you think I can't clear a room?"

But why are you here?

"I'll do you one better; what do you think your relationship is supposed to be helping? You should know better than anyone that all that 'acceptance' and adoration interracial relationships get is bullshit. It's all in the name; inter-racial; it's still not fucking normal. People have already made sure that it'll never be normal. And usually, interracial refers to white and black, mostly because it's an odd pairing considering how history went.

I don't like Iris because she's white; I like her because she has the kind of personality I like. You know what? I don't have to put up with your crap right now; I'm in the real world! I stormed out of the bathroom and went right back outsi-

"I think what you meant to say was 'right back into the bathroom'. Actually, seeing as to how there is no sanitary way to bathe in here, this would strictly be a restroom. If you decide to walk out again then you'll end up in another bath- I mean restroom just like this one. I can promise you this'll keep getting weirder if you keep going out the door, so unless you really want to see what else I came up with, don't try me." Roswell sat on the countertop all smug; smug bastard. I'm leaving anyway; he can't do shit.

"Cool, so I'll skip Scott's part and just tell what happened. Scott left the room and ended up back here like I said he would. This time I flipped the room upside-down and he fell on his head and cracked his neck. He didn't die because I make my own rules and now it's too early to kill him off. I gave the room a wallpaper of annoying political commentators and dancing elephants. I'll let him narrate again because we obviously see this this a different way."

What. The. Actual. Fuck? I hate Roswell and I hate all this shit he put on the walls.

"Hey, at least they're not men's rights activists."

What? They have those now? Why?

"Unfortunately, I can't take credit for that. I wish I could, but the world can outdo me without trying; it almost always does. Now before I go on, will you chill out for a bit and listen to me, or will I have to make things weirder?"

For some reason, a small part of me wants to see what else you can come up with, but I also have a date to get back to, so at least make this quick.

"You and Iris have some serious issues that I can't even understand how you, or why you'd stay with her."

Like I said, I don't like her because she's white. It gets harder and harder to prove that I didn't choose her because I have some self-hatred or that I put whiteness on a pedestal; she's just the person I was drawn to.

"I didn't mention race at all; you're lighting yourself up. However, since that's where you're at, I'll hang with it. Also, just throwing this out there; you're sounding really sporadic and…mentally unstable. It must really be getting to you, and you know, the funny thing is that other people where you're at would-"

*You mean black people."

"And other people of color; don't interrupt me again or

else I'll break your back and dislocate your shoulders. Selling out is usually a move people take to have themselves presented in another light. But you, you're a special case. I know you, Scott; you're not trying to get people to see you as some respectable member of society. This relationship is strictly about you, isn't it?" That's not the truth; he doesn't know shit! "I know that's what you're thinking, but let those words come out of your mouth; your back and your shoulders, Scott; your back and those shoulders. I wouldn't fix that either. Anyway, separately from that, you want to be seen as a person. You want to finally be a *person*, right? Well you'll only be seen as a *black* person and you can't be anything else. Won't be a deal to the people in your circle, but to the other people; people of all colors; the ones who don't know who you really are; are you afraid of what they might do? Is there any reason why you'd be scared? Any reason at all?"

I know exactly where he's going with this. Both those times were his fault and that's not even a technicality. I'm not going there; not now, not ever again. I seriously do have a date to get back to, though.

"But I'll humor you; say it isn't about race: why is your relationship so horrible? Occasionally, I wonder what it is you're trying to hold on to. You don't treat each other well; you treat each other like shit. Be that as it may, there's a huge contrast between her and the people that legitimately don't like your black ass. There are people from all walks of all colors and creeds that, for some reason or another, hate the fact you even exist in the same realm as them. And you wanna know who those people are? Your neighbors, people you casually pass on the street; your co-workers, if you had a job; your white friends who swear they're not racist because they're totally cool with you being in the same room as them. Hate doesn't discriminate, but then it does. It's everyone until proven otherwise."

350

Are you good, man? You sound like you're dealing with some issues way beyond me. I mean, I don't really care if you solve them or anything; as long as you leave me alone, I'm good.

"Can't do that. I have a big job to do and torturing you is my break from that. However, our issues couldn't be further apart. Your problems, my ranting; this is something that is unimaginable, for you anyway. I don't have your barriers; all of my opposition can be faced with death. I haven't come across a force I couldn't crush, but you, on the other hand, you're only human. There are laws you must abide by; a conscious that binds. I don't have that problem, thus, I can solve my problems. For some reason, it really bothers me that you see us as equals. This is, and this alone, is the only reason I can't stand you."

If you hate me so much then why are you pulling me aside to give me 'advice'?

"I take pride in my work. A warrior couldn't call themselves skillful if they led a sheep to slaughter. Fight an opponent who is well equipped in knowledge and skill; your victory will have merit. I want you to have a fair chance when I kill you. Otherwise, I'd be picking a fight with a cardboard box."

Are you calling me weak?

"Yes."

Okay so, you can get just put all this aside and let me get back to my date?

"I'm definitely more than capable, but I also don't feel like it. But, you know what would be the easiest thing? If you were finally desperate for the sweet release of death."

Why would I do that?

"Frankly, objectively looking at your life, why wouldn't you? Now I'll leave you to your date. Hopefully you'll take some time to separate your thoughts from impulsive actions.

If you're able to do this successfully, then you can have either impulsive proceedings with a faltering conscience, or a detrimental actions that are well thought-out. If you play your cards right, you could be looking at your reflection adjacent."

Hold on, before you go; what do you get out of this?

"Reflection adjacent" he laughed and it seriously got under my skin. That deep voice and his slow, raspy laugh are nothing short of evil. That haunting laugh echoed; it spiraled for...God knows how long. But there was something so strange; it was getting louder and fading out; he was never there, but he was staring me right in the face. I can't explain it, but I felt like I was in a real dream; like it was actually real, but it wasn't? Fuck, I don't even know; I don't even know what the fuck is going on with me anymore.

Everything was weird. Everything is weird; so fucking weird. I did a quick check to make sure no one else was in the bathroom, and I rinsed my face at the sink (where else would I do that?) once I was in the clear. I took a deep breath and released it all in a swift puff of air. I was supposed to leave; I wanted to, but for some reason I stayed. I stayed to look at myself in the mirror. I don't know; I had this compulsion; I had to make sure I was still there. When I looked everything was normal, but the longer I stared...that guy looking back wasn't me; it couldn't've been! It couldn't've been! He had my hair, my eyes, my skin, everything, but somehow, somehow that wasn't me! *What happened to you?* I couldn't stand it; not knowing, not understanding.

What happened to you?

My confusion had to be short lived; I have a girlfriend to get back to.

It wasn't a long walk back, I mean...you know; it was the same distance. Some things were weird; I saw them from the corner of my eye. People that were busy rushing off to

352

wherever they're going were now a blurred mash of colors. Just…shapes. There were a few dips in my hearing that I had to ignore; I have a girlfriend to get back to. Eyes on the prize, Scott.

"Scott, baby, are you okay?" I sat back down at the table with her and I admit; I might've looked a little off. These things are apparent to her by now. Also, this is the first time in a while that I've seen her concerned like this in a few months.

Would you believe me if I said I'm fine?

"Not one bit…per usual."

I'm doing fine.

"Scott" she groaned and dragged her hand down her face. "Why? Why are you so difficult?"

I thought you liked me when I'm hard. This wouldn't end well regardless of what I said. Figured I might as well amuse myself.

"Sometimes…sometimes you're fucking impossible! How am I supposed to be your girlfriend if you never let me into your life?"

Um…excuse me?! *Um…excuse me?! Did you forget who you're talking to? What makes you think you can raise your voice at me?*

"I-I'm sorry , I-"

Damn right you're sorry! We're gonna get out of here and go somewhere we can talk like we really need to, because apparently I need to set you straight again. And here I was, thinking a relationship would be a break from the rest of life. Maybe I should've said something nicer this time?

I stood up from that table so fast that it almost fell over. It probably would've if Iris wasn't pressing down on it. We didn't hold hands on the way out, but we did walk next to

353

each other. It was a cold, solemn walk, but at least we were close. This time I bought our tickets for the train. We were waiting by the rails; close as we could get without being over the line. It was quiet, between us at least. The only sounds were the ones around us; the buzz of the people passing through the subway and the liveliness of the shops and trains. People were doing all sorts of things, and we were there, standing. I had everything to say, and I'm sure she did too, but there were no words. After a while more people showed up; figured it would be weird just standing there so started up a game of Ultra Blox on my phone. It's another Tetris knock off.

"So now it's awkward all of a sudden?" Iris didn't look at me and her voice was calm, but I knew exactly what that meant. Her coldness always speaks volumes.

I have to pass the time somehow. I have three of these on my phone just in case one of them crashes. I put on a smoldering look but it didn't do any good since she still wasn't looking at me.

We got on the train with everyone else, but to my surprise, we didn't sit together. We've always sat together no matter what problems we were having. When I sat down she held on to the pole, and when I went to the pole, she sat down. At that point I gave up; she could've kept that up till we got to our stop.

What'd you even buy another crepe for? My effort for making conversation should be a success under normal circumstances. And of course, being mindful of our surroundings, I made sure to whisper.

"We were *going* to share it, but I'll eat the whole thing since you're already so full of shit." Well, doesn't look like that worked. Saying it could've gone better is the understatement of the day. Despite what she said, she kept the box closed with two green rubber bands stretched over it and held it close to her. On the upside, neither of us carried on in a loud tone. It's the whole reason I elected that we leave in the first place; nobody needs to hear our banter. I watched her from the corner of my eye to make sure she wasn't trying to make our business anyone else's.

When it came to our stop she was the first one off. A few people got off, but not enough for me to lose her in a crowd. I stepped out a while before the doors closed and she was on a bench that's a bit further down the platform from where the train let off. Mad as she was, she was waiting for me.

When I was making my way to her, I noticed the sun in the distance. It was at eye level; sunset. The clouds were dark, but they were lined in gold. The sky was a canvas covered in a spectacle of an artist's imagination. It was a painting that moved at a snail's pace. The mystic sunburst lying beneath the clouds looked to be a fusillade of the heavens. Things like this were normal, even for someone like me. I don't know why I took note of it today. I definitely don't know why the thought came at this time; I have a girlfriend to get back to.

But I will say that the masterfully painted sky placed a light on her that made that woman look even more beautiful. Her hair was glistening and all that jazz. I sat next to her and she took the bands off the box and put it in my lap.

"Here" she opened the box, unveiling the last crepe.

I looked smiled at her and nodded *Thanks.*

"For being an asshole." She swept the crepe right from under my hand and took a bite. She smiled; same way Roswell would. She's the reason I hate smug smiles and she knows I hate it. I have a counter for that; puts her back in her place every time.

Just like that, the smile was gone. She took the box back and carefully placed the crepe inside. Geez, I'm sounding kinda creepy right now. I think I'll stick to giving a general overview and leave it at that. Okay, okay, okay, so she sighed and she was like, really upset.

"Just hit me already, goddammit! Please, would stop looking at me like that?! Punch me, slam me, yell at me, just do something already! Why in the name of fuck do you give me such a cold look and make me feel like this is my fault? And you never tell me what I'm doing wrong! What is it Scott?! What. The fuck. Is. It?!"

And why would I stop if you didn't fix how you're acting?

"God, Scott; stop it! You make me feel like nothing whenever you look at me like that! Look, I'll do anything like that you want, just tell me! As long as it gets you to stop giving me that look! Hit me! Beat me! Just don't make me feel like nothing!" Her voice shone through as an urgent whisper. It made me feel guilty to some extent, but only partially. Also, I'll point out that she's not weak at all. I'll take a minute to explain: it's not the look that hurts; it's about what it means. It's actually something that I adopted from her. It was torture for me because it's the equivalent to beating me with a steel chair. I'm at the center of her world and she's at the center of mine. I love her and the fact that she could threaten to throw that all away with one look makes me feel vulnerable. Of course, I didn't want all the power, but I didn't want her to have it either. I've been trying to flip the tables but things don't always stay on my side. Maybe it's for the best; maybe that's what keeps us balanced. She's one of the most resilient people I know, but everyone can get hurt. As you might've guessed, this isn't the first time something like this happened, but- this really does make me seem like a bad person; I swear that I'm not.

Hmmm, I think it would take an awful lot for me to forget. I'm the poison you asked for; you'll have to do a little better to get it. It's an inside thing that we have. It sounds bad, but I promise it's...sweet...to us, at least. It has a totally different meaning for us.

"I used to know what that meant; I used to think it was

obvious what you wanted. When we first got together it meant sex, but that wasn't enough after a while. Your appetite is insatiable now and I'm not sure how I could manage it if I even decided to try." She was staring down at the box but I know for a fact that's not what she was looking at. I wanted to pay attention to her, I really did, but Roswell was sitting next to her. He couldn't've been there the whole time; I was looking at her the whole time! He wasn't saying anything and it bothered me for some reason. I kept wanting to pay attention to her, but it was so hard to focus. There was a demon sitting right next to my girlfriend and I couldn't just be like 'hey babe, there this guy sitting next to you that only I can see, and he's also a demon.' I don't think that'd be a good move for her sanity *or* mine.

"You'd never want me to buy you anything, sometimes you'd ignore my calls and texts; none of it bothered me until I started thinking about what could've changed." I couldn't say anything to him and he knew that, so why was he there? He wasn't smiling; he wasn't even looking at me! He was just...there! Iris, she was there too, but did she know Roswell was there? Does she know about Roswell too? "I don't think most people could ever understand how I felt. Heck, nobody could understand what it feels like to be addicted to someone; to be addicted to someone like you, specifically. Any time we have a problem, all you have to do is deflect the blame and I automatically feel the weight of it, some of the time, anyway. But you know, it's not the reason I try my best to do what you want; it's not because I feel responsible. It's because of that addiction; like I said a coupla' times before, you're the poison I asked for. I'm in love, I'm pretty sure; for whatever reason I can't think of. But now I'm starting to wonder if anything good I could do would be enough. There's some deeper issue I don't feel you're telling me about, and you won't tell me no matter how hard I push. I've been trying me hardest for you, but-you're not making sense anymore."

Roswell was struggling to get up from the bench; I watched it with my own eyes and I still couldn't believe it. He hunched over and vomited blood the same moment he finally gathered the strength to stand up. It was horrifying to watch, but thankfully it didn't last long. He took out a napkin from his left pocket, wiped his mouth, then walked down the platform until he disappeared into a faint cloud of light.

Wait, Iris was just pouring her heart out to me and I wasn't even paying attention! Uh...umm...how can I fix this? *Do you remember our first fight? You remember how you fixed it then?* Yup, that should do it. I hope that does it, but if it doesn't, at least it'll *feel great*.

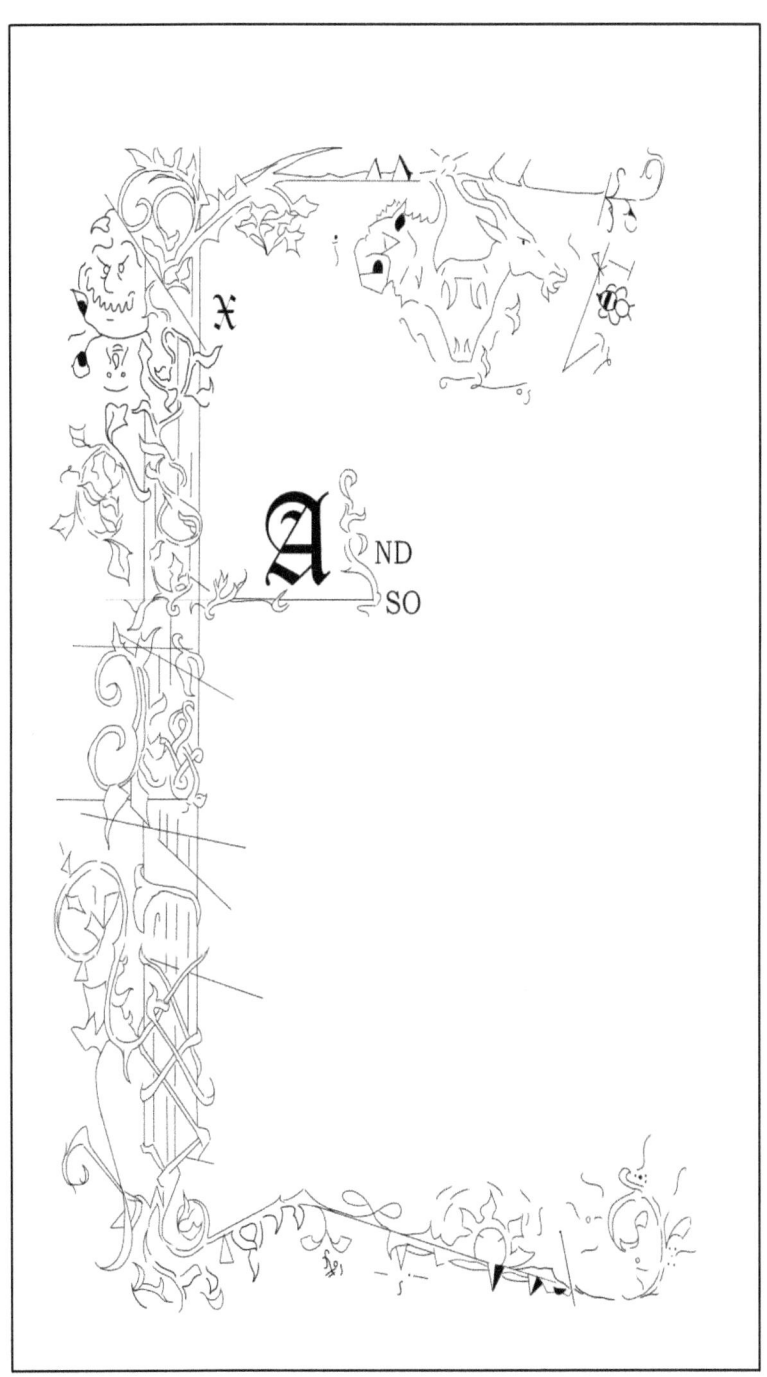

AND
SO

CHAPTER X
AND SO

It was great like I thought, but my mind was on a bunch of other things. Apparently, it wasn't as low key as I thought. She asked me if I picked up some new kinks out wherever I went. I told her she'd done more than fine. I know I wasn't lying; I needed to make her feel better. This was around the point where I'd need to mend things. Bad as it's been, there's a heavy fog in love and hate but there's not much that separates the two. As human nature goes, you're quick to search for an answer; I heard that from somewhere, but I can't remember where. But then again, I could try and turn things around; it's the one thing I haven't tried and I currently have everything to lose, but then I also don't; it's complicated. "I was thinking about...a conversation I had earlier; it's no big deal."

"Why? What was it about?"

"Um, I don't think this is your kind of conversation."

"If it's bothering you then it's bothering me. Plus, if it interferes with my sex life then it's definitely my problem; especially since you were practically demanding it and you were spaced out half the time. Scott, I love you and all, but I'm never horny just for you." My, what a catch she is.

"I don't think you'd understand."

"Be passive-aggressive, then aggressive, coerce into having sex with you, and then insult my intelligence? Scott, we're getting to the bottom of this."

"Alright, alright, alright, alright; I was talking to this guy in the bathroom about-"

"Which guy?"

"Woman, let me finish! Damn! So I was talking to the guy; you don't know 'em; I was talking to him about me and...uh...choices."

360

"This guy sounds a little sketchy"

"He's straight; believe me, he doesn't like guys. We're all straight, alright? He also didn't strike me as much of a people person."

"Got it; continue." Iris folded her arms and nodded her head once to show she was paying attention.

"Made me think a little bit about being comfortable in my own skin and about who I really am."

"Okay, you're black; you didn't know that? And some bathroom; you sure this guy wasn't sketch?"

"*No Iris, he's not gay and neither am I.* Anyway, it made me think about us. Why *are* we together?"

"Hmm, what do you mean?" Iris unfolded her arms and gently placed her hands on his thighs.

"It's not the interracial thing; you know I couldn't care less" I had to stop for a second and really think hard about the next words I'd say. The only good thing about messing up here is that I've got nothing to lose if I lose everything. "It's just that we're horrible to each other sometimes, and by sometimes I mean a lot. Every time I'm able to be dominant it feels liberating, but I hardly feel like myself. Maybe it should change; for real this time."

"Horrible?!" she accidentally (I'd like to assume) pulled some of the bedsheet off of me when she turned over to laugh into her pillow. After a few seconds, she looked back at me with watery eyes and a face that was trying its hardest to keep from erupting with laughter. "Horrible? In case you haven't noticed, that's our thing! What's horrible is different for us; this is who we are. The way we treat each other is like a cheesy, gushy romance novel as far as everyone else is concerned." She reached out and caressed my cheek with her hand. It made me feel so warm, but there was something different; don't know what it was. "You say it's not who you are and I can say it's not who I am, but this is who we are *together.*"

"But if this isn't who we are individually then why is it us together?"

"This is what we evolved into; people grow over time."

"But when did it 'evolve' into this?"

"Well" she sat up and leaned her back against the headboard. "I'm selfish at times and that eventually led up to me taking up any time you would've had for other people." She was getting so quiet that her words were almost inaudible.

"Yeah, I remember that pretty well; I heard through the grapevine that it didn't actually end."

"The grapevine, huh? You never could've got me to admit it back in the honeymoon phase, but I was scared, to some degree. I wanted someone like you and I finally got that, so I didn't want it to change."

"So you decided to change everything? Yup, that checks out."

"You could've left any time you wanted. We're still together, aren't we?"

"But is it the same?"

"You literally just said it wasn't. What's your point?"

"I want this to change."

"*This*? How come you've never had a problem with 'this' before and I know you definitely didn't have a problem with 'this' a few minutes ago."

"I never said I didn't have a problem with the way things were."

"Aaaaand now we're running in a loop. I'm *this* close to flat out ignoring anytime you want to 'talk about our relationship'. But if what you're saying is really the case, then what stopped you from saying something earlier?"

"The sex! It was great!"

"Well duh! Why do you think we banged so much? But seriously, where are you trying to go with this?"

"I want to change."

362

"But what is it that makes you want to change all of a sudden; you of all people? It's all you've been talking about for the last *two months*! I thought the heat death of the universe would come before you saw anything wrong with yourself. I thought the heat death of the universe would come before you saw anything wrong with yourself, and now you're doing…whatever this is. Hmm…Should I have made it 'death of the sun' instead?"

"It's not impossible for people to change."

"How do you think we got where we are?"

"I've experienced things that made me want to change. This talk keeps coming up like clockwork-" The room was already dark, but the faint lights from the window started to dim out; everything turned to nothing.

*

"Far as you can in the trial version. Unlock the full game to see more!" That voice; she wouldn't say that, would she?

I couldn't see anything ; all I could feel was the cold, hard floor beneath me. *Iris, is that you?*

"I'm your girlfriend now, Scottie!" NO! NO! NO! ROSWELL, YOU BASTARD! "Sorry to yank you from your quality time, but I've got some emergency business, so I'm gonna need to wrap this up fast. Some unforeseen circumstances have pushed my deadline up. I've got a story to finish, so you've got your work cut out for you. If it's any consolation, which it is, you'll get to hang out with you not-girlfriend Faaghira and save the world or something like that. Eh, I dunno. I haven't figured out all the details; I'm pressed for time. I hate to be so abrupt; my parts are usually a lot more organized. Kay, see ya at the big show! And one more thing: don't forget that I'm absolutely going to kill you once this is over because as much as I like messing with you, you're not moving things along at a good pace and *I'm getting bored*. Byeeeeeeeeeee!" I heard his voice but I never saw him. His voice echoed again but not as long this time. Odd thing; I could see fine right after his voice faded away.

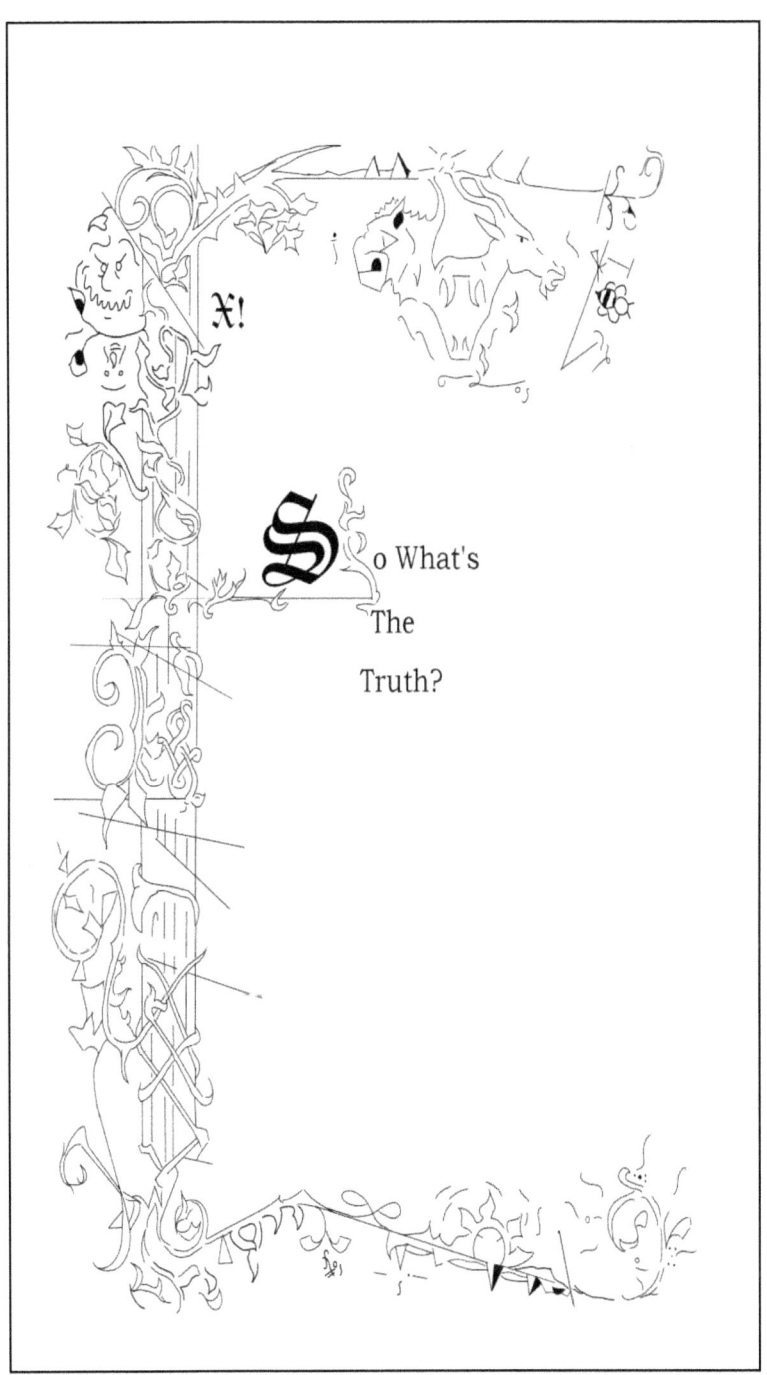

$\mathfrak{X}!$

So What's The Truth?

CHAPTER XI
SO WHAT'S THE TRUTH?

Scott opened his eyes and saw that he was back in Fae's condo; whichever one of the thousands he was in earlier. He was on the floor with a cover over most of his legs. It was morning; at least *I'm pretty sure it was.* The sun was peeking through the blinds, bashing his eyes with light. *Okay, so maybe it wasn't bashing, but it looks like it hurt.* He tried jumping up from the floor but all his energy was gone just from trying to tilt his head up. *I don't even know what just happened; one second he's in bed with Iris, then I'm in the dark and Roswell is mocking him or something, and then he wakes up on the floor all of a sudden.* "I don't even – I can't-why do I feel so weak?" *Beats me, kid. Hey, your voice is cracking a bit there, bud.*

"Faaghira! Faaghira! Faaghira! Faaaaaaaaaaaeeeeeeeeeee!" He called out to her as loud as *I* could. He probably didn't even know for sure if she was there, but he hoped she could hear him. "Everything felt so weird; not like physically, but it was weird mentally. I mean, it's usually that kind of weird, but it's never felt...so heavy. I needed some familiarity."

He went quiet when *I* heard footsteps coming down the stairs. "When you dedicate your life to something, sleep is sacred. You need to learn *now*; it's five thirty in the morning; Elle is still asleep somehow *and it better stay that way*. These hours are sacred in my house, got it?" She trudged to the couch; wearing a really long red t-shirt and dragging a cover over her shoulder. She was slow to sit down, but was so tired that she could only make it on the armrest instead of one of the actual cushions. Her hair covered most of her face until she parted it, specifically to show her, red, crusty, squinting eyes. Fae let the hair drop back over her face then she tossed her cover over mine.

"It can't be that early, the sun's already out!

"Broken Windows Patrol; that's not the sun." She started to walk away a bit faster than when she was coming to scold me.

"What's the Broken Windows Patrol?

"To put simply, it's a crime blimp that floats around from three to seven."

"Wait, does it commit crimes or stop them?"

"Yeah, look, I'm not telling you to go back to sleep, but for your safety, don't wake me up again."

"Oh, I remembered something I wanted to tell you." She was already back upstairs before I could finish. He wanted to tell her about the stuff that just happened with Iris and Roswell. Eh, she probably wouldn't've paid attention anyway; apparently she's real serious about her sleep.

Scott tried to go back to sleep but I couldn't hack it for some reason. He wasted some time playing all three of his fake Tetris games then I got bored so I read some clickbait articles and did some window shopping. Apparently, he must've lost track of time somewhere around there, because before he knew it, it was almost seven. "It's almost seven and my phone is almost dead." What's the problem? You know you can charge your phone, right? "Yeah sure, because I carry around a charger everywhere I go." Okay, the jury is in and Scott is a grump.

A screeching sound rang out through the air outside the windows. It didn't last long until it went away, but it was replaced by a really, *really* creepy song. It was echoing like wild which made it sound even creepier. It's this weird opera kind of song that's in Italian for some reason. Scott's eyes widened and did a double take on his surroundings. To say this is strange would be an understatement, and this also must not be a normal thing here. Faaghira came back downstairs and she was pissed. She. Was. *Pissed.* Phone in hand, she slid the balcony door open and leaned slightly over the railing.

"I promise that I had absolutely nothing to do with this. I repeat: none of this is my fault." Scott sprung up from the floor, shedding the cover and sheet that draped over him. He went out to the balcony to stand by her, though this clearly wasn't a good time.

"Nobody's said it was your fault; nobody's blaming you for anything," Her voice still held the same coldness and her face was stern. She seemed to be looking outwards, maybe at the blimp, maybe at the sky, but it might've been into something else completely. Regardless of what it was, Scott would've been lucky to be her fourth thought.

"What's wrong?" Scott tried to pull her attention like he had done before. It was easy for him to get upset with not getting what he wanted, and he definitely did. He made an effort not to show it, and maybe she really didn't notice, but his eyes widened and he furrowed his brows. His face read 'annoyed', but his words showed concern at a convincingly genuine level; at least I would've bought it if I didn't already know how he feels right now.

"Atticus!" She was still looking off into the distance, seemingly ignoring Scott. Faaghira was quick to trail some swipes on her phone and place it by her ear. "Larimar was trying to sleep; what the heck did you do?" She put her phone on speaker and held it below her chin.

"Oh my, you must not've been watching the news last night; I spent a good deal of time talking about daily initiatives to increase national pride, which seems to've been taking a dive thanks to a certain someone."

"You're seriously waking the entire city up at seven in the morning just to be petty?"

"No, I'm waking up the entire state for the sake of unity. A democracy that goes unattended will fail. Until I can be

368

sure that our unity is no longer in jeopardy, more unifying methods will be proposed in the following weeks. After the necessary period is over, the decision of whether or not to continue using these methods will be in the hands of the people," Atticus' gruff voice came with a swatch of confidence I haven't heard him use before.

"Turn it off!" She growled at him in such a way that I would've been paralyzed with fear if I was the one on the phone with her.

"Oh Faaghira, my dear, sweet, inconvenient niece; I'm obligated to do what the people voted for. The people vote for unity and excellence, thus, I must provide. And truly, as much as I'd like to publicly combat your efforts, it would justify your foolishness. While it is always...a pleasure talking to you, I have very important matters to attend to. Be sure to say hi to little Lari for me."

"No thanks, Elle is still scared of monsters. Also, die." She ended the call and sat down in one of the chairs close by. "Ugh! I can't wait till I don't have to deal with him anymore!"

Scott took a step forward but he stopped when Faaghira propped her feet up on the other chair. He was so blatantly offended that Fae raised an eyebrow at him. It does seem like a shift out of nowhere, especially since she missed that whole part with him and his girlfriend flipping out in the toxic Olympics. I actually was there for that one, even though I wasn't the narrator. Speaking of the narrator, he was pretty bad.

"Back to this bullshit again," He mumbled under his breath, but 'under his breath' turned out to be much louder than it was all the other times.

"And what bullshit would that be?" because Fae definitely heard him. Yeah, he's really whining at this whole life thing. Whoops, I meant winning.

He cleared his throat (because he never does that), pulled

a chair from the other side of the balcony, then set it as close as he could to Fae without getting in her now *very* personal space. "I-I wasn't talking about you; life-it's bull, you know?" Awesome save. There's no way she could think you're a dick *now*.

"Real talk-" Fae had her arms crossed, but her eyes were gazing at the city below, "-are you okay?"

"Uh, maybe; I wish I knew for sure. Do I seem like I'm not okay?"

"If you have to ask then you already know the answer. Was it Roswell that had you spooked? I know it couldn't have been Atticus; he's *my* nightmare."

"What makes you think it was- never mind. Roswell put in me in this dream; I don't really know if it was actually a dream, but I went to sleep and I woke up in the real world. Not to say that this one isn't real, it's- that's where I'm from."

"I know," she sounded worried, but something was different about this worrying. I don't know if this is the right way to describe it, but she sounded removed, kind of. "I think about that a lot. One of us is living in a dream. For one of us, everything will be a waste, but the answer gets blurrier every time I think about it. Something's always been off; I was either wise or stupid to believe any of that crazy stuff you told me. I couldn't say for sure exactly why I liked you in the first place, but maybe it was the universe showing me I'm not the only one taking things too lightly."

"Too lightly? This is serious for both of us! You're leading a rebellion and I'm trying to figure out my life! At least I think that's the point of me being here. See, I don't even know what the point of me being here is!"

"Scott, a demon put you in another dimension and you're acting like you're totally cool with it. My uncle took over an entire state, probably more than half the people here are in poverty, said uncle is a terrorist who has a terrorist organization in charge of the government; one of my ex-girlfriends is the leader of the rebellion fighting against my uncle; one of my ex-boyfriends is a loose cannon that hates the rebellion and my uncle. I live in the heart of it all, but I can't see any of that from up here. And now I sit casually, looking over the skyline, ignoring that everything's already gone beyond saving. Everything is a mess and I'm giving off the impression that everything will be fine. It's safe to say that we're both underreacting. Or at least we're trying to fool ourselves."

"If you put it that way then of course we are, but there's more to us than that."

"And what is it that makes you say there's more to me than what you've already seen?" Her words sounded ambiguous in intent, but that was probably just her voice. She has a really sexy voice, or at least I think so. Actually, I take that back; the sexiness of her voice isn't subjective.

"In that thing that might've been a dream, I met up with my best friend and went on a date with my girlfriend."

"What was her name again?"

" Iris. So Iris and I had a fight, kind of, but that was normal too. We made up, I think. She said I've been acting weird for the last two months, but I don't remember it being that long since we- I think reconciled would be the right word? I felt like we were talking about things for the first time, but apparently we weren't? I don't know; the whole thing was…weird. Speaking of Iris, you remind me of her. You look over the skyline and lean on the railing like she does. You like to have real conversations with me like she does, but you're not her."

"Hmm, what are you getting at?"

"You know how I told you Roswell made the dimension we're currently in?"

"Means he would've made me too; means he would've made everything in my whole life. I've been thinking a lot about that. If what you said about all this other dimension stuff is true then…maybe I'm supposed to remind you of her. Think about it; if he had to spend time creating an entire other dimension that's just as real as yours, wouldn't he skimp out on some parts?"

"But you're important! You're not some random person I run into every once in a while; you're the most important person here!"

"You're sweet, really, but you don't know what you're talking about. If you excuse me without a second thought, you're justifying Roswell too. If you haven't guessed already, what I am to you isn't what I am to him. I've still never seen the guy, but if he *is* real then he's more real to you than he is to me. If you're seeing a lot in common between me and Iris, then maybe that's because you're supposed to. All I see is that city, and most of what I think about is what I can do to save it. Again, it's wild that I'm even entertaining this whole demon thing, but this is your problem. His concern would be you above everyone else; me being different wouldn't be the priority of someone so…I might say it's 'determined'. Even when you're here physically, we're in different completely different worlds. I'm looking out for my world; you need to look out for yours. Be honest with yourself about all of this, it can get dangerous."

"Well, duh, it's been dangerous from the jump. After all I've had to deal with, danger doesn't mean a thing. I take that back; it definitely still bothers me to some degree. The point is that I'm used to uncomfortable things. I might've even grown a little bit after a while with all this weird shit going down."

"That's not what I meant. For some reason I doubt you'll get it now, but the kind of dangerous I'm talking about happens in your mind before it happens anywhere else. For your sake, I hope you get it soon. One more thing."

"What is it?"

"Don't ever bring this up in front of other people who won't take you seriously. On that note, what were you thinking of doing today?" Her voice was relaxed, a parallel to her worried eyes looking over the city.

"Nothing in particular; did you have anything planned out for us?"

"I had things planned out for me and you definitely can't tag along for most of them. Some of it is personal business, but I'm committed to Larimar for most of the day. You're a big boy and since you've been wanting to see the city, you'll get a chance today. If you want to do that then you definitely can. I'd been thinking about what Atticus said, the thing about you being pulled around, even though he was using it to shoot me down. Maybe you should take freedom out for a spin, just be careful. Atticus is still low key obsessed with you and you have a literal demon on your back."

"He's not literally on my back."

"Ugh, you know what I mean. Just be careful, alright? Here, gimme your phone for a sec," Faaghira held out her hand and ended the 'I'm not looking at Scott while I'm talking to him' thing that seems to be really popular in this book for whatever reason. It wasn't a look of longing or anything like that; it was a 'yeah, I'm talking to you' kind of look. Scott handed over his phone without hesitation and she gave it back in a few seconds flat. "If you get lost or you need me for anything then just call me up, but you'll have to use that sparingly today. Larimar gets to choose what we're doing today and sweet as she is, she gets bitter if someone interrupts our weekly 'sister day'. And Scott, please do yourself a favor and get some kind of security on your phone, or at least a lock screen or something. You may not have any money, but there are hackers around town that'll give you viruses just for the hell of it. Plus, you should charge your phone before you go out because unless you stay here all day, you're screwed if your battery goes out."

"Will your charger work with my socket?"

"Scott, now's really not the time, not that there ever is a time for that. I'd appreciate if you saved that shit for your girlfriend, and you got the lines switched up too so..." Fae reclined in her chair, folded her arms, and side eyed Scott in a way that yelled 'the fuck are you still doing here?' in the most polite way possible. Surprisingly he got the message, and quickly too. He turned to go inside-

"Hey Scott, Narrator, oh and uh Faaghira's here too. Hey how's it going?" No! Roswell is back. Why?! Why is he here?! "I kind of felt like showing up? I didn't know I'd need a reason to be somewhere."

"Who the hell are you?" Faaghira cracked her knuckles and was ready to jump up and fight.

"Yeah, we haven't met officially; I'm Roswell, you know; the demon. I know who you are but we haven't met, so this is weird, but it's also kind of isn't since you know who I am. I'm here for Scott, so you don't have anything to worry about."

"You're Roswell? You don't look anything like I thought you would."

"Yeah, I might as well start carrying around a card that says *'if evil looked as bad as it is, no one would do it'*. Look, I know, bad timing, but whatever it is I have to say to Scott is *probably* more important than whatever you were gonna say. I'm an asshole in case you didn't notice."

"For some reason, this is what I thought you'd-"

"And I'm also very proud of it."

"Really? And you're proud of it too? I'm sooo surprised." Fae let out a sigh of exhaustion, but there was no relief or anything like what she does with Scott. She was just straight up pissed.

"I'll pretend that wasn't sarcasm and I'll accept the shock as a complement. Thanks, by the way; you're so sweet. Hey so, like I was saying, I need to borrow Scott for a bit. This is gonna be real quick, but I'm probably lying so just don't try and stop me and you'll be fine."

"You remind me a lot of this guy I met before."

"Really? Did you like 'em?"

"He's trash; like I seriously want to punch him every time I see him."

"Well I like this guy; he sounds great! When can I meet him? Or how about we all go out for lunch sometime? It would be real cool, so we can do that, but after I finish talking to Scott about that thing." Roswell was donned in a brown aviator jacket with a faux fur collar and a smiley face with a big nose and a squiggly line for a mouth. It was the only insignia or sign of any type on the jacket, and it was painted on in a dark red color instead of embroidered. "Embroidery doesn't age well like paint does. You also can't wipe off embroidery. I mean, I can, but that's literally just me; rules of the universe are more of a suggestion to me rather than something I *have* to follow."

"Why are you even doing any of this in the first place?" Fae was braced for action.

"Okay, you're forcing your way into a bigger role here. Normally, I'd find that really annoying, but with you, I find it extremely annoying and *partially* gratifying." Roswell shifted his eyes between Scott and Faaghira…his pupils rolled to the back of his head. "They're solid icebreakers, these eyes of mine. Here I go, waffling again. So since we're all acquainted, I guess this talk can be for you too, Fae. Alright, here it goes." A violent cough attack overcame him before he could go on. It resulted in blood splattering on his sleeve, because Roswell's the kind of dude that always coughs in the bend of his elbow.

"Are you…okay?" Scott stepped back but contradicted the movement by starting to reach out to him.

Roswell smiled through his intense wheezing. When he

finally stopped, he flicked Scott on the side of his head. Fae tried to stop the demon with a strong swing of a chair, but she wasn't quick enough. Three small scars were left on the right side of his head. As for the chair, it turned into a mess of flowers as soon as it touched his back. "I lie about a lot of things, but I ain't like one of those other cats you might run into; I'm evil, kid. I say it and I mean it. I make a hell just for you and you ask if I'm okay when you see me coughing up blood? That's why it's you; you're one naïve dude. Your girlfriend seems to get it though."

"What the fuck did you do that for?" Scott yelled at the top of his lungs, but the echoing music from the blimps muffled it, so it looked a lot more dramatic than it sounded.

The demon laughed with a wide grin and strained, unblinking eyes. "I'm a demon; you're acting like I'd better have a good reason to be bad or somethin'. I hope your girl is planning to get you on your toes sometime soon."

"Fae is not my girlfriend!"

"You played yourself kid-" Roswell was interrupted by Fae locking him in an armbar and pushing him to the ground. "I never say who I was talking about; it's like sometimes you forget you have an actual girlfriend. Totally off topic, but lady, you're lucky I don't like it too rough, else I just might stick around. I never got around to what I was gonna say, but I really gotta get going; gotta set up for the big finale." Roswell flattened himself and slid out from under her. She was astonished and probably afraid. What else would she have encountered that's so weird and casually terrifying? "Casually terrifying is right on the money; I have the power of plot convenience. Like I said, none of this is what I came here for, but I've got a treat for the kid who sees the good where there isn't any. I left three clues for a scavenger hunt and the whole city's underworld just got into it. You're top billing on a hit list as of like, a minute ago, courtesy of yours truly. The same folks'll try and kill you dead. And Fae, don't hold me up any longer or I'm putting you at number two."

Fae clenched her fists and scowled at the demon, but she didn't do so much as step forward as she watched him revert to his original form. "We'll settle this later."

"Can't wait! As for you Scott, I have one last, very important message: Bye bitch!!!!!!" With the wave of his hand, sparkling beads of light came down over him, followed by a cloud of smoke. When it cleared, he was…still there? Turns out he was awkwardly standing there and grinning the whole time. So after the smoke cleared, he winked at Faaghira then promptly threw himself over the balcony railing.

"That guy is a nutjob! Geez, I can see why you have such a problem with him." Fae was still trying to catch her breath after being startled by whatever you call that thing Roswell just did.

"That's light compared to what he normally does. One time I think he killed me while I was in the elevator coming up to see you."

"What?! How often does he show up?" Fae was just starting to calm down

"I don't think he goes by a real pattern; he seems to show up whenever he feels like it. Don't worry though, he might've been bluffing about the 'hit-list' thing."

"Do you remember when we were on the ferry and I pointed out some of the contractors that were there?"

"Yeah." Scott sounded like he was drifting off, swept up in a dream. "We were dancing for the first time; your ass is great, by the way."

"Scott, focus! A demon put a hit out on you! Seriously, why does it feel like I care more about your problems than you do? We're lax, yeah I get that, but you still need to fight for yourself! It's like you're not even trying!" Fae was getting worked up, and rightfully so; Scott is pretty annoying. Then again, nobody's forcing her to help him.

"It's my problem, alright?! Let me handle it the way I want to," He raised his voice and while he didn't yell, lashing out isn't exactly any softer with a whisper.

"Scott, just go; you're being childish."

"Oh, so now you don't care about the hit list all of a sudden?" Scott threw a heavy fit, firing off at Fae.

She sighed, picked him up from underneath his arms, placed him back inside, then slid the balcony door closed. She sat back down in her chair and propped her feet up before scrolling through her phone again.

Scott stormed out the condo and slammed the door behind him, something he'd instantly regret. "Why would I regret it?" Um, let's see: your phone's battery is low; you don't have any cash on you, you don't have any other clothes, and most importantly, when's the last time you showered? "Shit, you're right! What do I do? I can't just barge back in and be like 'Hey babe, sorry I was being a jerk; I'm gonna take a shower real quick, but before I do, do you have some extra clothes and cash to lend me? Thanks, you're the greatest!'; she wouldn't let that slide. What do you think I should do? You're the narrator; didn't you catch on to something she likes or whatever? Maybe I could say that I'll buy her her favorite flowers." You'll buy her flowers…with her own money? You're a catch; somebody put a ring this man stat! Even if I did want to help, the only thing it says about flowers is 'Lol, Scott doesn't know Faaghira's favorite flower'; I can't help you much, but there's one person- um 'being' that would help. "Cool, as long as it's not Roswell then I'm game." Okay well I'm completely out of ideas.

Scott wandered the dimly lit halls of the eighth floor for a bit to kill some time. The walls are painted a glossy black (or dark brown; the lighting makes it hard to tell) and everything has a very streamlined luxurious design. The four windows lined at the corners along with the mini coffee tables, paintings, vases, panels protruding from the walls a high-class geometric aesthetic. The underside of every door glowed with a dim, yet radiant glow; as contradictory as the person who designed them. "This place is pretty dope. I'd totally live in a place like this if I could afford it." Scott, time to stop stalling. Remember our agreement; you want to get back home, don't you? "Mmmmm, I don't mind being stuck here for a little longer. Turns out I might be losing more by going back home." Dude, come on! Okay, we'll discuss this later, for now we'll focus on getting you what you need without bothering Fae. You'll need a set-up of your own if you're planning on staying here. If you keep depending on her for everything, especially with the way you are, you'll stay getting yourself into these kinds of situations. "I hate when you're right. Fine, fine I'll go and hopefully I'd have figured something out by the time I get off the elevator." You should take the stairs. Remember the time when Roswell showed up in the elevator and beat you to death with a guitar? "The stairs sound nice; I'll get to stretch my legs and get some exercise."

He started to run down the stairs at first, but he quit after he reached the seventh floor. That's right, one entire set of stairs. The steps he stopped at *pushed themselves up using their arms and legs, and then presumed to fly him down to the bottom floor*? What in the actual crazy? Roswell…what is he doing? "Hey man, I don't care what he's doing; it's keeping me from having to walk all that way." Why is this normal for you? Are you high or something? "At this point, I don't know if I would be the best judge of that. I'm drunk, I think? It feels more like acid, but that's Rozzie's thing I guess? Now that I think about it, I haven't actually been drunk in a long time." You got hammered at that party you and your girlfriend went to; that wasn't even four days ago." I mean, but how long before that? In reality I've had like, three months so far. Name a time I was drunk before that; I'll wait." Dude, I haven't even known you for a week; how often do you get drunk? "See! You couldn't even name another time! Like I was saying, it's been a long time since I was drunk other than that one time. Trust me, I know my own life." Whatever, I'll just move on to the next part. At least one of us has to stay on task. "Yeah, good on holding down the fort. You're the real MVP."

Scott was dropped off at the bottom of the stairwell *by the flying stairs with noodly cartoon limbs and angel wings.* Why am I the only one that seems to be noticing how crazy this is? So, Scott opened the door to the lobby, waved goodbye to the concierge (/head of security?), then headed straight outside. He rushed out into the city, going nowhere, doing nothing. He wanders aimlessly for two blocks; stopping in front of restaurants and bars, but never going inside; excitedly pointing his phone at buildings he was amazed by...but would place it back in his pocket begrudgingly after remembering how low his battery was.

Though it was early, the streets and sidewalks were almost fully covered, as they would normally be in the later hours. Nobody stopped to give him any questioning looks, no one tried to sell him anything, not a soul tried to mug him. I don't doubt that people noticed he looked stupid, but it didn't look like it crossed anybody's mind. Instead, he seemed to be the only one that was traveling without a purpose. Even the people he passed who were relaxing (or at least stationary), whether lounging on the steps of the city library, the grounds of various colleges intertwined with corporate buildings, elegant yet inviting restaurants, or one of the many lush and well maintained parks; everyone seemed to have some kind of purpose for being where they were. Scott, on the other hand, was out trying to kill time. The reason he was out in the first place is mostly, if not completely because of his childish behavior. It goes without saying that nobody else in the city would be stupid enough to throw a fit at the second most powerful person in the entire state. Considering that, Scott is definitely breaking records.

He took the phone back out his pocket then put it up to his ear. "I'm really hoping you get hit by a truck or something. Fae was being bitchy, alright? Am I supposed to sit there like a wuss and take whatever she bull she says to me. Shit, I hardly even get to talk when she's around! She's fine, yeah, but that doesn't excuse the fact that I feel like less of a man anytime we're in the same place! She needs to stop treating me like a kid! For once, for once I-"

Like the sound of thunder clashing against the sky, a bullet tore through the air, running right through Scott's thigh. People scattered and panicked, screaming and crying; pushing and shoving past each other; they were all desperate to get out of harm's way. Paramedics rushed to the scene to get Scott on stretcher and load him in an ambulance nearby.

But nobody called for them.

They were driving at a snail's pace, but the siren was blaring; it wasn't because of traffic. The police- I mean Justice and Peace Authority were nowhere to be seen. Also strange, nobody looked to see where the shot came from. The inside of the ambulance was normal up to the point where they started moving. The paramedics all had knives out surrounding Scott, ready to slash him, but nobody makes a move.

"Hey, so I get suspense is cool and all, but if you're trying to get that payout, why don't you kill me now and get it over with?"

"You're funny; wish it was someone else that made the top of the list. Eh, there's other funny people in the world."

"Cool, cool; still didn't answer my question though."

"And?" She put her knife over his throat almost grazing, but never landing on his skin. There was determination in her eyes and a terrifyingly serious look on her face. Scott slowly nodded his head and winked at the woman, turning her steely aggression into unamused confusion. "You're seriously expecting to flirt your way out of this?"

"Nope, I'm trying to flirt my way into it; lucky for you I'm into knife play." He winked at her again as he continued to nod his head, getting into some inaudible groove.

She cringed a little as she quickly put the knife back in its holster. Everyone else suddenly had other things to attend to, so they followed suit. The woman glanced at him from the corner of her eye, but she snapped her attention back to the nothing happening in front of her after he started rapidly flicking his tongue at her. "The only reason you're still alive is because we have to prove it to the clientele, so put your tongue back in your mouth or I'll-"

"Cut it off? Mmmm. Then what will you do with it?" Scott winked again and kept doing that nodding thing. The woman sighed and left the threat unfinished. By this point she was well aware that saying anything to Scott was the worst idea at the moment. However, there was a guy there who didn't get the memo.

"I'll shoot you right here if you don't shut up!"

"From what I heard through the grapevine, that translates to 'I'll blow the chance to do the job I was hired for so I can maintain my status as tough and impress my colleagues'. You think you're slick; you ain't slick." He sat up on the stretcher, curling his knees up to rest his wrists on them. "Shit, I know me when I see it." The rest of the contractors were silent. It might've been out of respect, but most likely nobody wanted to deal with his painfully discomforting sexual advances. The drive was smooth but very awkward. Nobody said anything, not even Scott. He kept fighting the urge to take out his phone as the boredom kept kicking in. And suddenly, the bullet in his thigh wasn't bothering him at the slightest. Yup, real solid writing.

CRASH!!!!!

The ambulance was hit with so much force that it flipped and crumpled on its side, moving against the ground with an ear-piercing skid. The inside of the ambulance was now a bloody mess. Scott scanned through the blood-stained faces and the crushed and lifeless bodies for some sort of answer; a sign of what happened. There was hardly any distance between him and what used to be everyone else. He tried to move to the back doors, but his leg was still shot with pain (literally). He took short rapid breaths in an effort to ease the pain, but I don't think it worked. He'd bite into his sleeve to muffle his pain induced yells. Tears poured out of his strained, bloodshot eyes. He bashed his shoulder into the doors in a desperate attempt to get out of the crushed van. He kept trying and trying; at one point he kept going even though he knew it was in vain. "This- has been…this is-" he was failing to catch his breath. "This shit's always happening to me. I couldn't even die like everyone else! Especially that one chick; she was cute; nice ass too. Goddam, the side caved right in; impaled her- then crushed her. That one was the only one I saw, but everybody- got dealt real bad. It was a split-second kind of thing, but I'm actually glad I didn't catch anything else. What I saw-" he thrust his shoulder against the doors, but all it did was crack his scapula.

He muffled his scream into his sleeve, but it made it sound so much worse. He sounded trapped, and though he actually was, the weight of defeat was carried through his agony. "What I saw is probably gonna haunt-" he was trying his hardest to steady his breathing down to a slower pace. "- It's probably gonna haunt me for- a long time." He held his breath and thrust his shoulder against the doors again. He screamed in pain, but this time it was so bad that he couldn't cover it with his sleeve in time. "Roswell! ROSWELL! I'll get through this; I'll get out of here, no matter how many of my own bones I have to break! And when I get out, I'm gonna find a way to kill you, just like I said I would. I meant it then and I never stopped looking for a way! Roswell, I hear you when you're trying to fuck up my life! I hear you

Roswell, and better, you better damn fucking well hear me!" Scott starts bashing the door with his other shoulder until it starts to give way. The small victory boosted his vitality, but it drained quickly when nothing else happened. He started using his hands to push the door but it was a faint attempt; there was hardly any strength left in his arms, but he kept pushing as if it would make a difference. "You better damn fucking well-" light creeped in from a small gap in the doors. Was he finally doing it?

Smoke began to seep into the inside, leading Scott to cough heavily. The doors caved outwards then jolted off. "No, this was my doing. I am sure that Scott tried his best to relieve himself of this stressful situation. However, his efforts would prove to be inadequate." It was Baron Sugar on the who stood outside the ambulance.

"Did you do this?"

"Yes. And no. And yes. I opened the doors. I did not cause this incident. I was hit into this ambulance by Roswell, causing this incident."

"So did you win or did he run off somewhere?"

"He is across the street."

"What? He's still here?"

"Yeah, surprise. Hey, so is everyone in there dead, or is it *almost* everyone?" Roswell shouted to them, even though he could've walked across the street so he wouldn't have to be so loud. "I mean, I could do that too, but I really don't feel like going *all* the way over there. Oh and Scott, you might wanna run off somewhere real quick; Sugar and I have a fight to finish. He ain't a dude that hits back too often, but he sure can take a beating."

"I didn't see anybody alive when I was trapped in there. Yup, I was trapped in a crushed ambulance with a bullet in my leg with a bunch of dead people. And before I forget to say it: Roswell, you're a dick!"

Roswell was prying off the door to the driver's seat…but

when Scott did a double take, he saw that the demon was still across the street. One Roswell excitedly waved to Scott, while the other pried off the door for the driver's side, mercilessly beating the driver's face into a pulp. It was out of Scott's line of vision, but the sounds went from something solid to a mashed pile of...something; that sound was unmistakable.

"Faaghira sent me to look after you. I was to appear immediately after you exited the building, but I was intercepted by the demon. Hurry, we must leave here quickly. Faaghira warned me of the contract that is now on your head, not to mention that you are no threat to the demon." Sugar looked down at Scott for a moment then looked straight ahead, still as a statue. Scott grimaced and punched Baron Sugar's arm with all his might. "No threat; I hold my stance." Baron Sugar tossed Scott on his back like a cinch bag. "Faaghira would be incredibly disappointed if you died. I will not allow this under my watch." Baron Sugar began to take off into the air when he was pulled back down by the one of the Roswells.

"Hey, hey hey; I didn't say we were done. This is still my book, you know. I ain't tryna have you ruining this for me. You've had a chance to have your own story for like, two centuries now; give someone else some time in the light."

"I have no time for your contractions." Baron Sugar's cloth 'face' unlatched itself from his head, revealing what could only be described as a miniature black hole. It let out a distorted, throaty shriek. It blasted the spots the Roswells were standing in. The both sides of the street were completely decimated. The ambulance and all the other vehicles on the streets were pressed and crushed flat by the sheer force of the increased gravity.

The Roswell across the street was crushed; his bones warped and pressed down just the same as the cars. He broke down immediately under his own weight. Some of the buildings were starting to fold in at the bottom. The other Roswell, however, stood perfectly, holding on to the end of Sugar's cloak. The skin of his face melted completely off. Otherwise, he was fine. Everything else gave into the crushing atmosphere, but Roswell hardly seemed to notice.

"Now Fae's got you being a hero? Not a twist I would've seen. I still need the city though, so you'd better fix it quick. Oh and in case you think of leaving your mess, other people need this city for real. It's a pointless illusion, sure, but isn't it all?" He chuckled; cracking lines his jaw to craft a sinister grin on his blood stained skull. Scott looked over his shoulder to see Roswell (why?), and his eyes were lit with terror when he saw the demon's bloody eye socket form an eyelid just so they could wink at him. Everything that was destroyed fixed itself, but this time everything looked fresh and clean; even better than it did before. The ambulance was back to how it was before the crash, but everyone inside was still dead. "Nice doing business with you, Sugar. Take care of the old man, kid; I can tell when he cares. Don't use contractions though, I heard he's not one of the people who jibes with that kinda thing." Sugar flew away with Scott after Roswell waved goodbye; his skin grew back rapidly, but it didn't finish by the time he was out of Scott's sight.

Sugar was up in the clouds with Scott draped over his back. It was quiet from high up there; surprisingly peaceful too. The city glowed with a spectrum of lights, creating a surreal abstract portrait. "Why do most of the lights cut off at a certain point?" Scott's eyes were drawn to the vast city below and the darkness appearing at its ends.

"As with all things, there is an end" Baron Sugar glazed over his words with his regular cold delivery. Aside from answering Scott's mundane questions like 'Do you get hungry even if you're immortal?' and 'How fast does a day go by for you?', the flight was silent.

"I've been wondering since Fae introduced you…"

"I existed long before Faaghira."

"That's not what I meant."

"Sarcasm. Proceed."

"How did you become…whatever it is you are now? Faaghira hyped you up, telling me that we have some things in common, but I'm not seeing it. Plus, and don't take this the wrong way, but Roswell said something that makes me think you might've been lying earlier."

The flight was stopped suddenly amongst a heap of clouds. Baron Sugar took Scott off his back and placed him on one of the clouds. Sugar stood upright even though there was no surface below him. "Faaghira is the first human with whom I have shared the tale of my rebirth. Under her insistence, you will be the second. Bear in mind that I will not be repeating this."

"You got it, Sugar."

"As a mortal your body, is not able to support itself on a cloud. In any event where you were to suddenly be reintroduced to gravity, you would be liable to fall."

"Oh come on! I'm just calling you what everyone else does!"

"To your death."

"Pfft, I never even said anything…you can go on with that story. I'm out of the way, I promise." Scott tried to play it cool by reclining into the clouds, but anyone could see that he was scared shitless. I would be too, though. That silly face painted on the cloth over his head is terrifying when it's paired up with his low, emotionless whispering voice.

"More than two hundred years ago; the same as the demon has been saying. I assume that you are familiar with the United States Civil War."

"Shit, I didn't believe you were really that old! But yeah, sometimes I think it never actually ended. Maybe on a surface level, but it seems like it still comes up from time to time."

"An observation, it seems, we have both made. You are wiser than you appear; that was a worthy interruption." He gave one solemn clap before continuing his story. "I am much older than the Civil War. I was already…this by the time the war broke out. Louisiana had just become a state, but my family and I had been there before that time, during French and Spanish rule. We were slaves, yes, but there was no insufferable cruelty akin to what would be in the years to come. Though at the core, ownership and power imbalances are cruel enablers of human nature. The most important thing for me since being born into that wretched life was that there were affluent people who looked much like myself, though objectively not as good looking as I. For sixteen years I had only known the United States as a young but isolated nation; it was far from my sight and my thoughts. Everything changed when Orleans was accepted as one of their states."

"Oh cool; history lesson."

"The 'colored people' as they called us, we would find that this country would have us defined as subhuman. All of the many *colored people* who had achieved affluence were stripped of their standing by an amendment that would restrict the right of suffrage to whites."

"Sorry to cut in again, but wasn't it just for white *men* specifically?"

"Separate 'w-i-c' from 'k-e-d' and you will not be able to read the word in front of you. By that point I thought it had already been, but I truly experienced hell for the first time when my home became their plantation. My family was kept together, but I wished so desperately that my parents and my sister could be far from this place. The rest of my family was apt to stay out of trouble, but being the free spirit I was, there was no end to my mischief. I was flogged both in the blazing sun and the humid nights. My parents scolded me out of love and fear for their child, but they stopped when they realized what had been done. They saw the scars it left, but they never saw the damage it did to me. Whether it was the hot iron mark on my chest or how my back looks like a cutting board from the days of relentless flogging, nothing my body endured was even close to the hell my mind went through. It would be my luck that I could work, be beaten with a fury, and still be alive the next day. I could not let that be the reality for my family. I knew my body would give out soon enough, but I had to do something before it did. I could not do much, but I was not totally powerless. It was a desperate move that sometimes makes me regret my willingness to take action."

"Never thought I'd hear that from anyone, let alone you. It's also surreal hearing about slavery from a former slave, especially when they're telling me in person. I never would've thought; I have to remind myself sometimes that slavery was a real thing that happened, and it wasn't even that long ago in the grand scheme of things. Even worse thinking that I'd be in it if I were alive back then. I'll level with you; you give me the creeps, but I can't even begin to imagine what it's been like having lived for so long and seeing how much the world changed."

"It has not. Since I forfeited the ability to see things from a small perspective, I am able to acknowledge that nothing is different. Law can deter the action, not the mind." Scott chuckled to himself, but he quit when Sugar's 'face' turned into a solid scowl. It was painted in a silly way, with one eye bigger than the other and looking very whimsical and kind of cute, but it chocks up to be terrifying when you see the rest of him draped in his long and tattered brown cloak. "My mother was pregnant; as fate would have it, I would have a baby brother in the months to come. I had time to plan the use of my power…and yield to the loss of my humanity. I waited three moons from the day he was born, and as my family slept…I took him to the river. I closed my eyes and turned my head away as I drowned my infant brother. I buried him far in the woods, but I could not bear going back to my family after that. I killed because I had a heart, and it is also the same reason that I decided not to return. Why would I go to my family after murdering my brother if I truly had a heart? I hate the fact that he lived the fullest life he could, but it was the best thing that could have been done. I had months to justify it before I followed through, but it was not until I committed the act that I began to realize the full stakes of what I had done."

"Did you get caught?"

"Worse; it was there when I was at my weakest that a squirrel came down from one of the trees. It spoke to me, offering me power. I swore it was my conscience, but the small creature said it was not."

"Roswell."

"I wish it would have made a difference to me if I had known the evil that stood before me. Desperation was not my flaw, but my predicament led me to a place where it would be my undoing. I will admit that I questioned my sanity when a squirrel was talking to me, but its words took hold of my heart. 'You can get the power you want', it said to me. The trial, slavery, had instilled so much despair in me that drowning my brother would be better than him growing up and living-pardon-existing in this wretched world. I saw no other viable options, and after living for so long, I came to terms with the brutal fact that I would have died a slave if I refused his offer. Yet, with time I also realized that no matter what I chose I would never be a free man."

"Was he just out to ruin your life like he was with me, or was he up to something different?"

"I can assume, but unfortunately I know nothing for certain. The deal itself was very strange. I asked how to receive this power and it told me that I was going to be a light in the dark. He changed to his normal form; the one you are most familiar with. He winked at me and my entire body was engulfed by a maelstrom of fire. I was screaming, but no sound came out of my mouth. I plunged myself into the river to extinguish the flames and…I wish I never tried to stop it. I saw my little brother's lifeless body sinking down below me. I went unconscious, but I was still able to hear what he said while I was submerged. I clearly remember him saying 'See you, number two'. I arose from the waters, still burning. I was a light in the dark; a light that showed the path to anger and destruction. The first thing I did was go back to the shack where my family lived. I was furious over everything; over nothing; I pushed the decrepit shack into the ground and incinerated it. My parents, my sister, they were all still inside; I made sure of that. I had finally had the power to save them, but I saved them in the only way I knew how. I burned everything and everyone; from the slaves in the field to the ones in the house; from the crackers to the master himself. It was not just fire; I pulled apart limbs and murdered with my bare fists. The owner prided himself on gaining his wealth from a short line of sugar barons. He said it was close to his heart, so I ripped out his heart and called myself and claimed the antithesis of his title, being that my slave name was just that; a slave name."

Scott was stunned by every part of Baron Sugar's story, but was horrified by the end where Sugar brutally murdered his own family along with everyone else. "I-I-why did you kill your own family; why the fuck would you kill your own family? Why would you drown a baby? How could you do that to your own brother? How- what did Roswell do to you?" his voice was trembling but he tried to mask it, as always. He sat up and clenched his fist like he was really gonna do something. Sugar's face changed to a frown; he put Scott on his back and started flying back down to the city.

"While I resent it, I am solely responsible for my actions. The only thing Roswell is responsible for is giving me the power I wish I had. My mind, I am afraid, was already set on

391

a mortal solution. I have had more than two centuries to strengthen my mind to the same level as my power; now I have created ways to solve problems that have long since passed. This power, I am slow to use it. I implore that you do not let desire or a void lead you to become the bane of your own existence. Leave this dimension as soon as you are able. You may look back, but do not let longing bring you back to this place. You are free; do not put yourself in chains."

"That's the problem, I'm not free!" Scott had to shout to be heard over the rushing winds. "My mom told me I'm a disappointment; hard as I try, nothing I do gets me anywhere good; I'm in a terrible relationship that I depend on physically, emotionally, and financially; I don't know what I'm even here for; I never asked to be born, ya know? I'm lots of things, but a free man ain't one of them." Scott was straining himself so much that a vain was popping out on his arms and- "Wait a second, why the hell do I have to shout while you can basically whisper and I hear you just fine?"

"As you said, you can hear me fine at a whisper. Calm yourself; your voice will be damaged if you continue to strain it under this wind pressure." Sugar slowed down, but from the looks of that means sixty mph at the least.

"Hey, so I've been wondering: why don't cars work when they get near your mansion?"

"I do not like to be bothered; I think cars are cool; I like to drink the gasoline. Though I know it will not, I like to imagine that it could kill me."

"You try to kill yourself?"

"Try is the keyword. I am invulnerable in most cases and immortal in all. For me, it seems that my existence will be spent keeping people off of my lawn. Perhaps I could liken to a millennia of being a grumpy old man."

"I don't understand you. I really don't understand you."

"From what I gathered, I am no special case. Be at ease,

Scott; I do not desire to be understood." Sugar finally landed back on the streets, but Scott still hung on to him like a koala.

"We are back in the city. You can get off my back anytime you would like."

"I know, but can you just carry me around for a little bit? I'm not even that heavy!"

"But you would like to get off my back immediately."

"Oh okay, I catch your drift." Scott lowered himself from Sugar's shoulders and awkwardly looked around with his hands in his pockets. He didn't have any trouble standing; it's like he was never shot. Sugar walked on without a word, but Scott didn't follow until he realized that Baron Sugar wasn't coming back for him. The two went on their way through the crowds of people there, Scott apologized every time he pushed past someone while Sugar, on the other hand, barged right through, though he's the one no one complained about. Scott was also the one stopping in the middle of the sidewalk to look around at all the lights and extravagant high rises. He kept reaching for his phone which always ended with him throwing a small fit. "Why do people look annoyed when I'm being polite and the they couldn't give less of a damn about you goddamn running them over?!" His jealousy taking off at full force. "And why does nobody care that you're a freakishly tall…um…well you're basically just a cloak!"

"I have been offended."

"Bet your ass you were! I thought you'd be a little sensitive to something, at least."

"I was joking. You are a pushover. It is also apparent that I am nothing but a cloak, as my physical form is an embodiment of astral energy that manifests through fire. Telling the truth will not make you tough by any means; specifically you. In regards to the first part of your question: The citizens of this state are ruled over by a tyrant that built upon existing class and racial disparities and keeps them in a perpetual state of fear. A tall figure in a cloak walking down the street is not a concern. If I do nothing to draw attention, then there is nothing to see."

"This is a weird place, but it's kind of like Times Square weird. I see weird stuff there all the time, but I dunno; maybe it'd be weirder without all that. Speaking of Manhattan, there's a ton of food places up there and all the ones I've been to were so good; it was wild! And speaking of food, there's this place I went to and Safira was there and the food was really good. I don't remember the name of the place, but I know the owner's name is Angelo."

"Concentrate on the name of the establishment. Do your best to recall the area in which you saw it." Sugar paused while Scott closed his eyes and took deep breaths. "The name of this establishment is *Ace N Dandy's*. It is located in the section of the Bellamy Quarter outside of the city central."

"Did you just read through my mind or scan through my memories or something?"

"No, I am familiar with the area. That was a good joke, was it not?"

"Ha ha, very funny. Now where is it exactly?" Scott crossed his arms and scoffed.

"From the corner of the part you are unfamiliar with to the other part that you do not know. I can take us there. We will walk." The walk was long and mostly silent, but with Scott being the kind of person he is, he couldn't let things be.

"What did you see after you…the incident? The one in your story."

"Elaborate."

"The world changed a lot from back then and you had a chance to see it all. That must've been crazy seeing how much things changed. You were alive during the Civil War, the first civil rights movement, both world wars; you were around before airports got that annoying 'security' they got after September eleventh!"

"You sound fascinated, but the truth is that immortality will aggravate more than anything. It did not even take me two decades to see the infinite loop of innovation, greed, and war. I hardly traveled and I hardly interacted with people. Frankly, I was expecting disappointment and I was not let down. This reminds me; Faaghira was sure that you and I would get along after I told her my story. At first I did not understand why she said that, and after meeting you I was more confused, but now I can see what she meant. One could not be faulted for mistaking her intuition for a supernatural ability." Scott chuckled to himself and Sugar's blank expression changed to a goofy smile. "She told me that you have feelings for her, but she did not say they are being reciprocated because she does not know the degree of your feelings." Scott froze and that smile drained off his face. "I am curious; how do you truly feel about Faaghira? Do not worry, this is purely for the sake of our bonding; I will not share any of these words with her. That is something that I will leave up to you."

"Um…well…you're putting me on the spot, aren't you?"

"The Earth has gravity."

"Okay, yeah, I'm stalling; you got me. I just- I don't know…it feels weird talking about stuff like this; especially with you. We just talked about how you straight up murdered your family and now you're asking me about my love life."

"Your father could walk into your room and say 'I just had sex with your mother. It is important to get valuable skills so that you can have a stable job and not have to struggle to make ends meet."

Scott was so stunned that he kept restarting different sentences till he could actually manage to finish. "That might be a false equivalency, but I see where you're going with this." He let out a heavy sigh then reluctantly continued. "It goes without saying that she's different from anyone else I've met, but there's something about her that resonates with me. I'm not sure about a lot of things; I don't know what a good relationship with parents would be like, I don't know what a healthy relationship looks like, no idea how I'd know what love is supposed to feel like. My life is normal for me, but I'm kinda shocked when I hear that's not how it is for everyone. Not that I think my life is the standard, but it's hard to believe that your whole life- none of it was normal. My life is the weird one, so maybe I am in love with her? I can't tell. I already have a girlfriend though, then there's the whole different dimension thing. We bicker and all but that's mostly because of me. She's right; she's been right, but I don't know what's supposed to come after that. What do I do? Iris and I argue all the time and it's the same thing with my parents; I don't know what's supposed to happen if everything is fine and she deserves everything to be fine. I remember that night we first met, which was just a couple days ago- I think; I'm not sure how time works here. Anyway, I remember Atticus saying that she didn't give me a chance to talk, but it was my choice not to. I wanted to hear what she had to say, plus she knows this place better than I ever will. How am I supposed to tell her what her home is like?"

"I was ignorant, but I was smart when I was human; we have this in common. There was no Faaghira when I was in your situation. There was no avoiding my unfortunate future, but you have the knowledge of my mistakes and Faaghira's care to help carry you back to your home. Your words to me have been few, but you have shown character."

"Is that why she cares about me?"

"Faaghira is aware there are things I will not tell her, and I know for certain there are things she will not tell me. Nonetheless, we hold respect for our mutual secrecy."

Scott nodded slowly in agreement and they walked the

rest of the way in silence. The gaudy, luxurious scenery was getting scarce the further out they went from the city central. The streets had entire patches riddled with potholes; abandoned buildings and desolate parking lots were beginning to be a common sight. Nestled in the deteriorating apartment buildings is the local favorite, *Ace N Dandy's*. While the streets should've have been desolate, they were occupied by people; so many people. Many of them looked to be happy and some were mildly irritated at the most.

"What's all this about?"

"Something of consequence, but not what we came here for." Sugar and Scott were greeted at the door by the owner himself, Angelo Whateverhislastnameis. He looked up at Baron Sugar with awe, but only for a moment. "It has been but a few weeks since we have last seen each other."

"I know, I know, but you're always a sight to see. Only person I've ever seen who's kind of close to how tall you are is that idiot Bellamy. Oh and Scott's here too? It's been a couple days, but I don't expect any of my customers to show up every single day; that'd end up being pretty weird. I'd be like 'dude, go get a life'." Angelo led them to the bar inside where the three of them sat and got caught up into a bunch of things ranging from love to the concept of time. Surprisingly Angelo was the one starting to get lost in the time conversation, so he changed the subject to sports, specifically professional air hockey; the state's official sport. He switched on the small boxy tv on the wall to show Scott why pro air hockey was such a big deal. Baron Sugar looked so unamused by the gesture that it was clear he's been through this before. Angelo took some playful jabs at Sugar, and Sugar's quips made Scott laugh the hardest I've seen. His laugh is also terribly stupid, so to say it's fitting is an understatement. But the revelry died out fast.

The PAHN (Professional Air Hockey Network) was interrupted by a live broadcast of Atticus's motorcade riding through city central. The roof of his car was down and he was waving excitedly and mouthing cheers to the rivers of people who were packed tightly together in the streets of his gleaming city. They were cheering for him. There were posters, flyers and banners, some being clearly homemade, but they showed out anyway. They all seemed to love the guy and it's clear that he loved how much they loved him. He stood up in the backseat of his car and started throwing out stacks of cash along with all kinds of candies, chocolates and jewelry. People were trampling on each other to get to his ever so generous handouts. As the motorcade proceeded outside of the city center he called out through a megaphone 'Soon we will no longer be in a perpetual state of war! We will achieve peace in our time very soon and I will lead us there!"

Then the screen showed the motorcade ride into the forgotten part of the city; the ghetto; the part he ruined. Yet, people were out there waiting for him just like the ones in city central. He threw around more money, candy, and the like, and they ran to it just the same. And there he called out over the megaphone "Prosperity will be for all! Once the terrorists are defeated my full attention will be on you! The very center; the heart of this state; the heart of this country!" His voice was electric; a gentle but solid force that resonated with the crowd. That crowd who scrambled for the money he so carelessly threw from his car. People of all ages and many colors unified by the salvation he provided from the hell he created.

Now the motorcade made its way to the neighborhood where *Ace N Dandy's* is. The tv now gave a clear view of their street. Scott and Angelo's attention was pulled from the small screen by the motorcade's presence being right outside the window. This time all of the cars stopped and more people than just Atticus were handing throwing out stacks of money and candy on the ground. Everyone out there rushed to grab whatever they could. The restaurant cleared out in the blink of an eye, leaving only Scott, Angelo, and Baron Sugar to look out at the chaos. Unlike the other two, Sugar completely ignored the situation outside. He was just chilling out on his chair while he sipped from a mug full of bourbon that he made appear out of nowhere. The way he drinks things is totally weird though. He lifts up his 'face' and calmly pours it in the fire that is his actual head. The sight wasn't something that garnered any attention from the other two. All eyes were on Atticus (except for Baron Sugar's, of course).

Scott and Angelo watched as more people poured out of the run-down apartment buildings, adding to an already staggering crowd. There were so many children out there; so many children, elderly, disabled; people of all kinds. And they were all rushing frantically to pick up as much money as they could. Economic mobility was an illusion until now. That money on the ground was the chance all of them have been dreaming for and now it was theirs. The same man who took opportunities from them was helping them, but it's safe to say that a significant number of people in the crowd weren't anywhere near old enough to know a time before Atticus was in power. It's possible they don't know a lot of what he's done. How many of the people that rushed out there know he's the reason they're far below the poverty line? And if they don't know that, what chance do they have of knowing that man is the reason there is a poverty line? None of that seems to matter, even to the ones who know.

He sat back and watched them take everything he threw out. He didn't smile or frown; he just watched. His motorcade continued down the street, allowing more people to fit in the crowd and fight over the countless stacks of money Atticus tossed around.

The motorcade didn't reach the end of the street before it was stopped.

A chorus of raging explosions shook the earth. The structurally unsound apartment complexes and houses collapsed from the sheer force of the blasts. As for everything that didn't fall...they would've been better off caving in. But as luck would have it, the buildings were the lucky ones. Most of those people desperately scrambling for money were left lifeless. Their bodies were scattered across the street and the sidewalks; some were contorted, others were sprawled out. The children...seeing their eyes still open; frozen in time. Seeing how they ran to carry as much money as they could. Seeing how they went to pick up those candies and chocolates. They were smiling; they've probably never been happier in their lives. It would be the happiest they'd be in their entire lives. Moments later Scott and Angelo saw their battered bodies be tossed aside on the street by the vicious explosions. Puddles of blood were staining the pavement, but Atticus was looking at a clean street. "The terrorists that call themselves the resistance have tried to destroy our hope for peace! They tried to kill me! These terrorists will pay with their lives!" He wasn't smiling or frowning; he looked at those gruesome surroundings with a trace of pride.

The motorcade drove on until all of the cars stopped shy of Ace N Dandy's. Nobody made any moves. Atticus looked straight at Scott, shot him a quick sardonic smile, then the motorcade started back up. Scott ran to the door and frantically pulled at the handle but it wouldn't budge. "Baron, I can't just let him get away! Let me open the door!"

"He killed countless people with no remorse. You will not stand a chance on your own."

"Then help me! You can actually do something! You probably could've even stopped it if you weren't afraid of using your goddamn powers!" Scott shouted his lungs out. Baron Sugar calmly ignored his ranting whilst pouring more bourbon on his head. "Well? Say something!"

"I sensed trouble and so I acted accordingly. However, I am unable to see the future and I am not obligated to stop a crisis belonging to someone else. I ask you this: why do you blame someone for not preventing a catastrophe and excuse the one that aimed to make it happen?"

"Because you stopped me from doing something and now he got away! How many more people will he kill, huh? Do you know? Oh wait, that's right, you don't even fucking care!"

"Bruh, what can you even do? Like, you saw what just happened right?" Angelo looked at Scott quizzically; in disbelief that him and Scott could've possibly seen the same thing.

"Anger does not grant you strength you never had. Do what you will, but when I have to save you; and I will by Faaghira's request; we will never speak of it again." Baron Sugar put his mug down on the counter and pulled the cloth over his face. Angelo tried to strike up a conversation, but it only lasted a few words before fizzling out. He was about to say something, but instead he resorted to a look; one look that said it all: You're an idiot, but don't stop trying to save the world.

Scott rushed out after Atticus and this time nobody held him back. All of the cars stopped and the security guards jumped to action when Scott yelled after Atticus. The guards had their rifles pointed at him, but Atticus told them to hold their fire. He just looked warmly at Scott for a moment; it was even creepier than it sounds.

"Scott, my boy! Seeing the danger that has pounced onto this neighborhood and yet, you run forth! It's in a time like this that I know I made the right decision!"

"Atticus what the hell did you do?!"

"My boy, I did nothing but care for these people; they had nothing to lose and everything to gain. It wasn't me but the resistance that targeted your kind."

401

"My kind? What do you mean 'my kind'?" Scott was livid. This wasn't the passive jerkwad we've seen in previous confrontations; this was one angry dude.

"The dark people like; the ones like you. You should be proud, really proud; you're the only black I wanted in my posse. You've got some balls; balls o' steel. You stood up to me *and* you were able to get in good with Faaghira, the first being the most important. Haven't seen a black so bold in decades. My niece that you fancy so much is the closest one, but that's a bit different; we can't directly harm each other because we respect each other's power. Also, neither of us can knock off the other without chaos ensuing."

"I'm fucking pissed off...but do you mean knock off in like a sexual way?"

"Talking to you, actually talking to you, you're worlds off from the gentlemen...and ladies she's had on her arm. Don't know why she'd keep you around. But me, on the other hand, I see a bright and powerful future for someone like you. You could relate to the other nig- colored people around far better than I can. My boy, you could set yourself up to lead the whole damned state if you made the right moves. You could have all the women you want waiting at your beck and call; you could even say you're related if that's what you're into."

"I'm not your boy! Stop calling me your goddamned boy! And you can miss me with all that underhanded shit you want me to do! I don't believe for a second that Faaghira had anything to do with this, you backhanded mother fucker!"

"My niece is back with the terrorists? Good to know. See, you're already helpin' me out; might as well make it a paying gig!" Atticus got out of his car, pushed aside his wall of guards, and stood right in Scott's face. (Given how tall he is, he was towering over Scott, but let's not make Scott seem like any less than what he already is, shall we?)

Judging by how pissed off Scott looks, he's about to do

something really stupid.

He quickly clenched his fist and- yup he did something really stupid. He sucker punched Atticus right across the jaw. One of the security guards fired at Scott immediately, hitting him in his right thigh. Immense pain pinned Scott down to the damaged street. He shouted in agony; an action that prompted Atticus to shoot him in the other leg.

"I'll have a wheelchair ready for when you come to your senses. It's a shame; I was only joking with what I said. You don't think I'd be that bad, do you?" He patted Scott's head then got his motorcade back on the move. Scott reached after the cars in the distance but it was pointless and he knew it. From his view he could catch it through his fingers, but they're almost out of sight at this point. He tried pulling himself up but the pain in his legs was too much for him to fight against. He kept trying in midst of all his agony.

"So this is what happens when I try to stand up; real funny, universe." Scott rested his back on the ground and crossed his arms, giving a weak chuckle to pad out his dry humor. "I don't get it; why can't I just give up? When I try to mind my business I get put into an entire dimension where I'm caught up in a giant mess! I stand back and I'm ridiculed! I stand up and I get shot in both my legs! I ask for love and I get someone I can't keep while I'm with someone I probably shouldn't! Why is this me? Why does this have to be me?"

"I wish I had the answer, but my own luck's been down too. Running a business and trying to bring hope to a bunch of people that are being shit on by-"

"Shat on" Baron Sugar cut Angelo off for what was *definitely* a deathly important correction. "But it was" Sugar whispered under his breath.

"Okay fine, they were 'shat on' by a tyrant they can never beat. I try to give people hope by thriving in the midst of all the hell he's putting us through, and sometimes I wonder why it even has to be this way. Why do I have to be the one to fight? How in the world am I supposed to do anything when no one else has been able to for the past twenty-five years? I ask myself this every single day, but I've still gotta do it even though I don't have the answers. People still need hope, and somebody's got to be the one to give it."

"That's very heartwarming," Scott did his best to sound sincere in spite of his pain. "But hope isn't taking the bullets out of my legs or stopping the bleeding" but that didn't mean much.

"For the sake of your safe departure, I will heal your wounds. However, I will not be able to fully undo what has happened without making you ill." Baron Sugar lifted Scott off the ground then placed him back on his feet. His right leg was buckling under pressure until he was able to steady it. He walked around in small circles, stumbling every couple of steps.

"That's great. That's just great. I've got a limp now. Fuck my actual life."

"You are welcome, but no thank you. As I said, I could not fully reverse the damage that was done to you without causing greater damage."

"That's weak; Roswell literally killed me multiple times and he brought back to life without a hitch every one of those times. And my clothes wouldn't even have blood on them!"

"I could bet my immortality that it damaged you in some way. Knowing Roswell, it would be no proper ailment, but devastating none the less. I will take us back to Faaghira's building; surely she has learned of this tragedy."

"Yeah" Angelo looked back at the massacre the bombing caused and almost broke down crying. "I'll bet she's pissed."

"Peace be upon you" Baron Sugar gave Angelo a solemn nod then disappeared into the air with Scott.

"Did you just tell him the Star Wars thing?" Scott broke the silence while he flew on Sugar's back.

"The what?"

"Bruh, I gotta get you caught up on pop culture."

"Only after you safely depart from this dimension."

"But then I won't see you again."

"A small price to pay. My agony will surely subside." Sugar raced them to her balcony without another word from either of them. When Scott climbed off Baron Sugar's back he looked confused.

"How do you always know which room Fae is in?"

"I do things that are convenient for the plot in order to prevent the narrator from having to describe mundane sequences. I have dealt with it before and it is irritating."

"I know, right?! This narrator is soooo annoying! They're always berating me and making fun. If I wanted any of that then I'd go talk to my parents!" Scott's laughing dried out when he saw that Baron Sugar wasn't laughing along with him (and I obviously wasn't).

"Scott, is there something you would like to talk about?"

Scott briefly cleared his throat and patted his chest. "I *hope* she's not still mad at me. I mean, she probably is because she wouldn't actually have a reason to stop being mad at me, but I'm still hoping she's not." Scott let out a deep sigh while he idly rubbed his cheeks with his hand. He paced back and forth until Faaghira showed up and slid the screen door open.

Well, at least he was expecting it to be Faaghira.

"You do know the door's not locked, right?" Safira was standing in the doorway with her arms crossed. Her eyes were watering, but her face was firm. Her focus shifted from Scott to Baron Sugar (of whom she was still slightly intimidated). "And you" her voice started to weaken, "you could've stopped this, couldn't you?!"

"So could Atticus Bellamy, yet only one of us is to be held accountable." Sugar made a point of brushing past her on his way inside. She flinched when he passed by but toughened back up when she realized Scott was watching.

"He still creeps me out too, but he's actually a pretty great guy. And not to mention that he's low key hilarious. I swear I'd be busting out laughing sometimes if he wasn't so terrifying!"

Safira almost cracked a smile and her face fought to keep it, but her sulking kicked it away. "Good to know, but bad timing."

"Too soon?"

"Way too soon; it just happened! You were there when it happened! You're a fucking mess!" Safira was beginning to puff up, but she calmed back down after taking a deep breath.

"I've been getting that a lot."

"By the way, Fae was worried about you. She's more messed up than me right now, so ease up on the joking around. She put her life into that, so this is especially hard for her. I know she can usually take it, but just don't go there today, right?" Safira is being way nicer than I thought she'd be. She's still totally hot though. Umm...where was I? Right! Scott didn't say another word; he made a moved past her politely and they nodded as they crossed each other. The entire room was dark save for a dim light He almost froze when he saw Faaghira weeping to no end. This wasn't like how Scott saw her shed a few tears the night they met; this broke her. She was a fortress, a strong tower with an embattlement of silver; but now she's shattered glass. It broke her. She sat on the floor in front of the couch; the glow of the television lit up her distraught face and glistened on her running tears. Her eyes were glued to that screen and it was clear that every second crushed her heart.

"I can't...I...I like to think that it'll all be a sham when I turn it off. I keep thinking of what I'll say to Atticus next time I see him. 'You really pulled the wool over my eyes with that one! It looked so real!'"

"How are you still so surprised? You know that old crusty

406

toothpick better than anyone; you should've seen this coming before any of us. You don't even like him!

"...But I know it's not true; I know it's real and I know he did it. You're right, I don't like him. But you know...you wanna know why I'm so fucking pissed off?!" Fae sighed and hugged Larimar tightly. "Elle, don't be like your sister, okay? Be better, please be better. I'm just really mad right now. Can you go downstairs for a little? I promise we'll talk later, I just don't want you up here right now; it's going to get *really* nasty pretty soon. Baron Sugar will be right there with you, and remember: he's not as scary as he looks."

"He doesn't look scary, he looks cool!" She tugged on Sugar's cloak and waved it around excitedly. He stood and watched her play around; someone who's not scared of him at all. "Hey dude, carry me." She stretched her arms up to him and he begrudgingly picked up the little girl then carried her downstairs. Scott almost laughed, but his empathy for Fae cut the happiness short.

"The reason I'm so angry right now isn't because he did something terrible; it's Atticus, so that's a given. I'm angry because he crossed a line he knew better than to step over. It was a direct attack on the people I'd been devoting my life to helping ever since I got all this money. He's the reason my parents aren't here right now; did you know that? They were supporting him, but I saw where it was going. He was going to kill them, so I found a way to get them exiled after Larimar turned one. It's been five years and he thinks I don't know what he did. I knew all along, but I thought that he'd back off if he saw I didn't know a thing. I was free to do my work if he thought I was ignorant, so I played the part and stayed active under the radar. He reached out to make an agreement with me after he found out how much influence I was gaining. He wouldn't target me in any way if I didn't directly target him either. We'd stay on our own courses and whoever got control of the city...it was a winner takes all kind of thing. If either of us broke that one rule then hell would follow."

"This is why we should've killed him off before it got to this point! I've been fighting him for longer than you have; he wouldn't play by any rules even if he's the one that came up with them." Safira pounded her fist on the nearest wall.

"Really?! We talked about this! How are we supposed to replace everything that we're trying to break down? We're not just trying to take him out of power; he *is* the government. He is the system we're fighting and it'll live on without him. If it was that easy to do it then a moral hang up wouldn't stop me from doing what would need to be done."

"So how are we supposed to fix this?" Scott tossed himself into the conversation, and this time I can't blame him. He was just standing there like a kid watching their parents argue, but unlike said kid, he had a better line than 'Please stop fighting!'. Safira tapped on her forehead but didn't protest him otherwise. She sat down and looked at Faaghira as if prompting her to say something.

"If I knew I would've done it already. If you have any ideas to fix the whole goddamn world then the floor is yours." She rolled over on her back and stared blankly at the ceiling. Scott patiently waited for her to say something else or signal him to start giving off his thoughts, but he ended up waiting for nothing.

"Emergency election? Emergency power? What if you had time to explain it to people so they wouldn't freak out?" He sounded less sure of himself with every word and his words drowned out completely by the end when he saw that Fae wasn't even paying attention. And so he cleared his throat and tried again. "What if you had time to explain it to people so they wouldn't freak out? I think that could save you from some major problems later down the line."

"Now that you've climbed in the same boat with the rest of us, all we have to do is wait for the rising tide to come in and lift us up into the magical land of prosperity where a good work ethic and a grateful heart can carry you right to the top of the food chain." There wasn't so much bitterness in her voice, but her words were still armed with a sting.

"I'm sorry, but when did I ask to be involved in any of this? That's right, I never did! I'm not a fucking political genius; I'm a normal guy! I'm trying, okay! And I'm trying to juggle a bunch of feelings and I like you but I don't know why you want me because you're really confusing!"

"Heartfelt, but this is a time for action, not confused feelings." Safira didn't sound as harsh as she usually does with Scott; she was more of a voice of reason here than a powerful force. She stood up and looked down at Faaghira, who was still spaced out with streams of tears. "I know you don't want to hear it, but now is the time for action. We have to kill Atticus; catching him and putting him on trial is like putting a fish back in the ocean. The people can't have their freedom if he's still alive."

"I already told you that he is the government. Someone that follows his agenda would fill in the void, and so on and so forth. What are we supposed to do about the rest of them; you wanna kill all of them too?"

"Yes, but that's more of a personal issue. I was thinking about the resistance filling in as a temporary government until we get rid of all his lackeys. You and me share the leadership role until we can get some proper elections in place. I don't like the idea, but nobody came up with a better idea. There's no clean way out of this, but if you feel like I overstep the boundaries at any point in time then kill me ASAP; I have good intentions, but I don't want to turn out like *him*. I say that unless you find a better alternative, this is what I'm following through with."

"Okay, fine, fine, I don't care at this point; we'll have to figure it out when we get there. And for you Scott, I care because you can be someone way better and the way you're dealing with all of this tells it all. Not *this* as in my situation, but this as in your… thing that you're dealing with. Don't get me wrong, you're still a dick, but it's clear to me that you can be a great guy if someone's willing to help you out. Hey, so we can talk later but I'm really fucking depressed right now and I need to talk to Saff about our next move. I'll see you later, and don't worry, I'm not mad at you; I never was. You're just mildly annoying and childish sometimes." She zoned out again when he left.

Scott was slow to get back down the stairs because he was trying to listen in on what Fae and Safira were talking about. He really picked up the pace when Safira loudly mention that it doesn't take that long to walk down some stairs. Faaghira could be heard laughing faintly but like with everything else, it went away too fast. Scott was startled when he saw Baron Sugar without his cloak; something he exclusively never took off. Larimar had it drooped over her body, and the three of them laughed at how she nearly got lost in it.

"I'm a wizard!" she shouted while she twirled around in Sugar's cloak. Scott laughed and rubbed her head.

"A wizard? What about being a princess? I thought little girls like that." He chuckled as he lifted the hood up from over her face.

"Princesses don't have magical powers, unless it's a magical girl and magical girls are princess wizards. I wanna be a super wizard instead, just like Barry Sugar!" She raised her fists up in the air and assumed her own power stance.

"Barry Sugar?! Oooh, can I call you Barry Sugar?" Scott sat down next to Sugar while he watched the little girl put on a most spectacular magic show.

"Call me Barry and you will not call anything after this day." With that said, Scott scooted away a little bit. He clapped along to her spectacular magic show with dragons, flowers, and a few sparks of fire (she might've had the tiniest

410

bit of help from Baron Sugar). After Larimar's show was over, her and Scott listened to Baron Sugar tell stories about weird people he's seen over the past generations. His voice was still very serious, but he talked with such character that Scott almost swore it was Roswell in disguise. He still didn't laugh, but he still sounded so cheerful (well, as cheerful as he's capable of being). Larimar loved it so much that she kept asking him more and more questions about his life. He answered everything until she asked him how he became a 'wizard'. This was the only part Scott actually understood. Sugar told him that story in full graphic detail, but Scott's an adult (not a very mature one at that, so maybe he's on the right track); what would Baron Sugar say to a six year old?

"My friend, I will not lie to you or downplay the truth; my power is a neutral chaos that has brought me much pain. You are too good for this story, but I would be willing to tell you when you experience more in your life. However, since I told Scott and he is nineteen, I will tell you near the same age. If you ask before then I will surely tell you; as long as you are close in age. My gift to you in lieu of that is my cloak; you can keep it." Larimar was excitedly snuggled up in the cloak and raised her fist in victory.

"I was gonna keep it anyway. Thanks, you're the second best Barry!"

"Oh? Second best, am I?"

"Don't feel bad. My sister is the coolest person in the world and that's not your fault." Her voice was a little muffled from being under the cloak, but everyone could still hear her giggles. Next, Larimar shared some of her favorite stories about Faaghira. A few blatantly embarrassing tales were thrown in, but it was mostly astonishing tales of how she helped people and fought the evil Junta by herself. Scott tried to tell her that the resistance helped, but Larimar made sure he didn't get it twisted. "She was by herself a lot of the time. Safira is really nice, but they were trying to do different things after a while."

"You're really smart for a six year old."

"You're pretty smart for an adult, but that's because a lot aren't smart." She was quick to fire back and Scott accepted it gracefully. Baron Sugar gave one solemn clap to show his support. Might be reaching here, but this could be the happiest he's been in…well…a long time. Scott was idly looking around the room when he noticed Safira sitting on the stairs watching Larimar and Baron Sugar doing magic tricks and being silly.

"Scott, I need to talk to you upstairs. It probably won't be quick, so don't plan on coming back so soon."

Baron Sugar offered to charge Scott's phone after 'suddenly remembering that was a grave issue that plagued Scott earlier'.

"Is it important?" Scott handed his phone over without a second thought and Baron Sugar followed though by making a phone charger out of thin air then putting it in an outlet. "You made a charger? I thought you would just use electricity or something." Sugar whipped up a quick line when he told Scott that he 'did use electricity, but he heard this way was slower'. Larimar cheered silently but enthusiastically for her friend, which of course Scott didn't notice.

"We don't talk casually, so trust that I wouldn't call you if there wasn't a reason." She stood at the stairs waiting for him to go upstairs, but he didn't get it message until she was tapping aggressively on the wall. He ran up there quick when he caught her death glare. He didn't try and strike up any small talk this time; he followed her back to Faaghira's room without a peep. Safira closed the door behind them then sat down in front of it. Her arms were folded and her face was stern, but that was offset by her hair falling over her eyes. She kept blowing it back from the side of her mouth, but eventually got so fed up that she just quit trying and tied her hair in a ponytail. Fae raised her eyebrow in disapproval and Safira rolled her eyes, as if saying 'I'm comfortable like this; get off my case'. Scott wasn't lost on the fact that they were having their own silent conversation, so he just sat there and nodded to an imaginary beat until he thought it was over.

"Anyway..." Fae trailed off after playfully shaking her head at Safira. "Me and Saff have been talking about what we should do about Atticus, and we haven't come to a consensus on that yet, but we did decide on a plan of action to draw him out. It's kind of shitty but we're fresh out of options."

"I don't wanna say I told you so, but I kinda do. I'll hold back for you, though." Scott lightly tapped his index finger against his forehead; making a conscious effort to look as serious as possible.

"Oh, don't let me stop you; brag to your heart's content."

"Okay, well I told you so."

"Feel better?"

"Yup." Scott smiled smugly, "But I kinda feel like a dick now"...until he remembered why they were having this conversation in the first place. I swear he has the attention span of a peanut.

"Well you are a dick; nobody here's surprised by this correct?" Faaghira looked at both of them questioningly until they both said 'correct'. "Okay, great; we're on the same page. Saff was telling me that we should start cutting off electricity and other resources to the central part of the city all at once. From there we'd strike wherever Atticus is at that moment then...still working on how we'll ultimately handle this. We'll hold him in custody first then we'll work from there." Safira rolled her eyes, which Fae clearly noticed, but it was mostly brushed to the side. "We'll work from there, but I was thinking that we should cut off just the electricity and do it gradually instead of in one fell swoop. I'd rather draw him out than starve people, mess up their water, and only have a chance at finding him. We wouldn't know where he is, and if we botched this then we'd have to come up with a whole new plan that would be even harder to execute. Not to mention that it'd definitely be an even shittier plan."

Safira went along with it, but she didn't hide that she was doing everything she could to hold back. She gave brief, slow nods, but her eyes screamed 'this is a terrible idea'. "I think that's a solid idea, but say he sees through it; what are the chances we'll still be able to catch him?"

"Anything is possible, but I know his emergency spots. If we sabotage the generators in a certain order then we'll be able to box him into one of the hideouts I choose. Things will be a lot easier to control if this gets done my way. It won't be the prettiest thing, it won't be the fastest, but it'll give the best results."

"Okay, doesn't explain what you need me for."

"I'd like you to ask Baron Sugar to help. Believe me when I say I want to keep you as far away from danger as possible, but from what I've seen on the news today you already know how ridiculous staying out of danger sounds in a city like this. I wouldn't be asking you if I could do it myself, but he specifically told me that he would never help me with any potentially violent issues unless it absolutely needed supernatural intervention. Apparently, none of this situation counts...but yours would."

"And what is his situation, exactly? Because someone forgot to tell me why this random guy is so important all of a sudden." Safira's tone sharpened but not to the point where she snapped at Fae.

"...It's more of a spiritual journey; probably some dissociation in there too." Fae struggled to make it sound casual, clearly.

"I'm dealing with a lot of demons right and one is particularly annoying. Baron Sugar is investing time in helping me deal with them." And so Scott chimed in. "While we're on the topic of Baron Sugar: you want to exploit my hardships to get a vaguely powerful supernatural being to help you take control of the government?"

"It sounds bad when you put it like that, but I've done worse without any help at all. Are you down or not? Don't feel like you have to do it, but it would make everything *so* much easier if you did. Scott, I really don't want this to drag out any longer."

"Fine, I'll do it, but you owe me."

"I've been letting you stay in my condos, I gave you one of my sweaters which you never even gave back, food, and, *and* I let you have some of my weed. Debt repaid; king me." Fae smiled faintly, but she was still worn from seeing the devastation from that explosion.

"She doesn't kill with kindness; it's the web she catches everyone with. I got caught in it too; turns out she's charming when she wants to be, like her despot uncle."

"It's my parents that were close to him. We're not even related; he's an adopted family member. I removed him in my head, but everyone knows him as my uncle, so I go with it. Family or not, he's the worst thing to happen to Louisiana since the U.S split. He's probably worse, but there's no way to measure that, so I don't dawn on it."

"What happened to America anyway?"

"The United States was cut between people who wanted changes and people who wanted power and familiarity. Fear of the unknown can put you high in the sky, and it looks like somebody flew too close to the sun. Canada and South America are still running, though. Things are a bit different around the world because of what happened, but this was more than forty years ago, so it's old news."

"You seriously didn't learn that in school? Which pile of rocks have you been living under for eighteen years?"

Scott huffed up and cleared his throat. "Umm, I'm

nineteen, actually. I was under a pretty nice set of rocks; you should visit sometime after this whole situation gets fixed." Scott could actually be genuine if he wasn't so busy being stupid and petty.

"If I ever run out of business to mind then I'll be sure to visit." She put her attention back on Fae, who was spacing out again. "*Fae. Fae.* Faaghira! You okay? If this is too much for you right now then we can take a raincheck. I know I was saying we need to do this now, but there's no point if you can't take it."

"Oh, no it's fine; I'm fine, really. If you were this caring before then maybe things wouldn't have ended so bad. I'll tell you, the last thing I need right now is time to think about what just happened. Doesn't help that the less I do the guiltier I feel. This is my fault; not all of it, but this couldn't've happened if I dealt with Atticus like I should've all this time ago. I need to fix this-"

"We need to fix this; the three of and whoever else you decide. The past is done, but life can be so much better for millions of people if we make it! You can't win this alone; nobody can." Safira dusted off her pants and headed for the door. "I'll have my forces ready to strike at a moment's notice; just tell me where to go first. Your plan, your rules; I'll play nice this time around since we've never been so close. Atticus gave us the leverage we needed; we can use this to finally push him into the ground. It's not the ideal situation; it hurt me too, but it's what we've got. And Scott, please take care of her the best you can. She'll do what she does, so just be there for her. She trusts you, man; don't let her down." Safira quietly left the room, and now it was just Scott and Fae.

"Fae, I don't even know what to say about what happened back there. I mean, I was right there when it happened; I saw it happen! It's...somehow, I feel responsible ....for the explosions, that is; I don't feel responsible at all in a regular

416

sense."

"What was it like?"

"It was hell on Earth. It was the most horrific thing I've ever seen." Scott's voice was shaken, dry and trembling. "I asked Baron Sugar why he didn't stop it from happening. He shielded Ace N' Dandy's, which we were sitting in at the time, so he was more than capable of doing it. I was furious with him, but then he asked me why I blamed him first and not Atticus. Why was my first thought to blame someone who could've stopped it instead of the person who caused it? I was still mad that he didn't do anything, but he told me that he couldn't stop every problem that people created. I hated what he said, but I hated it even more when I thought about it and realized I would do the same thing in his shoes. I felt bad for a second; I wouldn't save people either if I actually could. I wish I would, but I know I wouldn't. I don't know how you did it, but you were right when you said that me and Baron Sugar were the same. Now I don't know where to go or what to do."

"Maybe that's why he wants you out of here; you two were a lot alike, but look what happened to him. I definitely don't agree with him on a lot of things, but I don't think he's wrong on this one."

"It's- I have a girlfriend that I hope I'm in love with, but then there's you; you're everything I never knew I wanted."

"Hmmm, but I went over how that might be by design. Doesn't seem very convincing that you know what you want, because 'hoping' you're in love with someone is hardly convincing."

"There's something I haven't been open about. She fills in the gaps in my life: intimacy and financial stability. I've told her recently that I don't think our relationship is good for us. We were both different when it started, but we turned into emotional leeches; ruthless emotional sadists. I got addicted to whatever it is we made together; we both did. My whole life is tied into it. She helps me pay for college, but I never told my parents that. Mom wants me to break up with her, but she also cut me off financially and school costs money, so I can't please her even if I wanted to. She thinks I got a full ride scholarship or something like that, but she honestly couldn't care less about what's paying for school as long as nothing's coming out of her pocket. Iris is the exception but like I said, she doesn't know what my girlfriend does for me. That's why I hope I'm in love with Iris; she's a genuinely great person. I want to move on from her, but I can't move on in my life without her. I don't know what I'm supposed to do."

"You get on me for not explaining why I like you, but it doesn't look like you've been so honest with yourself with why you like me. From what you're telling me, I'd see me as an escape if I were you. I liked you because I thought you were cute. It's not that I thought you were special at all; I've been with better looking guys. Atticus had some kind of interest in you, so of course that got me wondering what all the hype was about. You ended up being a decent guy, but you're on the verge of being complete garbage."

"So why do you still like me if you think I'm garbage?"

"I said you were on the verge. I'm trying my best with you because you can be a really good person if you see a reason to be. Obviously, no one else is trying to help you grow, and that's a shame; they're really missing out on someone great. Since nobody else in your life is doing it, I figured I should be the one to believe in you."

"Fae, I know you want me to go back home, but nobody there cares for me the way I need it; not like how you care about me. What if I find a way to get Roswell and stay here with you? Maybe there's some way we-"

"Scott, this won't end well. There are many paths to Rome, but there's no way we wouldn't end up in Pompeii."

"Ah, I see what you did there!"

418

"Clever, right? Okay, the point I'm trying to make is that there's no way we could play it where we'd end up together. I may be everything you say you need right now, but as you learn more about yourself you'll outgrow me. I'm good for the guy sitting with me right now, but I'm no good for the guy that he should be. But I hope he never forgets me when he grows up, so in a disgustingly cheesy way, I'd always get to be with him."

"Wow, lucky guy. Who were you talking about again?" Fae shot him a dull look for ruining the mood. "Kidding, kidding, I'm kidding; I know it was me you're talking about! Gosh, it was just a joke!"

"I don't feel like joking right now."

"But you ju- never mind. I'm gonna see if I can warm Baron Sugar up to helping you. Damn, I didn't mean to make a pun; the fire thing totally slipped my mind."

"Thanks, you're a babe. I have to figure out which generator we're shutting down first by tonight so Saff can get a strike team out there. I'll see you later; I have to get this straightened out. Let me know if you need me for something." Fae got up to go the drawing boards (there are literally three on her wall) so she could start putting her plan into action.

"Real quick: why did Safira leave if you're not even done drafting your plan yet?"

"We're both actually very busy people; you don't see it as much because I live here and…well…she doesn't." She didn't explicitly tell Scott to leave, but the way she got so caught up in her work gave him the message. Scott was back downstairs again sitting with Larimar and Baron Sugar, but he didn't act like he was there in the moment.

Larimar brought him his phone and put in his hands. "Here's your phone. I have to aks you something." She lowered her voice to a whisper." Scott smirked when he leaned to the side to hear what was so important that she had to whisper.

"Go ahead, I'm listening."

"What's do neutral and lieu mean? I would aks Baron Sugar, but he would explain with more big words I don't know."

"But explain is a big word and you know that."

"Bun-bun says it all the time! I know what it means because she used it all the time and I asked what it means, but she teaches me a lot of stuff all the time."

"Neutral means something's not good or bad. Lieu means instead of. Don't be embarrassed if you don't know what something is. Tell ya what: I'll fill in the gaps where any time there's something you don't know; all you have to do is ask. Sound like a deal?"

"You better know a lot of stuff because I have a lot of questions."

"I'll do my best." Scott chuckled. Larimar bundled up in Sugar's cloak when Baron Sugar began putting on his own magic show just for them (which may have been slightly more complex than Larimar's). He made a pint-sized firework display then brought up a mini amusement park with its own Ferris wheel and carousel. It was a grand display that mesmerized her, but it wasn't long until she noticed that there wasn't any music playing in the miniature park.

"You can't come up with any music?"

"There will be music if you can come up with a song." All three of them smiled (Baron Sugar's face cloth thing had a smile on it, but his actual face is just a charred skull, so I don't think he's truly capable of smiling). Larimar began to hum her own tune and soon enough she was putting out words right off the top of her head. She sang wonderfully, though she stumbled with the lyrics every now and then, she did very well, especially considering this was improvised. The other two tried to sing along with her, but she changed the words so often that they gave up and hummed the rest. Scott would look up at the stairs every now and then and even though it was brief, he would keep looking back like he knew something was supposed to happen. Maybe Fae was supposed to waltz down the stairs then lay graceful in his arms. It could've been that she was supposed to call him upstairs to talk…or to 'talk'. Whatever it is, it never came. He wasn't so far out that Larimar noticed, but there were some moments that that his mind definitely wasn't there.

Almost an entire hour passed and it still never came. Baron Sugar made cannoli for both of them and Scott definitely ate his, but now he really seemed…out of it. Larimar was adamant about Sugar eating too so she tried to get him to eat one, but that only got as far as his mouth before it started to melt. He lifted up his mask (I'll stick to calling it a mask) and pushed the cannolo into his teeth. "You cheater, you didn't even chew! Bun told me that you always have to chew your food!"

"Mistake; she told you that *you* always have to chew your food. I am exempt because I am a wizard."

"So am I!"

"Addition: I am an undead wizard. I do not need to chew my food."

"No fair! I wanna be an undead wizard too!"

"No. No you do not, my dear friend. Your enthusiasm shows every reason why you should never be an undead wizard. Also, as you have seen, my mouth does not move at all." Baron Sugar pulled the mask back over his face. Larimar pouted, but you bet you she still ate the rest of her cannoli. He noticed Scott was still focused on something else, so he asked about it, but it didn't bear any fruit. "You have never gotten to properly see the city, so what would you think of the three of us seeing it together?"

"I'd rather go alone, but-"

"You'll get lost!" Larimar was quick to interrupt him, to

which Scott and Baron Sugar both laughed (though Sugar's gravely laugh made Scott's that much shorter).

"Yeah, that part. Why not make it a family outing? With you two it could fun."

"We are not close enough to even be considered family adjacent. However, I agree that it would be very good for the three of us to see the city together. Larimar is far too young to go out by herself and you have no idea where you would be going. While I have neither classification, I simply do not like people. We can leave right now; I will inform Faaghira." Baron Sugar disappeared for a moment then returned in what might as well have been the blink of an eye. "She said that it is okay for you to go, Larimar. However, you will not be able to have any ice cream because you are lactose intolerant. I have already went back and replaced the diary filling I used for the cannoli, so now it is as though you never consumed any lactose. However, you must be conscious of these things at all times."

"Ugh! It's annoying! Why can't I just be normal like other kids?" She huffed and made a point of crossing her arms.

"Normal is overrated; get used to loving the unique experience you are. That's something your sister taught me, just not through words; I'm surprised she didn't tell you somehow. You're also six, so I guess you just haven't picked up on it yet. And forreal, don't leave out the lactose intolerant thing; it's really important."

"Okay, okay. Barry, can we go now? I want to have fun already!" She didn't even finish the last word before they were in they were in the city. She was caught up in wonder with the fantastic. She was so fascinated by the unbelievable powers. She looked around wide eyed at the gleam of the city around her. All the different kinds of people, the streamlined geometric designs; the future so many people only dreamed of was right before her eyes, but that's not what amazed her. The city was always before her; it was as common as breathing or seeing the sky. The spectacular part for her was teleporting; specifically doing so without any grand gesture, was enough to astonish Larimar; the same one who tends to be unimpressed by most things. Scott, however, was used to the supernatural by this point, but he was astounded by the city's grandiose. Good thing Baron Sugar didn't feel anything because I'm fresh out of adjectives that start with 'a'.

Scott was the one dragging them from place to place, ooing and fawning over the closely knit modular buildings that crowded the sky from all the way on the ground where he was. They weren't all a glistening steel, but mostly vibrant hues of white, red, yellow; it got close to a rainbow in some parts. The structures, from fountains to bridges and even small stores were all based around a rounded, aerodynamic look. Everything was new and sleek. The streets were lined with small lights that let off a glow somewhere between yellow and white and it made everything look so fancy; from the asphalt to the few pieces of trash scattered far and few between. Even with all the phenomenal, post-modern architecture, there was still a healthy amount of trees and flowers; some wide trails of grass lined the opposite ends of the sidewalks leading to the main park. Everything was pristine and beautiful. "It's everything I ever hoped I could see at some point in my life. It's perfect. It's so surreal because it's perfect and I'm in it. It looks like this and I'm in it! Me! How the f-", he looked at Larimar for a second then had to think up something to say when he saw that she was paying attention. "-uturistic place like this is so normal to you Lari! Ignoring all the issues, you live in a real nice place."

"Thanks. Don't call me Lari; it's ugly."

"Huh, what should I call you then?"

"Larimar. Bun has another name for me, but she's the

423

only one that can use it. Saffie says it too but I like her, so that's okay."

"Okay, *Larimar*, where do you want us to go first?" Scott chuckled to himself.

"Hold on." Scott watched as she tried to climb on Baron Sugar's back. She ended up mostly tugging on his leg, so he picked her up and placed her on his shoulders. "Newt's Ice Cream!" Scott gave Larimar a scolding look. "I was joking! I wanna take the train uptown…I think it's uptown; then we gotta come back to the park because it's fun!"

"The train? I can fly us there much faster than a train could go; I could even teleport to where you want to go."

"I know, but I want to ride the train. C'mon, you can always fly, but how much do you get to ride a train?" She pulled back on his hood and he poked her stomach until she started giggling. "Stop! Stop! You're gonna make me fall!" She was laughing even harder when Scott started tickling the back of her neck. "Noooooooooooooo!"

"Alright, I doubt you will fit on the train while you are on my shoulders. Do you want me to carry you or hold your hand?"

"Hold my hand; I like walking." He knelt down to let her off his shoulders. She had to reach her hand up to reach his hand. They walked two blocks all the way to the train station. Larimar was happy with having Sugar there, Scott was still amazed with the city after walking all that way, and Baron Sugar was upset that Larimar wouldn't let him use his powers. It was funny seeing the three of them interact with the people in the station and on the train. A little girl holding an abnormally tall cloaked figure's hand, and then there's the dude with a slight limp that's looking wide-eyed at *everything*. Some people quietly backed away from Baron Sugar, some stared in awe, some in disgust; others didn't seem to care at all.

They got off the train and followed Larimar around

everywhere she pulled them to. She did such vile things as make them go up escalators (which Scott and Sugar both hated), buy snacks at convenience stores (criminally overpriced, especially considering Sugar had to pull money from thin air), and take her to a park where other kids were. Baron-I mean Sugar- and Scott mostly sat benches nearby to give her space to run around, but Scott would push her on the swings whenever she asked. She wanted Baron Sugar to do it, but he explained to her that other people don't see him as friendly the same way she does. She was bummed at first, but she understood. As a result, she played with other kids more than being on the swings, but she got along fine with Scott. When he wasn't doing that, he was talking with Baron Sugar about relationships and trivial things like his favorite foods. In turn, when Baron Sugar was meditating Scott tried joining him (he got bored, but he stayed quiet out of respect).

Larimar ran over with some of her friends, ruining Sugar's meditation; he was simply happy to see her having fun. She went on to brag about how cool Baron Sugar is and how they'd be able to visit her all the time after Faaghira fixed everything. Scott and Sugar waved to them and tried not to be awkward, but that obviously fell flat. Her friends were nice about it; they were amazed by Baron Sugar just being there. They played for a little while longer then she waved her friends goodbye.

Larimar, Scott, and Baron Sugar went on their way back to the terminal, with Sugar outright refusing to stop anywhere else. She buzzed her lips for a few seconds then sighed but didn't protest him. "But can you carry me?"

"Yes, but you are capable of walking. Ask Scott if he will carry you?"

Before she could ask, Scott knelt down to let her on his back. She wrapped her arms around his neck and he playfully choked, making her laugh hysterically. He put her back down when they were at the terminal because it would be too awkward to carry her around on a crowded train. He held her hand there and they walked hand in hand all the way to the city's central park. The three of them sat while she told of dramatized (but nonetheless captivating) stories from school. She got more enthusiastic when she saw that Baron Sugar and Scott were actually paying attention. Unfortunately, it wasn't long until Scott zoned out. He was stuck looking across the park, where something, or someone, got his attention.

Daphne was there, you know, the one he went to that snobby restaurant with? It's that one. He was looking at her halfway through Larimar's story. Not saying the little girl didn't notice; she totally did, but she ignored it. "Hey, I'll be right back" Scott got up from the grass to go to Daphne, leaving just her and Baron Sugar.

"Okay, but you're missing a great story." She whispered to herself. She shyly looked to Sugar, "You don't have to leave to, right?"

"Correct. Now tell me more about this 'Mitchell Banks' character; why do you think he bothers you so much?" Baron Sugar leaned in and patted her head (which he tried not to make awkward, but she probably wouldn't've cared anyway; as long as he was there).

Scott walked past a few flower patches to where Daphne was and stood in front of her, waiting to be recognized. She was lying with her back on the grass, reading a book called 'Introducing Astrophysics'. There was a half empty cherry soda bottle sitting next to her. She looked down from the book but went back to reading when she saw him. He kept standing there, casting a shadow over her. She was mostly able to ignore it, but she was fed up after he repeatedly called her name. "Can I help you?" Daphne was obviously aggravated, but Scott had a cheesy smile on his face when she finally acknowledged him.

"Daph, it's me, Scott!"

"Scott who?"

"Scott Blue!"

"That was lame."

"What? That's really my last name. Do you really not remember me?"

"Don't take it personally; I don't remember most of the people I meet. Most of them are weird and boring, like you."

"We went on a date a few days ago!"

She put the book down and looked at him again, squinting carefully. Then her eyes widened and the book fell out of her hands. "Oh, it's you! I remember you now! Dude, that wasn't a few days ago; last time I was on a date was last month."

"Um…no, that was definitely a few days at the most."

"If you say so, but it's been a month for the rest of humanity."

Scott pursed his lips and rolled his eyes, but ultimately decided not to go back and forth. Instead, he pointed out the agate stone necklace hanging from her neck. "Oh this? Don't you remember? It's the necklace I got from your creepy guy who paid for our date a few days ago."

"See?! I knew it was-"

"I'm messing with you; it was totally a month ago." She took a sip of her soda and smiled slyly. "I don't know why your friend bought me this. I didn't do anything with him and I said I wasn't going to; nice guy. Very, *very* weird, but a nice guy."

"Roswell is not, my friend. So anyway, what've you been up to?"

"Hanging out with different people I know; some I met pretty recently while I was skating around. Friend or not, that Roswell guy still left one hell of an impression. Consider telling him to show up more of your dates; might actually get you to score. Not with me, but it might get you to score."

"Whatever. You know what? It's weird that the first thing

you bring up is that I didn't pay for the date when I literally almost got shot to death!"

"Listen" Daphne sat up and idly rubbed under her eyes. "I don't know where you're from but boring things won't make headlines here."

"Boring? Getting humiliated and almost fucking killed isn't boring!"

"Hey man, be grateful you're still alive. A lot of other people are six feet under."

"And that's not alarming to you at all?"

"Seriously, where are you from? Things like that are as big a deal as blinking."

"This is really fucked up."

"Not my problem; that's a complaint for the higher ups."

"Is that one of your night friends?" Larimar hollered across the park. Scott tried to sink down, to avoid being seen, but then everyone would know he was the Scott she was calling out to. He sucked up his pride and nervously waved to the little girl. She probably would've embarrassed him even more if he ignored her.

"No, this is just a regular friend." He sighed, covering his face with his hands. Daphne chuckled to herself, as did a few other people passing by.

"Is that your sister?" Daphne asked, playfully jabbing his shoulder. "She's so cute!"

"No...I'm babysitting for a friend. I guess she can be adorable when she's not busy being annoying."

"Scott, your friend is really pretty!" Larimar was shouting again; she obviously didn't care what anyone thought about it. "You can bring her back with us since Barry says I have to go home soon." Baron Sugar was meditating peacefully a few feet away from her, unbothered by her antics. He waved back when Scott waved at them but wasn't involved otherwise.

"She really is adorable. I'm jealous; I wish I had a little

sister."

"Whaddya say? Up for a little adventure?" Scott was trying to pile on the sarcasm.

"If you consider going to someone's house an 'adventure', then yes." Daphne packed up her book and left her soda on the grass.

"Okay, well I better tell her now before she embarrasses me some more." Scott was about to leave, but Daphne took hold of his wrist.

"I'll just go with you now. It doesn't make sense for you to go, come back, then leave again; so much walking."

Now it was the four of them leaving the park and walking back to Faaghira's complex. Larimar didn't even wait a second to start dropping questions on Daphne. Scott was giving Larimar one of those 'don't mess this up for me' looks from the corner of his eye, but she was too busy talking to notice. "How do you know Scott?"

"Oh, we went on a date before; *a month ago*." Daphne leered at Scott just long enough for Scott to see it. "By the way, I didn't catch your name."

"I'm Larimar; there's no short version. Who are you?"

"Larimar, you ask 'what's your name' instead of 'who are you'; that was rude." Scott sternly nudged the little girl on her shoulder.

"No, I say 'who are you'. You can say the other one if you really want to." She elbowed him in his thigh. He grunted in pain, but that turned into a light cough when Daphne started to take notice. After all, that *is* the same leg he got shot in.

"Oh, that's such a pretty name! Do you know what you're named after?"

"My sister named me and she said that anybody that can't pronoun-prono-pr, say it right isn't someone I should be friends with because I'm too good for them." Larimar crossed her arms and held her head up with pride.

"Your sister is right; she sounds like a really caring and unique person."

"You'll meet her soon, but she might not seem so nice because she's really busy right now."

"It's okay, really; I don't want to interrupt her if she's doing something. I know I wouldn't wa-"

"No no, she likes meeting new people; she just won't talk that much if she's working hard." Larimar sharply cut Daphne off, but it was for reassurance rather than something ill willed. Scott tried to give cues to Larimar so she would be quiet (aka: stop 'blocking' him, even though he wouldn't get anything regardless), but she ignored those just the same. He was quietly sulking with his hands in his pockets until Baron Sugar chimed in.

"Get over yourself. You look pathetic."

"Gee thanks; just the words I needed to hear. I'm all good now. You're a miracle worker. Every single one of my problems is solved."

"Saying you are acting like a child is an insult to Larimar. You are much worse."

"Well excuse me if I thought I'd be the focus of my own damn story."

"You are, but not every story is yours." Baron Sugar sighed heavily but that's all the reaction he had. He saw that Scott was still sulking, so he eventually stopped trying to get through to him. "We are almost at her building. She will most likely be working, as Larimar mentioned, but I assure you that she is very kind. I would say that out of the two of us, I am far more intimidating."

"Really? Never would've guessed it." Daphne laughed, but it quickly went from lighthearted to nervous. To anybody who doesn't know them, Baron Sugar and Roswell don't seem all that different. She looked to have been panicking to some degree but must've thought about how weird it would look to be afraid of something a little girl didn't even bat an eye at. "The necklace is fake. It is not mine, but it is indeed beautiful. Perhaps you can craft your own story for it," Sugar spoke passively with a hint of playfulness.

Meanwhile, Scott tried to push himself into the conversation going on between Daphne and Larimar, but he was eventually reduced to laughing along with some of the things they said.

One of the times he was idly looking around, he caught a glimpse of Roswell instead of his own reflection. It was smiling at him with bloody teeth and a spark of death in his eyes. It laughed without making a sound. Those eyes, those strained, red eyes; they mocked Scott. The two of them were pinned in a brief encounter; Scott and the image of Roswell. The moment came and went, but it ended with a long lasting message:

Roswell was gone and Scott was left without a reflection. He didn't stop walking that whole time, but he had a hard time prying his gaze from those glass windows.

He could see everyone's reflection except his own.

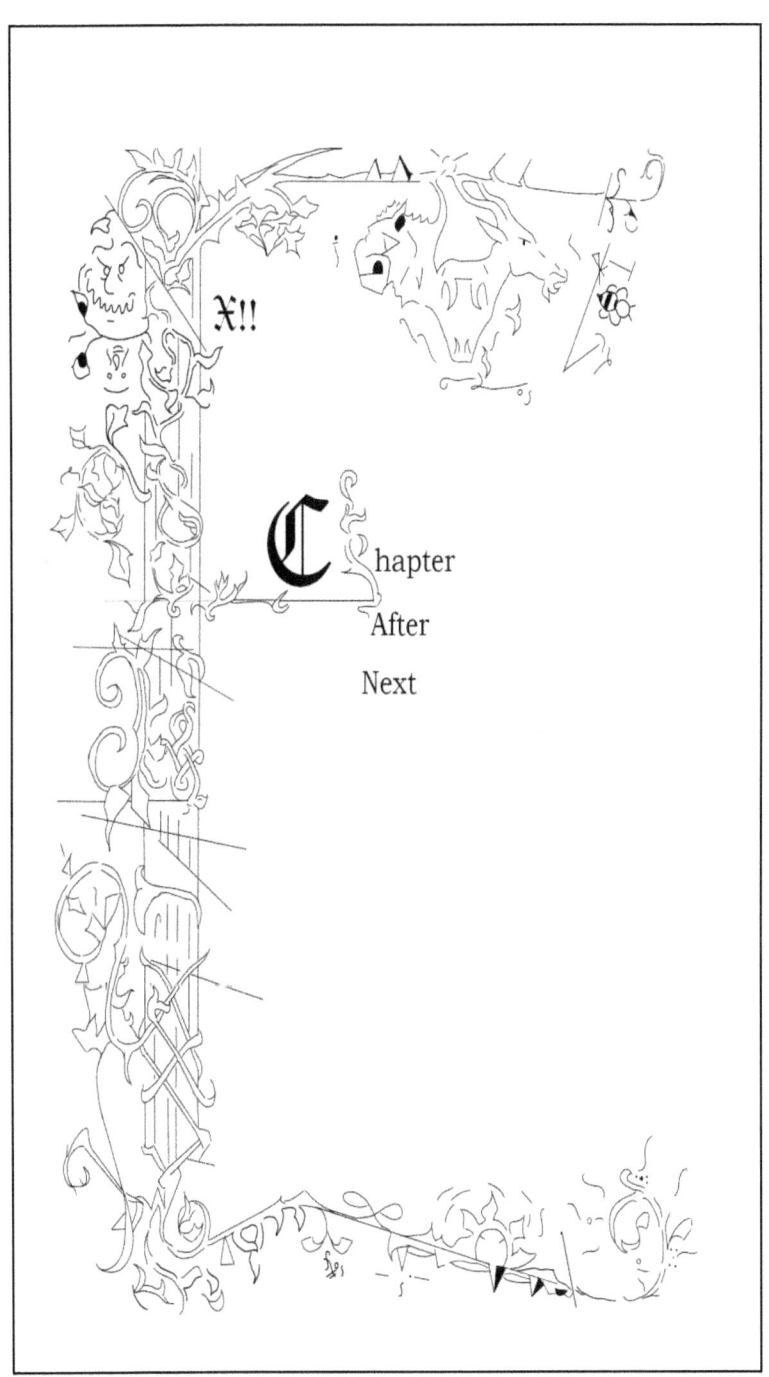

𝔛!!

ℭhapter After Next

433

INTERMI
CHAPTER AFTER NEXT

"Wow! This makes all the rich old dudes I know look like chumps!" Daphne was stunned by the opulence of the lobby; it's a whole lot grander than the one her and Scott were in *a month ago*. Everyone else went to the elevator unfazed any mind by anything around them; it wasn't anything special. Even Scott; wide-eyed 'wow this city is so beautiful so I need to stare at everything' Scott walked on like this was all part of the routine. Daphne wasn't frozen in awe like Scott's dumb behind, but the concierge scared the wonder right out of her (momentarily). He was getting ready to confront her but Larimar told him that she's a friend, so he backed off. It was a lot to process, but Daphne didn't get a chance to. The next moment was the four of them in the elevator, but the door didn't even finish closing before Scott had to get out.

"I'm sorry, really, but I just remembered that I've got this thing with...elevators." Scott rapidly pressed at button for the lobby, even after the door was wide open and they were back on the ground floor.

"Somewhere between now and when we arrived, you acquired a debilitating fear of...elevators?" Baron Sugar crossed his arms, but the face on his cloth mask was smiling.

"The easiest way to answer that is yes. Remind me to tell you later; it's something you're familiar with."

"Understood. Larimar and I will be taking the elevator."

"Hey Daphne, don't you have a thing with elevators too?"

"Nope, that's just you."

"But don't you want to take the stairs?" Scott kept pressing on.

"Just go with him so he doesn't get scared. I'll see you upstairs bye." Larimar waved quickly before nudging Daphne out. The elevator doors closed, leaving Scott,

Daphne, and the concierge in the lobby. He stared them down and they stared back. Scott did that weird cough thing again, Daphne stood there tapping her fingers on her thigh, waiting for Scott to stop being an idiot and go to the stairs.

The concierge looked at her then looked back at Scott. "He knows where the stairs are." He was on his way back to the room behind the counter when Daphne stopped him.

"Who are you exactly?"

"I'm one of Faaghira's bodyguards. If anyone in this area threatens Faaghira in any way, they will have various limbs broken, unless she specifies otherwise. You got in the building, so she's fine with you being here. The stairs are by the door, since Scott seems to have forgotten. Enjoy your time." He disappeared to the back room.

"Shit, this is Faaghira's building?! Faaghira is Larimar's sister?! Like, *that* Faaghira?!"

"Does she not have a last name? I never asked her about that. I'm pretty sure she knows mine, but I've never heard anyone mention her last name." They were making their way up the staircase, quicker than Scott had done with last time. Daphne was rushing up the steps and Scott was trying to keep up; only one of them knew where they were supposed to be going.

"How old are you? I meant to ask you that when we met, but it kept slipping my mind."

"Older than eighteen, why?"

"Hmm…how old exactly?" Daphne slowed down to a complete stop, resting her arm on the railing.

"I'm nineteen; how ol-"

"Yikes. We're definitely not doing anything. I'm twenty-four and you're not even close."

"What are you talking about? You're not even that much older than me; we're only five years off!"

"Honey, you can't even drink legally yet; we're worlds away. I'm sure you're mature and all, but that's reaching too

435

far for my radar."

"That's bullshit! My girlfriend is twenty-one and Faaghira is twenty-something! She's not that much older than I am; she told me that! We almost had- a falling out recently, but that's besides the point."

"Huh, really? I'm not going to say your age had anything to do with it, but I'm not saying that it didn't."

"What makes you so different anyway? You're acting like you're above me all because I'm younger than you, and only a couple years at that!"

"Depends; do you really want to know or are you trying to prove a point?"

"Yeah." He stepped around her and continued up the stairs ahead of her instead of trailing behind. "Since you were storming on without knowing where we're supposed to be going, can't say I'd trust your logic; that's all there is to it."

"I was going to get there eventually. Took you this long to call me out; trying to get on my good side?" Her phrasing was playful but ultimately dry.

"Good for you." He briskly walked up the stairs without looking back till he reached the exit on the eighth floor. He made a point of shutting it behind him. On his way through the halls his reflection on everything-from the glossy tables and vases to the glass in the over the framed paintings on the walls- was all Roswell mirroring him. Even with all of that he didn't look back. The lights were dim, but they caught on to any and every reflective surface for the whole stretch of the hall, but Scott, he walked on by. He stopped at the door labeled 'unit six', gently opened the door and quietly closed it behind him.

"You're back late; I was starting to worry you wouldn't show." Faaghira was leaning against the kitchen counter drinking out of a blue mug with the words 'Best Faaghira' printed in bold white letters.

"Really? *You*? Worried about me? You of all people should know that I always show up when I say I'll show up."

"I was joking." She placed the mug down on the counter then folded her arms. "And since when did you say you'd show up somewhere? There was that time on the ferry with Atticus' Junta garbage, but that was more of an obligation than a choice; no doubt he would've shot you if you said no. Besides, nobody thought you ducked out on us; we all know you don't have somewhere else to stay."

"What? Are you kidding? I could've stayed in Atticus' mansion this whole time."

Faaghira looked at him with tired eyes and a judging face. Not saying a word, she quietly took a sip from her mug. "Honey, he *shot* you in the leg. That's not even worth the joke."

"Baron Sugar told you?" Scott sighed in defeat.

"He told me *everything*. I'm nowhere near this calm when he tells me these things, but I'm usually mellowed out by the time you see me. I'm still freaked about Roswell putting a hit out on you; that guy gets under my skin. I'll see what I can do to get that hit taken off the market if that'll do any good. In other news, didn't you have someone you brought with you? Did they get to know the real you too soon? Are you actually worse than I think and you put on for me? If that's the case then that's sweet, but it's also trash."

"No, they walk slow. They'll find their way."

"You know there's twenty different units on this floor."

"Should I leave the door open?"

"Have at it, all the doors are locked. Quick tack on: you should work on that pimp walk you've got going on. Could maybe play it off better with a cane." She walked out to the terrace, sat in one of the chairs, and scrolled through her phone while drinking her iced tea. Meanwhile, Scott went to go prop the door open-

"Daphne? How long were you at the door?" Scott was

surprised, holding the same kind of enthusiasm he would before he was caught up in his little fit.

"Might've heard some things depending on whether or not you were talking about me."

"So you've been hiding out for most of the time?"

"I wasn't far behind you, you know. You must not have heard how loud your footsteps were. So I'm here now; you gonna let me inside or do I have to stand out here?"

Scott opened the door and motioned for her to go in.

"This is so surreal! This is her kitchen! This is the place she calls home! One of the places, at least. I'm actually here and…is that her out there?!" She excitedly pointed to Faaghira sitting out on the terrace. "I've only seen her on tv once or twice, but I never thought I'd get to see her in person!" She started to walk that way but stopped before she was even out of the kitchen. She looked at Scott, waiting for him to say something, which of course he didn't. "You go first. She knows you and I can't possibly give a bad impression if you're the act I have to follow." Scott was quick to walk; complying with a shoddy form of protest. Faaghira heard them but didn't acknowledge them until they were directly in her face and she literally couldn't anymore.

"You're Scott's friend." Fae glanced at Scott then Daphne.

"You're Faaghira!"

"Anybody here not know that?" She took another sip of her tea, folding her arms and crossing her legs. "What's your name?"

"Daphne; I just want to say that I really admire you!"

"Yeah, that's an image; that's not me. The public doesn't get to know me, but I'm glad you like *her*." Fae's nonchalance was dulling down Daphne's excitement, but she still pressed on.

"I think you're great, regardless of anything else." Daphne's brightness was waning even more when Fae only

438

gave slight nods while drinking her tea. "So what's it like having all this money? I bet you can have anything and anyone you want!" Daphne took one of the empty chairs and moved it closer to Fae.

"Hmm…if you really want to know-" Fae uncrossed her legs and leaned forward, "-I have some things I want that I can't ever get, but if it's got a price in dollars then I can get it tomorrow. But the hardest thing, I think…the hardest thing is not being able to get rid of what you *don't* want. Again, there's no price on that one, else I would've bought it just now." Fae spoke calmly, but with enough conviction that her essence was sharp enough to poison.

Daphne laughed awkwardly, but it shortly dissipated into silence. She shyly rubbed the back of her head. "Ha…I didn't know you were such a jerk in person."

"Comes with the territory." Fae winked then took another sip of tea, not taking her eyes off Daphne. "I'd say the same for you, but who are you, right? On another note, Larimar said you were pretty, which you are; she's always looking for another role model. Since she invited you, feel free to make yourself at home. You can also spice things up and make things even more awkward by asking me any other questions you have. I only have one spoken rule: leave if I tell you to clear out. Other than that, do your thing, whatever that is."

"Hey Daphne, I think Larimar is upstairs; we should go say hi." Scott was calling her back inside, to which she wasn't exactly jumping at the offer.

"Hey Daphne, I *know* that Larimar definitely isn't upstairs; there are other rooms in there besides mine and the living room." Fae sighed and took another sip from her mug. She looked over the sprawling city dressed with vibrant lights and glamour, watching the sun give off a radiant orange glow as it began to dip under the horizon.

"But…" Scott quickly trailed off. "Um, never mind; I'll

be back to see you in a little bit."

"You got it, babe." Faaghira struggled to feign happiness. Scott waited for Daphne to get up, but his eyes lingered on Faaghira sitting on the terrace, watching the sunset.

Him and Daphne wandered around through three different rooms before they saw Larimar and Baron Sugar playing a fighting game. Scott leaned against the doorframe and watched them battle it out. It was intense to say the least, but Larimar won (although it was a narrow victory). "Yes!" the little girl cheered; "I never thought I'd ever win in this game and I won three times!"

"I let you win." Sugar ruffled her hair while he laughed.

"Nuh uh, you won *three* times; you were trying!"

"Fine, fine, you achieved this on your own merit; congratulations, my friend." He put the controller down and began to meditate.

"Hey Larimar, me and Scott were looking for you."

"You found me, good job."

"Wow you've got a lot of sass for a little kid; has anyone ever told you that you're a lot like your sister?"

"I wish. You already met Bun; isn't she the coolest?! I wanna be just like her when I grow up!" Larimar is trying to mimic Baron Sugar's meditative pose and she's not getting it, right to say the least. "You should meda- medit-; okay, I got it; you should meditate with us!" Sugar gave her a brief side eye but he got over it fast. Scott sat down on the floor with them immediately, but Daphne only sat down with them when Scott stared at her with disapproval.

"So…what are we doing?" Daphne got bored from the silence between them, but probably didn't want to seem like a jerk to Larimar.

"Barry told me that it helps to talk about things. Do you have things you want to talk about? I have things; I always have things I want to talk about. I like to talk to Barry about how I feel; I don't talk a lot about school because I don't go to a school like other kids do."

"What do you do instead of go to school?"

"Bun teaches me almost everything, but sometimes other people do it when she's too busy. Instead of going to a school, Bun and I go into the city or around the…uh…I think she calls it a complex. There's another word with a 'p' but I don't know how to say it. She teaches me about lots of things and I take all my tests in the park or any other place I wanna go. X and some big people drive me to places if Bun's too busy but we always have family night when I come back."

"I'm guessing that Bun is Faaghira; that's cute. Does she have a nickname for you too?" Daphne beamed proudly.

"Yeah, but you can't use it. Okay so is there anything else you want to talk about?" Larimar sighs and crosses her arms.

"What's it like living in a place like this? It's really fancy and all; I want to know how you feel about it."

"I don't think I live a really different way that it would change what I'm like. Bun told me that you'll be whoever you are wherever you are. I really don't know what that means but she says it whenever we're looking at the city from outside or in a really nice place so maybe that's what it's for. Daphne, does it change anything for you?"

"I don't live in a really nice place like you do. You know what rent is'?"

"Yeah, it's moncy that-"

"Money that you have to pay monthly to live in a place someone else owns." Scott interrupted her in a split second (and everyone was pissed).

"Wow, you're so smart, *Larimar*," Daphne scoffed at Scott. "I have to pay that and nobody else in the whole state has anywhere near as much money as your sister, Atticus aside. I'm lucky to be able to afford it, but not everyone is so lucky." Daphne scooted over and propped her back up against the dresser under the tv.

"I know, but that doesn't make me feel bad. Bun-uh-Fae

is working hard to change that, but she's not the one in charge of how expensive things are. I axed her if there's anything she can do and she told me that she's doing what she can. We don't get to see each other all the time because of how much she works. Hmm…don't tell her I said this, but I know she's really tired all the time and she tries to make it look like she isn't. I know she can't fix everything …but seeing her be tired…I don't want her to." Larimar sniffled and wiped her eyes.

"As I mentioned to Scott before: if there are multiple people capable of doing something, the responsibility should not fall on the shoulder of one. Perhaps then, Scott, you and Daphne are of the same fabric; I believe that is the saying."

"I have something to share." Scott raised his hand but it lowered real quick when everyone ignored him. "I'm in a…so, say there's a hypothetical situation, and in this situation I have a girlfriend and I realized that we haven't been good for each other recently- but we still care for each other. And there's another situation in this situation where I meet another girl that I like-and she likes me-but she doesn't want to be with me. This girl is better for me in every way, but…we're not going to be together."

"Why doesn't she want to be with you if she likes you?" Larimar sounded like she was about to laugh.

"I don't- it's complicated. So, I don't know what to do-wouldn't know what to do when I saw my girlfriend again."

"In this *hypothetical* situation, you would need to be honest; with yourself and everyone involved. You mentioned that this other girl would be much better for you, something it seems the two of you would know in a situation like this. If the answer is so simple, ask yourself why nothing would change in this predicament." Baron Sugar's 'face' was blank as he meditated.

"He's got a point. Whether or not you had a better choice, why would you stay in something you know isn't good for you...unless...something about your first situa- *hypothetical* situation was keeping you from leaving." Daphne gave him an understanding look

Larimar quietly scooted her way next to Sugar, whispering "what does hypothetical mean?" He explained it as an imaginary situation that could happen, prompting her to slowly make her way back to where she was earlier.

"I've got something!" Daphne playfully raised her arm and flailed it around. "Say we've got another hypothetical situation-" Larimar throws her head back and groans loudly at having to hear 'hypothetical' again and again. "-and in this situation, there's a party. At the party is a bunch of rich snobs. The party gets crashed by...people who don't the rich snobs. So in this *hypothetical* situation-"

"Ugh! Get on with it, lady!" Larimar shouted.

"Geez, okay, okay! So the people crash the party, but they don't get to do what they came there for because someone sets some buildings in the city on fire. If this *were* to happen-" Daphne nodded at Larimar. "-then why wouldn't we hear about the torched buildings on the news. Why would we only hear about how the party was crashed by...the people who showed up?"

"Bun told me about that; you didn't have to say the *h* word."

"Which word? *Hypothetical?*" Daphne smiled slyly.

"Ugh! *Anyway*, she told me what happened and she told me why. My unca- unca- uncle, started the fire to make the people leave. He was trying to make it look like Barry did it, but not everyone thinks Barry is real. Uncle was going to tell everyone it was those people if they didn't leave. My sister told me that people can't say bad things about uncle on tv. Nobody said nothing about the fire because uncle didn't want them to." Larimar picks up her controller and goes into practice mode. At this point she's essentially in her own world.

"Scott, may we speak for a moment?" Baron Sugar stood up and the silly expression over his face returned. His cloak materialized over his shoulders. He walked out the room, which prompted Scott to follow suit. They went up the stairwell and stopped when they were on the rooftop. A light breeze grazed over them, while the lights from the city shed a radiant glow on their faces and clothes. "Since I am advocating for your immediate removal from this dimension, I feel that I should at least offer some aid to you regarding your personal issues."

"No need to stick your nose where it doesn't belong; I've already got one super-powered freak doing enough of that."

"Charming. Were I ignorant as in my youth, I would not understand helping you to be more than a cause of pity. I wanted to inquire about your actual girlfriend; why do you stay with her?"

"Definitely not to murder my whole goddamn family, if that's what you're getting at."

"I revel in the fact that you stand no chance against me in any altercation. I see this is a very sensitive topic; I would be fine with leaving this alone if you proved to be capable of handling it yourself. This is something you will need to face when you go back. I am simply asking what is keeping you with her if she does not make you happy?"

"It's not your fucking business, and I would'a said so earlier if Larimar wasn't in the room! Fuck off and get your own business to mind!"

"Then why did you mention it to us if you are so adamant about this not being our concern?"

"Because I can, you cold-hearted dipshit!"

"This is…out of character for you; or so I thought. I will keep trying; for whatever idiotic reason, I will continue trying."

"Out of character? Don't act like you know me. I can put on just like anyone else; it's something us regular people have to do to survive."

"If you would not mind explaining, I would listen to what you have to say. I will do my best to be receptive to what you have to say, no matter how much I should do the opposite."

"I get that you want to help; really I appreciate it, but this isn't any of your business. You may talk fancy and all, but the reality is that you lived your whole life as a slave; what I'm dealing with isn't something you could understand!"

"This is about a relationship; I never lived as a free man; I killed my family; if we are comparing lives, you have never experienced pain. Perhaps I would not understand why this situation is so monumental to you, but I will do what I can to help you resolve it since it is what you have binding you to this dimension. So tell me; tell me about this riveting thing that I cannot understand."

"No, you'd just mock me; I know your type." Scott sighed angrily.

"You know nothing. I can guarantee that your problems are too insignificant for me to mock. Now what is it that is so important that you must act a fool to guard it? It will sound more absurd the more you delay."

Scott walked to the edge of the rooftop and sat cross legged on the rough ground. He looked down at the illuminated streets; he was so high up that all the cars were specs. He was brooding, definitely, but he was also holding up something important. Sugar was standing right beside him in a split second, which startled Scott since he didn't hear him move. "You really gotta stop doing that! What if I jumped from shock and fell off the roof?"

"It would not be my fault unless I threw you off; otherwise, that would be your responsibility. Perhaps if the situation were not so dire, I would indulge in what I should."

"So you want to hear what's going on, huh? I'll tell you, but I won't be happy about it."

"Again, not my concern."

"Fine, fine; I haven't told Fae any of this so don't tell her. So the girl I'm dating is really *really* fucking gorgeous…our relationship is…it's not good. We've kind of broken up and got back together a few times, but we're together right now; we're trying to work through things. I tried to break up with her for good, but she pulled me back so easily; I can't help it, my feelings for her are so strong. I don't know if it's love, but it's a feeling all right. The problem is that it isn't good for us; we still do it anyway. Neither of us…neither of us are really willing to do what it takes to turn this around. There've been a lot of talks about it; lots of promises; didn't take long for those to fall through."

"If that is the only problem then leave her."

"…there's another part. I go to college; my parents couldn't pay for it. They were hounding me about getting good grades and getting scholarships. I tried as hard as I could; didn't get a thing. I felt like…nah, that's none of your business. My girlfriend, Iris; when I told her about it she said she could help. I was a little skeptical; what could my girlfriend do to help? Boy, if only I knew"

"Do not call me *boy*. Continue."

"It's just an expression, goddamn! *Anyway*, she told her dad a friend needed help paying for college and the next day she tells me I'm covered. I didn't know her family has money like that. I mean, the place I go to isn't that expensive, but it's somewhere actually I wanted to go; I wasn't settling. She doesn't go there, but she'd visit pretty often. After that I saw parts of her life that showed me how much money they really have. My mom straight up hates her guts and is always wondering why I won't break up with her, which, that's not her business. Ironic, you know, like Shakespeare. I told my parents I got a full ride scholarship; never been better at lying out my ass. They don't know; nobody else knows besides me, Iris, and now you. Maybe I did kinda tell Fae too, but

446

I'm having a tough time remembering what I said to her. The other reason I'll always run back to her; even if I hated her, she's the one holding up my life. I depend on her for most things; she knows that. My parents already cut me off, so if Iris cuts me off then literally my whole life is ruined. I'm not expecting you to understand, but that's what's waiting for me when I go back."

"In a way, I believe I understand. I take your decisions as foolish, though I understand. However, this is a situation that must be resolved. My advice to you is to act within your best interest at the moment. In whatever time you would be able to support yourself fully, it would be wise to do so."

"So you're basically saying I should ride this one out?"

"I am saying that it would be best to make a decision that will not complicate your well-being at this moment in time."

"Ah, I gotcha. Maybe you're not as bad as I thought. Still, it's easier said than done. I'm not with her just because of that; she's everything to me; that just adds to that."

"If you are serious, you will do what is necessary. As you said, this is between the two of us. Heed this warning of mine, Scott: You will be consumed by your problems, should you choose to avoid them. There are things I must discuss with Faaghira; I will take my leave." Baron Sugar left through the rooftop door instead of just disappearing abruptly like he does sometimes.

Scott was left on the roof by himself.

He laid on his back, looking up at the sky. He couldn't see any stars because of the endless amount of lights around him. He just laid there; staring up at the sky; staring up at the sky and doing nothing. Doing nothing while he was-

"Look this is usually the time when Roswell would show up and make things weird; I'm always expecting him to just jump out from somewhere, to be honest. That's what this whole thing is anyway; it's all weird. One thing that's cool though; Fae's got a nice fat ass. I'm just like, damn; I almost had that!" Scott, you're such a dick; like really, you're a dick. Is that what you like her for? After all this time? Really? "No, no, you've got me all wrong! That's not the *only* reason, but it's not something I'd always get to enjoy with Iris. We used to see other people sometimes, so sometimes I would get to enjoy a cutie with a nice fat ass, but that's not the case anymore; wasn't the case when it started though…"

You and your girlfriend cheated on each other? "I mean, I call it seeing other people, but yeah we cheated; a whole lot at one point. We were having some issues then, but not fixing problems never felt so good." I shouldn't be surprised; excuse me if you had me thrown off for *just about the whole book*. "Yeah, whatever. Stop talking like you know who I am; everybody's always doing that." Okay then, I have to narrate and you're not moving, so what do you expect me to do? "What am I supposed to do? Daphne's more interested in talking to a six-year-old than she is in talking to me! Heck, a walking corpse that was a fucking slave for Christ's sake has more business with Fae than I do! What am I supposed to do? I'm talking to you; you're not even real!" How are you talking to me if I'm not real? "Yeah, whatever, whatever."

Scott sat up with his legs hanging over the rooftop. He was waiting for something; he sat and waited. All that waiting never paid off; nothing changed; nothing showed up. No wisecracking demon randomly showing up, no explosions, nothing unusual; just…nothing. "He'll show up; there's no reason for him not to." Be real; there's no reason for Roswell *to* show up. "That's not true! I'm here!" Doesn't mean he'll show up. "Yes it does! He even said that all this was for me!" Why do you believe him? Better yet, why do you want him to show up? "It makes sense; because it makes sense. I believe him because…because…what other choice do I have? Whether I trust him or not, I'm going to end up doing what he says one way or another; that's how it's been."

Scott, you're sounding weird, even for you; especially for you. "Whatever, you wouldn't understand."

Things were quiet after that. "Maybe if I do something; maybe I have to do something to get him to show up." That is until Scott started muttering craziness under his breath. Then without warning, he jumped off the ledge. "He'll show up and stop me, you'll see." But Scott kept falling. The wind was rushing, blowing by his ears; but he swore up and down that the demon would show.

He waited for Roswell to save him.

Scott didn't even leave a crack in the pavement.

INTERMISSION

"What did you just do?" Roswell sighed, but he couldn't be seen anywhere. Strangely enough, it was a disembodied voice. "Where are you?" Scott shouted and his voice echoed infinitely. He was surrounded by...nothing at all. He floated in darkness; going nowhere; doing nothing.

"Here, where you shouldn't be...not yet. You're early; I had no time to prep; wasn't expecting company." A blue spotlight shone on Scott, and he tried to shield his eyes with his arm. A red spotlight flickered across the space, and under it was Roswell sitting in a folding chair faced forward while his back faced Scott. "So...wanna tell me why you're here?" The demon's voice was growing to sound dry.

"Because you brought me here. Hey, could you turn down the light? It's way too bright." The light over Scott's head got even brighter, causing him to turn away from it. "I said *down*; turn *down* the light!"

"Hmm, well I didn't. Since you're not telling me anything, I'll play detective to see if I can figure out what went wrong. So you did something, something I didn't plan for, that would get you killed. Now you're here, completely ignoring my questions pertaining to what you did to get here. By the way we're in my house; this is my house: The Orange Triangle Of Regret. Nobody shows up here unless I invite them or they screw up big time. I'm currently remodeling, that's why it's...uh...empty. Now like I said, you shouldn't be here, so why are you here?"

"You were supposed to show up on the roof. I was waiting for you to show up out of nowhere like you always do."

"You were waiting for *me*? Ain't that something? Look darling, I'll level with you; anyone's gotta be some kind of fucked up to want me to even be on the same plane of existence as them. *Oh, don't tell me it's getting to you.* House

451

always wins. I'd say, but there's no such thing as too soon, only right on time. Still, I've gotta run up the presses; we're about to be in the same boat; mine's sinking heavy."

"I don't have time for games! Why didn't you show up?!"

"You call on God this bad too? Or do you just like me cause I'm cute?"

"I'm not a gay, okay?! Stop trying to push that funny business! And if God is real then why didn't he show up when I needed him?! And put me on the ground, goddammit!" Scott yelled with unbridled rage.

"Though we're astronomically different, I take it we had the same reason. I didn't need to show up and you didn't *need* me to. You were bored." The demon was coughing so hard that he almost fell out of his chair. His throat was dry, he wheezed at some points; somehow he still found the time to laugh. "Maybe I've got to start putting up the braces. Didn't think for a second that I wasn't good, but I couldn't've guessed you'd be this bad." He carried on, with his dry laugh echoing; gradually distorting into a nightmarish sound.

It didn't stop.

An entire line of translucent rainbow-colored copies of Roswell were expanding infinitely on both sides of the demon and his chair. They all stood up and faced Scott; they all smiled with wicked grins.

Suddenly, streams of thick red smoke slowly poured from their mouths and flowed upwards from their eyes. All of their faces went blank and they started glitching out.

Worst of all, they did everything slightly out of unison; it was funny, until it wasn't. It kept going.

All of them together, they became a void.

They weren't moving, but Scott physically couldn't; he was stuck looking at them.

"And to think, bunch a shit I had mapped out; gotta cut most of it now." Roswell laughed slyly; the same as he used to. "A little short on words; next time be sure you can kick up a conversation before you call me on. And case you're wondering, you never jumped off that roof. Some poor shmuck took the plunge; maybe you were 'exploring the city at the time'. Right then. Catch you later, kidoo."

Scott was back in the city in a split second. Everything was normal; the streets were vibrant and a mass of people were out making their rounds. There was no demon, no terror; nothing out of the ordinary. Though, Scott was lost; he's only been in the city once and it wasn't even the same area. He checked around carefully then put his phone up to his ear, "Wait, was my phone on a hundred this whole time?" From what I remember, you were trying to find a charger for it. Hold on, I think I remember wh- "But it's fully charged now! I bet this was Roswell! Do you think this could be bad somehow?" Really? You're still worried about a demon? An actual demon? What's wrong with you? Aren't you worried about where you are? "I don't need to worry about that; I mean, you know where I am…right?"

You should show at least some concern for *something*. And yes, I know exactly where you are. "Good. Where am I?" You're still in Louisiana. "No dip, Sherlock." If you don't take your part seriously then why should I? "Fine, I'll take it seriously; whatever you want. Can you just tell me where I am now?" I did. Now do your part and figure out why you're *here* specifically. "And how am I supposed to know that if you won't tell me?" Last time I checked I'm not the main character.

Scott groaned and whined in protest, but he cut it out as soon as he saw some women looking at him funny. He was there in an open marketplace during the daytime. People were out buying fresh fruits, vegetables, produce from countless vendors on a cobblestone area that set out for two whole blocks. A couple of kids were playing hide and seek behind some of the vendors (much to the dismay of their parents). There were couples excitedly looking through all the fresh foods, and a picky chef painstakingly looking over every ingredient and every bit of food in their baskets.

Then it happened.

All the electricity went out in one fell swoop. People were instantly caught in a state of panic (the adults, at least; the kids were still having fun). Scott was trying to figure out what to do in the growing chaos. He didn't seem to mind any of it; his posture was relaxed, lazy even. He just...stood there. There were people opening the windows of their apartments; some yelled and fussed while the others were just checking to see if the street lights were out. There were people rushing, scattering out of the block...then there was Scott. Parents came back around to scoop up their kids that were still playing hide and seek; vendors were outright abandoning their booths. All this going on; the power went out in broad daylight and everyone was panicking. All of this and yet, Scott's reaction is...nothing. It didn't occur to him *once* that there's a reason all these people were freaking out?

"I'm not everybody, I'm Scott, remember? Really though, you know people overreact. A few lights go off and everybody loses their mind. Why would I get caught up in all of that? Lots of people aren't rational like I am. If they would chill out then they'd see that there's nothing to worry about." Right on que, the Peace Officers arrived in the market. Squad cars piled in from every side, helicopters were flying overhead; it was turning into a warzone. "You're being dramatic; it's not a warzone, there's no explosions or anything like that. It's just the police; maybe this is a normal thing... kinda."

One of the squad cars opened up and an officer in full riot gear. He lifted up the visor on his helmet and waved to Scott. Their face was very tough looking; a smile definitely wasn't natural for it. Still, Scott waved back at him eagerly; a mocking gesture directed at me. Boy is this guy a sucker.

"Friend, there is nothing to worry about; there was an attack by the terrorist group in our fair state. If you would be so kind as to accompany my squad back to City Hall then we'd really 'preciate it. It's where people go to be safe during a crisis, if you know what I mean."

"Uh, yeah, yeah sure; lead on man- uh- officer."

Scott got into the officer's car and the entire sea of police vehicles followed. The car picked up speed rapidly, whipping past every high rise as the wheels screeched against the road. "Ha ha…you drive like Faaghira!" Scott laughed nervously and combed through his hair. The officer smiled and turned the radio all the way up. And of course, country music; it's not even good. "Yup, I'm cool with this!" Scott was trying desperately not to panic.

"Good, good; I heard most people get worried around this part." The officer yelled over the music instead of just lowering the volume. He brushed down his bushy moustache with his left hand and reached for a box of donuts in the backseat with his right. "You want one?" Scott let out another nervous laugh while his shaky hand took a jelly donut from the box. The windows were down just enough to let the violent winds push at Scott's ears. He winced for a moment, but he cleared his throat and tried to look like he's relaxed.

"Hey…uh…can you slow down? I don't think the City Hall is so far that you have to drive so fast. And-and what if you hit somebody?" Scott's voice was beginning to shake.

"Nobody's on the streets; orders from Atticus Bellamy himself." The officer pressed as hard as he could on the gas pedal. Some bumps under the tires jolted the car. He let his hands off the wheel, using one to rest his head on and the other to eat a heavily glazed donut. Scott was careful not to look uneasy when looked what was down the road. He tensed up his hands to stop them from shaking, but the terror showed in his eyes. At the end of his gaze was a large body of water at the end of the road; a road that got increasingly worse the further it went along. "The irrigation lake; somebody said it should be a pond; they- you'll meet them pretty soon."

Scott immediately tried to open the door, but it was locked. None of the buttons on his side worked, so he rushed to take the wheel. The officer steered with his knee so his hands would be free to push Scott away. In retaliation, Scot fought with all his strength...and the officer didn't even seem to notice. He pushed at the officer's face with one hand and steered with the other. When the car started swerving, the others in the escort pulled up and bashed into the sides, slowing it down. Scott took off his seatbelt and tried to push his way through to the backseat, but officers in the cars behind them were shooting the windshield.

"Never thought I'd say this, but I wish Safira was here. She can handle all this action movie crap, and she's a girl! She's a lesbian on top of that! I have to man up for real if I'm expecting to get out of this one."

"You think you're a man? I'll show you a real man!" The officer tried to bash Scott, but Scott pushed him back, throwing the officer's head to the steering wheel.

"You're not gonna show me anything! Ugh, you nasty!" Scott stomped on the officer's foot, pressing the gas pedal all the way down. The car floored it past the vans at its side, leaving sparks on its trail. Scott took hold of the wheel; he was going for a daring turn. If he made it then he'd get past the rest of the convoy by the skin of his teeth. If it doesn't work then-

Yikes, they rammed right into him! They rushed him while he was turning! Three vans crashed into the car, crushing the driver's side; officer and all. Every vehicle in the ensemble closed in, bumper to bumper, ramming Scott, and themselves, off the road.

Scott was desperately trying to find a way out of what would become a metal coffin soon enough. He looked behind him to see the rest of the cars falling behind him. It was a long drop and there was no way out of it. Every vehicle plunged in the lake one after the other. He maneuvered his way past the officer's crushed body to get out the car. Scott pulled himself up on the roof as the car floated up to the surface. He coughed up water then gasped for air. "Shit, how did I get out of that?!" Oh, I don't know; do you want me to read that whole part again? "Nah, you don't have to be rude and stuff, man. I mean, it's crazy that I'm still alive! It's crazy that any of this is happening, to be honest. And shit, why don't I care? I should be freaking out or some shit. At the end of the day, I act like this is normal; I know it isn't. I've gotta get out of here." Oh, just like Baron Sugar was saying. "No, not here as in this dimension, here as in this lake; this situation specifically. Even with all the crazy stuff that goes on, this whole scene is still better than my old life."

That 'old' life is your real one; don't forget it. "Nah, forget it. As soon as I find a way out of here I'm finding Fae; I'll help her with whatever it is she's doing then we'll hang out or something." You really think that's a good idea? "Unless you can fix my whole life by the time I'd go back, this is the greatest idea in the world." Scott stood, but he carefully crouched back down when the car began to dip into the water. He desperately scanned the high concrete walls surrounding the lake; he was looking for something, anything that could get him out of there. He spotted a ladder…at the other side of the lake. He repeatedly sighed as loud as he could, then he tried to paddle the car forward with his hands.

It didn't move; big surprise. "It was worth a shot. I really don't want to swim *all* the way over there." You could try using the other cars to jump across. "I don't see how that would work." There are enough cars there. You can make it across; it says so in the author's notes. "Cool, now I can get out of here and find Fae." He braced himself to jump, closed his eyes, then took a leap.

The car tilted over as soon as Scott landed, flipping him into the water. Whoops. He was plunged down and he swam up frantically to breathe. "Dammit, you said I would make it!" I say a lot of things; looks like you'll have to swim after all. "I hate you." Scott trudged through the cold lake until he finally reached the ladder. He looked up at how far he had to go and groaned. From where he was it appeared to be a mile high. He took a deep breath and started to climb. It felt like an eternity to get all the way up the wall. The ladder was shaky at some points causing Scott to shriek (which he denied doing immediately after). The sun was out, and so was the electricity, but the people definitely weren't. The city felt so…lifeless. Peace Officers were quietly patrolling the streets in squads of five that moved on foot. They were armed with flashlights, assault rifles and body armor; all adorned with the smiley face insignia of the Junta.

Scott was about to call out for help, but after remembered that these are the same kinds of people that killed themselves while trying to drown him. They come from the same fabric as the guy that almost killed him the night he met Daphne. And it's this same group that was still a terror even in broad daylight. Scott was running, excited to be free; trying to find somewhere familiar.

"You hear that?" Scott heard a guard whispering. He panicked and rushed to find somewhere, anywhere to hide. He crouched behind a dumpster careful not make any more noise. One of the patrols stopped and shined their flashlight down the alley. "Found him" the officer turned off the flashlight and headed back to his patrol. Scott peaked out to see what was happening, but hid well enough that he was sure they couldn't see him.

Scott saw a man running out to the officers. He was

panicking; going on and on about how he lost keys to his apartment during the rush in the marketplace. They assured him there was nothing to worry about. One of them asked for his identification papers, which he frantically got from his coat. That man had fear in his eyes; beads of sweat were running down his forehead. "There's nothing to worry about, you'll be fine; accidents happen." The officer lifted up her visor and smiled when she patted the man's shoulder. She drew the revolver from her holster and shot him in the chest four times. One of her squad members passed her a wet wipe and she wiped the splatters of blood off her face.

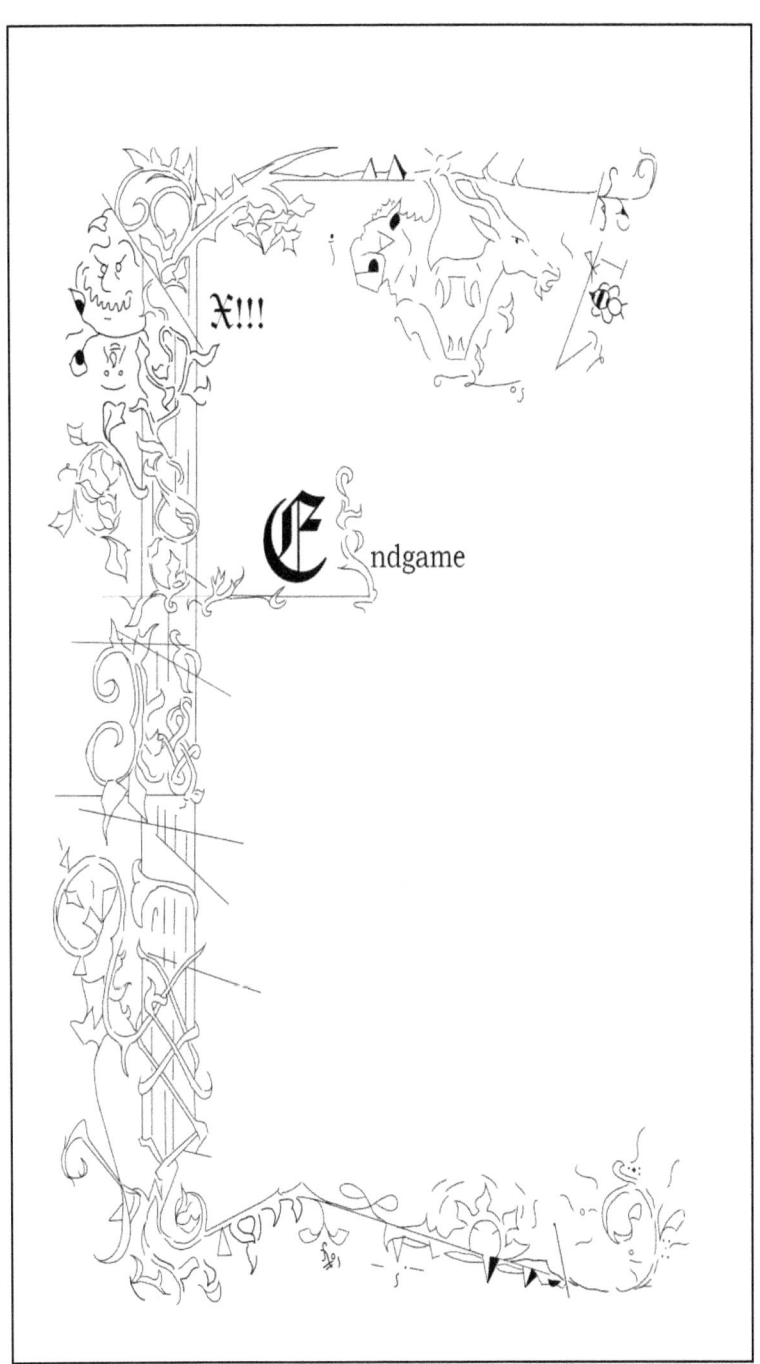

X!!!

$\mathfrak{E}$ndgame

CHAPTER XIII
ENDGAME

"Captain, we have to move, the resistance is taking advantage of the blackout. Our orders are to take out the resistance, not civilians."

"He could've been resistance. If you're arguing the morality of my actions, I might get suspicious. This is war. Take the body and throw it in the dumpster; trash gets burned anyway." She put her visor down and put the revolver back in its holster.

"What do we do with the identification papers?"

"Keep them; Atticus wants to have things covered on every avenue. On the chance I did want it burned, I'd probably get 'swept off my feet' in the middle of the night." The captain chuckled, brightening the mood in the strangest way. She placed the bloody wet wipe in the other officer's hand and patted them on the shoulder. "Oh, and thanks for the wipe; it's way harder to get blood off these visors."

The captain and two of her squad members were walking off while the others stayed behind to dump the body. Scott was careful to not make any noise as he left his spot when the officers were on their way to the dumpster. He wandered quietly into any space he could get to where the Peace Officers weren't. He wouldn't admit it, but he was hopelessly lost. The sun was beating down on him, he was moving noticeable slower, he was tired, he was in a place he didn't know, but he couldn't just stop because of how he felt. He had to find Fae; he had to figure out what was going on. Most importantly, for the moment, he had to keep away from the Peace Officers. That sounds a little weird out loud.

"I know, right? But think about this: I'm tired, I may or may not know exactly where it is I'm going; why don't I just let them catch me? Roswell will bring me back and probably even put me with Fae in one of her condos. We all know that's what would happen anyway." Scott, I think you have too much confidence in Roswell. He's a demon and he even said that he wants to kill you; he said it multiple times! I know you don't have a lot to work off of, but you really shouldn't be so dependent on him. I'm not supposed to be mentioning this because Roswell is definitely listening right now. I don't know how he'll react to what I'm saying, but I can't count on it being pleasant. "Don't sweat it. I have to find a way to go, so make yourself sparse and get me some idea on where I should go next." Fine, I'm only helping because it's my job.

Scott wandered past the areas with pristine vehicles and exquisite high rises into the 'poor' district where the buildings were smaller and in poor shape. There were only handful of cars there; all of them were lucky to be holding up. There were broken chain link fences around some of the properties, grass peeping through some of the cracks in the sidewalk, potholes in the road, but how bad it truly was got the spotlight because nobody was outside. Scott didn't see any Peace Officers patrolling this side of the city, but it was understandable that no one would want to be out there. It was a cesspool. There was a-

"Scott, over here, quick!" Scott looked up and saw Angelo on the second floor of Ace N Dandy's, waving aggressively. Scott made a (quiet) dash to the restaurant. He pulled at the handles but the doors were chained from the inside. He pounded his fist on the door until Angelo unlocked it. "You don't need to bang on the door. If you saw that the handles were chained then why would you punch away at the door as if that would open it? I was going to open it; I was the one who called you over here! Tell me why *I* wouldn't open it? Why wouldn't *I* open the door?" Angelo took the lock off the chains, letting them fall to the floor.

Scott pushed at the handles, but the doors still didn't open. "It's a pull door; I didn't think I'd have to put a sign." Angelo shook his head until Scott pulled the doors open. "You can take a seat somewhere where you don't think you'd be seen. I have to lock this door back up."

Scott slouched in a booth in the back of the restaurant. The room was dark aside from the glisten on parts of the chrome counter from the sunlight that snuck in through the windows. "Hey Angelo, I haven't seen you in a few days; what's been going on?"

"Days?" Angelo's face was scrunched up in disbelief. "That bombing was almost two months ago!"

"Oh, uh…I lose track of time…easily." Scott slumped down into the booth.

"You should sort that out. There was a debate going on between Fae and Atticus on what should be done about the bombings. Everybody was tuned in and the power just went out everywhere. Word has it that the buildings run on their own power grids. Meanwhile, Atticus has his troops looking for anyone in the resistance, and to him that's anyone they find out here. You have to be careful; those are ruthless bastards."

"I guessed that much" Scott sighed heavily. "Do you know where Fae is?"

"I just told you; she's debating Atticus. For everyone's sake, I hope she wins."

"No, no, I meant like physically, where is she? Like where is she now?"

"They're at City Hall. *Don't tell me you're actually thinking of going there.* The only way you could get there is if you could fly. Scratch that; you'd get shot down if they saw you up there." Angelo's voice lacked any excitement.

"So what the hell am I supposed to do?!"

"You don't know? Man, how am I supposed to tell you what to do? You're grown; figure it out. I didn't know Fae's type was getting worse these days. It's her life; not really my business." Angelo let out a sigh weighed down by stress.

Scott noticed how clean everything was; the room looked untouched compared to how he saw it the first time. "Were you closed today?"

"When we heard Fae and Atticus were going to debate, everyone in the neighborhood knew better than to try and run things like normal. I gave everyone their paychecks yesterday; let anyone who didn't have a safe place to go stay upstairs until this blows over. My only regret is not having more space. It'll only be a day or two, but still, anything I can do alone is just a temporary solution." Angelo sighed again. "If there's really something you think you can do then there's a service tunnel that can take you to Fae's complex; they won't look for you down there. That should be a safe spot; if Atticus sends anyone there then he forfeits control of the Junta to Fae, and that's a line even he wouldn't cross."

"Thanks Angelo, can I get a meal on the house?"

"Tell you what: just for you, you can get anything you want off the menu for free, if you give me twenty dollars."

"But that's not free!" Scott whined.

"Neither is making food; I run a business, not a charity."

"Eh, I can't argue with that." Scott shrugged and slouched further into the booth.

"Here, take a water" Angelo tossed Scott a water bottle from behind the counter. "Fae was worried about you. She came around twice to ask if I'd seen you."

"Aww, she really is in love with me. I don't know why she keeps denying it." Scott smiled warmly.

"I wouldn't be so fast to say that. Faaghira's the type that would go looking for a bullet that was removed from her leg if it was in there long enough."

"Damn, that's harsh."

"I call 'em like I see 'em." Angelo sat down on a stool in front of the counter.

"You better not let her hear that."

"I said that said that to her face last time she was here."

"Hey, so…thanks for the water; I'll get going now. Is that tunnel behind an abandoned house?"

"She showed you that? You must really be something. You're not the reason she got caught, are you?" Angelo voice was suddenly stern.

"What?" Scott was panicking. "Mercury didn't get caught! What are you talking about? What would she even get caught for?"

"Man, stop playing, I knew that was Safira; we've been friends for…I'd say about three years now. She changes her name and colors her hair when she's in hiding. She even wears regular clothes instead of the military super-spy getup she usually has going on. Mercury: someone you only get to see when Safira's trying to lay low. It's not that nobody can recognize her; it makes it easier for her to blend in around people that don't know her. I know I shouldn't have told you any of that, but it seems to me that you've already gotten to know her on a somewhat personal level, so it's not like it matters."

"What do you mean?"

"She showed you where the service tunnel is; whatever you said to her must carry some kind of weight." Angelo got up from the stool and took the lock off the door again.

"Guess so." Scott picked himself up from the booth and got ready to leave.

"Yeah, be careful, man."

"If I could promise anything, it would be that." Scott was back outside, and the door was locked behind him shortly after.

He walked on the cracked sidewalk, littered with some confetti and scorched spots. Scott looked across the street for a quick second, but he was frozen in disbelief when he saw the debris from the bombing still looming. It was left virtually untouched; a haunting image suspended in time. The biggest difference now was the police tape barring off that area. There were still hands reaching out from underneath the rubble and destroyed wood frames. Of course they weren't alive; they were encapsulated by the statue of death. Any bodies that were apart from the debris a month ago were long gone, but the spots where they died were stained with their blood.

"I feel responsible for this somehow. I know it wasn't my fault, but I feel like it is. They didn't even clean up the damn thing. Now I have to keep looking at it." It's not your fault; you know that. What are you going on about? "You don't get it. This is a shot at me! None of this…it's real, but it's not. That's…I don't know, it means something, right?" What are you talking about? "There's all this going on; everyone sits and lets this happen! Worst of all, Roswell is behind all of this. Other people don't know the truth like I do, but I can't even do anything about it. Unless…" Scott, ran off to the abandoned house and busted through the cellar (even though he could've opened it in a non-dramatic way). He walked briskly, still taking note of the graffiti on the concrete walls. There were unexpected ones like 'Resistance are terrorists', but of course there were the classic hits such as 'Atty is a bitch' and 'Freedom Now!'.

Scott clutched the front of his jacket; an effort to keep warm in the harsh cold air in the tunnel. He shifted his eyes around the room, carefully watching his surroundings. "Roswell…I know you're here."

There was no response. Things were quiet.

"You always show yourself when I'm alone…well, except for that one time with Fae. But it's the times like this; when no one's around you always show up." Scott could see the breath flow from his mouth, slowly suspended by the air.

And yet again, nothing. Scott looked around the pillars and pipes, but eventually went back on his way to Fae's complex.

"Roswell, I know you're here. I'm about to reach Fae's house. You know you can't let other people see you. If you're gonna show up you better do it now." He didn't give up on Roswell after all, how sweet.

Scott slowed his pace waiting for the demon to appear from somewhere. He grew agitated when Roswell didn't show. He started punching one of the walls surrounding him. He kept this up until his hands were bruised, then he sat on the chilled concrete floor.

"STOP. CALLING. ME." Roswell stood over Scott. His arms were crossed and his face was stone cold. The demon's eyes were filled with the fires of hell. Yet for some reason, an empty smile grew across his face. "Listen, I've things to do; I have something I'm doing right now. You- I keep having to stop whatever it is I'm doing so I can show up; get you to stop feeling lonely. And hopefully, if I do that right, you'll leave me alone just long enough for me to get through with my prior engagements. Now I just had to leave a confrontation with someone really important because of you. It'll probably come back to bite me- probably you too, so make this worth my while. Why did you call me all the way down here?" His voice was drenched in anger, but he never lost his smile.

"What's all this supposed to lead to? There's this whole thing between Atticus and Fae, the resistance and the Junta, rich versus poor; how's this supposed to end? How long is all this conflict supposed to last?"

"As long as people make it; basically forever." The demon acted surprised.

"So what does all of this have to do with me? Not that I'm complaining...about the good things that came out of that, at least, but why do I have to go through this *with* them?" Scott whined.

"You'd really make me laugh if you weren't so busy

468

making me frown. So I've this thing; you remember the two supernatural beings I warned you about early on?"

"Yeah, Sugar- I mean Baron Sugar is one of them."

"Okay, so the other one, you know, you've seen him…it. You were in that absurdly expensive restaurant; you and Debra were in the elevator-"

"Daphne; me and Daphne; her name is Daphne" Scott cut him off sharply. "You were there too. You're the reason that weird tiger and all that other stuff was there when the elevator opened."

"Funny, I doubt she'd remember your name if it weren't for the perks of hanging around you. Though, it's a bit sad she's able to get along better with a six-year old than she does with you. Now as for the tiger, yeah, that's the one. When you and Daphne were in the elevator and you saw the tiger thing. That's the other supernatural being, Terbold; real dorky name." The demon began to laugh, but it was cut short by a coughing fit that ended in him spitting out blood. He knelt down then rested on his back, stretching his arms across the floor.

"That's who you say you're trying to fight?"

"Succeeding, like in everything else I do."

"You think so? You're failing hard when it comes to making me want to die. That's your goal, isn't it?"

"Such a big oversight, you'd swear we're related."

"Ha ha, very funny." Scott had a deafness in his voice.

"It is, really. I'm surprised your parents could ever stop laughing after making such a good joke." Roswell chuckled a little bit, but it ended in him coughing up more blood. "Welp, there goes my heart! Lol."

"And you're a shitty excuse for a villain." Scott tried his hand at a quip, but it didn't gain any traction.

"Darling, no need to make it a kitchen if you know you can't take the heat."

"What's the use of showing up if you're not even going

to make yourself useful?" Scott snapped at the demon.

"Whoa, helpful? First I'm a shitty villain and I'm also supposed to help you? What's the truth, Scott Blue?" Roswell cupped his face in his hands and gasped in the mmost overly dramatic way. "Scottie, have you been seeing *other* demons?"

"Enough with that gay shit, alright?! It's not funny!" Scott yelled at the demon feverishly.

"The way you're so adamant, I'd swear that gay people routinely kicked you off your tricycle when you were a kid…and that they did it again a couple days ago. Brings me to ask; do you still ride a trike? Cause if you do then I'd kick you over too."

"When will you get to the part where you start telling me something useful? That's basically what you do every time you show up."

"I'll tell you what I'm supposed to be doing: I'm supposed to be fighting a jerk with superpowers; sonething I already mentioned to you."

"You're supposed to be fighting yourself then?" Scott smirked.

"No, the other jerk with superpowers. See, there's a time I wasn't so smart, naïve even. I did my job, but I didn't always do it all that well; I wasn't Roswell, The Demon. I was just any ol' run of the mill demon back then; I wanted to chage that. I started 'sharing' my powers with my clients. I thought it was a good idea; I'd give needy people more than they could ever handle. It worked for a very long time, but I failed, though it was only twice. The first, Sugar told you that one, but the second was a short while after; twas the nineteen fifties. I forgot what the guy's name was, not that I ever cared. One day I-"

"Can you get to the point already?" Scott pushed his hands in his pockets.

"You call me here and you want me to leave; you say I'm

a jerk and you expect me to help; she loves me, she loves me not. Being honest, you put the fun in fundemental operator error. I was right about to get to the point. Scott Blue; I say this with courtesy; you're a complete idiot. This one, Terbold, it calls itself, is also a complete idiot, perhaps in the same way as you. Long story short, he used his powers to copy me. It was flattering at first but recently he's been getting in my way. Listen, he even had the audacity to interrupt me while I was interrupting your failing date with Debbie…that you couldn't pay for-did I save your date? Damn, I'm getting rusty!"

"You may have paid for dinner, but you weirded out my date, then you straight up stole my date!" Scott grunted and huffed angrily; he even kicked one of the columns, and of course he tried to play it off like it didn't hurt.

"Alas, redemption!" Roswell sat up to put his fist in the air, but he was back on the ground within a second. "I am evil yet! Thanks for pointing that out; in return I'll drag the plot on for a *little* longer. Mostly because I have to fix the problem you literally just made for me, so….uh, yeah- big thanks for that one."

"I didn't force you to come here; that's not my fault."

"You're despicable; shame I stopped giving out powers." The demon sighed heavily. "Right then, time to see what I can salvage. Kay, bye." Roswell stood up then jumped down a red warp pipe. Scott tried to look around to see if the demon was still around somewhere, but he eventually gave up. I'm surprised he tried at all; he should be used to this by now. He passed by a door with a sign on it that read 'service tunnel' on his way out of the main tunnel. Scott was in the old train station that Safira led him through the last time he was there. It was still a grand, but undeniably depressing sight. The beauty of its extravagance survived, yet it had dilapidated over time.

Scott was ready to go up the stairs and into the warehouse

above the station, but he heard some Peace Officers laughing and joking at the top of the stairs. "Shit!" Scott quietly panicked while he rushed back down the stairs. He remembered Angelo talking about a service tunnel that led straight to Faaghira's complex; the same one he passed. He expected it to be cryptic or some kind of maze, but it was just a matter of going straight down the service tunnel and climbing up a ladder.

He emerged in a room he didn't recognize. The only light source came from the five monitors bunched together on one wall. There was a coffee maker, water bottles, and a mini fridge on a table tucked away in a corner. The concierge was at his desk scrolling through something on a tablet. "Faaghira isn't here" the concierge looked at Scott from the corner of his eye. "She instructed me to let you up to the eighth floor; Safira is up there. You can head up now."

"Thanks. You know, you should pay close attention to that service tunnel. All kinds of people can sneak through here."

"I saw when you came in. If she wasn't cool with you then we wouldn't be I here. You can go now; I have work to do." The concierge continued swiping on his tablet, unbothered by Scott.

"Geez, you don't have to be so rude!" Scott stormed out and slammed the door behind him. He took the elevator up; for some reason he looked around, expecting Roswell to show up. The demon didn't show again, which left Scott disappointed for some reason. When he arrives on the eighth floor he sees the door for unit six wide open. "None of the doors stay open like that!" Scott whispered to himself (though he was so loud that it defeated the purpose of him whispering). He moved carefully on- oh okay, I guess not. He ran into the room, throwing all caution to the wind. "Saffie, are you okay?" He shouted when he got in the doorway

Of course, this was just another move that made him look stupid.

Larimar and Baron Sugar turned around to see who was making all that noise. "Oh, you arrived…again." Sugar shook his head solemnly and resumed painting on a canvas in front of him.

"Cool! Scott's back! Where did you go?" Larimar waved at Scott with both arms; a move that nearly got Sugar to laugh.

"Hey kiddo! At least *somebody's* happy to see me." Scott side eyed Sugar (who wasn't even paying attention) then sat on the floor with them. "I was out…you know, I like to explore. It's a really nice city; you live in a really nice city and I wanted to see it. You sister is very busy, so I didn't want to wait for her to have time to show me around. So where's Saffie?"

"She is not here" Sugar spoke hastily.

"The guy at the desk said she was!" Scott's voice was filling with anger.

"Safira had a very dire situation to handle."

Larimar poked Scott's shoulder to get his attention. "She said she had a mission she had to do right away so Barry- how do you say the word?"

"Teleported."

"Yeah he teleported her to the place and then he came back."

"You left her out there by herself?" Anger built up in Scott's voice.

"Should I have brought a child into a potential warzone?" Sugar poured a stream of water on his paintbrush then swiped the water out of existence.

Scott cleared his throat and pounded his chest. "Hey, so Larimar, I was visiting a friend…out of state; that's where I went." Baron Sugar nodded with approval.

"Wow! I thought you were homeless! I've never been to

473

another state before!" Larimar jumped with excitement.

"Uh...thanks?"

"It is understandable why she believed that you were homeless."

"So what has everyone been doing while I was visiting my friend?"

"Safira and Faaghira have decided on a plan of action that was initiated last week. Part of that requires Safira to partake in dangerous operations. Also, the concierge is unaware of my existence, therefore she could not leave the normal way without raising any questions." Baron Sugar was almost finished covering the whole canvas with paint. Oddly enough, it was a scene depicting him painting a scene of himself painting Larimar, Scott, and himself sitting on the floor, just as they were in the present time.

"The guy at the desk doesn't know you're real? Why didn't Fae introduce you?" Scott laughed awkwardly.

"You have seen me, correct?"

"Yeah, I don't see the problem." Scott chuckled and snorted a little bit."

"You were terrified when you saw me for the first time; admit."

"That's different! I wasn't expecting to see something like you! I thought I'd get to..." He paused when he remembered Larimar was still in the room.

"Because you're one of her night friends?" Larimar sipped from an apple juice box that she picked up from beside the canvas. Her expression was a mix of innocent and knowing.

Scott was left blushing "Uh...maybe so. Just imagine if Barry never showed up."

"I have; it was a vision of sorts. To say honestly, you would no longer be night friends." Sugar's jabs at Scott may have been lighthearted, but his monotone voice makes it so hard to tell.

474

"Then maybe it...was best that nothing happened." Scott's words were wrapped in hesitation.

"What did you want to happen?!" Larimar jumped up and down excitedly. "Bun Bun never tells me this part!"

Scott's eyes widened in shock. His eyes shifted over to Sugar as a cry for help, but Sugar simply shrugged and gave Scott two thumbs up. "So Barry-"

"Do not call me that"

"Uh...Baron Sugar, what's our next move?"

"I will wait for Safira; she will contact me when she needs my help."

Scott stood up and brushed the non-existent dust off his shirt. "Don't you mean if?"

"No."

"What are we supposed to do while we wait?"

Baron Sugar put down his brush and put the painted canvas on the floor. "Here Larimar, this is for you. As for time, I can tell a story."

"Tell me about Roswell." Scott demeanor switched to something very imposing, though he toned it down when he saw Baron Sugar was unbothered.

"Be wary of your questions, for the sake of your audience. I will tell you about a problem someone had long ago; a problem with power. They felt powerless- rather helpless in their normal life. Something changed; a power was bestowed upon them, something they believed they were ready for. It was actually care that was placed in their hands; they were the one who twisted it into something it never should have been: power. As-" Sugar was interrupted by the sound of static cutting through radio on the kitchen counter.

"There's snipers at the power plant! We've been intercepted! We need immediate extraction!" Safira's voice was muffled, but the urgency of the matter struck through clearly.

"Unsurprising. I will arrive." Baron Sugar brushed off his cloak then prepared to leave.

"What about your story?" Larimar whined.

"Surely it has been told before. I never did plan on finishing the story."

"No Fair!" the little girl crossed her arms and huffed.

"Safira, how would you like to proceed?" I could've sworn Sugar was joking, but I still can't tell; I didn't see anything about it in the author's notes.

"Extraction! I literally just said that!" She yelled, making the signal even fuzzier.

"I assume your mission is incomplete. I hoped that you would reevaluate your position on extraction if you were given the chance." Oh, so maybe he wasn't joking?

"Fine! Just do something and do it soon!" A rain of bullets could be heard from her end of the line.

Baron Sugar stood up then looked down at Larimar. "Be well my friend, will return. Make sure Scott does not act up."

The little girl saluted excitedly. "Yes sir!" She fought to keep a straight face but couldn't hold back her chuckling.

Sugar's expression was the dopey looking neutral one he usually has, but something about the way he carried himself in that moment showed discomfort. "Larimar, I know that you say this in good fun, but I would greatly appreciate if you did not call me 'sir' or any other authoritative title." He knelt down and hugged her. "Of course, this is of no fault to you; it is my past that haunts me still. I will tell you that story at a time of peace. You did absolutely nothing wrong. You are a shining jewel. I will return." He stood up again, and with a swipe of his cloak, Baron Sugar disappeared.

Larimar picked up the canvas and struggled to walk with it; even more so when she tried to take it up to her room. She nearly dropped it a few times, but she (barely) managed to catch it.

"Hey…uh…need help with that, kid?" Scott lacked the

brazen confidence he normally has.

"Nope! You wanna see my room? It's really cool!" Larimar sounded extremely excited for someone who was having such a tough time moving a large canvas up a set of stairs.

Not really knowing what else to say, he said "sure." Larimar was going on about how her room was "probably the coolest thing you've ever seen," but was quick to pass him the canvas when he got to the steps, mumbling "here, hold this."

"I thought you didn't need any help!"

"I need to open the door because you don't know where my room is." Larimar's a smart girl; there's no way she *didn't* know that's a flimsy excuse. It worked, nonetheless. She opened the door for him like she said, then she asked if he could hang it up on the hooks Sugar put on the wall. Scott smiled at the fact that she actually asked for his help, but he realized how he looked like an idiot having a dopey grin out of nowhere; needless to say, he fixed his face real quick.

Larimar's room was modestly sized but incredibly comfy. Transparent violet drapes with lines of diamonds and beads hanging over a mound of pillows and covers that were scattered on top of a fluffy white rug. Blue Christmas lights were pinned up around the edges of the ceiling, giving off a cool and comforting light. A dresser and a small brown bookshelf sat against one of the walls, though there were hardly any books on it. Her closet was completely empty; seriously, there wasn't anything there. She had a NES, Super Nintendo, Sega Genesis, N64,….then an Odyssey. Some of the game cartridges were in disorganized stacks on the floor and the rest of them took up room on the bookshelf.

The light from the glowing sunset shone through the only window, illuminating the crystals strung around the room. The sparkling diamonds contrasted with the walls painted with a beautiful dark blue and purple gradient, creating a kind of cosmic atmosphere. Scott was mesmerized, but Larimar went to turn on the Super Nintendo without giving the atmosphere a second look. As soon as she pressed the power button, everything shut off. Aggravated, Larimar repeatedly tries to get the tv back on, going as far as unplugging the cord then putting it back.

A sudden tremor pulls at the building, throwing Larimar and Scott to the floor. Scott's eyes immediately dart to the window; they were met by a red streak of light that soared across the sky. He panicked when it fell out his line of sight. He rushed over to shield Larimar, but an explosion erupted outside before he could get to her.

"Larimar! No!" Scott picked her up, to which she responded by repeatedly hitting his arm.

"Put me back down! Bun told me to stay on the floor if bad things ever happen around me!" She shouted at him partially out of anger, but mostly because the explosions outside made it hard to hear. Scott panicked so much that he dropped her. "OW! WHY'D YOU DROP ME?"

"I DON'T KNOW! YOU STARTED YELLING AND YOU WERE ANGRY AND I DIDN'T KNOW WHAT TO DO! I'M SORRY!"

"I FORGIVE YOU BUT THAT WASN'T OKAY! DON'T DROP ME AGAIN!"

"THANK YOU! WHY AM I YELLING AT A SIX-YEAR OLD?" Scott threw his hands up in the air.

"OH YEAH? WELL WHY AM I YELLING AT…A HOWEVER OLD YOU ARE?"

"WE NEED TO STOP YELLING!"

"YEAH, 'CAUSE I CAN HEAR YOU NOW!" Larimar was trying her hardest to keep a straight face but she couldn't help breaking into laughter.

Scott wiped off some spit that landed on his face and started chuckling. He snorted a little bit which made them both laugh even harder. "You know, I forreal thought the glass would break!"

"It can't break. Bun Bun told me that it's re-in…re-en-for…it's really strong. She said it's really strong."

"Huh, that's cool. So tell me how you were able to spit when you said 'yeah cause I can hear you now'. I wasn't sensing any part of that that could even remotely cause somebody to spit, so what happened kid?"

"Bun Bun makes fun of me for that too! She says it's cute, but I know she's just trying to make me feel better. You do that too." Her laughter dissipated; her face slowly grew into sadness.

"Me? Hey, since when did I have to get blamed too?"

"I know something bad happened. The building shaked and the power went out. I think these are the bad things Bun Bun was trying to stop." She picked herself up off the floor and solemnly trudged to the window. She looked on as fire and smoke spread over part of the city, clouding out the nearly collapsed sun. From the high rises to the smallest buildings around, they were turned to rubble and ash. The true impact of the blast couldn't be seen from so high up. Larimar was frozen, staring at the damage with terror in her eyes. There was no rain, there was no snow, there was no wind; nature appeared to be gone. At that moment in time there were only ashes floating through the air. She stood and watched as a handful of ashes scattered past her window. "I'm scared. What if Barry isn't okay? What if Bun Bun isn't okay?"

Scott was at a loss for words. What would he tell her? How would he comfort her? "Hey kid, so you know if Fae keeps any juice in the fridge?" Of course he'd say that. Even worse, he was in the doorway ready to leave.

"Yeah," Larimar sniffled then wiped her nose on her sleeve.

"Oh, my bad. I don't know what I was thinking. Not the kind of juice that *you* drink, it's the adult drinks. Does

Faaghira have any of that? The stuff you can't drink? You know alcohol? She have any of that here?"

"Yeah," she sniffled again. Her voice was trembling. Larimar buried her face in her arms then pressed her forehead against the window.

"Hey...uh...thanks Larimar" Scott quietly exited her room and went downstairs to the fridge. He zeroed in on a mostly-full bottle of red wine that quickly became nearly-empty. Now this poor excuse of a man is looking to get wasted while a little girl is upstairs crying her eyes out! "All of first-" Scott's speech was heavily slurred. "-Larimar is not crying her eyes out; I promise you her eyes are still in her head. And the next one is-" He flat out gave up on the entire sentence. He dragged out one of the stools from under the counter and sat next to it. Yeah, I guess he's done with whatever he was saying.

A stern voice called out from a speaker upstairs, but in his stupor Scott was checking everywhere around him, paranoid it could be right under his nose. He heard them asking if everyone was okay up there. After not hearing a response, the voice said that they were coming up to check on things. Scott realized the voice wasn't from someone that was physically there, but then he got scared at the prospect of answering. It was the concierge; what would he do if he found out that Safira wasn't there? "Hey Larimar, can you get that? I'll give you a dollar."

Scott heard Larimar shuffle her feet across the hallway and go into another room. She quietly answered the call, assuring him that everyone was fine. When the concierge asked why she was crying and Larimar hung up after she said she was thinking about her parents. She dragged her feet down the hall again and went back to her room. Way to go Scott, you're a real hero. "Lay off my back, okay? I'm having a- this is stressful. I think it is. For all of us. I'm drinking for me *and* Larimar, so know that. What was I supposed to do? What's easier for me to fix: somebody crying or me being drunk? Actually, don't answer that," Scott pursed his lips. "It's easier to get a little girl to stop crying."

He chugged the rest of the wine and put the bottle back in the fridge. How courteous. Not telling you what to do, but it would be nice if you tried to not be a jerk to Larimar. "Yeah, yeah, I'll go check on her; I was done anyway." Scott was careful going up the steps since he didn't want to trip and cause a scene…or give me another reason to laugh at him. "Nah, nah, I don't want her to be startled; she's already crying. Plus, I don't want to trip" Scott mumbled. Her door was still open but Scott knocked anyway to get her attention. "Hi Larimar, can I come in?"

"I don't want your dollar; I'm already rich." Larimar was nestled in a cover on a mound of covers. She was still staring out the window; the lower half of her face was buried in the cover to hide the fact that she was crying.

"Yeah…so…hmmm…I guess I should apologize for you being upset by what I said. Did that work?" Of all the people, why does it have to be him? "Ignore that; act like I didn't just say whatever it is that could've possibly made you upset."

"When is Barry coming back?"

"That's a little hurtful." Scott was going to walk in, but he stopped and stayed in the doorway.

"I don't like you."

"Ouch, you really are Fae's sister. Can I come in? I wanna explain some things; I could listen if you'd rather have me do that."

"I can hear you so you don't have to come in." She rested on her side, landing on a mountain of pillows. She was still sniffling, but at least she wasn't staring at the chaos that fell on the city.

"Okay, guess I deserve that. Alright, I'm-you might've

481

guessed that I'm not all that good with kids. Just between us, I'm not all that good with a lot of things. With that considered, I wanted to know if it's okay for me to ask you some things. I figure you don't want to hear much about me, and since I'll be around Fae so much I don't want you to not like me. If it's okay with you, I want to get to know you. You don't have to answer anything you don't want to and I'm not expecting you to think I'm cool or anything. Maybe if you can tolerate me at the least? How do you feel about that?"

The room was so silent that you could hear a pin drop. She eventually responded with a faint "sure," which caused Scott to let out a sigh of relief.

"Great....how'd your parents die?" Wow. Seriously?

"My parents aren't dead. Bun Bun said she put them in another state. She said they were good people who did some really bad things. I don't remember them; she sent them away before I was one. I never met them. Sometimes I wonder what they're like. Bun Bun raised me and she said it isn't hard, but I know it's hard for her. Sometimes she gets really sleepy when we watch movies or have dinner or talk about stuff. I don't get to see her all the time, but she helps a lot of people a lot. She makes a lot of stuff that people use and she's really smart and she's also really nice. I wanna be just like her when I grow up."

"I didn't know that. And I don't blame you; who wouldn't want to be like Fae when they grow up?"

"But you are grown up!" Larimar chuckled a little bit.

"Your sister taught me lots of things; I'm still trying to learn them all. And one of the things you just taught me is that I might have some more growing up to do."

Baron Sugar suddenly appeared in front of Scott. "We must leave now! This building is protected only when Faaghira is present!"

Scott's face scrunched up. "I thought you said-"

"We will leave now!" Sugar picked both of them up and

flew out the window. Within moments they landed in an abandoned grocery store outside of the city. The interior was dusty and decaying, but everything was still standing (somehow). Safira and the remaining members of her squad were the only other people there. Sugar put Larimar and Scott down before checking on Safira and the others. Larimar and Scott sat up against one of the empty shelves; both sat in silence trying to figure out what just happened.

Eventually, Larimar poked Scott's arm and whispered "Do people never grow up? Because that sounds hard."

"Just wait till you start dating!" Scott smiled until he thought about his own love life.

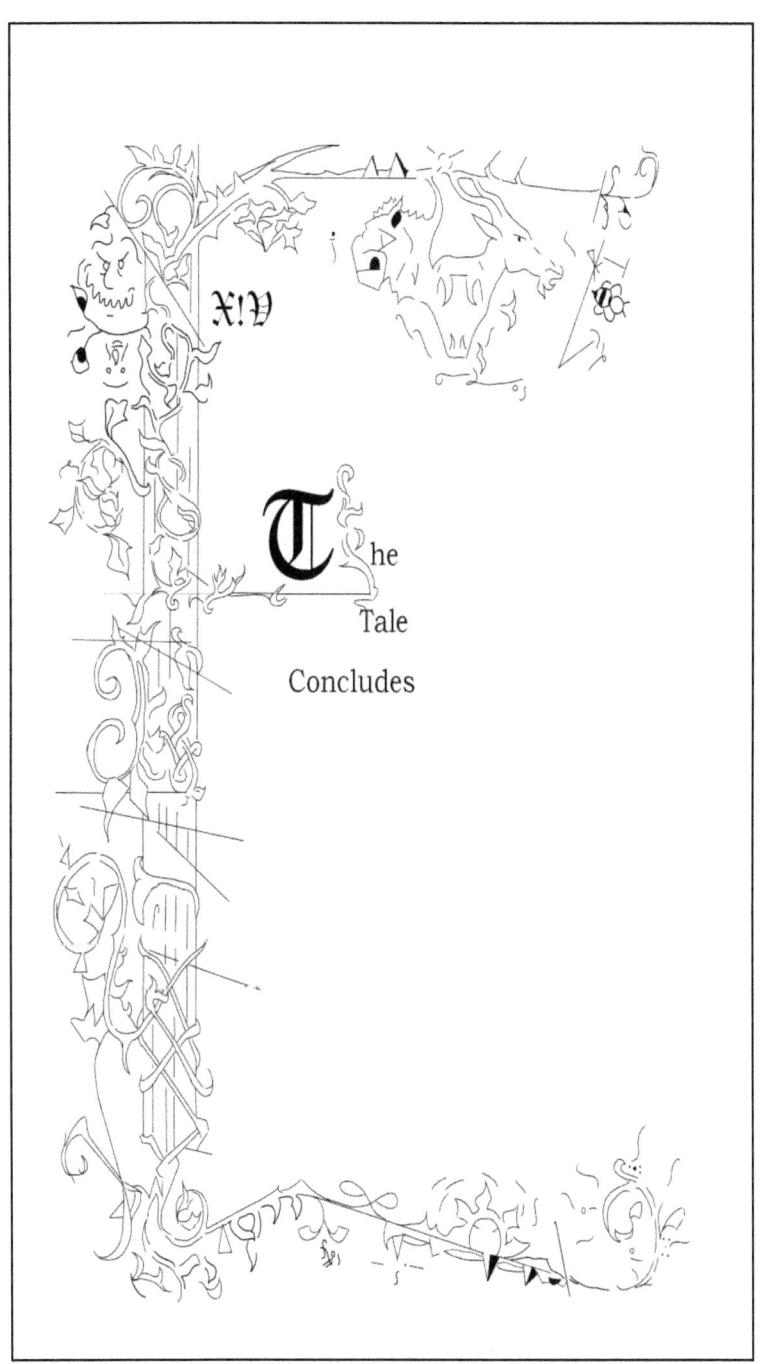

XIV

The

Tale

Concludes

CHAPTER XIV
THE TALE CONCLUDES

The situation was bleak. Part of the city was bombed to dust, Atticus was still in power, and the grocery store smelled kind of bad. One of Safira's squad mates angrily questioned Baron Sugar as to why he didn't save everyone else. Safira watched and shook her head in disappointment.

"To me, this was everyone. Any casualties sustained should be attributed to your leader; they are the one responsible." Baron Sugar looked straight ahead, ignoring the rest of the rebel's antics. However, when their ranting continued past a certain point, Baron Sugar met them with a disheartening stare. "You do not have permission to talk to me. Turn your foolishness elsewhere." The rebel retreated to the area the rest of the squad was gathered in; there's no doubt he was gossiping something in the realm of how tough he was.

"We've got to get back out there! Bellamy is planning on us not doing anything!" Safira intentionally put herself in a spot between Sugar and the four remaining members of the resistance.

"So what then? You'll run back out there just to cry to Baron Sugar that snipers found you again?" Scott's quip almost landed him an express ride to the hospital, courtesy of The Resistance's leader.

"I'm seeing one problem I can handle right now." Safira rolled up her sleeves.

"An action that will not be necessary." Sugar's voice was fiercely stern.

"I want to see her fight! Hit him Safira! Hit him!" Larimar stood up and cheered.

"And the last thing *you* need is encouragement." Sugar looked over at Larimar who was still cheering shamelessly.

Scott nudged Larimar with playful agitation. "Hey! I thought you were supposed to be on my side!"

"Whatever." Safira relaxed her fists and called told two of the rebels to report outside. She told Baron Sugar that she was going to carry out one of the contingency plans her and Fae put together. He took her and her squad to the site she pointed out to him. Sugar returned promptly, but only to take Scott and Larimar back out with him. They soared through the moonlit sky, first going through lush forests then breezing past the extravagant high rises. Soon the sights shifted to the apocalyptic images of dented metal frames left from the buildings that were bombed into submission.

He brought them to City Hall so they could find Fae. As per her agreement with Atticus, it was highly unlikely that she was hurt in any way. There were Peace Officers stationed on the roof and from what they could see through the windows, in every wing. The streets were crowded with people scrambling in every direction in a desperate attempt to find somewhere safe. There were large groups of people flocking to City Hall, but the doors never opened for them. Instead the Peace Officers opened fire on them. A hailstorm of bullets poured down on masses, regardless of where they were headed to.

Baron Sugar gently placed his cloak over Larimar and Scott and pulled off his cloth mask. People were being mowed down left and right. Only a handful of people made it off that block. The Peace Officers put down another barrage when they saw Baron Sugar was still standing. He dissolved into mist then flew up to the roof where the officers were. He rematerialized and stood idly. They were quick to shoot at him; he incinerated them without hesitation. He looked down at the massacre they caused; from the main road to City Hall's steps, everything was stained red. Sugar's face was a fire fueled by rage; the only trace of humanity left was a charred jawbone.

He dropped back down in front of the steps. He warned Larimar to cover her eyes before he picked up his cloak. She did as she was told, but Scott's eyes were subjected to the horrors of corpses piled up all around him. Similar to what he saw at the Junta Jubilee; lives frozen in a brief moment. That image, the atmosphere; it was so much for him that he vomited on the spot.

"Barry, what was that?" Larimar's voice was shaking. She was about to take a peek through her fingers to see what it was.

Sugar's mask formed back over his face within a second. "That was just a bird, Larimar. Keep your eyes covered. He dashed up the steps and rammed the doors down with his back. He incinerated the Peace Officers waiting in the main hall the instant they laid eyes on him. A chilling breeze funneled the remaining ashes and bones outside. "You no longer have to cover your eyes. However, do not look behind you; look straight ahead."

"Where's Scott?"

"...recuperating."

"From what?"

"We will look for your sister. She is safe, we simply have to find her." Sugar gently placed her down on her feet.

"How will Scott know where to find us?"

"I will leave a trail for him. I promise to you that he will be fine." They walked down the corridor to the east wing which is where Larimar said the side broadcasts were recorded. She wanted to stop show him every painting and vase they passed by, but Baron Sugar gently reminded her that they didn't have much time. Meanwhile, Scott was still catching his breath outside. After much deliberation, he wiped his mouth on his jacket's sleeve and threw it off. He tried not to pay any mind to the scattered ashes and charred bones that were pushed outside by the wind. He almost tripped on the door Sugar knocked down. The floors were polished with a mirror finish, something that was different from the last time he was there. And as Sugar promised, a black line on the floor ran through the east wing to where he and Larimar went.

"Oh for real? Barry promised to leave behind a trail for me?" Yeah but don't let him hear you call him Barry. Did you see what he did to those people who shot at him? "He threw that cover over me and Larimar, how would I have seen anything? It was weird under there; it was surprisingly very spacious and we couldn't hear what was going on outside. It was also kind of boring so Larimar asked me what my friends are like and I froze." Why'd you freeze? "What was I supposed to say? My life's complicated; what part of that am I supposed to talk about with a six-year old?" I don't know, you could've said how they're nice or something. Look, you need to get moving; if I don't do my job then bad things could happen. "Dude, dead people, literal war; this is already bad." It'll get worse if you don't get moving. "Oh wow, I better follow this arrow so I can catch up with Barry and Larimar."

The arrow led him to a large theatre with countless rows of empty leather seats. He scanned the room until he found something that-oh snap, Daphne is in one of the seats! "For real? Where's she at?" In one of the back rows to your right. "Oh yeah I see her. Give me one second, alright?" Um, okay? "Daphne! Yo Daphne! It's me! It's Scott! Whatchu doin' here?"

Daphne was sitting back with her kicks propped up over the seat in front of her. She had her headphones in, grooving to whatever she was listening to. She did a double take when she saw Scott trying to get her attention. She took off her headphones slowly, still in disbelief that he was actually there. "Faaghira really needs to come get her man," she muttered to herself. "Dude, why'd you find me?"

"I came here to find Faaghira and I saw you sitting way

over there."

"But why'd you find *me*?"

"You should come over here so we don't have to keep yelling at each other. Baron Sugar and Larimar are somewhere here too."

"Word? Where's Larimar at? She's mad cool." She got up to meet Scott at the path between the aisles.

Scott told Daphne he was in the process of looking for them; she underhandedly mentioned she wasn't surprised he couldn't find them. After reminding Scott she hadn't seen them, he suggested they search together. She passively agreed, but only on the terms that he didn't try to make any small talk. He followed the arrow to the backstage and into a clean white hallway. Daphne asked him why he kept looking at the floor while he walked and he gave one of his generically awkward responses that would get her to stop talking.

It took going up two flights of stairs to find Larimar and Sugar, who had already found Fae a while ago by this point. She was sitting in a corner of the debate room with her legs curled up and her arms wrapped around her knees. Larimar was leaned against Fae, having locked her arm around her sister's. Baron Sugar was…present; he stood by the door but didn't do much else.

"Hey Faaghira. Hi Larimar! How are you?" Daphne excitedly ruined what was an obvious moment of grief. Larimar waves halfheartedly while Fae didn't respond at all. This is what must've given Daphne a clue. "What's wrong?"

"Anything I try; I do everything I can just for it to spit in my face in the end." Fae stared off into nowhere. The only other thing she did was loosen her grip around Larimar's arm. Scott went to sit on the floor with her. It was awkward because when is it not with him, but endearing nonetheless.

"Fae, you didn't do anything wrong. There's no need to cry; I'm here for you, okay?" Scott leaned his head on her shoulder.

"I know I didn't do anything wrong and I'm not crying, but if I was then that wouldn't be a problem. Did no one tell you that it's okay to cry or do you have to be taught everything?" Fae was calm, but her words stung Scott so bad that he moved away from her discretely. Daphne offered to leave, but Fae told her not to. "I have to leave anyway; Atticus is around here somewhere. He ducked out after the missile dropped, but he didn't go far. This is the safest place in the city right now; he knows he could get caught in crossfire if he goes out there. He has a bunker down in the basement, but there's also a safe room two floors up. I'd bet he's in the bunker, but he has cameras everywhere and monitors in both, so we shouldn't all our money on one thing and get it wrong."

"Okay, me and Daphne will check upstairs." Scott called out without the slightest bit of hesitation.

"That leaves Shaggy, Velma, and I to check downstairs." Fae laughed dryly for a brief moment, but afterwards it was as if it never happened. Larimar giggled which made Baron Sugar begin to wonder why he didn't understand the joke. They split in their groups, Scott leading the way to the safe room and Fae led her sister and Sugar to the bunker. Of course, Scott had no idea where the safe room was but he stumbled his way into everything else so far, so why would this be any different. Still, he was eager to get up the staircase until Daphne mentioned the likelihood of heavy security. His excitement died down but he didn't turn back (there's also the thing of having nowhere else to go).

Surprisingly, nobody else was there; it's like all the officers he saw from outside disappeared. There were only two rooms to check and no one was in either of them. The safe room was up there, monitors and all; just like Fae said. There was also a mini-fridge with a full bottle of red wine and a bag of chips. It soon became an *empty* mini fridge after

Scott stocked up on what he claimed to be trauma care supplies. "It would be a tyrant like Atticus who would put a bag of chips in a fridge."

"You're taking the whole bottle of wine?"

"One drop for each of my problems. And what else do you expect me to do? Am I supposed to pour some in a cup and leave the rest?"

"You're not even old enough to drink. I should be the one drinking that."

"The law is just a societal construction. Here you go baby, you can have the cold chips." He twisted of off the cap, took a loud sip of wine then handed Daphne the bag of chips.

"You wouldn't be so bad if you were older."

"You're saying that like I'd change in two or three years. Hey, since we didn't find anyone up here that means Atticus is in the basement."

"Faaghira said it was a bunker; and this whole idea of me jumping into the same place as the most dangerous person probably in the whole continent- I'm not really feeling that. Him not being where I looked is a sign for me to dip."

"There's a war going on outside; you'll probably get killed. Dying seems to be a real big thing around here; everybody's doing it." Scott took his bottle with him, and it didn't take long for Daphne to follow him again. She made a hollow joke about how much better the weather was inside City Hall. They went to the other wing after getting back to the main floor (it says in the author's notes that they could've went straight across from one of the upper floors). The guards he saw in the west wing through the window outside were on the floor now (along with a few others he didn't see earlier). They were all alive, but it's like they were glued to the floor. Scott tried picking one of them up (not that he was strong enough), but they didn't budge.

"That's weird."

"Lately, everyone's weird became my normal." He found

the next sets of stairs and descended until they met back up with the others at the bunker. Kasabian and Safira were there too. Atticus sealed himself behind a door and had enough explosives within the building to bring it down on everyone.

"If either of my nieces leave then I'm setting off every bomb in City Hall, so you better not move." Atticus sounded extremely pleasant over the intercom (aside from the content of words). He could be heard munching on kettle corn and it sounded like there was some bossa nova playing in the background.

"We know; you already said that." Safira was working on getting the door open while Kasabian searched frantically for any explosives that could be around them. Baron Sugar could have done both of these without a problem, but he wasn't sure if how sensitive the explosives were, and he knows doesn't have a clean record of pulling punches. Larimar said she wanted to watch a show, but he doesn't like using his powers that much in one day unless he deems it absolutely necessary. He suggested that they tell each other stories instead. Since Fae didn't have to watch over her sister, she was free to make some calls she had been putting off.

It wasn't long until Fae had to interrupt Larimar's storytelling to get Sugar's attention. "Sorry Elle, but I have to tell Barry something important."

"Why can't I hear too?"

"Because you're…no, you're right." Fae sighed heavily. She made sure that Safira and Kasabian were still occupied, afterwards she continued. "Atticus…he's not behind the door; he's not here at all. Safira and Kas would be pissed if I told them. Also, Kas might think that I was in on it and try to kill us. Barry, I need you to go to one of his mansions and bring him back here; Scott knows the one I'm talking about. Make sure you take him with you; knowing him, he'll try to 'fix' something and get us killed. Plus, I don't want him drinking around Larimar. Elle, stay away from alcohol, but if you ignore that and try it anyway when you get older, don't drink so much, okay?"

Sugar went to go get Scott who was sitting off to the side somewhere, nodding off in a pleasant stupor. Sugar carried him over to Fae so she could tell him about- "Faaghira, why is your skin patchy in some places. I mean, you're still hot...so yeah?"

"I have vitiligo; why is this important now?"

"I wanted to...does it make you feel bad being different?"

"Scott, I need you to go with Sugar and show him where the mansion is; it's the same one we went to."

"Sometimes I feel bad being different...you really think I can find where it is?"

"I'm counting on you; I can't leave."

"I won't let you down. Scratch that; I'll do my best but we'll see how that goes." Scott shrugged. Fae pointed to where the blind spot for the cameras was so Sugar would know where to teleport from. Her and Larimar waved goodbye discretely, but they didn't say anything so that they wouldn't draw in any attention. Baron Sugar appeared in the sky with Scott clinging on to his back. He waited patiently for Scott to point out a location and went in that direction without a second thought...

...Every time Scott pointed out a place. See, he wasn't pointing to the mansion the first time around; he spotted a liquor store he wanted to check out, but of course Baron Sugar didn't know that. Scott came up with a (poor) justification for each stop. First there was "I'm almost out of wine and I need it for trauma, then "That girl looks like someone I know. She was cute wasn't she?" and after two other stops, the last one was "I really wanted a burger; I was hungry." Scott had him circling around in the air until he finally spotted the mansion...or at least what he thought was the mansion.

"Yeah that's the place! Right there! It's down there! You see it?" Scott's mouth was stuffed with the hamburger he was chewing. Sugar dove down at a blinding speed, but gracefully landed in front of the front doors. Scott pounded on the door then it was being littered with bullets in the blink of an eye.

Baron Sugar pushed the doors down with one measly breath. Bullets were flying at him, tearing into his clothes. He uttered the word "declined" and none of the bullets could travel further than a few centimeters from the barrels. Next, all of them were frozen in place. They could talk and move their eyes but were otherwise rendered immobile. Scott peaked in at the after the gunfire stopped to see if it was safe. "Why would you knock? They did not know we were here."

"I was angry! They were gonna find out anyway!"

"Your anger nearly cost you your life. *I* am not endangered by your foolishness, you are. I do not want to use these powers; they are not at your disposal." Sugar's voice is normally stern, hence that lack of exclamation marks. He never yells, he just always sounds intimidating. "I am helping you not out of obligation; I seek to rid the world of this demon and prevent his power from spreading back into humanity. I will guarantee your safety up to the completion of my goal, but this is not for you to abuse."

"Let's just find Atticus and get back to Fae; no need for all the yapping." Scott held his head up high and his red wine with a loose grip. Baron Sugar smashed the bottle with his fist and stormed up the main room's opulent staircase. Scott, being the petty person that he is, went in a completely different direction than Sugar. He went looking for the music room Fae showed him the last time he was there. He stumbled every few steps because of the slight limp in his right leg, worsened by the fact that he couldn't walk in a straight line to save his life. He knocked over a vase (allegedly an accident) when he was trying to find the holographic wall the music room was behind.

He eventually resorted to throwing himself at different spots on the wall until he found the entrance to the music room. He was able to make it down the carpeted steps by holding on to the railing. Unfortunately, the door was closed and he never saw the sequence she used on the keypad. Yet another thing he didn't think through. He tried pushing the door open anyway; surprise, it didn't work. He leaned against the wall, staring inside; all those beautifully crafted instruments were teasing him. But there was nothing he could do. "Fae really thought of everything; inventing all this stuff. She's gotta be the smartest person I've ever seen; I'd tell her that if it would make a difference." He curled up on the stairs and kept staring at the instruments on the other side of the glass. Why is he even here?

His sulking was cut short because he was teleported into Atticus Bellamy's office. "This is what we are here for; it is still part of your responsibility." Baron Sugar stood firm with his arms crossed. He had the cloth sack back on his head, but this time it had a blank expression instead of the normal dopey smile and goofy eyes. The office had the elegance and space of a ballroom but was filled with tributes to Atticus, whether by paintings or awards. There was no furniture aside from the chairs that hugged the corners of the room, his desk, and his chair that was, at that moment, overlooking the city. The large windows were sealed shut but the curtains flowed as if wind was winding them around.

"Atticus Bellamy, you're under arrest! Huh, I've always wanted to say that."

"Scott Blue, you're fresh outta luck." Roswell, The Demon rolled out from behind the curtains. He wore an annoyingly fake smile from the time he got off the floor to when he looked at Scott and Sugar. He spun Atticus' chair around and revealed a man who was beaten so brutally that he was almost unrecognizable. "Hi guys. Sugar, how've you been? How are the kids?"

"Why are *you* here?" Sugar's mask burned until his jaw and the raging fire that surrounded it were all that were left.

"Same reason you are; he was getting pretty annoying, wasn't he?"

"Was?" Scott was getting queasy. "Don't tell me that you kil-"

"M'kay, I won't, but who do you think you're looking at? The Archduke- nah, never mind; I'm pretty sure that one's been used to death by now." Roswell sat on the blood-stained desk with one leg crossed over the other and his eyes peeking over his shoulder.

Scott shuddered upon getting a closer look at what used to be president Bellamy. Some of the only ways to tell for sure it was Atticus is because of his suit and how tall he was. "What did you do?"

"I punched his face in; sucker was ruining my story. I had this whole spiel set up about good and evil; what drives someone past their limits-" The demon got off the desk and put his hands in his pockets. "-But then I find out this guy was constantly putting up things I didn't plan for. Let's be honest, there was no way he was getting to the end of this story alive." Scott sharply turns away from the corpse dressed in white. "Peep this; lemme show you something here."

Atticus' face healed and he sprung back to life. The first thing he saw was the demon's wicked smile. "No! No!" Atticus panicked, his heart raced furiously; beads of sweat ran down his forehead. "Get away from me you freak!"

"Freak? That's the best you got?" The demon spoke calmly. "Hold up, I'll get back to you on that one later; I gotta show 'em what I did first." Roswell picked Atticus up by his forehead and slammed him onto the desk. Each of his punches left behind an increasingly louder echo. "See, dude was going around like- you know tryna be a god and all that shit." He was relentless; blood was splattering all over his clothes, but his voice was horrifyingly calm. "That in itself doesn't bother me cause you either got it or you don't; that's not something you ascend to."

The sound of bones cracking fell away and was replaced by mush. Blood splattered on the window and the curtains. The demon's laugh was pleasant. Oddly enough, the only other emotion he showed was mild annoyance. I personally would be more comfortable if he got angry for once like everyone else. "See, mans was ruining my story; tried to make it his own. I'm running on a tight schedule and interferences aren't cute." Atticus was back to that grotesque state, slumped on the desk. "And then he looked something like this. Of course, I put him back in the chair *before* I was done, but you get the picture, right?"

Scott shivers at the sight; Baron Sugar stands firmly in silence. Scott's immediate reaction was to take a few swigs from his bottle of red wine, but he was quickly reminded that Sugar broke it. Despite this, the top of the bottle never left his grip. Cuts from the glass stretched along the bottom of his right hand; he still didn't let go. "Why didn't you stop him? We were supposed bring Atticus back alive!"

Baron Sugar stood still, but there was restlessness in his demeanor; it's like something was holding him back. "For the turmoil that man was said to have caused, even I would not save him. Why did you do nothing?"

"I don't have any powers, unlike *somebody* here."

Roswell threw off his jacket and pulled out another from his pocket. He zipped it up and clasped the buttons over its side, then ruffled the faux fur surrounding the collar. It was identical to his old one, minus the poorly painted smiley face and blood stains. "He's pretty useless. Just about anyone else in the world would be a better main character, but on the bright side, he's in a story that needs him more than his parents do."

Scott's breathing was rapid; he was caught in a space between fear and fury. He swung at Roswell, with the remains of the bottle and the demon dodged it effortlessly. He put his hand over Scott's face and pushed it to the ground. "Remember when you said you'd find a way to kill me? *We're still waiting on that.*" Roswell knelt next to Scott and patted his nose. "You didn't have any powers then either, but you had anger. Given the fact that you had no idea who you were talking to, what you said is still very bold. So for your sake *and everyone else's*, you better find a way to kill me." The demon raised his head and waved to Baron Sugar. "Better look out for your friend here. They didn't see you on the cameras, just him. When Atticus turns up dead, they'll have just one person to blame. Hey Scottie, on the bright side, there'll finally be a lot of people out there that want you. *You'll love the way this one ends...unless you find a way to stop me.*" The demon gently shut the door on his way out.

Baron Sugar stood unmoving. He looked at the disfigured body that used to be Atticus. "I have to get you to safety. I do not know what the demon has planned, but you must avoid it. You should be safe with Faaghira for some time. I will do what is necessary to end the vile actions of this demon."

"You'll kill him?" Scott sounded like he was caught between hope and fear.

"If possible."

"Why don't you go after him now?"

"I will be right back." Baron Sugar left to find Roswell, but Scott tagged along because he didn't want to be alone around the leader's dead body. Turns out that Roswell was right outside in the hallway.

"You're still here? I thought you would've teleported or something." He was on the floor, clutching his stomach. "If you're wanting to kill me then you can go ahead; I've been in the market for a replacement. Everything will be rectified; the world will be saved. It'll be like what you did the first time, Sugar. Don't worry, I'll say hi to your family for you. Remind me again, how old would your brother have been if you didn't drown him? Oh, my bad they'd all be long dead by now. Looks like you did a favor and saved them some time." Roswell got up slowly, smiled, then disappeared though a portal. Baron Sugar let him get away and took Scott back to Faaghira to tell her what happened.

Faaghira was redoing Larimar's braids when they told her the news. A heavy sorrow dropped on her, though she was still focused on fixing her sister's hair. "...People will be looking for Scott; mostly to thank him, but he'll have the whole government trying to snuff him out. Hmmm...it won't be a popular move, but I can appoint myself acting president, make up a charge then pardon him of all crimes."

"How will you surpass the next person in line?" Sugar

"Nepotism. I am the next person in line; it's part of a deal I tricked him into signing off on. He respected that I outsmarted him, so he went with it. Besides, I already made copies."

"An oversight they will no doubt regret."

"I don't want to keep the position, so make sure Scott's out of here soon."

"What position?" Safira picked up on the conversation and got curious, which in turn made Kas suspicious. They got the bunker door open, so they already knew Atticus wasn't there. Fae explained that he was killed but left out the details on how it happened. She also reluctantly explained that she'd be assuming the position of president. Surprisingly, Kas didn't give much of a fuss. He told Fae to lead wisely and make sure The Junta dies too, then promptly removed himself from City Hall.

"Your request will be fulfilled. Roswell will still be a

looming threat; however, I will handle this upon my return." Sugar was ready to take Scott away, but his efforts were met with protest.

"Don't I get a say in this?! Fae, you can't be serious! Are you ready to just throw me away like that?!"

"Goodbye Scott," Faaghira spoke halfheartedly; she was focused on re-twisting her sister's braids. Larimar waved and said goodbye before Baron Sugar teleported Scott to the grounds he went to with Fae after leaving the Junta Jubilee.

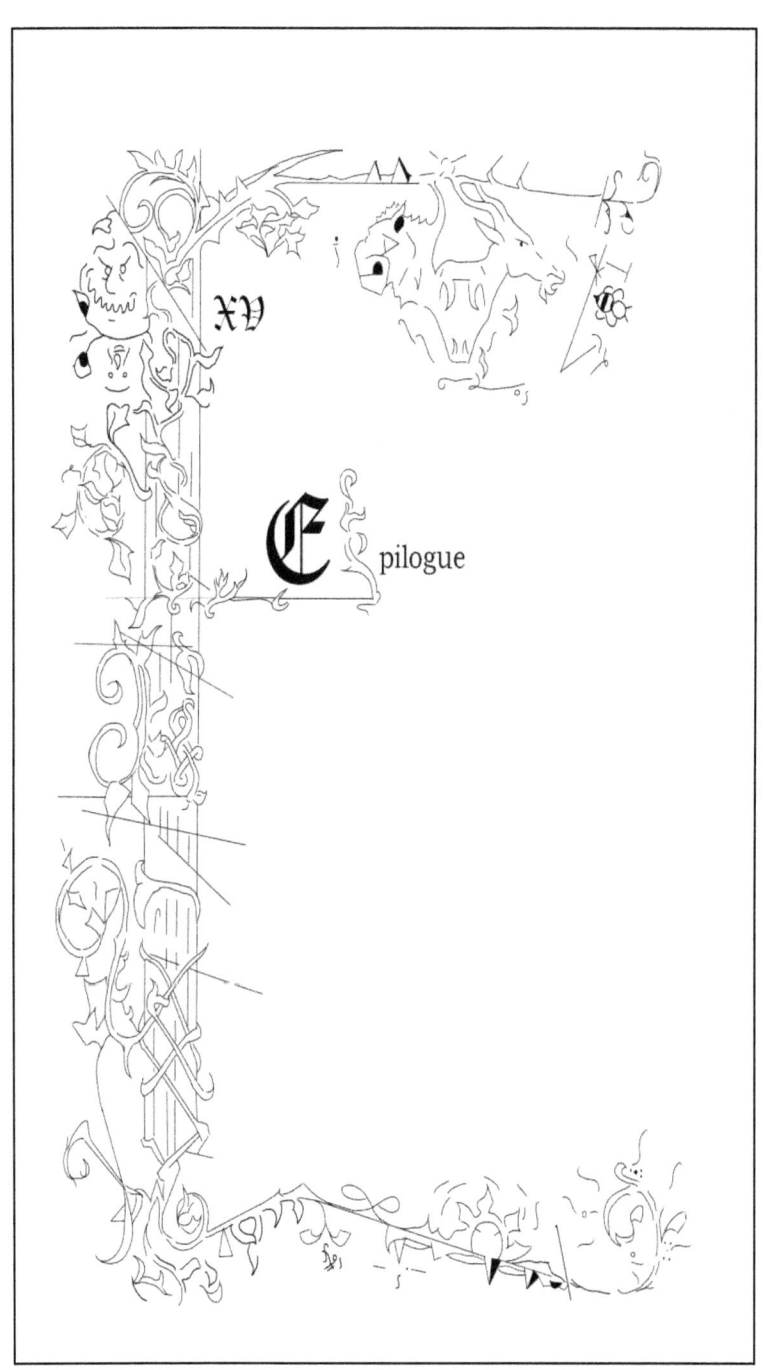

XV

$\mathfrak{E}$pilogue

CHAPTER XV
EPILOGUE

"Man, look at this place. I haven't been here since…how long since we left that party?"

"*We?*"

"Uh…oh…right. When Fae drove here and jumped out the car."

"Ah yes, I remember that. I healed her arms; she was in great pain. Unfortunately, this is the only place that I can return you to your home without an extensive use of my powers. As I am left with no other choice, I take it that this location was reintroduced for plot convenience. The demon is getting much lazier." Before they could go in Baron Sugar's house, they were teleported back to the city center.

"Why'd you being us back here?" Scott got agitated.

"I am not the cause of this. Watch your tone." But he's still wise enough to back down when Baron Sugar got on him.

"So why are we here then?" Okay, maybe he hasn't learned that much after all.

"It must be the demon." Sugar teleported them back to his estate, but they were brought back to the city center within a second. "What foolishness is this?"

"Hey man, stop buggin; stop bringing me here!" Scott backpedaled when it looked like Sugar was ready to tear him apart. "Ight, ight, how about this: I'll break up with Iris if you take me back home. That's what you wanted me to do, right?"

"As I said, this is not my doing. However, I find it interesting that you now refer to your dimension as your home."

"I mean, *it isn't*. I've got nowhere to go, but I don't want to die! I see the writing on the wall. They'll hunt me if I stay here; I'm not an idiot!" Scott observed the beautiful buildings and glistening lights around him, but none of that was enough to overshadow the weight of the chaos that encapsulated the city in that moment.

"It is unfortunate that it took this predicament for you to rea-"

"And once Fae fixes everything I'll be able to come back." Scott spoke with a sense of pride.

"You are an idiot."

"Look, matchstick, only fine girls get to call me an idiot and even then, I don't always let it slide!" Oh boy. Scott must have the attention span of a doorknob.

"I sincerely hope there will come a day when I will not regret helping you." Scott threw a little tantrum while Baron Sugar kept his cool, but for the people crowds of people that were still outside there was only one thing worth paying attention to. The sky was torn open by a beam of energy, but nothing happened beyond that.

Even Scott and Sugar got curious about; it was the center of everyone's attention. A jasper eye dripped out of a nearby fire hydrant, enveloped Scott, then dissipated into pixels. Now, Sugar wasn't too distracted to notice this, but he was hesitant to do anything but stare. He went back to City Hall and looked for Fae to tell her what just happened. People were blowing up her phone with texts and various notifications telling her about the whole in the sky, but she told Sugar she thought it was just him taking Scott home. She already sent Larimar with Safira to a safehouse outside of the city to keep her out of harm's way.

"This is my fault for not acting when I should have."

"Was it Roswell?"

"No, there is another with his power."

"There's more than one? Why is there more of *him*? Anybody could've been cloned, and it just *had* to be him. Why couldn't it be me? I'm supposed to get sworn in soon and I really don't want to do this."

"It is not a clone. Roswell hates them also."

"Doesn't matter to me who that asshole hates, I have a city to run now. Since Scott's back home where he should be, you don't need my help. That whole superpower battle thing you have going on is way above my pay grade, and nobody's richer than me." Oops, looks like Baron Sugar forgot to mention something.

"Scott was abducted before I could bring him back to his home. I did not notice until the being was nearly gone. I was under the impression that something would spawn from the opening in the clouds."

"So how do we get him back?" Faaghira quickly sent a text then stood up, ready to leave.

"I will get him back; you will do nothing. Your duty is to your people. You are to be sworn in soon."

"I just texted the Junta commission that I just appointed myself acting president; I'll go through all the formalities later. All due respect, you're ridiculous if you think I'm not going with you."

"If it is knowledge you seek, then I will question the demon and relay that information to you. However, if you want to take action then I highly advise against it."

"Look, if Scott's in trouble then I'm going to do what I can. I'm not asking for your permission, I'm asking for your help." Fae sized him up and crossed her arms.

"And how would you find the demon without my help?"

"Try me and I'll find a way."

"If you are truly so determined then accompany me to see the demon in his home."

"That means Roswell, right? Or are you talking about the one that took Scott?"

"Roswell."

"Can you just call him Roswell instead of 'the demon'? It's pretty confusing."

"Apologies. That demon is no man, but I will use his given name for your convenience." They were warped through a void of eight-bit clouds and poorly drawn flowers until they were on an empty grid that stretched endlessly in every direction.

"This is my house, The Orange Triangle Of Regret. It's not orange *or* a triangle; it's an old name I made, and I couldn't come up with anything better. To believe I used to think this was cool." Roswell was on a step ladder, pinning a banner over his silver throne. Of course, since this was Roswell the banner wasn't being pinned to anything.

"Where's Scott?" Fae grunted.

"It's funny how I never invited *any* of the people who show up at my house." He got down from the step ladder and sat on his throne.

"I don't have time for your games." Fae was fierce.

"He's obviously not here. Give me a second and I'll get back to you; I have to go do a thing." Roswell was back up, though he struggled to get out of his chair. He walked far off to one side of the grid and returned on the other side with a walking stick made of oak.

"Since when did you need a walking stick? You could easily fly if you so desired." Baron Sugar carried suspicion in his voice.

"I'm trying the whole walking stick thing out this chapter; wanted to see what all the rage was about. So why are you here?" Roswell sat back down in his throne.

"Something took Scott when I was trying to bring him back to his home."

"Tell me what this thing that took Scott looks like."

"An eye; it was made of Jasper."

"A jasper eye? This sounds like the handy work of my least favorite supernatural being."

"Why would you accuse me of this? I would not-" Sugar's defense was interrupted.

507

"No, not you, my *other* least favorite. Why are you pressed over what I said? Don't tell me you have feelings all of a sudden. It's Terbold; you know who that is, Sugar."

"Does this make it any harder to get Scott back?" Fae asked sternly.

"He's the only real thorn in my side; he vies for my power. Though, if he were anything like you, Sugar, we wouldn't be having this problem. He's got a silly name, but he's the carrier of unadulterated evil. I might've been proud of him if he wasn't trying to kill me and take my job. Overall, this won't be too difficult for me if I have some time to plan things out." Roswell rested the walking stick on his lap.

"Will you help us or not?" Fae sighed.

"Just to be clear, I'm not a hero. I don't care to save anyone from that loser. This time, and only this one time, it serves me twofold. He'll be out of my hair and I can go back to what I was doing. If and only if you agree to help me kill Terbold will I help you rescue Scott. We can seal the deal with a hug; handshakes are too cliché." Roswell used the walking stick to prop himself up then stretched his arms out wide. He was smiling for so long that it got really awkward.

Fae leaned to the side slightly to whisper to Sugar. "Don't you have the same powers as Roswell? Can't you rescue Scott and get out of there?"

"He won't do what needs to be done. He's physically capable of doing everything I can, but there's no way he'd actually do it. He knows it too; you can ask him right now if you want. You don't have any powers, so you got your choice. Make a deal with me or die an early death. Take all the time you need, but hurry up because this is time sensitive." Fae sighed then extended her arms begrudgingly. The demon gave a gentle hug, then looked at Baron Sugar and motioned for him to do the same. "Come on and get in on this! It's not official till you do it too!" Sugar was initially unwilling to move.

"If I have to do it, so do you." Fae's no-nonsense attitude got Sugar to agree. Roswell gently hugged them both and whispered, "After we kill Terbold, I'ma beat both ya asses." Afterwards, he let go.

"I wish I could be surprised, I really do." Fae sighed yet again.

"I will see to your death after Scott is recovered." Baron Sugar still has a very dry delivery, but I'm sure he had some emotion deep down somewhere.

"Man, now I'll be sad if you don't go through with it! Now whadd'ya say? Want to work together till I screw you over?" Roswell grinned.

"Nah, not really." Fae shrugged.

"There is no way I would ever want to." It's assumed that Sugar frowned.

"Wonderful! Can't blame you; I wouldn't want to work with me either. Heard through the grapevine that I'm a real asshole." He swiped the air with his index and middle fingers which caused a miniature black hole to appear. "Well then, off we trot."

XV!

Seriously,

When will

This

End

CHAPTER XVI
SERIOUSLY, WHEN WILL THIS END?

Scott was in a steel chair with his legs and torso chained down. The air around him was dry, the atmosphere was dreary. He was in a dilapidated factory. With the sound of an industrial engine, all the lights turned on and gears brought all the machinery to life. He desperately tried to wriggle free from his chair, but he ended falling on the floor. Scott crawled out of the light, away from the conveyor belts in that were in front of him. The chair dragged across the floor, adding to the shrieks and grinding from that projected though the factory. He didn't know where he was going, but he was determined to get somewhere, anywhere else.

He pushed off the floor and bashed the chair's legs against the side of one of the engines; its back and legs were bent. He tried to pull the chains off his torso since his hands were free, but they weren't loose enough to move. He put in all that effort and exhausted himself for nothing. A distorted howl layered with a bloodcurdling wail drowned the cries of the engine. A green chimera emerges from the shadows; it moved in a slow, calculated rhythm. "There's no need to play a fool anymore. Roswell's coming for you. Go on and use your powers to get out of those chains. We have time before Roswell comes to get you back."

Scott was paralyzed with fear; the only thing he could manage was mumbling "what the fuck?" seven times.

"Dammit, I said to stop playing games! Use the powers Roswell gave you to get out of the chains!" The chimera roared.

"What powers?! Roswell never gave me powers!" Scott's heart rate was increasing sharply.

"Liar!" The chimera roared again, but this time there was a devastating power behind it. "You are lying to me!"

"Why are you acting like it's normal to be a monster and chain people to chairs in a musty factory?!" Scott stuttered, but still tried to show some aggressiveness amid his panic.

"Why are you calling me a monster? I didn't do anything bad. Is any of this unusual to you?" The chimera spoke in a mocking, yet sinister voice.

"You're a chimera!"

"But I didn't do anything bad." The chimera teased.

"I'm chained to a steel chair! None of this is normal!"

Terbold dragged Scott back into the light. "Even though you're trying to fool me- no that doesn't matter. I'll show you why you're here." Car parts moved down the assembly lines, but nothing got put together. "Can't you see what's missing? Workers! There is nothing without them! Do you see how barren this is? How useless this is?" With one vicious roar, the parts run through the assembly line faster and were machined into a sleek green convertible. "Do you see what's possible with solid machinery and some team work?"

Scott gulped then cleared his throat. "I don't-I didn't see any team work. That was literally just you doing telekinesis." He laughed nervously.

The chimera's goat head stared him down and the cobra hissed viciously. "There is nothing like hard work!" The lion roared and pounded its fist on the rugged floor. It yanked parts of the assembly lines and crudely mashed them together. "And Teamwork!" The chimera banged its fists on the pile of metal. "The blood, sweat, and tears." The heap of metal goes through a very sloppy transformation process that turns it into a luxury car with the atomic age design reminiscent of the nineteen-fifties. "Things like this could only happen because of American ingenuity! Not that you would know anything about that. Never seen a blackie that could handle this kind of work."

"A racist chimera; that's new."

"Things were good; the best they've ever been. I think it's a hoot that I lost my job, everything, when employers here weren't had right to say that they only wanted the best taken away from them. It's more than a little funny how the whole industry here started going downhill when you started putting yourselves in places you didn't belong. "

"Damn, I know people like to blame me for everything, but I ain't have a single thing to do with you getting fired."

"Making jokes; what else could I expect? If you keep provoking me then you'll need to use those powers I know you're hiding!"

Scott cleared his throat. "I already told you that I don't have any powers! Let me go!"

"Or do you not know how to use them? I'll tell you a story. This was nineteen fifty-eight; that's around five years ago in case you can't count. My wife took my kids and left because I was laid off; she wanted to take it to court but she knew I'd say no; she knows I'm a fighter. A squirrel broke into my house and while I was having dinner, but I was always ready to defend myself. I got my hunting rifle from the fireplace and was ready to shoot. This thing opened its mouth and Roswell jumped right out. I shot him and he spit the bullet right out. Then he took my gun and turned it into a bunch of flowers. He called my dinner bland then he said he'd give me powers like his. He did after I shook his hand, but he never showed me how to use my powers; I had to learn on my own. He said he'd show me if I beat him in a mountain chopping contest. He said that I'd be put in a different dimension and timeline if I lost, so of course he cheated and broke my wrist. I got a new name since then, but that's the honest truth."

Baron Sugar, Roswell, and Faaghira appeared through a miniature black hole.

"Square up man, I'm coming to get you." Roswell pointed at Terbold with finger guns.

"Wow it's musty in here!" Fae held her nose and swatted the air in front of her.

"What is this place?" Baron Sugar sounded extremely confused.

"Detroit." The chimera hissed proudly.

"*His* version of Detroit; this is not at all what Detroit looks like. Pretty cool for a fanfiction though," Roswell laughed obnoxiously.

"What is...Detroit?" Sugar crossed his arms; his confusion sounded just as serious as he always does. Fae looked facepalmed, Roswell smiled proudly, and of course, Terbold was furious.

"I would say something smart, but you barely have your house; you've been a recluse for over two hundred years, so I'll let you off easy." Roswell nudged Sugar's arm.

"Letting me off easy? You truly are gracious."

"You mock me in my own home! Detroit is what I know! I won't let you spit on everything I love; everything I worked for; everything I'll get back!" Terbold pounced at Baron Sugar, but Roswell grabbed the lion by the throat and slammed its face into the ground. Meanwhile, Fae ran to Scott to see if he was hurt.

"What did that thing do to you?"

"Can't you tell?" Scott shivered and breathed heavily. "It was just some light foreplay, but I'm glad you showed up when you did."

"Faaghira, darling-" Roswell called out to her, "-the deal goes first. Step over here and help, will ya?"

"Sorry, I have to go." Fae propped Scott up against a table that was far away enough for him to be safe. She ran to Terbold held on to the goat's horns, pulled herself up, and stomped on its head. The cobra swoops in to bite her, but Baron Sugar intercepted it. He pried its jaws open and turned it to ash.

"Enough!" Terbold struggled to get up, but it gathered

enough strength to emit a wave of energy that destroyed the entire factory. Ten copies of him materialized from the atmosphere. It was revealed that they were somewhere in space on an unfamiliar moon.

"What the-" Fae was extremely confused, but who could blame her? This keeps getting so much weirder.

"Have we been in space this whole time?" Baron Sugar sounded just as confused as Fae.

"Is this how you wanted to greet your kids? That's what you wanted to dish out to your wife? You couldn't even make your own dimension; you had to get a moon far out in one of mine. This is basically like crashing in my house. I did a pretty good job though; this galaxy is beautiful!" Unsurprisingly, the only one who was excited was Roswell. Terbold shouted at the demon to be quiet (and all its clones repeated it). "You can't even beat me though, so I'll just put you out of your misery. You've nothing to gain and nothing to lose but your life; make this easy on all of us, will ya?"

Three of Terbold's clones surrounded Scott; each holding fury their eyes. "I have what you want! I've realized how to use these powers since the *decades* you abandoned me! But there are still things you know that I don't! Show me what I need to know to get my family back; to get me life back! Show me or I'll kill him! I'll tear him limb from limb!"

Roswell yawned, and all the chimera's clones melted. "You don't threaten me, loser. I made the ground you're standing on; I made you what you are. Nah, I'll backpedal on that; I'm not responsible for that ugly ass makeover." The chimera created dozens more clones…that the demon wiped out of existence with two weak punches. "You can start putting up a fight anytime you want, just so you know." Roswell put on an obnoxious smile. The chimera grew to the size of a titan, but it was having an even harder time standing up. It limped when it walked and its muscles were strained. "Okay, Sugar, Faaghira, do that one thing that I told you about."

The chimera increased the gravity within a small radius to protect itself. Nobody moved; the defense was a waste. The titan wheezed momentarily, but it eventually regained its composure.

"Hi guys." Scott called out nervously from under the table Fae propped him up against. "I'm still over here, you know…in case you wanted to know. I still exist."

"We didn't forget about you, just hold tight." Fae attempted comfort him from a distance since he was so far, but it didn't give off warmth like she'd hoped. Baron Sugar jets of lava from his face (did I mention this book is weird) that left the giant chimera's limbs severely burned. It slumped over and crashed into the moon's surface. "This was *very* anti-climactic."

"And look at this thing! No one can tell when I get hit, but you burn this embarrassment and it actually has the audacity to show it off! Pathetic!" Terbold's wounds were miraculously healed, but it no longer had the strength to stand. Roswell nodded at Sugar and Fae. "You did your part; I'll handle the rest." His fist glowed with a dark red aura; it pulled in matter from the stars and planets behind him. He threw one powerful punch…but he stopped himself before it connected. The chimera shielded with all its might, but it all amounted to nothing. Terbold shriveled and started rotting as it gasped for air.

Roswell broke off one of the goat's horns and stabbed the chimera repeatedly. "Eh, I'm bored." He stuck the horn in the ground and impaled the rotting chimera. Afterwards, he tossed it into a black hole. The demon broke Scott's chains; he pulled him off the floor, then tucked him under his arm. "You already knew this was coming. Drop in and get him when you're ready." Roswell dropped down a warp pipe with a halfhearted smile.

"Why didn't you stop him?" Fae was wrapped in a state

of exhaustion and disappointment.

"I will explain, but first I must take you somewhere safe." Baron Sugar voice was solemn.

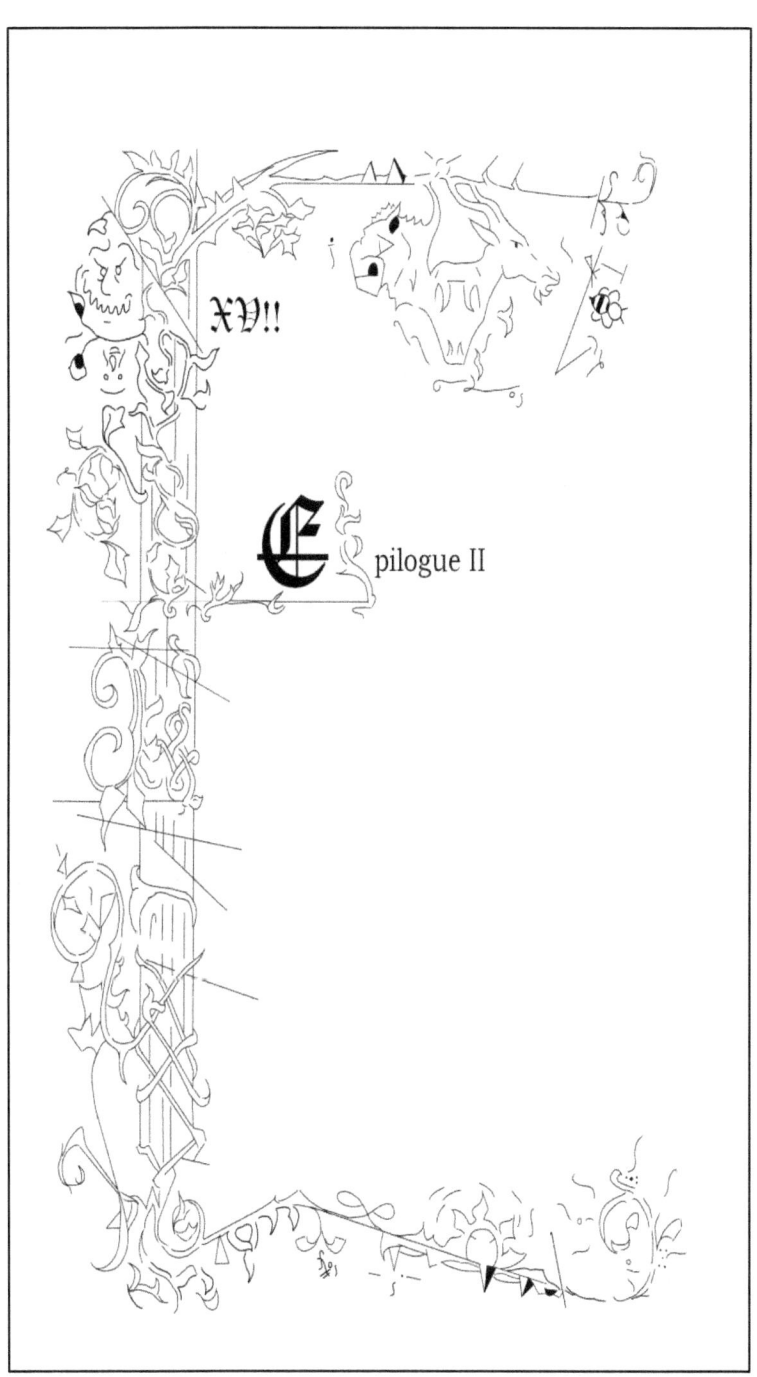

XV!!

Epilogue II

CHAPTER XV
EPILOGUE II

"What we discussed before; Roswell is nearing his death. Should we pursue this, he would die during the encounter...? I have been adamant to inform you that the dimension and everything in it will perish with him."

"...I know. I tried to tell him before; for some reason I just couldn't say it. The most I did was hint at it; we know he's bad with hints."

"Have you decided on what you will do?"

"I'm not ready, I doubt I ever will be." Faaghira's eyes were watering when she took out her phone and saw the picture of her and Larimar she had as her screen saver. She gave herself a moment to regain her composure, then she called Safira. "Saff, I need you to replace me as acting president."

"What? What happened? Why can't you be president? What's going on?"

"I'm coming to get Larimar. I've been so busy that I hardly get to do anything for her. I want to take her somewhere better for a while; we'll go on a trip somewhere nice."

"Oh...I understand. Fae..." Safira's voice trailed off.

"Talk to me Saffie, what's on your mind?"

"I know I've been selfish, and I know you don't like apologies, but do you think you'll be able to come back soon? I'm not fit to be the leader everyone needs! *I can't do this without you!*"

Fae sniffled then cleared her throat but did so quietly enough that Safira wouldn't hear her. "Well I believe you can; you just need some time to prove it for yourself. Tell you what, next time you see me we'll be running things together. How's that sound to you?"

"I can't wait! Oh, and Fae…there's one other thing."

"You already know you can tell me anything."

"If you have time to think about it…"

"Come on, don't be shy Saff."

"I still have feelings for you and I've been thinking about it, with the time that passed…I think it might be love after all. I know I'm laying this on you out of nowhere, and there were a lot of times before when I didn't treat you right. But I just wanted you to know that before you go."

"You don't have to wait on me-" Fae giggled, "-but if you're really not seeing anybody by the time I get back, guess we'll have to see how things pan out. I have to pack up Elle's stuff; I'll talk to you later."

"Oh, okay…have a safe trip."

"Bye Saff." Fae hung up and let out a deep breath. "Barry, can you go pickup Elle from the safehouse? I don't think I'll hold up after seeing Safira. I know her; she'll think I won't want to see her. It's easier for me like this; bad enough I have to smile and lie right to my sister's face. She thinks the world of me, but I don't want that to hold her back from being better than me." She sat on the edge of the roof top and dangled her feet over it. "I'm leaving her to Scott. He'd do better to give her the kind of life she deserves; something better than anything I could give her. It'll be tough for her whether he's rich or not, which I know he's not. I just wish I could come up with something better, but this was the best I could come up with so soon. Maybe it's on me for not taking it serious till the last minute."

"Do you think you will be able to say goodbye to her?"

"Not in front of her. I wrote her bunch of letters in a journal; there's some pictures in there too. There'll be two bookbags full of everything I could pack for her. Can you do one last favor me? Make sure she doesn't want for anything. It's the last thing I can do for her."

"Your request will be carried about to the best of my

abilities."

"Thanks-" she hugged Sugar tightly, "-I owe you"

"You do not owe me anything."

Fae laughed a little bit, "yes I do."

"If you insist. We have not much time, so you may ask me any question of your choosing and your debt will be cleared." The light brown knit cloth reformed over his head. It was repainted with a dopey grin, a teardrop shaped nose, two round eyes (one being noticeably bigger than the other), and curved lines for eyebrows.

"Hmmmm, why do you wear that goofy cloth bag over your head?"

"Many suns have set since I was human; now people fear me. It is this silliness that provides comfort for others. This humor is one of the last remnants of who I once was; who I would have been in a better world."

"Remember when we met? I was terrified; kind of hard to believe now."

"Why do you find that hard to believe?"

"I was scared of you my whole life. Atticus brought me on the grounds where you live a long time ago; I don't remember anything about that day other than seeing you. You were in all of my night mares, but I wasn't even sure you were real. You were a rumor, a myth...but I saw you. It felt so far away; the older I got the more it haunted me. I felt so many things; inadequacy, confusion, helplessness...feat. The further along I got, the more scared I was. It got to the point where I thought about that moment every day. The more I knew, the more I got frustrated at what I didn't understand. I was mad I could never understand the nightmares you were in."

"I am deeply sorry to have caused you so much turmoil. It is not your fault; turns out it was never your fault."

"After hearing your story and getting to know you, I realized that I was just afraid of being afraid."

"Very insightful. Thank you for sharing that with me; it must have been difficult to do."

"Do you remember what happened that day Atticus brought me there?"

"He stood on my property holding a baby for more than ten minutes. He was trespassing; I was annoyed. I told him to leave; I was not calm. Once again, I apologize for frightening you. His intentions are unknown to me, but whatever they were, they have been ruined by our friendship."

"Sorry for making you out to be a monster." Fae paused briefly, taking in the mesmerizing views of the sprawling city below. "If you could do anything with your powers, what would it be?"

"I will go get Larimar. We will leave whenever you are ready. Be well, my friend."

XV!!!

Triangle
Of
Regret

CHAPTER XVIII
TRIANGLE OF REGRET

"How are you enjoying the party?" There were a bunch of Roswells throwing darts, playing charades, riding imaginary horses, and playing tennis. There were streamers and banners that said 'happy new year', as in they actually *said* happy new year. The long wooden table from the third chapter had all kinds of alcohol and cheesecakes. Confetti fell from the atmosphere since there wasn't a ceiling.

Scott was...he didn't know how to react. How was he even supposed to react? "It's not my scene; I'm sure you put a lot of effort into it, though."

"I didn't, actually." Roswell smiled while he sat in his throne. His back was leaned against one armrest and his legs were hanging over the other. "I was waiting for the main attraction, but you're okay too, I guess. As far as I can tell, I'm the only one that can smell; oh how you reek of cheap liquor." With one swipe of his hand, all the duplicates disappeared, and by disappeared, I mean 'walked off into the horizon while booing and hissing at the original Roswell'. A banner fell over his head that had the words 'Destroyer of worlds' written on it. The demon suddenly had the oak walking stick balanced on his shoulder.

Scott was confused, of course, but there was a whole table of free drinks so he (over) indulged.

"Oh, my bad-" the demon was staring past the banner and off into the nothing beyond him, "-am I sittin' in your chair?" He used the walking stick to prop himself up with every step he took. His eyes were red and dry; they had bags under their bags. "I had lots of stuff planned; good ideas; never did get around to most of it. Back in the beginning, the other stuff around was supposed to mean something at some point. It took the second chapter for me to realize I had so much potential I would be throwing away if I stuck to my original ideas. Imagine all the good things I could've thrown away for the sake of being stubborn!" The demon was swept up in a violent coughing fit.

"What else were you gonna do? The way things turned out, I might've liked whatever the other option was better."

"You wouldn't, believe me. I'd put in all that work and you'd want to leave waaaay before the end. As you might've noticed, I caught a *small* case of the sniffles; made this out to be my last job. If you never came back I might've even retired, but I knew you would. My kind; we live big but we don't die in peace. I take my misfortune in strides. Of course, I had detailed stuff written out, but I would've had to force people to do things they otherwise wouldn't, just so I could keep all my ideas intact."

"What I don't understand is-"

"There's lots of things you don't understand."

"I don't understand why you chose me. Why am I the one that had to go through all of this? You could've picked anyone, right?"

"You must be hoping that I've been lying this whole time and will finally reveal the truth now that my health is failing. I'm a jerk; what about that is so hard to understand? You're optimistic, though misguided. You want to believe in people, or at least see the best intentions they could possibly have. I'll make this clear *one last time*: I did this because I had the power and it's what I felt like doing. This was gonna be my last job and I knew you wouldn't give me a tough time; simple as that."

"That's it? You could've at least made me sound less pathetic! I know I'm not the most courageous guy out there, but you could at least try to not make me seem so useless! And it's not just with words; the biggest problem that made me want to go back to…my dimension I guess I should call it, is that nobody *needed* me here. I felt like a plus one to everyone's party! And you know what else? I'm tired of being the butt of everybody's jokes! Especially yours!"

"*Especially yours*; sounds like a cheap perfume. I dig it. I was starting to forget you can say more than two sentences at a time. Speaking of time, we have plenty of that. You can ask me absolutely anything, and I might as well answer truthfully. Don't be shy there's not much of a reason to be at this point. We've known each other for how long now? Well, time's an illusion, but we've known each other for long enough."

"You said this was your job; what do you get out of doing this?"

Roswell coughed up a puddle of blood. "Death, eventually. I'm not trying to sound edgy or anything; I get a fun time, then I die. I used to be more reckless in the past, but I mellowed out; that's when I got dangerous. I have a question for you: why do you live your life the way you do? Who are you? This is informal; just you and me."

"I think I saw this one coming. Don't you already know me though?"

"I'm a demon; you think I never lied to you?" Roswell had a playful tone.

"I didn't think too much about that."

"I know you believed when I said I 'specialize in love'. I was lying; I was lying the whole time. Maybe I said that once. I was the source, so nobody could fact check me. I know you do that too, but I'm getting off topic. Say whatever you want to about your life; say whatever."

"I make a lot of my way on luck. I have parents with high expectations, and I slip by so much that they think it's because I'm really making it. They got the wrong child; I fall into things and they work a lot of the time. I have a girlfriend that loves me and parents that do too, but not in the same way, obviously."

"Right."

"But I don't think my parents like me. I think if I wasn't their son and they saw me out somewhere, I think they'd say people like me are what's wrong with the world. Iris likes me, and she's really sweet, but I don't always get to see- but I don't always get to see that. Our relationship is…complicated. I said once, she's a *little* controlling. Her and her dad pay my tuition and other stuff, dorms too if I'm being honest for once, but one of the conditions she made is that I can't get my driver's license. There's no chance I'd even be able to afford a car anytime soon, but she drives me wherever I want to go."

"You've got yourself a good set of problems."

"None of those problems include gas, parking, insurance, or tuition, so I'm good. She checks through who I talk to, but it works out because most of them aren't reliable anyway."

"New York's parking fees are so bad I'd've sworn I made them!"

"It's not one sided though. I don't like when she talks to other guys and I don't want her hanging out with people I don't know or that I don't like. We both cheat on each other and it's not a secret, but we don't bring it up until we fight. It gets heated pretty often, but one of us always comes around. Either I apologize or she does, and we say things'll be different, but we both know that's not true. Well, that's my fault…somewhat."

"This is very abusive; couldn't've done much better myself. Kudos to you!" The demon winked.

"It's not abusive; we don't hit each other. Hitting is off limits. What we have isn't the cleanest, but that's what works for us."

"Airplane statements really are a wonder. What about drinking? I've had my fun saving your liver and screwing with your reality. What happens after I bow out?"

"Me and Iris bond over drinking sometimes. Some things I dealt with- the way somebody dealt with me when I was drunk; I've been thinking about slowing it down just a little bit. Maybe if I had a life that didn't make me have to cope then I wouldn't drink so much."

"You say your piece and pay lip service to what people want to hear. You know what you will and won't do, so why lie? Do you feel like you have to? Do you feel like you can't do anything else? What's holding you back?" The demon smiled warmly.

Giant bronze arching doors materialized and were broken down by Baron Sugar and Faaghira broke it down. Roswell tapped his foot on the grid and the doors were repaired themselves. "You showed up the one time I invited you; good job."

"Bother the world no longer, demon." Baron Sugar's 'face' dissolved when he prepared himself to fight.

"You're here for your man? To imagine that Scott wouldn't have anyone in his corner if he didn't go off course back then…it's something. Even better, he wouldn't need anyone in his corner if didn't come back. Shouldn't've placed your bets on winning a game of tic-tac-toe. It's bittersweet. Right then, you know what comes next."

"Just give us Scott back and we'll leave; I for real don't even want to fight you. Barry can do all that; that's not what I'm here for." Faaghira looked exhausted and the tone of her voice was unusually dry.

"I wouldn't go this far for nothing." Roswell smiled quietly; his eyes shifted around the grid. It was really awkward. "I've never been in a boss battle before, so I'm not exactly sure how this is supposed to work. Do I attack first, or do you hit me? I'm bad at monologues, so feel free to jump in any time." One Roswell appeared behind Sugar, but Fae was quick to notice and lay hands on the demon. Sugar slammed it to the ground and burned it.

"My, my, unprovoked; I dig the way this is going so far!" Roswell hit Baron Sugar with the walking stick, causing him to fly back a few yards.

"Is that the most you can do with your powers?" Fae taunted the demon. Scott warned her that she could get hurt, but he didn't do anything to hold her back.

"Is this…a challenge?" Roswell's smile became crude. He was noticeably frail, and his movements were slightly rigid. Still, he dusted off his faux fur collared bomber jacket with all the smugness and pride he had before. "There's lots of things. I've always wanted to build a castle or palace for myself. Maybe I'd celebrate a shallow victory there."

"Can you show me what that would look like?"

"Hmmmmmm, since you asked nicely." The blandness of the grid was replaced by an opulent opera theatre. "I gotta admit, this is pretty nice." Faaghira was starting to sound more like her normal self, but she never quite made it back.

"I didn't even bother to come up with something new; it's the theatre in Versailles. I'm surprised I can still remember what it looks like." Baron Sugar became a raging comet and charged at the demon with power so immense that it broke the sound barrier and eventually went the speed of light. Most of the theatre was left in ruins by Baron Sugar's rampage. However, Roswell caught him by the face and drove him into the ground with his left hand. The demon was completely unbothered; he never took his eyes off Faaghira and Scott. "I'm so tired these days that I can hardly come up with anything new. I envy my old self and their creativity…but not their creativity- but not their lack of vision."

"This isn't a fair fight."

"Looks like you'll have to get good th-" Faaghira elbowed Roswell in the chest so hard that he was wheezing.

The theatre was beginning to fade away, but Roswell fixed it immediately. "No fair, I just put that up!" His legs dropped and that's when Baron Sugar attacked him again. This time Roswell was bowled over. Baron Sugar was beating him down relentlessly when Scott urged him to stop.

"He's not fighting back! Don't keep hitting him like that!"

"You can't kill evil. Slash it with your swords, shoot it with your guns, strangle it with your hands; it may not win, but it'll outlive you." Roswell's laughter turned into coughing. He barely had the strength to stand, having to resort to using the walking stick to prop himself up again.

"Scott, let's go! He's too weak to keep going; we can get you out of here." Faaghira pulled at Scott's arm, but for whatever reason he didn't pull his eyes from the dying demon. Baron Sugar created a portal for them to get through while he stayed behind to fight Roswell

"*No, no, no, no, no, I can't lose*. You don't understand how this works; I set a goal and I reach it. You don't get to throw away what I worked for because it's convenient for you. *I already made sure of that; you know it, don't you?*" Roswell threw the walking stick at Baron Sugar and pushed past Scott in one swift move. He lifted Fae up with his fist at her stomach and drove her into the stage. "You knew there was one way this was going; *you'd lose.*"

Scott was frozen for a moment. Instead of threatening the demon with death, he just stood there; his body went cold. Fae was invincible, she could do anything...he actually killed her. He killed her...he didn't even care. He was acting like the most he did was brush dust off his jacket. That bastard! "Life is spun through my hands. You believe that? Sugar, I'll let you kill me now; I'm pretty sure I got what I was looking for."

"Why did you kill her?" Scott was struggling to speak.

"Run that by me again; your voice is a little hard to hear…wait, are you crying?" The demon's warm smile was interrupted by him choking suddenly.

"Scott, we must leave."

"Stay out of it! You didn't save her and you had the chance!" Scott snapped at Baron Sugar. "Why did you kill her? She had nothing to do with this! I'm the one you wanted! Why did you-" Scott broke into tears. He dropped to his knees and cried over Fae.

"All the tenacity is gone. Now you get that you can't hurt me; nothing you could ever do would hurt me. Just; six hundred and seventy-two and counting." The demon knelt down next to Scott. "You wanna know why Baron Sugar didn't kill me yet? Because when I die, my creations, my dimensions; everything dies with me. Faaghira's life; all her struggles, all her wealth, all her achievements…*gone*. What would she go back to after you went back to your reality? Would you want her go with you and start all over? Sure, she'd be alive, but she would amount to nothing…*just like you*. I can bring her back, but there's something I'd want from you before that could happen. You remember what I said my job was? *You gonna tell me what I wanna hear?*"

"Take me instead." Scott fought to talk through his tears.

"What was that?" The demon put his hand to his ear. "I'm having a little trouble hearing today."

"Take me instead! I don't have anything in my life worth living for, but she does! I'm living by the skin of my teeth and I won't get anything out of it! My parents hate me, my girlfriend controls my life and makes me into someone I don't even know; I have to drink just to get through my day to day! Fae has everything to lose! Don't take that away from her because of me! Bring her back and you can do whatever you want with me! I don't care! Just don't take her! Take me instead! I have nothing to live for!"

"No." The demon smiled and shook his head. The theatre disappeared and the grid returned. A whole opened up under Faaghira and pulled her into an abyss. The grid slowly began to dissolve. Roswell was slumped against a wooden crate, holding an empty wine glass in his hand. "To Scott Blue, destroyer of the universe." A spotlight flickered on the demon until it went out permanently. Baron Sugar urged Scott to get through the portal before the grid evaporated completely. Scott refused to leave Fae, so he ended up having to be carried out.

The last he saw of that reality was Faaghira falling through an infinite vastness of existence. It was paced; a beautiful and tragic dance through the atmosphere.

The portal brought them to the other side of the bronze doors. Larimar was sleeping on two backpacks when Baron Sugar woke her up. "Larimar, we have to go. I will have a portal send you somewhere you will be safe. Your sister has trusted Scott with your care; this place is not safe for you."

"Where's Bun Bun?"

"We will be right behind you. My friend, you must go now." Baron Sugar picked both of them up and walked through the portal.

Everything collapsed before the portal closed.

Scott and Larimar were on a boardwalk in Coney Island. Baron Sugar was nowhere to be found.

EPILOGUE III

"Where'd Barry go?"

"I don't think he could come with us."

"Where's Bun Bun?"

My throat feels tight; it's like something's cutting off my air. I'm tearing up, but I can't let Larimar see me like this. "Looks like it's just us now."

Larimar held on tight to her backpack straps. "Why isn't Bun Bun here too?" I'm carrying the other backpack, so it's not exactly easy for me either.

"Boy am I hungry? Are you hungry? I could go for some fries and a milkshake." Shit, I can hear Larimar crying. I'm not looking at her, I can't! I can hear her sniffling and wiping her eyes; shit what am I supposed to do? She's gonna have me crying to if I don't think of something. "Larimar, you don't have to make yourself stop crying. I'm sorry; I got uncomfortable and- we can talk instead. I don't have a place to live at the moment, but we got dropped off at Coney Island and Luna Park is pretty close. I'd hold off on the roller coaster they have, but we could sit on a bench and talk. I know I'm not- this is gonna be tough for both of us."

"Why did Bun Bun leave me with you?" Ouch. That's...ouch. That hurts. Not totally undeserved, but it stings.

"I know I can never replace your sister; nobody could ever. She never told me why she thought I should have a part in that. She wanted what's best for you. Honestly, I don't know, and I can't blame you for being mad. Would you talk to me, still? Please? I don't know what to do right now and I think nobody understands how you feel right now more than I do."

"Where do we go to talk?"

We go to a bench in Luna Park and Larimar sits down

first, but she takes off her backpack and puts it next to her. I feel like she's blocking me off, but at least she's willing to talk. "Fae did a lot of things I don't understand. She did a lot of spectacular things, but she did a lot of things I don't get. She believed in me; yeah, just between us, I don't know why she did that. She trusted me to take care of you. *Me.* I don't get it."

"Me either." I waited for her to say something else besides that, but she left me with nothing.

"Yeah…I don't blame you. I don't want to let her down, though." What else am I supposed to say? My other best friend just died and that's her sister! Plus, she's a kid; I don't know how to talk to kids! "What was she like?"

"You met her."

"But-uh-you knew her better than I did; better than anyone, probably. You two were really close; there's a lot that only you know. Can you tell me some things about her?"

"No, I don't wanna do that." Shit, I'm trying my best here!

"…Okay, so what do you want to talk about?"

"Where's the rollercoaster?"

"Err…I'll bring you back for that when you're older. Hopefully it'll still be around by then. Might not be so safe, but that's always been part of the charm."

"I'm hungry."

I don't have that much in my wallet. Just twenty-six bucks and my voter i.d. "I have enough money for a milkshake and some fries."

So I take her to a diner nearby. It's a pretty clean place and all. She made the order herself since she said I'd mess it up. I heard he say something about 'dairy-free' to the waiter, so- right! She's lactose intolerant! Yeah, good thing she handled that. Even though it wasn't cheap, I bought the milkshake for her and the fries for me, but I let her know that she could help herself to as many as she wanted. She still looked sad, so I put two fries up my nose while she wasn't paying attention so I can get her to laugh. "Look Larimar! I'm a walrus!"

"Throw those away, that's nasty!"

Not at all what I was expecting. "What? I was just trying to make you laugh!" I laughed to play it off, but it doesn't look like she's buying it. Now she took some napkins from the dispenser, put two on the table and used the other three to pull the fries out my nose. She wrapped them up in the other ones and got up to throw them away. When she came back, I asked if she'd share with me. I mean, it would only be fair since I offered her some fries.

"No, you play with your food." I'm getting served up by a little girl, but I couldn't help laughing; she got me on that one! I laughed so hard that I snorted, which is the only thing I was able to do to get her to laugh.

I texted Charlie and told him I was at Coney Island and I needed to be picked up. He's a dependable guy, and today he's back to best friend numero uno. Charlie said he was 'on the way' which means he didn't get out of bed yet. I suggested that me and Larimar dance to pass the time, but she said there was no music and she also flat out didn't want to. We went to a souvenir shop and she saw an overpriced snow globe that she wanted, but I didn't shy away from the fact that I couldn't afford it. Charlie texted me saying he was around the corner, so I'd say we about fifteen minutes or something like that.

I felt bad about the snow globe thing, so I took her to the flea market in Luna Park and told her she could pick out something. One of the vendors said my daughter might like to look at some ribbons and hair clips. She's a nice lady, sure, and she was just trying to push what she was selling, but hearing her call Larimar my daughter felt weird. I'm a good guy, but not so sure I'd be a good dad. Larimar tugged on my arm and pointed out a fancy looking white silk ribbon. I was going to suggest another color since white usually gets dirty easily, but I just bought her a blue one too; it wasn't that much money. I bought her a pack of butterfly hairclips too because I think they look cute. Charlie called me to tell me that he's outside and he's waiting on me, which means he just got here.

"Man I haven't seen your-" I know what he was about to say. He didn't say it because he just saw Larimar; he doesn't curse around kids. "-Face in a long time! It's great to see you! Why are walking with a limp? And who's this?" He was definitely happy to see me but it's weird for him to see me without Iris; even weirder to see me taking care of a kid.

I was waiting for Larimar to introduce herself, but she got cold feet all of a sudden. "This is Larimar; she's a friend's baby sister." She nudged me in the side of my leg, so I had take a guess at what she wanted me to change. "This is my friend's *little* sister. You happy now?"

"I didn't know Iris let you have friends other than me. How'd you manage that?"

"We met at college. Iris doesn't know about her."

"*Her*? Yeah, best not mention it. Where's your friend now? I can drop Larimar off whenever she needs to go back home."

"...It's just me and Larimar now."

"Shi-Darn! What happened? No, don't answer that; let's get going." Larimar held onto my hand before we got in the car. I was gonna sit in the back with her but it would've been weird for me. I don't know what to say and I think she still doesn't like me. I would've put her in the front, but she doesn't know Charlie; apparently she gets shy around people she doesn't know. I wouldn't do that to her; she must be going through a lot. She misses Fae; I do too.

The ride was really awkward because it was quiet, so Charlie turned on some music. I'm surprised he didn't put on any of his of his own music, but maybe it would've felt too weird for him.

"Thanks for being Scott's friend because he's homeless." Larimar's sudden comment got Charlie to laugh so hard that he hollered…and it made me want to sink into the seat and disappear.

"You're ruthless; you're a cool kid! Hey, Larimar, don't worry about anything, alright? Long as Scott's my best friend, you'll have a place to stay for as long as you want."

"Scott, don't get a better friend or be mean or else we'll both be homeless." This little girl is out to get my self-esteem. At least Charlie's getting a good laugh.

"You can stay as long as you want whether or not Scott's my best friend!" Not helping, Charlie. I peeked behind the seat and saw Larimar was smiling. How'd he get her to smile?

We get out the car then Larimar asks me to give her a piggyback ride. I told her we're literally right in front of the house, but she could care less.

"Carry me." She reached her arms up and next thing I know I'm carrying her on my back. I acted like I hated it, but it was so fun that I had to make sure she couldn't see my face when I was smiling. I don't think she's not sad anymore; I'm smiling but I'm still devastated. Makes me think about Fae; when we first met I thought she was switching through emotions all night, but maybe she never stopped feeling however she felt. Maybe this is how she felt.

Charlie unlocked the front door, but we didn't go in right away since Larimar kept making me go around in circles. He was carrying her other backpack for me so I could carry her around. We did go inside eventually; Larimar was getting tired. "It's not the cleanest right now, but cut me some slack because I wasn't expecting more company. By the way, I never properly introduced myself, I'm Charlie Davis."

"Hi Charlie Davis, I'm Larimar."

"Scott knows where the other bedroom is. I can change

the sheets real quick if you want."

"Did you use them?" It's been a while, but I know Charlie really well. He's a neat freak; he wouldn't offer to clean things out of nowhere since he already does it.

"Nah, I changed them a yesterday, but I was just saying cause I have to change the sheets in my room, so if you wanted me to change the other ones too then it wouldn't be a problem."

"...We're good. I need some extra covers though; I'm sleeping on the floor. And I need some extra pillows too." It's getting close winter in New York; I get chilly.

"What about me?"

"You'll have to sleep with *only* two pillows and *two covers*; you and your greedy self." I miss being able to make jokes like that. Between what happened with Roswell and Iris keeping me close here, I hardly get to let loose.

"Alright, alright. I missed you man; it's good to have you back. You've been spending so much time with Iris that I haven't heard from you in months. I got around to thinking Iris had you write me off."

"What? I'd never let that happen! You've been my best friend since we were kids; you're always looking out for me, man! There's no way I'd ever drop you!"

"Past few months sure could've fooled me." Shit! What's been going on? I've only been back from the other dimension like...twice not counting now! I know I haven't been gone for months! I have to see if I can get a hold of Baron Sugar somehow and see if he knows what's up, but I'll figure that out tomorrow. It's time to get some sleep. I let Larimar have the bed because there's no way I'd let her sleep on the floor and I'm regularly accused of being a cover hog. Also, her sister died and now she has to live a completely different life with me at the wheel. Saying she deserves a bed all to herself is an understatement. She was talking to me about something, but I fell asleep at some point. I don't know

540

how long it took her to notice, but I was out cold.

"Your existence was simultaneous in multiple dimensions. Time passes differently in these dimensions. A paradox was created when you shifted between realities. When you were not mentally present in one, that version of you would act accordingly with the direction you were already headed in. For the sake of order and my own commitments, I will no longer appear physically. However, I will honor my promise to Faaghira in whatever other way I can. Though my explanation is vague, I hope it finds you well. Give Larimar a hug for me." I don't remember exactly what happened in my dream, but I remember Baron Sugar explaining the whole time difference thing. I woke up right then and tried to talk to him, but he wasn't there.

It was already morning so I go to have breakfast, you know the whole morning routine. Larimar was still asleep and I didn't wanna wake her up. Her braids were still okay, but I asked Charlie if he knew anyone that could do her hair. What Fae did can't hold up forever. I wish it could, but I'm trying to stay ahead of the curve, plus it's something nice I could do. Iris calls, telling me she's picking me up for dinner with her parents tonight. Apparently I agreed to this last month? It might be that she told me I was going and I didn't say no. I wanted Larimar to be there with me, mostly because I'm the only person she knows and I don't want her to by alone, but also because Iris' parents aren't the most progressive people. By now, not being low key racist shouldn't even be considered progressive, but I take the good with the bad; my tuition gets paid for and I get some other nice perks too.

Charlie got one of his friends to come over and change up Larimar's hair, but she insisted on leaving her hair out so she wouldn't have to sit down forever while it gets braided again. This time she wanted a side ponytail, but using the butterfly clips and one of the ribbons I bought her. I was right there and talked with her the whole time, and I even paid attention a little to how everything was being done. I think Charlie's friend said she had 4a and a little bit of 4c in some strands, but I don't know what any of that means. But who knows, one of these days I might end up doing Larimar's hair.

Iris was shocked that I had someone with me, but she didn't berate me like she used to; she was really nice about it. I rarely ever see her be nice. I didn't even have to explain why she was coming with us. Larimar worked like a charm. The dinner was…awkward. Iris's folks live in a really swanky apartment; nothing much compared to what Fae had, but I can bet it costs way more than I'll see in my lifetime. Her dad asked me what I do for a living and I said "study hard"; he didn't really respond.

"Daddy, can you pass the garlic rolls?" Iris gave me the perfect opportunity for a power move, and Larimar being there meant I'd probably pull it off without too much of a problem. Me and her dad both reached for the basket.

"She was talking to me." I smiled like the smug bastard I know I am, but it was hard not to look *too* happy. Larimar laughed, but I doubt she understood the context. "Here you go sweetie." I passed Iris the basket and she blushed so hard, but she did her best to ignore it. I swear that man was biting down on his tongue. The most her mom did was make small talk and ask if Larimar if she wanted more lasagna. Things went pretty good considering the circumstances. My tuition's still getting paid, my relationship is still the same, but I thought it would be good for me and Larimar to take the train back to Charlie's.

It's the next day and I'm still having problems readjusting. Larimar and I decide to go out for a walk, and somehow it turned into her sitting on my shoulders while I carry her around. "Where to, Captain Larimar?"

"I dunno."

542

"Wanna go to a park? I can push you on the swings."

"Am I old enough to go on the rollercoaster now?"

"Not yet Larimar, let's see in around seven years."

"I want you to see Bun Bun's letters with me, but you can't show anyone else."

"Okay Larimar, we'll go back to Charlie's right now."

"Bun Bun called me Elle. You don't have to say my whole name anymore." I could hear Larimar start sniffling. Shit, now we're both crying. I want to do so much more than this. I want to relive all the memories. I want everything back; the good and the bad. I want another chance to do things different; I want to save her; it doesn't matter what would've happened to me. I wish I could-"I wish I could've saved her. I wish I did better. I'm sorry Larimar."

When we got back, Charlie asked if we were okay; I told him we need some time. I closed the door then wrapped myself in covers on the floor. Larimar was curled up on the bed. We both cried ourselves to sleep. I woke her up to make sure she got something to eat, but other than that I left her alone. We slept so early that neither of us were tired when it was late at night. Larimar got some of Fae's letters from one of the backpacks and put them on the bed. She's reading them out loud. She's letting me hear what Fae left for her. It's all she has...and she's sharing it with me. "Thank you, Elle." She wasn't able to get through the first letter without breaking down again, but I couldn't either. She got through more of it than I could. I picked myself off the floor and scooped Elle up into the biggest, warmest hug I could. This is my fault. None of this is what I wanted; this wouldn't've happened if I'd grew a pair and just walked away. I can't change the past, but I'll do what I can to make it up to her. I don't think anything will ever make up for what happened, but I have to try. If I don't fix anything else in my life, this'll be the one thing I'll get right. "Elle, I promise I'll do everything I can for you! I know I'm not good like Fae was;

no one could ever be as good as she was! I know that but I still want to take care of you! Elle, if it's all good with you, I want to adopt you! You don't have to call me your father or anything like that; I just want you to know you have a family! You have someone who understands!" I'm crying so hard I don't have any energy to process what I'm saying, and my throat's so dry that I can't go too much louder than whispering, but I mean every word.

"Scott…"

"Yeah Elle."

"I'm never calling you my father." I'm so happy to hear that she can still joke right now! She's amazing! I'm going through so much I can barely string two thoughts together!

"You never have to! I'm just Scott, I'm just Scott Blue. You'll be Larimar Blue- only if you like the last name though. I have to go through Barry to do some reality warping thing to make things official and get you everything you need to live here. You can change it to anything you want!" "That's okay. Larimar Blue; I have a last name now. Can I get a middle name too?"

"Anything you want, Elle." I didn't break up with Iris, but now I have a better reason to stick this out besides free tuition and housing. But even if I didn't need her for anything else, I can't go too long without her. What we have is a part of me, and I can't just let all of that go just because I have someone depending on me now. I called my dad; we're on good terms, but that stopped being my home a while ago. I'll try to slow down my drinking, but my life needs some big changes before I'd ever be able to cut down like I want to. I'll have to leave Elle with Charlie for a day or two if there's ever a time I can't hold up.

"Sapphire, I want my middle name to be Sapphire. Larimar Sapphire Blue." "Well miss Larimar Sapphire Blue, family starts with us. Let's see this through."